HUNTED

TELICIA MCSWAN

Cover and Interior Book Design and Editing by Sarah Lemcke
www.allintheedit.com
sarah@allintheedit.com

To all those who read this book,
thank you for taking a chance on me and my quiet dream.

~ PROLOGUE ~

This guy is literally a waste of money but to appease my family, I'm here. Talking. Not wallowing, bottling things up, getting angry, or whatever it is my family and friends think I'm doing in order to force this upon me. I stare out the window in an attempt to avoid the most recent question I'd been asked. The rain was splattering against the window in a heavy downpour that had been threatening for several days. The weather matched the feeling of this cold dark room, nothing like the calm and peaceful environment I would've expected but apparently this guy is the best. I knew the rain would bring a nice reprieve from the heat and humidity but it also meant wet shoes, wet clothes, wet hair, wet everything. Great.

Doctor Martin clears his throat, redirecting my attention back to him, "How would you describe Hunter?" He gently asks again.

For the second time, I contemplate how I would answer that question. I study Doctor Martin's features instead. The man sat like a stone. He rarely moved except to change his posture. The questions he asked were deep and meaningful, and some were completely random. It felt like an emotional roller coaster. I knew I needed to do this though.

~ PART 1 ~

CHAPTER 1

Nobody tells you how tough it is starting at a new school. Coming into Grade 11, second year of high school, wasn't any different, and that's what was making me anxious the night before I started at Rosetta Grammar School in January. I sat up late that night, picturing the friendship groups that had already formed and the struggles I might face trying to fit in with people that have already spent several years together. How should I introduce myself?

Do I keep it plain and simple? "Hi, I'm Hayley?"

Or was this a time to be creative and come up with a nickname?

Whilst I was comfortable with my personality and my ability to make friends, a skill I'd learnt several times thanks to constantly moving around due to Dad's job, it was still a nerve-racking experience. When it was finally morning and I was getting myself ready, I couldn't help but worry if the other kids would like me. Would I like them? Would I be judged? What would they even think of me? All of these thoughts crashed into one another as I dragged my brush through my shoulder length naturally brown hair. Was it even cool to have your natural hair colour these days? Sometimes it was hard to keep up with what was considered trendy. New schools meant new trends and as much as I tried to defend my fellow sisterhood, girls could be mean and vindictive when they wanted to. There were even some boys from my old school that had dropped a few harsh comments. As I finished tying my hair up, I couldn't help but study my face in the mirror. I consider myself to be quite ordinary. Our family heritage was Spanish however I didn't inherit any of the beautiful olive skin tones that my dad was so fortunate to have. Instead, I was fair skinned, taking after my mother, but after several years of practice, I had nailed a minimalistic make-up routine that made me look a little more bronzed and like I wasn't wearing make-up at all. Whilst thinking about it, I pull out my makeup bag and start applying some foundation. I had about ten more minutes before we needed to leave. I know I look more like my mother. I even have the same ordinary brown eyes that I was about to border with black mascara. I wished I had a sibling to talk to about my fears as we both started a new school together, but I was an only child. Now that I was a bit older, I had a better understanding of the stress and pain that my parents went through just to have me. They were never able to conceive a second time and the cost of IVF was too much for them at the time. It wasn't too bad though. I had my parent's sole attention, and they tried hard to do a lot of things with me and play with me when I was little, even when they were tired after work. They encouraged me to try after-school sports a few times over the years, but after realising my hand-eye coordination was average at best, Mum suggested dance lessons. I fell in love with dance immediately and the fact that this new school taught dance as a subject made me even more excited to attend. Now that I had finished my makeup, I double check my bag to make sure my dance gear was packed, ready for today's class. I zip up my bag and take a deep breath. I could do this.

As we drove the short distance to my new school, hidden away in the valley of one of Cairns' up-and-coming suburbs, I started to feel anxious again. We moved frequently for Dad's work as a project manager. He was paid to relocate to wherever a major project was taking place but this would be the last time we moved as he decided it was time to settle for good. It was another tick in my book. I'd finally be able to make some friends that I could keep for longer than a few years. There was a great university here that I would apply for when the time came as well. I reminded myself of this as we approached the school gates. Everything was going to be okay.

⸺⟡⸺

Reflecting on who I was, I couldn't work out what made him attracted to me. What made me different from all of the other girls in my grade or in this town? He was your typical cool kid with a bad boy vibe. And who wouldn't be attracted to him? Even at sixteen, he was already tall—like, really tall—and you could tell he was starting to grow into that whole effortlessly hot guy look with the body to match. He had a wicked way with words. His dark brown hair flicked up in a way that looked natural, but was a phase that all of the boys were going through, even at my old school. Except he just seemed to get it right. It suited him so well. And his eyes. Bluer than the ocean, mesmerising, deep, dark, dangerous. Meeting Hunter was no different to meeting anyone else. He seemed like the average teenage boy: into sports, strong, funny, well-liked, and handsome. Girls wanted to date him and guys wanted to be him. He just seemed to be a natural at being what everyone fantasised about. And he knew it, too.

Chapter 2

Mum offers to walk me into school as she pulls into a car park outside of the administration building of my new school situated in the sunny and green valley of Cairns. Her beautiful brown hair was pulled into a braid and her olive-brown eyes made her look younger, regardless of the odd few greys sneaking through. I politely decline as I open the car door. Now that would be lame if my parents walked me in!

"Just be yourself, Hayley. You will do great." Dad gives me a reassuring look. "Now get out," he jokes as he runs his hand through his greying hair. His hair was the only thing that made you realise he was older than you probably thought. He gave off strong George Clooney vibes.

Dad always knew how to ease my nerves.

"Bye, Mum. Bye, Dad." I close the car door, slinging my backpack over my shoulder, waving as they drove away. I fix my uniform one last time. It was a simple white button-up shirt with a weird crossover tie and a mid-length teal plaid skirt. I wasn't pleased about having to wear a skirt, but Mum and Dad were lucky enough to get me into one of the up-and-coming private schools in the region. Thankfully it wasn't anything ridiculously long as Cairns was a hot and humid town. At my old school, I was able to wear a school t-shirt and shorts. My old school was comfortable. I had made some really good friends and now I had to start all over again. I shake my head, trying to push the negative thoughts out of my mind.

My admissions letter asked me to go to the administration office first and a student from my grade would be there to take me to my homeroom and show me where my classes were. There weren't many new people in my grade from what I understood in my entry interview. As I walked towards the administration building, I couldn't help but notice how new everything still seemed. All the buildings were freshly painted an odd mixture of red, white and green. The grass was freshly manicured and there were plenty of scattered lunch tables under shade sails between each building. Some of the buildings were single storey and others were double with a flight of stairs at each end. I could see lockers in the middle of each building and there were students slowly making their way to their designated areas. Most of the kids looked happy. That was promising, right?

The administration building was well signed so I easily find my way in. There were a few parents already there with their kids but I could tell they weren't in my grade. There was one girl standing to the side. She had a teal blazer on and a few badges pinned to it. Her dark brown hair was braided and a headband kept the strays out of her face. She seemed friendly enough. She was smiling at me. Another good sign.

"Hayley?" She hesitantly approaches me.

"Yes," I smile back as relief washes over me. "That's me."

She throws her hands in the air. "Thank goodness! I've been asking so many random students if their name was Hayley." She laughs. "I'm Kate and I'm here to show you to your homeroom and a few other areas of the school."

I laugh with her, sensing she had already embarrassed herself enough this morning.

"Follow me!" She walks out of the administration building and up the path to where I could only assume was the senior school area. "Are you ready for a big year?" she asks.

She keeps a slow pace so it was easy to walk beside her. "Definitely," I reply. "Only two years to go!"

"Tell me about it," she laughs. "It'll fly by though and then we'll be in the real world."

"It's scary to think we have to be adults in a couple of years!" I joke.

Kate laughs again as we walk along the pathway.

"This is the middle school area," she points to a few rows of two-storey buildings. "Usually we all keep to our areas. Senior school is up the back. That's where most of your classes will be, and our lockers are there too. What classes have you got this year? We will have to compare timetables!"

I take in all of the buildings. These ones were a dark blue, and I soon came to realise the colours represented the different grades at the school.

"I've got English, math, business, tourism, dance, and drama," I answer.

Kate grabs my arm in excitement. "No way! Me too! Well, except tourism," she laughs. "You'll love the dance studio," she continues. "It's so beautiful and big. It doubles as the drama room, too."

"Awesome," I reply. "I also enrolled at ACE Dance Studio. Do you know anything about it?"

We were starting to get close to the lockers and I could see groups of students around the lunch tables and outside of the classrooms all huddled in their groups.

"Oh yeah, I've heard of that studio. I think it's good. I don't know too much about it. I just take dance as a subject so I don't have to do a science one," she chuckles.

I let out a laugh. It wasn't the worst idea I'd heard to get out of science. I definitely wasn't keen on the subject. When we get to the lockers, Kate hands me a key to locker 15, which was thankfully in the middle row so I didn't have to bend over or reach up to access it. I unlock it and put my bag away, only keeping a notepad and pen with me. I let Kate lead the way to homeroom. If all the girls—hell, if everyone here—were like her, then I think I was going to like it.

I had nearly made it through my first day. It was now lunch time and Kate had already introduced me to several of her friends, and her boyfriend, Ethan. He was tall and had an athletic build. He kept his short hair styled with gel so it flicked up at the front. His brown eyes complemented his tanned skin, and he had sun-kissed golden-brown hair, all probably due to the amount of time he spent outside playing sport. Kate and Ethan had been dating for nearly a year already. He seemed down to earth and flitted between seeing Kate and his own group of friends during the first break of the day.

I was racing back to my locker to grab my gym shorts for my dance class. I considered dance to be my therapeutic release and a common language that would help me connect with other people. I was so excited for the first class that I had completely forgotten to grab my shorts. It was hard to get used to a school where the girls and boys had strict uniform guidelines and you had to bring shorts or tights on the days you weren't permitted to wear your sports uniform so you could comfortably move around in class. Luckily, a few other girls had done the same thing, and we went our separate ways back to our lockers that were spread through the senior section of our school. I had just unlocked my locker when I heard his voice for the first time.

"Hi," he says. Even his voice matched his looks, incredibly attractive and alluring.

I turn around to face the mysterious voice. He was leaning against the lockers across from mine. I had seen this boy around a bit today. He seemed to be a friend of Ethan's.

"Hello." I smile back.

He didn't look as though he was going to say anything further so I keep digging in my backpack for my shorts.

"I'm Hunter," he eventually says.

"I'm Hayley," I respond politely, slightly averting my gaze to him as I search my bag so I could get to class quickly.

"What class have you got now?" I hear him push off against the lockers and walk towards me.

"Dance," I answer, still going through my stuff. *Where were my shorts?*

He leans against the locker next to mine and I couldn't help but look up. How could you not?

He was so tall and his blue eyes were mesmerising.

"So, the new girl can dance? Now I'm intrigued to know more." He stares at me, a small smile escaping his lips,

I feel myself blushing. "Well, there's not much to know."

"I doubt that." His smile widens, and then he turns and walks away.

I let out the breath that I didn't realise I was holding before closing my locker and walking back to my dance class. My heart was racing but I decided not to tell anyone about this because there was nothing to tell and I didn't want to start anything. What if he was someone else's boyfriend? Surely a guy like that wasn't single.

CHAPTER 3

Time was flying by and we were now two weeks into the school year. I didn't have many other interactions with Hunter. He either kept to his crowd of friends or he simply walked off if Ethan ever stopped to talk to Kate. I guess I just wasn't his cup of tea.

Kate and I, along with a few of the other girls, were headed back to our lockers for our last break of the day after dance class.

"I love it when he waits for me!" Kate grins as she catches sight of Ethan.

I look ahead and see Hunter and Ethan, along with a few of their friends, leaning against the row of lockers where Kate and mine were.

"Aren't you two just the cutest!" I poke my tongue out at her.

"You've got your own man amongst that group, sweetie." She giggles. "Hunter's only there because your locker is there."

"What do you mean?" I ask, trying to keep my voice even.

"I think he's got a thing for you. He's always looking at you and he asks me about you sometimes, and he definitely asks Ethan to ask me about you."

I roll my eyes. "He does not."

Inside, my stomach was full of butterflies. Tall, brooding Hunter had a thing for me?

"Are you blushing?" Kate laughs. "Come on, you don't have to be shy. Everyone at some point will have a thing for Hunter."

"Did you?" I ask.

Kate laughs harder. "Of course I did! But then Ethan happened, and it went away like that." She snaps her fingers. "Hunter is one to watch, though. Super unpredictable. Always surrounded by girls but never has an official girlfriend."

"Really?" I frown. "What does that even mean? Surely he's got a girlfriend?"

"He has… 'things' with girls. He's not really interested in committing to anyone long term," she responds.

"Who has he had things with at this school?"

"Look at you asking all these questions," she grins before continuing. "I'm pretty sure he's had a thing with Hannah and maybe Kyla." She shrugs. "I don't really know. I zone out when Ethan talks about some poor girl Hunter has been terrorising with his charms and commitment issues."

"You make him sound awful," I laugh.

"He's just a guy who knows he's good looking, until you came along that is."

I blush again. "Well, I'm not going to make any moves. I've got my own world to concentrate on and I happen to like my planet revolving around me and not some guy," I say confidently. "No offence!"

Kate laughs. "None taken. I'm always my top priority and Ethan knows that. One day you'll find a guy like him. Maybe Hunter will surprise you!" She grins.

I grin back but it drops when I see Hunter approach us.

"Talking about me, ladies?" he asks.

I shake my head quickly as Kate smirks. "Talkin' 'bout ya not to ya," she says with her hands on her hips.

"Now I'm curious." He leans against the locker. "Why would you possibly be talking about me? Clearly, you're filling the new chick in on your obsession with me, Kate."

Kate rolls her eyes. "Am I that transparent?" she gasps dramatically.

I can't help but smirk. She has so much confidence and I couldn't help but admire her for it.

Hunter even cracks a grin. "Well, what do you want to know, Hayley? Or has Kate already told you everything there is to know about me?"

"We were actually talking about how arrogant you are." I have no idea where that came from, but it came out of my mouth. *Was I flirting?*

His jaw drops in mock horror. "Ouch."

Kate chuckles and pushes Hunter away from my locker. "Move along, little boy."

Hunter grins and walks away.

If my interactions with Hunter were as fun and as effortless as that one had just been, I think I was really going to enjoy it here.

⸻⬧⸻

English class was next, and Kate and I sat together with Ethan on her other side.

"Lend us a pen, will ya?" Hunter pulls out the chair beside me and sits down.

I turn and give him a look.

"Please?" he adds.

"How about you try again, and in English, please?" I can't help but flirt with him. He just made it so easy.

Hunter breaks into a grin. "Hayley, can I please borrow a pen? My arrogant self has lost my one true pen."

I let out a laugh. "Sure." I unzip my pencil case and hand him a pen. I felt Kate's eyes on me the whole time but I choose to ignore her.

The teacher starts the class and before too long she has us working on a group task.

"We should hang out sometime, away from all this crap." Hunter waves his hand around.

I feel my jaw drop. Was he asking me out on a date? This was random. He was doing it in front of everyone.

"Well, that's a new way to ask a girl out. You really have no shame, do you, Hunter?" Ethan laughs.

Kate tries to keep her expression neutral, but I know she's buzzing inside.

"I'm not asking her out," Hunter says bluntly. "She's my friend. Why wouldn't we hang out? You and I hang out on weekends when you're not with Kate."

Well, that was a kick in the guts. I don't know what could be more embarrassing, being asked out in front of everyone or being somewhat friend-zoned in front of everyone. At least he acknowledged me as a friend, I guess?

"Well, aren't you just a charmer, Hunter? You should really work on your delivery if you want to be my friend. I generally have friends who are nice to me." I add a flick of my hair and continue writing notes for the task.

Hunter laughs. "Fair call. I'll do better next time."

We slowly work through the task the teacher has given us.

"The new Marvel movie is out this weekend. Let's go, Hayley," Hunter says out of the blue.

"What about me?" Ethan asks dramatically.

"Kate doesn't like Marvel. So, unless you're going to make Kate suck it up and go, or the three of us can go, then why would I ask you?"

I couldn't help it. I burst out laughing. "Do you even know how to have a friend, Hunter?"

Kate and Ethan laugh with me as Hunter chuckles himself.

"What do you mean?" He continues to laugh. "I'm a great friend."

"Clearly." Ethan scrunches up a piece of paper and throws it at Hunter.

Hunter demands to present our work and we let him. God only knows what would come out of his mouth. I'll just sit here and watch. In my safe space, the friend zone. Was it a good thing or a bad thing to be here?

CHAPTER 4

I was finishing up at ACE Dance Studio on a Friday afternoon after a long class discussing our plans for the year and the types of performances we would be giving. ACE was an incredible studio with modern sprung floors, floor-to-ceiling mirrors, air conditioning and funky lights that would flicker with the music. The teachers were fresh and forever watching videos of other dancers all around the world to ensure our routines were on trend and relevant. I took jazz, hip hop, and contemporary classes. Contemporary was my absolute favourite as it was more thought provoking and emotive rather than the 'spirit fingers' vibe of jazz and attitude of hip hop. I was thrilled to be able to have a say in a few things since I had been offered to teach the little kids after my first week at the studio. As I was walking to Mum and Dad's car, I open my phone to see several messages. One was from a number I didn't know.

So when can we see the new Marvel movie this weekend?

I didn't have to ask who it was; I knew it was Hunter. I wonder how he got my number?

Well I have dance class on Saturday mornings so we could go Saturday night? What time can Ethan go?

He responds nearly instantly.

Ethan's not coming. Just us.

Just the two of us? At the movies? On a Saturday night? *Just go with it*, I tell myself. It seemed like it was just the way Hunter was. *At least you'll get to spend some time with him and try to get to know him a bit better.*

Yeah ok, what time?

7:00pm, see you there.

⸎

It's Saturday afternoon and I had spent the last hour on the phone to Kate trying to work out what to wear. Mum knew all about Hunter and his lack of commitment whilst being the most attractive guy out there. She seemed to be supportive of at least being his friend and to let any further relationship happen on its own. The day was going by fast and I felt like I was going to run out of time trying to put together the perfect outfit.

"Hayley, just be you. If you want this boy to like you, in whatever way, just be you. You don't want to have to pretend and then explain yourself later." Mum sits at the end of my bed.

"I don't know why I'm being so pedantic about it. I know what he's like," I sigh and flop on the bed beside her. "I've heard the rumours."

"I think you should go with your signature look." Mum ignores my comment. "Jeans, that navy shirt and your cardigan. Throw on some sandals, and you're done." Mum gets up and walks to the door. "You've got half an hour until we need to leave."

Crap. I start to pull my hair out of my hair tie and run my brush through it before tying it into my messy signature bun. I straighten the strays that don't quite reach so it didn't look like I had been electrocuted. I change my clothes and get started on my make-up. With just the right amount of make-up, I could pull off looking like I wasn't wearing any at all. I grab my shoes and my bag. It's surprising how quickly time flies when you're trying to impress someone.

"See? Perfect, just like I told you." Mum smiles as I walk out onto the deck where her and Dad are sitting having their afternoon tea and coffee.

"Do I need to meet this kid?" Dad lowers his voice and puffs his chest out.

"No," I laugh. "If he becomes more than just my friend, then maybe you can meet him."

"You're no fun." He relaxes back against the couch. "I had a speech prepared and everything."

"Let's go, honey." Mum grabs the car keys, and I follow her outside.

When we arrive at the cinemas, I promise Mum that I'll text her if Hunter doesn't arrive within 10 minutes. She agrees to wait in the car during that time, thankfully, just in case. I didn't need a chaperone. My mind is racing. What if he didn't come? What if it's a mean prank? My worries don't last long as I see Hunter sitting on one of the benches inside the cinemas, playing on his phone. I should've known better that he was already here. I send a quick text message to Mum and I see her start to drive away.

"Hey friend," I say as I approach him. I was trying to make it glaringly obvious that we were just friends, just as Hunter had pointed out. This was not a date.

Hunter looks up and smiles, putting his phone in his pocket. "Hey, Hayley. How are you?" He unfolds himself from the chair.

"I'm good," I reply, hoping my nerves weren't noticeable. He turns to walk towards the ticket and snack counter. I take notice of how he's dressed: dark blue jeans, a white crisp plain t-shirt, and vans. His hair was how he usually wore it at school. Surprisingly, he smelt of peppermint.

"How was class today?" he asks, referring to my dance class, as we wait in line. He remembered. My heart fluttered.

"It was the same old-same old." I try to be modest.

"Is that all I get?" He grins. "Do you put on shows and stuff like that?"

"Oh." I feel myself blush. "Yeah, there's an end-of-year concert I think, but I haven't been there long enough to know too much. I just like dancing. It's my hobby, I guess."

"At your old dance school did you do that stuff then?"

I nod as we move forward in the line. I don't remember ever telling him that I danced where I used to live. He was always surprising me.

"You're not giving much away," he laughs. "How about competitions? I hear some of the girls talk about that stuff."

I feel a pang of jealousy at the thought of what he did with other girls. I try to clear my mind though.

"Sometimes. I did at my old dance studio as I'd been there for a few years."

"Did you win anything?"

"Sometimes," I say again. He gives me a look which encourages me to elaborate. "Most times I was in a solo or a duo, and then a group routine. I think we won a few times but it's pretty cut-throat stuff. I try to just enjoy it, rather than let the competition get to me," I laugh.

"That's a lot to remember." He looks shocked. "How does one go about watching these concerts you speak of?"

I raise my eyebrows at him. "You just want to see girls in tight outfits and all done up."

"Do I really come across that shallow?" he laughs. "No, I'd go to support you. Plus, if it's a public thing, you can't say no. So, one way or another, I will get to see you dance."

I lightly shove his arm. "Whatever."

He grins just as the cashier calls us forward. "You can get the next one." He faces me briefly before addressing the cashier. "Two tickets to the Marvel movie please."

"Sure, any snacks for you and your friend?" The cashier looks me up and down in a judgemental way. She's a young girl, maybe around my age. I watch as the 'Hunter-effect' takes hold of her. He probably doesn't even notice. She stares him up and down, taking in every inch of him. I look up at Hunter as he frowns. Maybe he did notice? He looks almost embarrassed, yet frustrated at the same time.

"Yep, we'll share a popcorn and some Maltesers and two cokes." He swipes a credit card over the eftpos machine.

She gives me one final glance before grabbing our food and drinks and placing them on the counter.

"Can you get the tickets, babe?" Hunter asks as he balances our snacks in his arms and takes a sip from his drink.

Based on this girl's reaction to Hunter's comment, I decide to play along. Clearly, he did notice. It still made my heart skip a beat hearing him call me 'babe'.

"Sure thing, hun." I smile as I take the tickets out of the girl's hand. "Have a good night!" I say to her as we turn and walk away.

"I hate that girl," he whispers in my ear, sending tingles up my spine with his closeness.

"Hate is a strong word." I laugh. "I think she liked you."

He groans and takes another sip of his drink. "Thanks for playing along. I didn't mean to put you on the spot." He pauses at the bottom of the cinema auditorium. "Where do you want to sit?"

"Middle section, middle row," I reply confidently.

He starts to walk up the stairs and I follow him.

"It's the least I could do after you paid. Thanks Hunter." I plop into the seat next to him.

"It's not like we won't do this again." He shoves a handful of popcorn in his mouth. "So, you can shout us next time."

I'm pleasantly surprised that he saw a future of some kind between us. Whether we were friends or a couple, at this point I didn't care. I just enjoyed his company.

"You're not one of those people that talks throughout a movie and asks if I saw what happened?" I ask, grabbing a handful of popcorn too.

He laughs. "Nope, and if you are, I'm leaving now."

I laugh with him. I'm surprised at how natural it felt being around him and I could feel myself relaxing. This evening wasn't going to be a total disaster if I just acted like my normal self.

"So, tell me more about yourself." I test the waters with him to see if I could find out anything more than the limited information I already knew.

He hesitates slightly as though he was trying to work out what to tell me.

"What do you want to know?" he asks.

"I don't know. How about your birthday?" I ask.

"Why? We're all the same age."

I sigh. "Dude, you don't need to be so defensive. I'm just trying to get to know you. Do we really even know much about each other?"

I could see his face change.

"Sorry, I didn't mean that to come out so harsh," I say quickly, worried that I had ruined the vibe.

"No, no, it's okay. You're right. My birthday is June second," he responds. "You?"

"September sixteen," I answer.

"Come on, ask me something juicy! This could actually be fun."

I decide to pluck up the courage and quell my curiosity.

"If you had to date someone at school who would it be?" I ask before quickly adding, "If you don't already have a girlfriend." I avoid his glance.

"Come on, you know I don't have a girlfriend and I'm not interested in dating, too much work. I just like to have fun." He shrugs his shoulders. "Your turn."

Conveniently, the lights started to dim in the cinema. "Shhh, the movie is starting," I cheekily reply. I'd never been more thankful for the timing of the universe.

⁕

I turn to look at Hunter when the movie finishes and the lights come up. "That was so good!" I beam.

He smiles back at me without saying anything.

"What?" I ask. Did I have food in my teeth? Did my make-up run?

"Nothing. I'm glad you enjoyed it. You still haven't answered the question, by the way."

"What question?"

Then I remembered what I had asked him before the movie started, and he had in turn asked me the same question.

"You thought I'd forget, didn't you?" he smirks. How did he still look so good even after sitting still for two hours?

"Well, more like I had hoped you had forgotten," I reply. "Nope, no one has caught my eye yet," I answered.

His face drops but only for a second and I decide to call him out on it.

"What? Did you think I'd say you?"

He laughs and shakes his head. "Come on, let's go."

I grin at his response. I had put him on the spot. I think I had worked out how to talk to him. So long as I called him out on his crap, I would get the response I wanted. Hunter stands up and I follow him out of the cinema. From inside, I could see my parent's car in the parking lot.

"Is someone coming to pick you up?" I ask as I wave to my parents.

"Nah, I'll probably just catch the bus or something." He puts his hands into his pockets.

"I'm sure my parents wouldn't mind dropping you home," I offer. I knew that they wouldn't like him walking around late on a Saturday night.

"Maybe I can get them to tell me who you like at school." He grins.

"The bus sounds great! Have a nice night," I laugh and spin on my heel to walk off but he grabs my arm and pulls me back. It makes my heart skip a beat.

"I promise I'll behave. Are you sure they wouldn't mind?"

"I'm sure that they would prefer it if my friend got home safely," I say, again reminding him of the friend zone he had so wonderfully put me in the other day. I lead the way to the car and can see Dad share a glance with my mum. Trust them to come together. Dad would've taken any chance to meet the mysterious Hunter.

I open the rear passenger door of the car and stick my head in.

"Do you think we can drop Hunter home? He was going to take the bus."

"Sure honey," Mum responds, almost too quickly.

I slide into the backseat and Hunter follows, shutting the door behind him.

"Mum, Dad, this is Hunter. Hunter, these are my parents, Miranda and Antonio." I buckle my seat belt.

"Hello," he politely says. Courteous, good-boy Hunter was on display.

"It is so lovely to meet you Hunter. We've heard so many wonderful things about you," Mum responds.

I feel my jaw drop and Hunter looks at me with a smirk on his face.

"Really, like what?" He grins. "Like how incredibly good looking I am?"

My parents laugh.

"More like incredibly annoying." I cross my arms over my chest.

"Where are we dropping you off tonight?" Dad asks as he starts driving.

Hunter gives him instructions on how to get to his house. I was not familiar with the area, but Dad seemed to know exactly where to go. It doesn't take long to get to Hunter's house and when Dad starts to slow the car, I look out the window, amazed. The house was beautiful. The windows were floor to ceiling length and there were water features in the front garden. In the driveway was a nice shiny black sports car.

I glanced at Hunter to see if he would give anything away.

"Thanks Miranda, thanks Antonio," Hunter says as he opens the car door.

"You're most welcome," Mum replies.

"See you at school, Hayley." He gives me a smile and closes the door.

I watch as he walks up the driveway and into the house.

"I like that boy," Dad says as he pulls away.

CHAPTER 5

"Define close?" I ask. How detailed did Dr Martin want me to go? Why was I even here again?

"Inseparable, never apart, almost to a point of obsession," Dr Martin responds. I wonder if psychologists received training at university on how to keep a poker face. Sometimes I wondered if the details of this whole thing, and probably other people's stories and mishaps, ever affected Dr Martin. How do you listen to all of these stories and then go home completely normal? Does Dr Martin ever wake up in the middle of the night after a terrifying nightmare based on what someone's told him? Does Dr Martin hurt like I do, knowing that this is how it ended?

"Do you need a break? I know bringing up old memories must be tough for you," Dr Martin interrupts my inner thoughts.

"No, sorry. Um, I guess at one point it did turn into an obsession. But it never seemed extreme. I didn't see an issue with two people in love. Do you? There are healthy obsessions and unhealthy obsessions, right?" I respond.

Dr Martin looks over the rim of his glasses. "Obsession can be a very powerful thing and is often misunderstood. Teenage girls claim to be obsessed over a boy band, teenage boys can be obsessed over a football team. This is a material thing, but when obsession becomes unhealthy, this is where you see a complete one-eighty in behaviour. A person's attributes are still there, but their every thought revolves around that other person. What are they doing? What are they thinking? Did what they say really mean this, or did it mean that? Keeping track of someone's every move, monitoring their whole life. That's when obsession becomes unhealthy. Let me ask you again, do you think it was a healthy or an unhealthy obsession?"

I bite my lip. Dr Martin has got me there.

CHAPTER 6

Kate and I dawdle down the path past the classrooms on the way to our lockers. School hadn't started yet but Kate and I had met up to get started on our dance routine early this morning while it was nice and cool. We would be performing it in several weeks for our first assessment of the school term. It was Valentine's Day today and Kate was excited to see what Ethan had in store for her. She was telling me, in great detail, what he had done the previous year and how it would be hard for him to beat that effort, but she was sure he could pull it off.

We walk past some of Hunter and Ethan's friends sitting at the tables outside of our homerooms. I spot Hunter easily as he's sitting on top of the table with his feet on the bench below. Ethan is there too, and I watch as Kate races over to him, surprising him from behind. I keep walking to my locker as I didn't really feel like watching their lovey-dovey display.

"Hayley!" I hear the group of boys call out. I turn my gaze and smile back at them.

"Happy Valentine's Day!" they sing out, laughing with each other.

I never celebrated Valentine's Day. I never had someone to celebrate it with, so why bother getting caught up in the hype of it all?

"Thank you." I smile back at them again.

As I got to my locker, I could feel a pair of eyes on me. I ignore them, knowing very well who it was. Hunter and I were friends. Nothing more, nothing less.

"Aren't you going to wish your girlfriend a happy Valentine's Day?" I hear one of them laugh, followed by a light scuffle.

I open my locker to find a small bouquet of flowers. I could feel a smile escape my lips. I try my best to turn casually and look at the boys seated at their table. That's when I notice that Hunter was no longer there.

⸻ ◆ ⸻

It was after our morning break when Hunter seemingly storms over to me as I get my books out of my locker.

"Got a secret boyfriend I don't know about?" he demands.

"Excuse me?" I reply, shutting my locker and turning to face him.

"Who sent you the Valentine's Day thing?" He waves to my locker.

Disappointingly, the gift actually wasn't from Hunter. A part of me deep down wanted it to be from Hunter, but it was from Kate. She had given all of her close girlfriends a Valentine's Day gift.

I thought about his question for a moment. Why would he be asking me this?

"Why are you so interested?" I cross my arms in front of me.

"I'm not." He stands up straight. "It's called making conversation."

His abruptness startles me.

I begin to stutter an apology before he breaks into a grin.

"So easy to stir you up," he grins. "It's cute."

I blush.

"See you around, Hayley."

⸻◆⸻

"Hayley, wait up," Hunter calls as he catches up to Kate and I.

We were walking back from the tuckshop with their newest flavour of frozen drink in my hand. Kate keeps walking as I stop to talk to Hunter.

"So, I found something that I thought you'd like and I thought what better day to give it to you than on this silly made up day that the world calls Valentine's Day." Hunter pulls a small box with a white bow out of his pocket and places it in my hand. He doesn't meet my gaze at all when his hand gently touches mine. I was speechless. I couldn't believe this was happening.

I hand him my drink so I could open the small box.

"Don't drink any of it," I instruct. He grins back at me.

I could feel his eyes on me as I open the box. I'm surprised to see a small ballet dancer charm for my charm bracelet. A bracelet he didn't know I had.

"Wow, Hunter," I say quickly as I admire the charm. "It's so beautiful, thank you."

"Well, yeah, I thought you might like it." He shrugs as he takes a sip of my drink.

"I didn't get you anything," I blurt out.

He frowns. "You're my friend. I saw it and I thought you'd like it. That's all there is to it. I don't expect you to do something in return just because it's Valentine's Day."

I feel my eyes widen. That was blunt.

"Don't read into this, Hayley. I'm not looking for a relationship," he continues.

I put the charm back in the box and into my pocket. It was time to go on the defence and call him out. That tactic had worked in the past.

"Who said I was even interested in you? I was just being polite," I say as bluntly as I can manage.

He laughs. "Wow, okay. I can take a hit to my ego. Got to admit, this is a first for me. I'm usually pretty popular with the ladies."

I had forgotten how arrogant he could be and today, I just didn't feel like dealing with that kind of attitude. I push past him and he doesn't try to follow.

———◦———

It was the end of the school day and I hadn't seen Hunter since lunch. Not that that surprised me. We didn't have many classes together. I walk back to my locker to get my school bag. As I turn back around to head off for the day, I see Hunter leaning against a post with his back to me. I attempt to breeze past him to show that I didn't care.

Instead, he gently tugs the handle on my backpack. "Hayley."

"Yes, Hunter," I respond as I turn to face him.

"Can I walk with you?" he asks.

He was so random. It was kinda cute, but I had to be strong. I wasn't going to let him play me.

"I'm walking up to the pick-up zone," I reply.

"Good, so am I." He holds his arm out for me to lead the way.

I don't know what to say to him or if I even wanted to say anything to him at all. I saw his true colours again today.

"Do you like the charm I got you?" he asks, like earlier had never even happened.

"It's very nice. Very unexpected, especially given your reputation. Tell me, do your statistics always get a gift before you play them?" I can't help but be blunt. He needs to know that I knew exactly the kind of person he was.

Hunter lets out a laugh. "Where on earth do you get your information from?"

I shrug. "People talk, Hunter."

"Are you asking around about me?" He grins.

I sigh. Of course he thought everything was a game. "No, I'm not, Hunter. More like people see us together and feel the need to tell me about you. Or warn me."

"I don't give a fuck about what people say about me." This was the first time he had sworn around me. "How many girls do you think I play around with?"

I must've pushed one of his buttons.

"That's a bit of a loaded question."

"How many girls, Hayley?" he asks again, forcefully.

I sigh once more. There was no getting out of this one. I had to finish what I started. "I don't know, five? Surely you've got girls outside of the school?"

"Wow," he lets out a blow of air. "That's what you think of me?"

"It's what everyone thinks of you." I shrug.

Hunter stops to think about this. I couldn't tell if he was proud or hurt by this.

"I don't care what people think about me," he says again. "What do *you* think?"

I stop and look up at him. Now was my moment to be truthful again. That's what he told me he liked about me. "That it's all for show. You haven't had a girlfriend at all. You're scared of commitment because you know you're good looking and you're constantly thinking someone better is going to waltz in and you don't want to miss out."

"You think I'm good looking?" he smirks.

"Is that really all you took out of what I just said?" I let out a frustrated sigh. One day we'd have a serious conversation from start to finish without him being immature.

"Well, you think you've got me all figured out, don't you?" He crosses his arms over his chest.

I let out a laugh. "Far from it, Hunter. You surprise me daily."

"Good, that's what I want you to think about me," he smiles softly.

"I'm so confused." I scrunch my face up. Is this how he tricked all his girls? He just ran them in circles until he said something cute or mysterious?

"Hayley, I don't have a girlfriend because I don't want one. I haven't found the right girl yet. Sure, I've messed around with a few, but I'm not a man-whore." His face was serious, and I was slightly surprised.

"You're a rollercoaster to deal with, you know that, right?" I drop into step beside him.

"Keeps life interesting, I think." He jogs away to join a few of the boys at the bus stop as I keep walking to my parent's car.

CHAPTER 7

"Was he happy, though?" Dr Martin continues with his questions.

Every single memory he was forcing me to bring up was now plagued with what ifs? Had I really missed all the signs? Why did it matter if he was happy in high school? Everyone is allowed to change.

"I thought he was. He never made me think otherwise," I answer truthfully.

He always seemed happy to me. Sure, there were good days and bad days. Just depends on what had happened really. Everyone has the ability to get under someone's skin. He was a teenage boy so his attitude and temperament were going to change constantly. I know mine did.

"Was he a troubled boy?"

"Well, I wouldn't say he was troubled. Things could've been significantly different at home to what he let on." I shrug.

I knew Hunter though. I knew everything about him. If I had seen the red flags, believe me, I would've done something.

"What does that mean? Did he have a troubled home life?" Dr Martin continues to poke me.

"He wasn't abused or anything, if that's what you're getting at." I cross my arms over my chest in defence. "He just didn't like to be told no by anyone." I try to move on from the subject of his family.

Dr Martin narrows his eyes at my last statement.

He just didn't like to be told no.

That in itself was a red flag now that I reflected on it, but I didn't mean it in a bad way. He just liked attention so he would argue his case to be the leader of a group, or tried his luck on teachers to see what he could get away with. He was also a loud and confident person. I didn't think these traits were a bad thing. He didn't exude this power though. He knew and respected boundaries.

"Did you ever feel pressured by him?"

"Absolutely not," I spit out unintentionally.

This was not the person I knew. They had twisted everything.

~ PART 2 ~

CHAPTER 8

"Ready for our last year of school ever, Hayls?" Hunter asks me as we walk down the pathway to our homerooms.

"As ready as I'll ever be," I reply. We were in our second week of our final year of high school and I was trying to work out ways to drop hints to Hunter that I wanted to be his girlfriend. I had decided over the Christmas break that I'd had enough of our back-and-forth flirting and I wanted more from him. I glance over at him. "I wonder what's in store for us this year."

"For us? You'll become a dance teacher, and I'll be the king of everyone. Sounds reasonable." He swings an arm around my shoulder and grins. Little did he know how that made me feel inside. I almost want to shake his arm away because I didn't want to live in a fantasy land where we were actually a couple when I knew that wasn't what he wanted.

We hung out all the time over Christmas. We went to the beach together, the local water park, even the beautiful Lake Eacham for swims. Most of the time, it was just the two of us, as Kate's family went on their annual holiday over the summer break. I fell into the trap of feeling like Hunter and I had a special connection and that we could actually work as a couple. He had a reputation of never having a girlfriend, but I didn't know that Hunter. Apparently, he had changed after he met me. Or so everyone told me. If you didn't know our history, you would have thought we were dating with how we acted around each other, so why not make it official? I wasn't expecting a miracle, and I certainly wasn't delusional enough to think I could change him, but I could only try, right?

"You're so modest," I laugh, stepping out of his reach.

We were walking past the administration building when our year coordinator, Mr Edwards, called out to Hunter. Behind him was a boy. He was shorter than Hunter, though not by much, and had a friendly smile on his face.

"This is Theo. He'll be joining you both in Grade 12 this year. Can you show him where his home room is?" Mr Edwards says.

"Sure," Hunter responds half-heartedly and I try to hide a smirk. I knew that he wouldn't be pleased to show the new kid around and I was surprised he was asked at all given his reputation. "What home room are you in Theo?" Hunter asks.

Theo looks at his timetable. "12B," he answers, looking back at Hunter.

"That's my home room!" I beam. "I can show you where to go!"

Theo smiles back at me and I feel Hunter stiffen beside me as his demeanour changes. I decide to ignore it. I would hate to feel unwanted on my first day of school.

"Well, my name is Hayley," I offer out my hand for Theo to shake and knowing Hunter won't do it, introduce him as well. "This is Hunter."

"Nice to meet you both," Theo smiles back. As if they could read each other's mind, neither offer their hand out to shake.

"Well, let's go." I try to break the tension by starting off in the direction of the classrooms.

Theo was tall with dirty blonde hair that stuck out in all the right places. His green eyes bore into mine, like they were trying to read my mind. Theo was a good-looking guy but when I looked back at Hunter, he just didn't compare. Theo starts to tell us about himself and how his family had an emergency pop up which was why he was starting a week late. I lightly nudge Hunter with my shoulder. His head snaps up to look at me and I mouth at him to smile.

He rolls his eyes. "This is my home room. See ya round, Hayls. Enjoy the new school." Hunter finally offers his hand for Theo to shake.

Theo eyes him for a second before accepting his hand. "Thanks."

I feel Hunter's eyes on us as we begin to walk away.

I try to casually look back at Hunter. He stood talking to Ethan and I could tell by his posture, his hand running through his hair, that he was annoyed.

CHAPTER 9

"Who the hell does he think he is?" Hunter asks as he slumps against the locker beside mine. It was only a month into the new school year.

"What are you talking about, Hunter?" I respond as I get my books out.

"Theo. Like he waltzes in here thinking he owns the place." Hunter crosses his arms over his chest. "I don't like the way he talks to you."

"What do you mean?" I sigh. "He speaks to me just like you."

"He's nothing like me," he snaps back.

"Are you jealous or something, Hunter? I'm pretty sure everyone knows your place at the top. Plus, there's nothing wrong with a bit of healthy competition."

"You think I'd honestly compete with someone just to get you?"

I'm stunned by his words. *What did he just say?*

It looks as though he is stunned too, because he turns quickly on his heel and walks the other way.

⚬

It was lunch break, and I was walking back to my locker with Kate and Theo. Hunter was less than pleased to hear how many classes I had with Theo but there was nothing I could do about that. I couldn't help that Theo and I had similar interests.

"Jeez, if looks could kill I would be six feet under now," Theo laughs. I look up and see Hunter giving Theo a death stare whilst whispering something to Ethan. They were leaning against the set of lockers next to mine.

"Ignore him Theo. That's just Hunter," I laugh. A part of me was wondering if Hunter was talking about me, especially after what he said this morning. Butterflies filled my stomach with even the thought of Hunter liking me back.

"What's his deal, anyway? He just seems full of anger every time I talk to him," Theo looks down in frustration.

I almost want to laugh. The Hunter I knew was so different. "I'm not sure. It took me a couple of weeks to figure out Hunter and there's no other way to explain him, except 'that's Hunter'."

"And you put up with that? You're a good girlfriend," Theo nudges me lightly with his shoulder. I could just tell he was trying to get an understanding of my dynamic with Hunter.

"Oh, no," I try to laugh it off. "I'm not Hunter's girlfriend. We're just friends." Deep down, I knew that I wanted more, but Hunter seemed to be okay with just cruising along like we were.

"Right," Theo gives me a look to say that there must be more to it. "Does he know that?"

"Just friends," I try to assure him, as well as myself.

Hunter and Ethan were still there when we reached the lockers except Ethan made his way towards Kate. They were so cute together.

"Hey Hayley," Hunter says as I open my locker. "Theo." His voice turns to stone. Theo acknowledges Hunter in return before packing his books away in his locker.

"So much testosterone in the air," I whisper quietly under my breath.

Hunter moves himself casually in front of me, blocking my line of sight of Theo.

"So we've got English next," he says and I nod. There was a hint of excitement in his voice.

"Ryan just had English and they're doing another partner assignment." He crosses his arms, and leans against the lockers. "So, are you ready to get another A? We always do so well together," his voice was now slightly raised and he was trying to subtly look over his shoulder. You didn't need to be a genius to figure out who he was hoping was listening and watching us. I really did wonder what Theo thought of Hunter, especially now that he knew we weren't a couple.

"I would not have thought you'd want to work with me again after last time." I laugh, trying to continue as we normally would. "You said I was too much of a hardass."

"Someone's got to pull me into line," Hunter laughs. It's so adorable. "Well, save me a seat, babe."

He kisses me on the cheek and walks off.

I immediately turn to look at Kate. Her eyes are wide, her expression likely mirroring my own surprised face. Ethan grins but he turns and follows Hunter around the corner.

"Just friends, hey?" Theo interrupts my thoughts. His face was stone cold as he storms off.

I put my hand against my cheek. It was such a small, simple gesture, and he was so gentle. A wave of anger floods over me and I feel as though I had been slapped in the face. He used me to make a point to Theo. That's all it was. He never would've done this if Theo wasn't here. I was angry. I felt used.

"What are you doing?" Kate asks. "You okay, Hayls?"

"No, I'm not okay, Kate. I'm going to ask him what his deal is," I say, finally mustering the confidence to approach him and marching off in the direction Hunter went.

I walk around the corner and could see him talking to Ethan at the tables. They were sitting on the tabletop with their feet resting on the bench. Hunter had his head in his hands and it made me immediately want to comfort him. Clearly, he didn't see that coming either. Ethan catches me staring and tries to signal me not to approach. Hunter notices though and looks up to see me staring. He drops his bottom lip. You can see the confusion on his face.

I start to move confidently towards him. He sighs and gets up to walk over to me. When we're finally face to face, he remains silent. I would have to be the one to break the ice.

"Is everything okay between us, Hunter?"

"It was dumb. I shouldn't have done it. It meant nothing." He crosses his arms over his chest. "That's all it was. A mistake. Don't read into it," he says bluntly.

I can't help but feel hurt by his words. He was so quick to dismiss what happened and was now being rude. My inner child comes out. "I think I'm going to work with Theo in English instead."

"What?" Hunter gasps as his arms drop to his sides. "I fuck up once and you drop me for him, out of everyone? It was just a stupid kiss on the cheek."

"I'm not dropping you, Hunter, but clearly you've got something going on in your head. You can't just kiss me on the cheek and then expect it to go back to normal." I put my hands on my hips.

"There's nothing wrong, Hayley. You know I don't like Theo. We're supposed to be friends." He looks at his shoes and crosses his arms back over his chest.

"Hunter, we are friends and that's why I want a better answer than 'it was a mistake'. I don't want to be used in whatever imaginary show you're putting on to prove a point to Theo."

He bites his lip. "I can't give you a better one other than it was a mistake. Brain snap. Surely you have them too. You just had one when you picked Theo over me."

I couldn't help but let out a laugh. Tension broken.

"Fine," I smile as relief washes over his face. Hunter turns to walk away but I gently touch his arm. I wasn't finished with him just yet. He whips back around to face me, eyes wide from my touch. "You'd tell me if there was something troubling you, or if I did something to upset you, right?"

He smiles. One I had never seen before. "Of course I would. You're my girl." He lightly squeezes my shoulder and starts to walk away.

"Hunter," I call out and he turns back to me, "If we're just friends, you can't really say stuff like that. It's super misleading and I'm getting tired of having to convince people we're not in a relationship."

"Who's bothering you? It's none of their business what we do." It's almost as though he grows another foot taller, as his arms fold back over his chest.

"You're missing the most important part of what I said. Even now, Hunter, don't you realise people are trying to hide the fact that they're watching us?"

Hunter looks around us and it instantly becomes a bit louder.

"Hayley," he places his hands on my shoulders and leans down to look me in the eye, "You are a girl, and you are my friend. That's it. Everyone jokes around."

"Hunter, you're doing it right now!" I shrug away from his hands.

He groans. "I'm not doing shit with you, Hayley! We had a good thing going and now you've ruined it by adding feelings. Pick Theo for your stupid English assignment. I couldn't care less! I wouldn't want to mislead everyone about an 'us' that doesn't even exist." With that, he storms off and it becomes loud again.

I'm too stunned to move. How could he be so rude? I look up to see that Ethan has caught up to Hunter. Ethan says a few things to him and absentmindedly points back at me. Hunter turns to look and I could see the worry on his face. I watch him start to walk back towards me but instead I glare at him and he stops. His bottom lip drops as we lock eyes. I linger in his gaze for a moment and then turn on the spot and walk away.

⸺⸺◦⊙◦⸺⸺

In English class, Kate and I strategically choose our seats so that I was at the end of the row of desks. Ethan, bless him, follows Kate's instruction to sit in front of me instead of next to her and one of our dance friends, Louise, sits beside Kate. I didn't want Hunter to sit near me. I didn't even want Theo to sit near me. I didn't want to add more fuel to the fire.

Ethan leans back in his chair to talk to us before the teacher arrives.

"You have that boy wrapped around your finger, Hayls," Ethan chuckles as he balances himself on the back two legs of the chair.

I feel a grin escape my lips.

"What did you even say to him?" Kate asks.

"I asked him point blank." Ethan shrugs. "I took a note from Hayley's book. Plus, if he upsets you, Hayley, it upsets Kate and then I have to deal with it," he jokes. "So it's in my best interest to help sort it out."

"Fair call," I laugh.

Whilst we're chatting with Ethan, I see Hunter pull up a seat beside him but he doesn't turn to face us. Ethan looks between Kate and I. He shrugs before turning back around in his seat and claps Hunter on the back as they engage in a hushed conversation.

The teacher finally arrives and calls us to attention. As they start going through the content, I could see Hunter strategically using his phone so the teacher couldn't see. He hadn't once looked back at me.

I had started drawing in my notebook when I felt my phone vibrate in my pocket.

I check the notification and see Hunter's name appear. I peek to see if he's watching. He wasn't, but my curiosity got the better of me.

We all good? his text message read.

I send back the red X emoji to say 'no'. He leans back in his chair with a sigh. I want to go to him and comfort him, but I have to stand my ground or otherwise he would keep doing it. When I look back up, I meet Hunter's eye before he quickly whips his head back around to the front.

"Alright everyone," the teacher pulls my attention back. "Time to pick your assignment partners!"

I sigh softly. I knew that Kate wanted to work with Ethan and I wasn't going to hold her back just because Hunter and I couldn't get our act together. Theo probably thought that I was still going to work with Hunter anyway. Everyone starts to move around the room. I was about to turn to Louise beside Kate when I realise Hunter was crouching down in front of my desk, leaning on his forearms. Kate squeezes my shoulder and Ethan grins, mouthing the words 'told you so' before he moves to sit with Kate.

Hunter's face is full of concern and he doesn't meet my eye.

"Hi Hayley," he mumbles.

I decide to keep up my strong woman stance. "For the sake of this assignment, I will act as though our lunch time argument didn't happen but outside of this classroom, stay away from me. I don't want you to walk with me or wait for me," I say sternly.

I could see his face drop, but he simply nodded. Maybe Ethan was right. Maybe I do have him wrapped around my finger. This was clearly a first for Hunter.

"Miss, can we work outside?" Hunter calls out to the teacher. This would be interesting.

"Just at the tables outside, Hunter," she responds with a hint of irritation, but she probably knew he'd put up a fight if she said no.

"Come on, let's go," Hunter gathers up his books as well as mine and heads outside before I have a chance to protest. I feel Kate's eyes on us as we leave the room. Hell, I felt the whole class's eyes on us. Everyone was watching.

I follow him to the tables and sit across from him.

Hunter clears his throat. "So, I'm not very proud of the way I handled things before. I didn't mean to be so harsh. I don't know why, I just don't like that Theo guy and it's so obvious that he wants to be with you and he's simply just not good enough for you," he keeps his head down. It was clearly hard for him to be mature about this instead of a hard ass.

"Hunter, I am not interested in Theo. So, snap out of whatever theory you have in your head that I'm trying to ruin our friendship by getting with him."

I could see him smile, even though his head was bowed. He looks like a kid getting told off by his parents for doing something he thought was funny.

"So, stop showing off in front of him because I am not a toy you can use and abuse," I finish off my rant.

He looks up at this, his expression shocked. "I'd never do that to you, Hayley."

"You did though, Hunter. You've been doing it all year," I snap. "So, unless you have a secret reason why you keep acting this way, then no more."

"I need to get something from my locker. Come for a walk?" he says as he stands up.

I let out a laugh. "Seriously? You flit from a serious conversation to just something so random!"

"What did you expect from me?" He smiles as I stand up and follow him.

Hunter walks ahead of me and I see him look around. It all happens so quickly. He grabs my hand, pulls me towards him and gently pushes me against the lockers. Hunter takes my face in his hands and kisses me ever so tenderly. I'm nearly too surprised to move, but it melts away and I could feel myself relax into the kiss. I could feel his smile as he realises I'm not resisting. When Hunter pulls away, it seems as though we were both holding our breath and we let out a small laugh.

The bell rings, signalling the next class. He drops his hands quickly and clears his throat.

"I'll text you," he says shyly as scratches the back of his neck and then puts his hands in his pockets and walks away.

I don't see Hunter again after that.

⊷◆⊷

"Hayley, can I talk to you?" Theo catches up to me on my way to the pick-up zone.

"Sure," I answer sheepishly. "I'm just walking up to where my parents pick me up if you're going that way?"

He nods as he fixes his bag on his back and joins me.

"What's up?" I ask. I had a hunch as to where this could be going. It wasn't very often that Theo asked to talk to me, or even made an effort to find me just to talk to me. My mind flashed to Hunter instantly.

"Well, um, I was wondering if you wanted to maybe go to dinner with me on Saturday?" he was so shy and I could see it had taken a lot of courage for him to ask me out. This would be a fun and awkward conversation, especially after today's events with Hunter. *Not!*

"Oh, um," I begin to utter an excuse.

He laughs lightly as he immediately realises what's happening. "It's Hunter, isn't it?" he says. "I didn't even think! Just because you're not dating him, doesn't mean you don't like him."

My eyes went wide in embarrassment. Yes, Hunter and I flirted a bit and people may have thought we were a couple but to be called out on my feelings made me flustered.

"I get it, Hayls," he scoffs. "He's the complicated bad boy. What girl wouldn't want to date Mr Bad Boy?" His voice is cold.

I stop in my tracks. Was there a full moon tonight or something? Why were all the boys being so disrespectful? "Theo, just because I say no to going on a date with you doesn't mean you have to be so rude. Yes, Hunter is complicated but I've known him for a while now and you seem to be the only person who has a problem with him. No one else does."

Theo scoffs again. "You're blinded by him, Hayls. He's not good for you." He turns away from me, throwing his hands up in frustration.

"Funny. He said the same thing about you." Theo spins back around to face me at what I just said. I could almost see the steam come out of his ears with my comment. Clearly, he thought he was Mr Perfect, too.

CHAPTER 10

As usual, Hunter was waiting for me at the drop-off zone at school. I was trying to work out how to tell him about my encounter with Theo all night but I didn't know how. I didn't want him to do anything to Theo but then I thought it might push him to ask me out officially. I settle on not telling him, especially after how angry Theo seemed to get about the whole thing. No one else knew about the exchange I had with Theo. Plus, Hunter really didn't like him so why even bother? I didn't want to deal with whatever attitude he would get as a result.

Hunter doesn't try to hold my hand as we walk nor does he act as though our kiss even happened. I don't try to force anything either as I was still worried that I'd scare him away. I keep the conversation light and just talk about nonsense. He would add his commentary whenever he felt like it but otherwise he kept quiet. I think he was appreciative that I didn't bring it up. He was definitely acting very shy but he has a smile on his face and I could feel his eyes on me the whole time.

"Are you sure he kissed you yesterday or were you imagining it?" Kate asks me in one of our classes together after our morning tea break. I had called her last night to tell her what happened with Hunter.

I laugh. "What do you mean?"

"He seems like his usual self. I would've thought he would act a bit differently," she shrugs.

"So did I, Kate." I brush a stray hair out of my face. "But this is a first for him, so maybe he's just really shy?"

"Maybe." She shrugs her shoulders and returns to her work.

I look away from her and accidentally catch the eye of Theo. I had nearly forgotten about our encounter yesterday. Now that I had seen Hunter, he was all I could think about it. I had to tell Kate. She'd know what to do.

"Theo asked me out yesterday," I whisper.

Her eyes widen before she starts to chew on the end of her pen. "He what?"

"I said no," I say swiftly.

"How has it taken you this long to tell me?" she demands, dropping her pen on the table.

"Sshh!" I look around to see if she had attracted anyone's attention. "I want to tell Hunter but I don't know how and now I'm worried he's going to find out from someone else." I rub my forehead.

Her eyes widen again. "Hunter doesn't know?"

I shake my head.

"Well, I'm sure it'll be a fun conversation when he does find out. I just hope I can tell him before someone else does," I drop my head on my forearms. My stomach was in knots.

⸎

"What the fuck happened after school yesterday, and how come I'm the last to find out?" Hunter storms up behind me as I walk to class.

"What do you mean?" I try to play it cool and decide to keep walking. I didn't want to draw attention to ourselves, and I also needed to show him that I wasn't bothered by Theo.

He lightly grabs my arm to turn me to face him. It sends electric currents up my arm and I was hoping that he didn't let go.

"Theo asked you out, Hayley, and you didn't tell me!" he crosses his arms over his chest.

"It's not a big deal, Hunter. Remember, I'm not interested in him and I know you don't like him so why would I make you mad by talking about him?" I respond.

"I knew he had intentions above being just your friend." He was definitely frustrated. "I wish you'd told me, Hayley. I didn't want to have to find out from everyone else. It made me look like an idiot!"

Gosh, gossip travelled fast in this school.

"Hunter," I try to keep my voice steady. "Please don't make this into something it's not. Theo asked me out, and I said no."

I could see he was trying to choose his words carefully. Inside, I start to feel butterflies. Maybe this was the moment he finally asked me to be his girlfriend.

"Was I kissing myself at the lockers yesterday?" His voice is low and I blush at the memory. "Hayley, we've known each other for ages now. I wait for you every morning, and we walk together every afternoon. We hang out all the time and damn it, Hayley, I know you kissed me back yesterday, or did I dream it? You're supposed to be mine!"

I could feel my bottom lip drop at his honesty. At least I wasn't imagining it these past couple of months. Hunter really had liked me all this time.

"Fuck it," he snaps. "Hayley, I need more and I've just been enjoying how close we are and I didn't want to fuck anything up, but I want everyone to know that I'm your boyfriend. Not Theo."

I could feel a smile escape my lips. He looked so frustrated yet shy all at the same time.

"Are you going to ask me on a date?"

"Whatever gets me the title of being your boyfriend," he huffs.

"A date would be nice." I smile.

"Hayley, will you be my girlfriend and do me the pleasure of going on a date with me Friday night?"

I couldn't believe it. My dreams were coming true and he was admitting it to me.

I nod as he takes my face in his hands and kisses me. It was just as magical as it was yesterday. We just seemed to fit together so perfectly.

"See you later, girlfriend," Hunter grins and walks back towards his classroom.

—◈—

I say goodbye to Kate and grab my bag from my locker. I could see Hunter at our meeting spot and I could feel a smile escape my lips. He shyly smiles back before getting pulled over for a chat by one of his friends.

"Hayley," Theo's voice distracts me and I turn to face him. Theo had avoided me all day but must have clearly told people he had asked me out if Hunter knew. I wondered what else he said whilst gossiping to everyone.

"Theo," I respond coldly.

"Look, about yesterday, I was completely in the wrong—" he begins.

"Yes, you were." I cut him off, stealing a glance at Hunter. He was still talking to his friend but I could see him do a double take when he saw Theo and I together.

"Let me finish. I guess my ego took a hit and I overreacted. I still don't like Hunter and think you're too good for him. I'm sorry Hayley, I shouldn't have spoken to you that way."

"In what way?" I feel Hunter loom behind me. I could see anger flush over Theo's face.

I turn and place a hand on Hunter's chest which causes him to look at me instead. "Leave it alone, Hunter. I can handle this." I turn back to Theo. "Thank you for apologising, Theo. You shouldn't have said those things when you hardly know Hunter. And for the record, Hunter and I are very happy. Together."

Theo's face drops as Hunter wraps an arm around my waist and I lean back into him. Thanks to him, it was finally official with Hunter and he knew it.

"I'll see you around, Theo," I mutter and walk away, taking Hunter's hand as I go.

Hunter chuckles. "You have no idea how badly I want to kiss you right now," he whispers.

I feel myself blush and lace my fingers with his.

"Like really badly. Thank you for standing up for me, Hayley." Hunter smiles at me but then I see the cute boyfriend act drop and get replaced by the jealous boyfriend act. "Now what the hell did he say to you yesterday that made him need to apologise? Apart from him trying to steal you away from me?"

I fill Hunter in on what happened yesterday and he listens intently. People do a double take when they see Hunter and I holding hands on our walk up to the pick-up zone. I guess it was something I had to get used to.

When we get to the pick-up zone, Hunter turns me to face him before he brushes ever so gently a strand of hair out of my face. He hesitates momentarily before leaning in and kissing me.

"Finally, Hunter's got the girl!" I feel Ethan smack Hunter on his back. A few other people around us start laughing at Ethan and Hunter's exchange and someone else wolf whistles. I could feel the heat rise to my cheeks.

Hunter pinches me lightly on the cheek. "It's only just getting started, girlfriend." He smiles and then goes to join the bus queue with Ethan.

CHAPTER 11

"Well, well, well." Kate approaches us from the lockers the next day at school.

As usual, Hunter had met me at the drop-off zone and held my hand as we walked down to the senior school area.

"Two little love birds are finally sitting in a tree!"

Hunter slings an arm around Kate's shoulders. "Jealous, Kate?" he smirks.

Kate pushes away his arm. "Ew, in your dreams!" she groans. "Girl, you better watch those hands of your man. They wander."

"Hey, whoa, that was uncalled for," Hunter snaps. "You know damn well I'm not going to hurt her."

I could see that Kate was stunned from his response until he finally breaks into a grin.

"Otherwise, I'd have you to deal with if I do." He continues to grin as she starts to swat at him.

I shake my head in laughter as I open my locker to get ready for my first class.

"So, when's your first date?" Ethan swings an arm around Hunter's shoulders.

"Babe, can you see this? Tell him to get off me. I have a girlfriend," Hunter jokingly tells me.

He genuinely looked happy to call me his girlfriend, and it made me feel warm inside. I can't help but laugh in response to Hunter before catching the eye of Theo. He quickly looks away and keeps walking.

"What the fuck was that?" Hunter must've noticed the fleeting exchange.

"What was what, Hunter?" I sigh. Of course something had to ruin this nice moment.

"Were you just making eyes at Theo?" he demands.

I could see Kate and Ethan start to slowly distance themselves from us. I couldn't help but feel embarrassed. I needed to do something that would settle him down.

"No, Hunter. He came into my line of sight. That's all it was. Calm down," I say matter-of-factly as I close my locker and turn to face him. He was facing the direction that Theo went. I walk up behind him and wrap my arms around his waist. I could feel him instantly relax at my touch.

"I don't like him, Hayley." He turns around to face me as he wraps his arms around me.

"I know you don't, but if we have to keep having the same conversation about him, I'm going to lose my mind. It wasn't even a choice, Hunter. I can't believe I'm admitting this but this—" I point between us "—has been a long time coming."

This relaxes him further and he smiles shyly.

"I knew you loved me from the start," he jokes.

I roll my eyes. "Come on, class is about to start."

Hunter walks me to the door of my classroom. I could see he wanted to say something but was biting his tongue. No doubt, Theo was probably right inside the door.

He leans down to whisper to me. "I'm going to kiss you now."

I laugh as he gives me a quick peck on the lips.

I walk in the door and the classroom erupts into applause and cheering. I could feel the blood rush to my cheeks and I turned to see Hunter grinning at the door.

"See ya next class, girlfriend!" Hunter calls out.

CHAPTER 12

My heart was racing. I was going on my first date with Hunter tonight. I had been nervous all day at school. Even Hunter was nervous but it was so adorable.

"How do I look?" I ask my parents as I walk out onto the deck where they were sitting. I picked a dress this time, much to my mum's delight. It was navy blue, and nice and flowy, perfect for early autumn weather in tropical north Queensland. I paired it with white sandals and silver jewellery.

"You look beautiful, honey." Dad beams.

"Let's not be late," Mum says as she grabs her car keys.

Hunter had picked a restaurant that overlooked the boardwalk and the man-made lagoon in town. I had never heard of it but it served Italian food, hence the dark dress, as I was notorious for spilling food whenever I wore white. I hope I wasn't too dressed up.

"Ok, let's go," I agree with Mum and follow her to the car.

"Now, we trust you, Hayley, but remember, this is a first date so no funny business. You are to be where I dropped you off at 10:00pm and not a second later. I'm sure Hunter will understand," she says as we start to drive away.

"I understand, Mum," I reply. I knew I was lucky to have progressive parents. Some parents wouldn't be as relaxed about their kids dating but I had luck on my side that my parents already knew Hunter.

"What if he doesn't show, Mum!" I start to panic as she drives into the car park of the restaurant.

She laughs. "That boy will show. I can guarantee it. This moment has been a long time coming, Hayley. I doubt he will do anything to mess it up."

I take a deep breath. She was right. He would be there. If he wasn't, I would just move schools. Problem solved.

"Remember, 10:00pm, Hayls." Mum leans over the passenger seat as I turn to shut the car door. I nod and she drives off.

"Hayley!" I hear Hunter call out and I immediately relax.

I turn to where his voice came from and smile. He looked so handsome with his nice black jeans and a crisp white button-up shirt. The sleeves were rolled at his elbows and he had left a few buttons undone, exposing his toned chest. I could see he was looking at me the same way I was looking at him.

"Wow." He embraces me in a hug. "You look so beautiful."

I feel a pang in my heart. He used the word beautiful, not sexy. It made me feel which made me feel butterflies in my stomach. I wasn't just a toy to Hunter. I was a woman who he really liked and thought was beautiful. I didn't want him to let go. It felt so right in the moment to be in his arms. He presses a kiss into my neck and I feel my knees go weak.

"Let's go," he says, breaking us apart. "I'm starving."

His hand automatically finds mine as he leads the way to the restaurant.

"Have you been here before?" he asks as the waiter takes us to our table. It's one overlooking the water and there are hundreds of fairy lights creating the most romantic scene for our first date.

"No," I reply as we took our seats. "It's beautiful here, though."

"Not as beautiful as you." He smiles.

I feel myself blush and pick up the menu to distract myself.

"You have no idea how good it feels to not have to hide the way I feel about you anymore," he grins. "I don't know why I didn't do it sooner."

"You're not the only one to blame in this situation, Hunter," I admit to his surprise. "I could've acted on my feelings, too." With this admission, he blushes as well. "I guess we didn't want to ruin what was already good. Imagine if I didn't like you or you didn't like me? It would be hard to admit feelings and not have them reciprocated," I try to explain.

He nods. "Yeah, I know. We were kind of a couple already anyway. Right from the second I saw you at your locker one the first day of Grade 11." He grins.

"Is that why no one else asked me out? You scared them all away?" I joke.

"Yep. That was my plan all along." He rolls his eyes in a joking manner. "I was doing alright until Theo came. Guess I have him to thank because now I've finally got you all to myself."

I love hearing the way he talks about us.

"What?" he asks sheepishly. I must've been staring at him too much.

"Nothing," I shake my head quickly. "Just thinking that you were brave to wear a white shirt to an Italian restaurant."

"Oh." He looks down at his shirt. "Yeah, guess I didn't think that through."

The waiter arrives to take our order. Hunter chooses a spaghetti bolognese and I opt for the lasagne.

We talk constantly throughout the meal, and I'm almost sad when Hunter said it was probably time to leave.

I try to hide my disappointment. It was just after 9:00pm so I still had a little bit of time until Mum said she would come to get me.

"What time is your mum coming?" Hunter looks back at me as we leave the restaurant.

I feel a smile escape my lips. The night was not over yet.

"Mum said she'd meet me back here at 10:00pm."

Hunter looks at his watch and smiles. "Plenty of time. Let's go for a walk." He offers his hand out to me and I take it happily.

We follow the path around the lagoon which had scatterings of fairy lights in the trees. The night was going to be over before I knew it. Time just seemed to be flying. I marvelled at how easy the conversation came. We never ran out of things to talk about. One topic always lead to another. How amazing would it be if I met my soulmate right now, at this young age? What if Hunter was it?

"Look!" Hunter points. "Ducks!"

He walks over to the railing surrounding one side of the lagoon. I watch as the ducks swim slowly in a formation. Occasionally one would dive under the water only to resurface a short distance from where they originally were. Hunter stood behind me, with one hand on either side of me, holding onto the rail. I lean back and rest my head on his chest. This moment felt so perfect. I want to turn around and kiss him but I was scared to ruin the peace. Then I thought back to our conversation about why we didn't act on our feelings sooner. I turn around abruptly to Hunter's surprise. Now I was facing him, I can feel the butterflies in my stomach but I push through them as I slowly move my hands to either side of his face. A smile slowly creeps over his face in anticipation. I stood on the tips of my toes and he responds by bending slightly, closing the gap. His lips were warm and I could feel the smile still on his face. His arms wound around behind me as he presses my body to his.

Hunter is the one to eventually break off the kiss. "Wow," he breathes.

I blush and rest my forehead against his. Every now and then he would stop me and give me a quick kiss on the lips. When I ask the reason why, he said, "Just making sure you're still here and this is real."

"I'm not going anywhere," I smile. "Well, at least until Mum comes to get me."

"Which will be—" he checks his watch "—soon. We should walk back now."

I feel my face drop. I didn't want the night to end.

By the time I eventually flop into bed, I still had a grin plastered on my face.

CHAPTER 13

"Did you see a change in him with this new status change?"

God, I was sick to death of talking about my feelings now. I was really tired after all that had gone on and I nearly cancelled today's appointment, but I knew it was important to talk about this. I needed to talk about this. The more I talked about it, the easier it was to recall certain memories or even things Hunter had once said. I could picture him clear as day and could almost hear his voice in my head as I remembered certain memories. It made me want to cry.

I clear my throat to conceal any emotions that were building. "He was the happiest I'd ever seen him, Dr Martin. He was in love."

CHAPTER 14

School retreat was approaching soon. It was our third term of Grade 12 and I had officially been Hunter's girlfriend for nearly six months, but our friends joked that we had been together since my first day of Grade 11. Being with Hunter was so easy. He made me so comfortable and I never worried if he was out with other girls or potentially cheating on me. We would text until late at night and I'd wake up to a good morning text. He was the perfect boyfriend. I felt deliriously happy. Even my parents adored Hunter, and he came around most weekends for dinner or to hang out. Well, not necessarily to hang out with me. Dad would often see if Hunter wanted to help build something or to work on the car and they would disappear for hours. But he never stayed the night. That was as far as it was allowed to go, and I was okay with that. I was only 16.

We were headed to a private campground surrounding a big lake with dorms for a week as a little 'getaway' to us relax and prepare for our final few months of the school year. I had heard great things about the retreat and the amount of time we got to spend just hanging out around a campfire. It was still winter, so it was perfect jumper—and snuggle—weather.

Mum and Dad drop me off at school Monday morning. The teachers were all there, along with quite a few students already. Everyone had their suitcase and a pillow for the bus. After meeting up with Kate and Ethan, I see Hunter out of the corner of my eye and I turn to watch as he effortlessly swings his duffle bag at the bus driver to catch and load. I was always amazed at how attracted I was to him each time I saw him. He just seemed to get 'it' right. The plain blue t-shirt, the dark blue jeans, the grey jumper, it all just worked for him. When Hunter turns and looks in our direction, he nods to signal that he'd seen us. Such a simple and small gesture made me giddy inside. He looked for me first. *Is this what love felt like?*

"Take a picture, girlfriend," Hunter says as he approaches me and slings an arm around my shoulders.

"My screensaver of Chris Hemsworth isn't going anywhere," I respond cheekily, knowing it would get a rise out of him. Even the mention of another male made him squirm.

"No, he's not." Hunter reaches for my phone in my back pocket.

"Don't touch what you can't afford." I playfully slapped his hand away.

He bites his lip with a grin and I had a feeling I knew what was running through his mind at that moment. I blush as my mind flashes back to a time in his room when I made a joke about not being able to touch what he couldn't afford.

Harmless banter. He stood up very seriously and backed me up against his wall.

"Please, you're dying for my touch," he whispered. My heart was fluttering with possibilities. He was so close to me. He leaned down to kiss me but teased me instead. His hands slowly slid down my back before resting on my butt. With ease, he lifted me up and my legs curled around him, all whilst still teasing me with kisses. "Well, if I can't have any, neither can you," he whispered and put me down with a smirk. He started to walk away but I pulled him back, pulling his face to mine, his hands travelling all over my body.

I look away to distract myself. He'd been becoming a bit more confident in the way we kissed and where he could touch. He was also very happy with teasing me.

Hunter leans down to cuddle me. "I think I know where your mind just went," he whispers and I feel goose bumps rise. "If only we were alone." His voice is hushed and low, sparking a tingling sensation in my body. He was really good at this.

"Gather around students. It's time to board the bus," the teacher calls us to attention.

When we're all finally on the bus, the teacher calls out, "No funny business, kids".

"No funny business here," Hunter whispers in my ear before gently moving his hand further up my thigh.

I bite my lip. "Don't," I warned him.

Sure, Hunter and I had fooled around but we never went too far. Hunter was good like that. Very respectful even, stopping us before we did go too far. He was so different from what I had expected. I knew he was experienced. Well, actually, I didn't. We had never spoken about our sexual partners. I wondered how many girls he had slept with, even at our young age.

"Earth to Hayley?" Hunter looks at me.

I shake away my thoughts.

"Where did your mind just go?" he asks curiously, his eyes looking me up and down.

"Nowhere." I shake my head again.

"Tell me!" he whines.

"It's not a conversation for the bus, Hunter," I reply as I quickly look around me. I did not need people overhearing our chat.

"You're not breaking up with me, are you?" Concern crosses his face.

"No," I laugh.

"Did I do something wrong?"

"No! Hunter, stop it," I continued, laughing. "Why do you always assume the worst?

"Then what is it? Why can't you just tell me?" He grips my arm in desperation.

"God, you're annoying!" I lower my voice and place a reassuring hand on his. "I was thinking that maybe we should talk about past partners if you're going to keep pushing boundaries with your hands."

Hunter sits up straight at the seriousness of the question. "Yeah, okay, we can talk later, but yeah, probably something we should discuss." He looks awkward, almost ashamed of what he would need to tell me. He moves on quickly though as he snuggles back against my shoulder.

I was glad to hear that he was willing to have this conversation and didn't push me out based on his past reputation. Rumours swirled constantly about Hunter and his antics but I'd never heard concrete information from him. If I went into the conversation assuming the worst, then I guess it wouldn't hurt so bad if it was true.

Hunter tells me that free time was easy to come by on retreats. The teachers would make you do group activities in the morning and then you had the majority of the afternoon to yourselves, followed by evening activities. Kate and Ethan agreed from across the aisle, joining in our conversation every now and then. I was excited. If what they said was true I would get to spend some more quality time with Hunter. He said he was actually looking forward to retreat and said that camping on the lake was stunning and I would really enjoy it.

We finally arrive at the retreat and I'm blown away. The lake looked stunning, surrounded by lush greenery. The serenity was incredible. This was definitely going to be a great five days away. Hunter sticks as close to me as possible while we listen to the teachers give instructions on dorms and when we were due to have lunch. It was as though the teachers then switched off from 'teacher' mode.

After lunch, we had the rest of the afternoon to ourselves. We would be given dinner and then have to participate in a group activity before bedtime. Ethan and Kate had gone off on a bush walk somewhere, leaving Hunter and I to have the afternoon alone. We walked down to the lake and found a nice grassy spot to sit down. I convinced Hunter to swap jumpers with me. Being significantly shorter than Hunter, it was a real treat to see him in my tiny jumper. His jumper on the other hand was amazing and I didn't want to take it off.

He motions for me to sit in front of him and lean back against his chest. I wouldn't say 'no' to that.

"I want to talk to you about something, Hayley, and what you said on the bus this morning has encouraged me to say this." I could hear him take a deep breath. I swivel around to look at him.

"Hayley, we've been together for what, two years now?"

I chuckle. "No, we haven't. We've known each other for that long."

"But let's be honest. You were mine from the second you walked in that door." He smiles and gives me a quick kiss. "But it's something a bit more serious and I want to be mature about this. Hayley, I would like to take our relationship to the next level."

"What do you mean?" I could see he was really nervous about this. He was studying the grass instead of meeting my eye.

"Hayley, are you really going to make me spell it out?"

Oh.

"I want to have sex with you." He dips his head as he mumbles his words.

I'm stunned. I wasn't expecting this at all. Maybe a chat about what our plans were to move forward in our relationship but not the conversation about 'it'. I didn't feel prepared. My face must've given away my emotions though as he quickly starts to speak again.

"I'll never force you into anything, Hayley," he says. "I want you to know that. But I also want you to know that it's what I've been thinking about and I was hoping you would take some time to think about it too."

I didn't know what to say but I was touched at how he was behaving so maturely and I was proud of him for doing so.

I lean in and kiss him softly in response. His arms wind around me.

"Thank you," I whisper when I pull away. "I'll definitely think about it. Thank you for being honest with me."

"Are you going to ask me that burning question I know you want to ask?" He looks out at the lake.

I pause to look at him. I need to choose my words carefully but before I could say anything Hunter start talking.

"Despite what you may have originally thought and what I'm guessing everyone thinks, I'm not the big player everyone says I am. Okay, I've had sex before," he admits. "It was just once but we weren't necessarily official or anything but I thought that maybe after we did it she would want something more and I was prepared to do that. I was prepared to have a girlfriend. I really liked her. I thought we would have a future together."

I try to keep my expression neutral. I couldn't believe how open he was being with me.

"But it turns out she didn't want any of that. She just led me on for weeks, dressing up, or down, when we hung out and she'd say things that would make any guy weak. Before I knew it, I was in love with her so why not have sex?" He shrugs his shoulders. "But then she texted me the next day, asking for one of my older brother's friends numbers as she had a thing for him. When I asked her why she spent all that time leading me on and having sex when she wasn't interested in me, she said we were just friends in her eyes and she just wanted to get it over with so older guys would have sex with her."

I feel my bottom lip drop.

"Yeah, can you believe that?" He laughs half-heartedly before looking away, wiping at his cheek.

Hunter had his heart broken already? Was that why he was the way that he was?

"I felt so used. I knew from that moment that I wouldn't let anyone hurt me like she had hurt me, and that I'd never go too far with another girl until I was certain I was ready. I didn't want to hurt anyone. I thought sex was meant to be so special and I was so crazy about her—ask Ethan, he knew. The whole experience actually made me rethink my view on having sex with just anyone just because it felt good so I decided to wait for the right person again," he continues. "I'm not going to lie to you, Hayley, just because I haven't had sex with another girl since doesn't mean I didn't mess around with them. I know my way around the female body and I've accepted my fair share of favours, if you catch my drift, but I always shut it down if it went too far."

I'm blown away by his honesty. He must've lost his virginity at an early age. We were 16. Based on his story, I would say even as early as 14.

"Please say something." His eyes urge me.

"Sorry Hunter. I'm just digesting what you're telling me. I'm very thankful that you're being so honest with me. I know this must be hard to talk about," I reply.

He smiles. "I guess you just make me feel comfortable to talk about this stuff. I kept my guard up for so long and then you came around and my whole world changed."

I lean in again for a kiss and let him deepen it when I feel his tongue trace my lips. He pulls away though and rests his forehead against mine.

"She doesn't go to this school anymore, just so you know," he whispers. "I think she dropped out of school entirely and fell into a bad crowd. It was probably for the best I didn't chase her for too long. I don't want to end up like that."

I feel relieved to know his old flame wasn't at our school. I feel like I would've been told by some busybody by now if she was. Or she would've had the pleasure in telling me herself. How could someone of his age have so much wisdom to know he would've been headed down a bad path with that girl? How did he have such mature thoughts about sex when he had a reputation like that? I honestly didn't think there was much truth to the rumours, but it turns out they were mainly true. He was experienced.

I know I need to give him some reassurance. "You're not going to end up like that, Hunter, I'll make sure of it," I say confidently. "I'm not like her at all."

"She is nothing compared to you," he says sternly. There's nothing but love in his eyes though and it makes me want to wrap my arms around his neck and smother him with kisses.

"Now turn around. You're missing a great sunset!" he says as he helps me shuffle around.

I lean back into his chest, interlocking our fingers. "Thank you for being so honest."

"I think it's important that we're honest with each other about this stuff. You deserve to know and I don't want there to be any secrets. Who knows what the gossipers out there say. I want you to hear my sexual history from me. It doesn't freak you out though, right?" He gently pulls my face to look at him. A hint of panic crosses his face as he searches mine for any signs of concern.

I squeeze his cheeks. "Nope, not at all. Thank you for trusting me and sharing this with me." I kiss him gently and I can feel his smile grow.

"Do you have anything you want to tell me?" he asks quietly.

I feel my face flood with embarrassment and had to think quickly of how I could respond.

"Nothing to report," I say quietly. "Read into that what you will."

I could feel him rest his forehead on my shoulder and I was hoping that meant he understood that I had zero experience in the sexual department.

All I could think about though was what he'd said. *Did this mean he was in love with me? More importantly, I think I was in love with him.*

⸺◆⸺

On our walk back up to the rec room for dinner, we run into Kate and Ethan. I wanted to get Kate alone and ask her what she thought about Hunter's proposal. I wasn't going to share Hunter's experience, just ask her for her opinion on sex in general. I already knew that Ethan and Kate had had sex before. Kate was an open book on most topics. She would even make comments of their bedroom antics whilst Ethan was around. He'd simply shake his head and walk off. Either that or Hunter would stir the pot and they'd end up having a pretend fight, distracting Kate from saying anything further.

I was consumed by the thought of having sex with Hunter and what that meant to me. Was I even old enough to have sex? It's not really something that comes up in conversation at school. I must've been more quiet than normal as Hunter kept looking at me throughout dinner with concern written all over his face. I tried to keep giving him reassuring looks and push my thoughts to the back of my mind so I could get through dinner and the activity they had planned for us after. I didn't want him to worry.

"You're okay, right?" Hunter whispers in my ear as we take a seat on the floor for the evening activity. "Like, we're okay, right? You're not going to dump me?"

I give him a quick peck on the lips to calm him down but he doesn't look convinced. That girl really did a number on him.

"Right!" the teacher interrupts. "Tonight, we're going to take you through a guided meditation to help teach you tricks to get through stressful times, something we think will be very beneficial as we approach the end of your schooling careers."

"Wonderful," I mutter under my breath causing Hunter to chuckle. I quickly looked at him and he looked less than enthused to do meditation but I think for a different reason to mine. Maybe it could help me put the question of whether or not to have sex with Hunter out of my brain.

⁕

Hunter gave me one final kiss goodnight before he went back to the boy's dorms.

Kate closes the door to our room behind her and flops onto her bed.

"Okay, I can't hold it in anymore," I burst. "Hunter asked me to have sex with him."

Kate's eyes widen. "What? He asked you? How sweet! What did he say?"

"He asked me to consider it and that it's been on his mind."

"How mature of him. This shows you he's serious, Hayley," she says as she starts to take her hair out of her braids. "He wants to move at the right pace for the both of you and not just for his needs. I can't believe he waited this long to be honest."

"I'm just so conservative, Kate. I don't even know what to do or how to prepare for it. What does it feel like?"

Kate pats the spot beside her on the bed.

"I'm not going to lie, Hayley. Your first time will not be comfortable. It'll feel like a rubber band snapping inside you but once it's over, that's it. It'll get better after that, trust me!" She smiles.

"Oh." I feel my stomach turn.

"I would much prefer you be prepared and ready to be awkward around Hunter, rather than not. It's a big step in your relationship."

"I know, Kate, and thank you, really. I appreciate it."

"Do you think you're ready?" She raises her eyebrows at me.

"Is there a way to know you are?" I ask shyly.

"Do you want to be with Hunter?"

"Yes."

"Do you trust him?"

"Yes."

"Are you prepared for the feelings you may have about him being your first if you don't survive as a couple for long after?"

"I don't know. I mean, I plan on being with him for a while." I shrug my shoulders.

"Hayley, let me just put it out there. Everyone has mixed opinions. My opinion is that it is inevitable to lose your virginity, and if you trust the person you're with, you'll be okay. So long as you are safe and know the consequences if you're not."

I smile weakly at her. I needed to trust my gut on this one.

CHAPTER 15

There was a light knocking sound that woke me from my sleep. I slowly sit up in bed and can see Kate was already up and rubbing the sleep out of her eyes.

"What's that?" I mumble, half asleep.

"I don't know." She yawns as she approaches the door.

The knocking starts again and I check my phone. Yuck, it's 1:00am. I watch Kate push the curtain to the side so she can look to see who was there first. She lets out a light chuckle before unlocking the door and pulling it open quietly. Surely the teachers weren't doing random checks of our rooms.

I rub my eyes, trying to get them to focus in the dark. I must've been in a deep sleep.

"What are you two doing here?" I hear Kate whisper into the dark.

"Shut the door and be quiet, you'll get us in trouble." Ethan's voice is hushed as he rushes to close to the door behind him.

I'm still processing what is happening when Hunter nudges me.

"Move over, babe," he whispers and I happily oblige, pushing up to one side of the bed.

He gets in and makes himself comfortable against the pillows before extending his arm out for me to snuggle in against his chest. Being wrapped in his arms like this was the most wonderful feeling ever. I had never felt more safe and secure. How could I convince my parents to let Hunter stay over now that I knew how amazing it was to fall asleep snuggled against him?

I could feel my own eyes getting heavier as Hunter drew patterns on my back. It was so relaxing. He had to be the one, right? How could I feel this calm and serene and not trust him with something as serious as sex? I think my mind was made up.

"Hunter," I try to whisper.

"Mmm?" he responds.

"My answer is yes," I mumble as I nuzzle against his chest.

I feel his heart beat faster and his arm tightens around me. He places several kisses into my hair and I know he was smiling.

An unfamiliar alarm goes off, startling both Hunter and I awake. Begrudgingly, I open one eye. Yuck, it was so early that it was still dark outside. I didn't want it to be morning already. I had slept so well, wrapped in Hunter's arms. Even in this small bed, it felt huge.

"Rise and shine, girlfriend." Hunter places a kiss on my forehead.

"No," I groan and pull the sheets up over my head.

"Oh yeah, she's not a morning person." Kate laughs as she and Ethan crawl out of bed.

"I have to get back to my cabin, Hayley," Hunter chuckles as he rolls out of bed and follows Ethan to the door. "I'll see you soon."

"Yup," I mumble as I drag myself into a seated position. I clue on that Ethan had set an alarm for earlier than normal so that he and Hunter could sneak back to their room.

Kate locks the door behind them once they leave. "Come on Hayley," she says. "We've got to wake up soon anyway. Let's get ready and go get a cuppa by the fire."

Once we're dressed, we headed towards the rec room where all of the students gathered for a drink. The retreat was so different to what I was expecting. The teachers were actually laughing at some of the things that the boys did instead of rousing on them. I think this helped relax Hunter a bit, as he knew that they didn't constantly have their eye on him. On the other hand, Hunter's behaviour in general seemed to be more mature. He was even being pleasant to Theo, having been forced to interact with him more than usual. I knew that if we were at school, it was likely that Hunter would've started some sort of scuffle, but he kept his cool and even managed to talk to Theo without throwing in a snide remark. I could see the confusion on Theo's face at times. He didn't know what to make of Hunter's new attitude. Hopefully it continued when we got back from retreat. Theo wasn't that bad of a person. We had our differences, that's for sure, but before he asked me out, we were actually friends.

Kate hands me a mug for my cup of tea. I prepare my tea while Kate finishes making her coffee. I gazed around the rec room, smiling when I met the eye of another student. I couldn't see Hunter or Ethan yet but we still had time. I could see Theo helping the teacher get the fire going again.

"Let's go sit outside." Kate takes a sip of her coffee.

We walk back outside to the campfire and sit down on the log.

"Good morning, ladies." Ethan's voice came from behind us and it wasn't long before I felt a warm hand on my shoulder as Hunter jumped over the log to take a seat beside me.

"Morning, Hayley." He gently kissed my cheek.

I smile back at him and rest my head on his shoulder. "Tea?" I offer my cup out to him.

"Is it too hot to drink?" he asks, taking it in his hands.

"Maybe, but I like it hot," I reply.

He takes a sip but pulls a face. "Just a little bit too hot for me."

I laugh. "You're weak!"

He takes another sip cautiously. "Nope, I just value my taste buds that I've now just burnt off."

"Where's my strong man?" I joked.

Hunter stands up, stretches and points towards where Theo was standing. "He's about to build a better fire. That's where he is." Hunter turns to face Theo. "Let me give you a hand, mate."

I feel my eyebrows raise in shock. He called Theo 'mate'. I never thought I'd hear Hunter say something like that to Theo. I look over at Theo, who pauses before deciding to ride the wave of Hunter's new attitude. I share a glance with Kate and Ethan. They both looked just as surprised as I was.

"Well, hell must have frozen over," Ethan says under his breath before kissing Kate on the cheek. "I'm off to play, too."

CHAPTER 16

The teachers leave us to get on with this morning's activity. We had to work in pairs to paint our partner's face with symbols and colours of things that we thought made up that person. You could pick any partner, so Hunter and I were together.

"I'm painting you first!" I get in before Hunter.

He grins at me and takes a seat next to the table of paint.

"Make it good." He crosses his arms in front of him.

Kate and Ethan are on the station next to us. Kate is painting Ethan's face first. She had already started painting a heart on his cheek.

"Hmm," I bite the paint brush absentmindedly whilst I thought of what to paint. What made up Hunter? How did I paint what he is, or even what he meant to me?

"You look so cute right now," he grins up at me, making me smile. I knew what to paint now.

I start with oranges and reds, trying my best to paint a fire. A fire could represent multiple things: strength, tenacity, uncontrollable, irresistible, hot.

"I wish I could see what you're painting," he whines. "This sucks."

"Quiet in my studio please," I joke as I try to focus on getting the flames right.

"Yes, ma'am." He laughs.

I move onto my next section of his face painting. Much to his delight, I would be painting a heart because he had been so amazing at the retreat. The maturity he had displayed and his affection had made me fall even harder for him and I hoped it continued when we got back home.

Ever so slowly I watch Hunter's hand reach up to my face to brush a strand of hair out of my eyes. His hand lingers against my face before working its way down to my shoulders, my waist, to where it eventually stops. I bit my lip trying to ignore what he was doing.

"PG13, Woods," Ethan quips up.

I feel the heat rushing up to my cheeks. Hunter's face breaks out in a grin and his hand drops away quickly.

"You made her lose her concentration," Hunter replies, ever so quick with the comebacks.

"She needed no help from me to lose her concentration," Ethan jokes back. "Hands to yourself, you sicko."

"Not my fault that she's irresistible." Hunter places both of his hands on my lower back this time.

I raise my eyebrows at him. *Really?*

"What?" He shrugs. "They're not on your ass."

I shake my head before focusing back on the painting. I move on to greens and blues to paint a sporting jersey. Sports were a big part of Hunter's life, too. That now made three items I had painted. A heart near his jawline, a fire on his cheek, and the jersey on his other cheek. I decided to paint my initials in the heart, just to be cheeky. I also paint a measuring tape to symbolise his height, and a black circle on his nose to represent his clown-side. Then I attempt to paint a chain wire linking the ideas altogether. I couldn't believe that I'd actually pulled it off.

"Alright, I think I'm nearly done," I stand back to admire my work.

"Wow, Hayley, I didn't realise you could paint," Kate gushes.

"Thanks," I reply as I quickly clean my paint brushes for Hunter to use next.

"You're just saying that, aren't you, Kate? I bet it looks like shit." Hunter laughs.

"Hey!" I lightly punch his arm. "I can always fix it to look like shit."

"Alright." He grins. "My turn."

We swap positions. Hunter brushes the hair out of my face again before turning to the colours he had to work with. I could almost see his mind turning ideas around. It was like he was trying to work out which path to take. Did he paint something silly, or did he paint something serious?

"Okay, I have a plan now. Sit still." He picks up a paint brush and starts to paint. I could see he was using purple. A chill runs up my spine due to how cold the paint was on my skin.

"Do you want my jumper again?" he whispers as he continues to work.

"No, but thank you," I reply. "The paint is just cold."

Hunter grins but doesn't say anything else. I wonder what he's painting. I try to steal a glance at Kate. It looks like Ethan was painting a big flower that covered a good portion of her face. It actually didn't look too bad.

The teacher walks around to let us know that we have ten more minutes to complete our looks before we could show each other.

"Nearly done, girlfriend," Hunter says. I watch as he studies my face as though he was trying to figure out if he wanted to add something or fix something. He lands on a decision and adds one thing more before dropping his paintbrush in the water cup. "Nailed it!" he announces before offering me his hand so I could stand up.

I look over at Ethan and Kate. Ethan was adding a few more things but I was so impressed. Half of her face was painted as a flower and the other half was painted as a love heart. The designs met in the middle with a combination of little things like the words 'family' and 'friends'. It was absolute perfection. I didn't know Ethan had an artistic ability.

"Ethan!" I exclaim. "That's amazing! Kate, you should never wash your face!"

Kate beams back at me. "I'm so excited to see it!"

"I really want to see mine!" I was somewhat nervous to see what Hunter has done. He wasn't laughing whilst he painted and he wasn't trying to get Ethan's attention either so it had to mean he painted something seriously and not as a joke.

We watch as the teacher walks around to each station. He has a smile on his face as he inspects everyone's work and even gives Hunter a light nudge with his shoulder. "I hope you're all happy with what your partner has painted. You can now pick up your mirrors and have a look."

I look at Hunter and he's grinning. I hope he likes what I did. I certainly wasn't a painter at all but being able to work with make-up, I had some level of skill that helped me.

"On the count of three?" he asks as he hands me a mirror.

I nod. "One."

"Two."

"Three!" We both quickly turn our mirrors around.

I couldn't believe what I was seeing. I feel like if my jaw could really drop to the floor, it would. I was completely blown away. He had managed to paint a perfect ballerina with her tutu in the Spanish flag colours. The ballerina started near my temple on the right side of my face and she curved down my cheeks. As I watched her trail off I realised he'd painted many little ballerinas that went around my face like a clock. Curving with the flow of the bigger ballerina's tutu was his name. I look back at him, gobsmacked. He had a beautiful smile on his face, one that I didn't see very often.

"Do you like it?" he asks sheepishly.

I look back at what I had painted on his face and it just did not compare.

"I had no idea you could paint, or even draw for that matter. Hunter, this is amazing. I honestly can't believe this." I give him a quick peck on the lips before returning to look at my face in the mirror.

"Why do you look like you're about to cry?" he asks, concern covering his face.

"Ever heard of happy tears?" I ask.

"Nope, usually I only cause sad tears because of all of the hearts I break." Now he has a smirk on his face.

I frown but decide to move on. It wasn't worth picking apart every little thing he said when he was new to the whole commitment thing. "What do you think of yours?" I say instead as I focus back on what I had painted on him. My painting was nowhere near as good as his.

"Yeah, not bad," he jokes as he wraps his arms around me. "I like the images you chose because they represented what I meant to you and honestly I wouldn't have cared what you did, the fact was that you did it and that's all that matters to me."

Gosh, he just had a way of making me feel all warm inside.

"What's with the fire though?" he chuckles. "Do you think I'm a pyromaniac after my handy skills of getting that fire going this morning?"

"Fire is also hot," I say cheekily.

He bites his lip seductively and I grin. I could be a tease too.

"We're going to take some photos, everyone!" The teacher interrupts as he walks around with a camera.

Hunter and I stood together for our photo and then we took one with Ethan and Kate before a big group photo.

"If you want to wash it off, you're welcome to. Please meet back here at 12:00pm for lunch though," the teacher calls again. "Until then, free time!"

⸻◆⸻

After lunch, the teachers had scheduled a water-based activity. We had to work as a team to build a raft out of random objects and to see if it would float with us on it. The water was still quite chilly but I enjoyed it. They split us all up into teams but luckily I was put on a team with Ethan. Theo ended up on my team and whilst Hunter didn't say anything or give away any hints that he wasn't happy with it, he did whatever he could to tamper with our raft. I actually found it amusing and every now and then Theo would crack a grin as he and Ethan began tampering with Hunter's groups' raft. It resulted in both our teams failing miserably but god, it was so much fun and it was amazing to see Hunter behave around Theo again. Afterwards we were able to go for a shower and then it was free time until dinner. It was probably planned this way to ensure we really did wash our faces after this morning's face painting activity.

"Let's go for a walk, just the two of us," Hunter pulls my arm gently. We were standing around the campfire with a few other classmates after having showered back in our respective rooms.

"Sure," I smile. "What's the special occasion?"

"Making up for lost time with you when you were with him," his eyes flick to the side momentarily where Theo was likely to be standing, albeit he was a short distance away from us.

I roll my eyes. "Please don't start."

He laughs. "I trust you completely," he says, much to my surprise. Maybe he really had turned a new leaf and realised that Theo wasn't a threat now.

"Let's go down to the lake." He takes my hand and leads us down towards the water. "Was it a nice surprise last night when we stopped by?" Hunter grins at me.

I can feel myself blush as I recalled the memory. "You're lucky you didn't get caught!"

"Why do you think it took us so long to get to your dorm? We were monitoring the situation!" He laughs.

"Fair," I reply.

"So last night you said your answer was yes. That was to my question about having sex, hey?"

I chuckle. "Yes, why's that?"

"You weren't half asleep, were you? You knew what you had said?" Hunter has gone all shy again.

"I knew what I was saying and my answer is still the same."

"Well, cool," he replies and I laugh.

"It's so awkward to talk about isn't it?" I say through laughter.

"You have no idea," he breathes out heavily, like he had been holding it in.

"But I don't want it to be planned because I think that would be awkward," I try to explain. "It should just happen naturally. You know, if we were alone and you were prepared then it could happen, but I don't want it to be like at 6:00pm we meet and do the deed and then we part ways."

I hadn't really thought about what I wanted my first time to be like but I knew I had to be open and honest with Hunter, and more importantly, with myself, for this to work.

"Okay, first of all, boys are always prepared. We get a sex talk just like you girls do at school too! Secondly, I agree, I don't think it should be planned either. If it feels right in the moment, then I think we'll know."

"I do want to make one thing clear though, Hunter. I'm not going to be one of those statistics they talk about in sex-ed. I don't want to be a teen mum. I don't want to have to make the decision about whether or not we keep the baby. I want to be smart about it," I say confidently and truthfully.

He laughs. "I don't want to be a teen dad either. Why do you think I've avoided having sex since with all those girls? One of them would've tried to trap me, no doubt!"

I can't help but feel sad that he even had those feelings where he thinks a girl would try to trap him by tricking him into having sex with the aim to get pregnant by him.

He must see the change in my facial expressions. "Hey." He lifts my chin gently so I'm looking up at him. "I know you're not like that. That was the old me and the concerns I had back then. I don't have to worry with you. You're so different, in all the best ways."

I feel shy but also reassured by his words. "Also, if you don't have the *thing*, I'm not going to agree to it. I don't care how into it we already are," I cross my arms over my chest.

"You know they have a name?" he chuckles. "You can say the word condom."

I laugh and turn away in embarrassment. "I told you it was awkward!"

He laughs with me. "God, I love you."

"What did you say?" I spin around to look at him.

His eyes widen. We had never said those words to each other. I was sure that the feelings I had towards Hunter were love, and the fact that I agreed to have sex with him meant I was in love with him, but we had never actually said those three words to each other.

It doesn't take him long to recover, though. He stops in front of me and takes my face in his hands.

"It's true. I love you, Hayley." He smiles shyly. "And I'm not afraid to admit it. I love you. I'm pretty sure I've loved you since you first walked into my life."

I blush again as I wrap my arms around his waist. "I love you, too."

He kisses me so deeply and passionately that it takes my breath away.

CHAPTER 17

"I think I'm going to sleep all weekend." Kate yawns as we get off the bus.

"What? Didn't you get a good night's sleep?" Ethan jokes.

"Sharing a single bed between two people isn't exactly comfortable," she retorts.

I laugh at how funny they were as a couple. They had no secrets and always told each other the truth. It was admirable really and I guess that's what made them work so well together. On the nights that Hunter and Ethan came by our dorm, I slept surprisingly well as I snuggled against Hunter. I didn't want to come home. I wanted to stay at retreat forever, just so I could share the bed with Hunter again. As I go to grab my bag from the bus, my phone rings. Surprisingly, it's Mum. She must be running late.

"Hey Mum, how are you?" I answer.

"My darling child is alive! Are you okay? Did you get hurt? Do you need food?" She laughs.

I shake my head and laugh too. "Yes, your one and only child is still alive. We just got back."

She proceeds to tell me that her and Dad had to leave early for an award show tonight and wouldn't be able to pick me up but she had already spoken to Kate's mum who would be able to drop me home.

Out of nowhere I feel a surge of confidence. "Would it be okay if Hunter came over and kept me company?"

She went silent. I knew the look she was probably sharing with Dad.

"Hayley, you know we love you and we really think Hunter's a great guy. You can have this opportunity to prove that we can trust you because we really want to," Mum starts.

"I'm too young to be a grandfather, Hayley, is what we're trying to say," Dad interrupts.

I feel my jaw drop and embarrassment flood my face. "Dad!" I cry. "Are you serious? Give me some credit, please!"

This attracts Hunter's attention from his conversation with Ethan and he walks over, a puzzled look on his face.

Both of my parents laugh. "Of course we trust you, honey. We just wanted to make you sweat it out! You're a grown woman now. You know how the world works and we trust that you'll make the right choices."

"Hilarious, Dad. I hope you feel good about yourself!" I try to laugh but was still so embarrassed that they would even bring up the topic of teenage pregnancy, and over the phone too.

"We will speak to you tomorrow!" Dad wraps up the conversation.

"What was all of that about?" Hunter asks, confusion written all over his face.

"Uh, I asked my parents if you could keep my company tonight whilst they were out of town," I feel shy even asking Hunter if he wanted to spend the night. Given our conversations at camp, I didn't want him to think I was hinting at anything, but now I was more curious than ever as to what sex would feel like. Damn teenage hormones.

"Uh, yeah, if you want me to?" he says casually.

"Okay then," I reply. My shyness has turned into nervousness now that it would just be Hunter and I completely alone with nothing stopping us.

"I'm ready when you are," he replies before leaning down to whisper in my ear. "Every type of ready, if you are."

I feel goose bumps rise. This was it and we both knew it.

CHAPTER 18

Kate's mum drops Hunter and me at my house.

"Do you want a drink?" I ask after we dump our stuff in my room.

"Yes, please, whatever you're having is fine." He sits down on the couch.

I grab two soft drinks from the fridge and sit down next to him.

"I need to unpack my stuff and put some washing on. Then Mum and Dad will think I'm an angel child." I laugh as I take a sip and put it on the coffee table.

"Yeah, then they can leave you alone more often and we can hang out." He winks.

"Are you nervous?" I bite my lip, addressing the elephant in the room. "Like you'll be seeing me naked and I'll be seeing you naked. It's a really vulnerable time."

Hunter pulls me onto his lap and rests his forehead against mine. "No, I'm not nervous, because I'll be with you and I love you. You make me feel comfortable so I know that yes, this will probably be super awkward, but we're in this together so if anything, it'll just become a super funny awkward memory."

"That's a really nice frame of mind, Hunter." I hadn't thought about it like that. Trust Hunter to put my mind at ease.

"If you're worried or nervous, or whatever, it's okay," he says. "We can just take it slow or not at all. The last thing I want to do is rush you." He brushes a strand of hair behind my ear.

"Okay." I kiss him gently. "Thank you."

I let him deepen the kiss and it's not too long before I can feel his hands on the bottom of my shirt.

"You know what? I think I'll feel better after I shower." I jump up off him, quickly overwhelmed by where this was heading.

"We could shower together," he laughs nervously. "That way you're getting one thing out of the way. Seeing each other naked, that is."

I think about it. This was a lot more daunting than I thought but if we broke it down like this, perhaps it would be more manageable? It shouldn't be this way though. I shouldn't feel like I need to break down each step. It should come naturally. Maybe I wasn't ready after all?

Hunter breaks my train of thought. "The fact that you've hesitated makes me think maybe not," he says.

"I don't even look at myself naked, Hunter. How do you expect me to let you?" There's certainly nothing wrong with my body but I've never looked at it and tried to imagine it through someone else's eyes. "I'm going to shower by myself and just make sure I'm ready," I reply confidently. This is probably the first time I will have had proper time to myself to really consider the whole thing anyway. Clearly I was hesitating on something.

"Okay, works for me. I'll shower after you though. I don't want to smell like a campfire for much longer." He laughs.

I smile at his concern before going back to my room and grabbing a change of clothes. Once in the bathroom, I peel off my clothes, forcing myself to look at my body in the mirror and imagine what it looks like with fresh eyes. I couldn't shake the negative thoughts from earlier but when I look at my reflection, I couldn't fault my body. It's strong and toned. Everyone has rolls if they slouch, everyone always thinks their thighs could be thinner, but if Hunter truly loved me, he would look past all of that stuff and just see me, Hayley. His girlfriend. The one who made him rethink having a girlfriend after he was deeply hurt by that other girl. He'll see a good person who loves him. I turn away from the mirror and get in the shower. I wash my hair and my body and then do a quick shave. I give myself a nod of approval after I'm happy I've washed the smell of fire out of my hair and skin, and have smooth skin in all the right places. I know that I'm safe with Hunter and that I can trust him. I know that he respects my boundaries but tonight was the perfect opportunity and sometimes you just had to trust the timing in your life. I'm just nervous because I've never had sex before. Surely everyone gets nervous their first time? What Hunter said made me feel better though. There's no one else I can imagine going through this awkward experience with.

Once I get out, I wrap myself in my towel so I can blow dry my hair. I walk back to my room and get dressed before meeting Hunter outside the bathroom.

"I'm going for a shower. Where do you keep your spare towels?" he asks.

I pull a towel out of the cupboard and he closes the door behind him.

My mind tosses up the thought of joining him in the shower but the fact that I just dried my hair makes me stick with my plan of unpacking my stuff and putting a load of washing on. Hunter's not in the shower for very long and he reappears in my doorway with the towel wrapped around his waist.

"I forgot how good a real shower was," he laughs before he realises that I'm staring.

It was the first time I had seen him properly without a shirt on. His body was toned and muscular. Everything was defined. I can't help but walk over to him and trace my fingers over his muscles. A smile creeps slowly over his face. My finger stops at the top of his towel and it snaps me back to reality.

"I should check to see if Mum's sent me any messages about Dad's awards dinner," I say quickly before walking to my bed to pick up my phone. Hunter bites the inside of his cheek with a smile and returns to the bathroom.

I open my messages and there is one from Mum.

There's money in the microwave for pizza x

"Pizza for dinner?" I call out to Hunter as he gets dressed.

"You're amazing," Hunter replies from the bathroom.

I walk into the kitchen and dial the number for the local pizza shop. I order a BBQ Meatlovers and Garlic Prawn pizza and a garlic bread.

"Reckons 30 minutes," I say to Hunter as he enters the kitchen.

"Sounds good because knowing you, that's how long it'll take to choose a movie." He plops himself on the couch.

I sit down next to him and switch the TV on and find the Netflix app. We scroll through movies before finally landing on one. I hear the washing machine beep that it's finished.

"Oh, hang on a minute. I'll just put the clothes in the dryer," I say as I move to stand up.

"Wow, you're a little housewife, aren't you?" I poke my tongue out at his comment. "Do you want any help?"

I laugh. "It's okay, it's just moving clothes from one machine to another. I think I can manage. Money's in the microwave if the pizza dude comes."

I walk off to the laundry to swap the clothes around and put the dryer on.

I come back and find Hunter balancing the two pizzas and garlic bread whilst he talks to the delivery driver. It looks like a young female.

"Perfect timing," I say before taking sight of the delivery driver. She was maybe a year or two older than me with a black pixie style haircut. The tips were dyed hot pink and they matched the accessories she wore with her uniform. Her eyes were heavily coloured in black everything: mascara, eyeshadow, eye liner. Her lips were coated in hot pink lipstick. She was just so different from me. It looked like her boobs were about to pop through her shirt and she chewed gum in the most annoying manner. Was this the kind of girl Hunter played around with before I came along? What on earth did he see in me then?

I see her face drop as I come into view.

"I didn't realise you two were still together." Her voice is shrill and full of attitude.

"Can I help you?" I snap, crossing my arms over my chest.

She scowls at me and then turns her attention back to Hunter. I can now see that he's fuming.

"Look, I've asked you to leave multiple times. Can you please just go or do I have to call your boss and have you fired for harassment?" Hunter's tone is rough and I can see he's getting angrier by the minute.

"Whatever, enjoy your boring evening. I'm off at 10:00pm if you want a good time." She winks at Hunter.

He responds by slamming the door in her face.

"Wow," is all I can manage to say.

Hunter storms back to the lounge room, dropping the pizza and garlic bread on the coffee table.

"Why the fuck are people so fucking rude? Yes okay, I fucking hooked up with her in the past a couple of times. She used to bring pizza over for my brother and I always got stuck answering the door and, as you could see, she's not shy. Fuck, if I had known it would cause me all this shit with girls I would've gotten into a relationship a lot earlier." He sits on the couch and puts his head in his hands.

"Hunter," I whisper as I quietly sit beside him.

"I'm sorry, Hayley. I really am sorry. I want you to trust me, especially tonight of all nights, and Amber just had to be the delivery driver, didn't she? I don't want there to be any doubt in your mind about how I feel about you. I swear, no, I promise, I have not spoken to any other girls that I used to hook up with since I kissed you that first time at school. I realised what I wanted and that was you, so I cut ties with those people. I love you, please believe that!"

I've never seen Hunter get this upset over something before. Sure, I've seen him angry in the past over Theo but not about our relationship. He really was showing his vulnerability tonight.

"Hunter, it's okay. I believe you." I put my arm around him and rest my forehead against his shoulder.

"I didn't know she would come, I swear!" he continues.

"Hunter, calm down, please. It's really okay. I know that you didn't have anything to do with this." I squeeze his arm. "She didn't know you would be here. How would she know that I lived here?"

He still looks really upset and I know he thinks he's ruined the night but I'm honestly not fazed by that girl. He picked me and I know how to take his mind off it. Now was the right time.

I stand up and grab his hand, pulling him up off the couch. He follows me with a confused look on his face. I head towards the bedroom and walk him to the bed where he sits down quietly. Since we first talked about sex, I started picturing how I'd want my first time to be so I decide to take it slow, just like I'd seen in the movies. I light a few candles and turn off the lights before I walk back to stand in front of him. The whole time he remains quiet. I take a deep breath and sit on his lap. He knew exactly what I was doing. I play with the collar of his shirt, unsure of what to do next. But he knew and I trusted him.

"If at any point you want to stop, just tell me." His eyes search my face for any signs of hesitation as he wraps his arms around me.

I nod and press my lips gently to his. He responds softly and slowly but it doesn't take long before our kisses become urgent. He lifts me slowly and places me on my back before propping himself on top of me. Hunter pauses briefly to take his shirt off. I sit up with him and raise my arms above my head as he takes my shirt off too. As if he needs guidance, I place his hands on my chest. He starts to kiss my neck and I can feel his hands moving lower, playing with the hem of my pants. His breath on my skin makes goose bumps rise. Awkwardly and silently we both take our pants off and he reaches for the condom he must've put nearby earlier. I can feel my heart racing but there isn't a doubt in my mind that I'm ready for this. I grab for his face again and he starts to move my bra strap down my arm before reaching around to undo it. I can feel his bare chest against mine and it's warm and comforting knowing that he isn't looking straight down at me. My heart is racing. Surprisingly, I find myself starting to push the waistband down of his underwear and he obliges. He slowly reaches for my underwear and stops to look at me for permission. I nod and he continues to pull them down. He then returns to pressing kisses into my neck as his hands travel up and down my body.

"Are you ready?" he whispers.

"Yes," I reply as he reaches to unwrap the condom and put it on.

He pauses above me before gently kissing my lips and then he starts to move.

Luckily Kate warned me because it's more uncomfortable than I would've imagined and sure enough at one point I feel like a rubber band has snapped inside me. But then it starts to feel good and I feel as though we are moving and breathing in sync.

"Fuck Hayley," Hunter mumbles into my hair. His breathing is getting faster.

And then it's over. Hunter collapses on top of me and takes a big breath in.

"Wow," I finally say.

"You're telling me," he responds before pushing himself off me and onto his back beside me. "Wow, I feel like I've run a marathon."

"Fun fact, apparently when a boy finishes it's equivalent to eight hours of work," I randomly blurt out. Hunter gives me a look. "Sorry!" I laugh. "I have no idea where that came from!"

"Kate, that's who it came from." Hunter laughs at me. "I'm going to go and uh, get dressed."

I realise that's code for cleaning himself up. I grab my blanket and wrap it around me. I collect my clothes and go to my dresser while he does his own thing.

I quickly peek behind me to see if he's looking and when I can see he's not, I drop the blanket and start to get dressed. I've just put my underwear on when I hear him wolf whistle.

He takes me by surprise and I swing around to look, with only my arm covering my chest.

"Jesus Christ, is that really your body? How did I get so lucky?" He walks towards me and takes my arms, pulling me quickly against his bare chest. "See, you're safe now. I can't see anything. Guess we'll just have to stay like this forever."

I laugh before I swivel myself around so my back is then against his chest. I reach down for my bra.

"Uh, I wouldn't do that right now, Hayley," Hunter says quickly. I realise the position I put him in and laugh.

"Look at all this power I have, which I can now hold against you!" I grin as he backs himself over to the bed. He grabs a pillow and places it on his lap.

I turn around and put the rest of my clothes on.

"Hungry?" I ask.

"Starving." Hunter beams at me and follows me back to the kitchen.

I stick half of each pizza in the microwave.

"I'm really hungry now," I laugh. "I don't know about you but I worked up an appetite."

"I know, right!" He leans against the bench. "How do you feel?" he asks but his eyes are focused on the floor.

I pause for a moment and let what we just did sink in. "Honestly, I don't feel any different."

I say truthfully. Hunter grabs at his heart jokingly.

"I didn't mean it like that," I chuckle. "It was great, Hunter. I just meant I don't feel like an adult or a different person because we slept together." I shrug.

He laughs and walks over to me. "Yeah, I know what you mean, but far out. When do your parents get home?"

"Tomorrow at some point?"

"Well, eat up girl, because if you think that's the last time we're doing it before your parents come home, you better think again." He bites his lip in a seductive way.

I giggle. Having sex just opened a whole new cheeky personality that Hunter had hidden away and I was certainly a fan.

Hunter was right. We had sex another two times that night and each time felt better than the previous time. I couldn't believe how comfortable we were together now, like two puzzle pieces that just melded together. He was so mature about it, always checking in to make sure I was okay and if I was happy to keep going. We eventually fell asleep around 1:00am and I felt so serene and peaceful, content with my choice to lose my virginity at my age. I trusted Hunter completely.

When I wake up Saturday morning, it's around 8:00am. I was still naked from our last time. He too was undressed still and curled around me. I can feel his soft breathing on my neck. I don't want to wake him but at the same time, I want to make sure the house looks okay and the evidence of what we did is destroyed before my parents get home at 9:30am. I try to slowly roll over so I'm facing him. He stirs slightly before his breathing returns to normal. I place my hand on his cheek, marvelling at how far we had come. In this moment, I'm so happy with my life and I could honestly see a long future with Hunter. My only hope is that now that we'd had sex, Hunter didn't change.

Confident that Hunter is still asleep, I get out of bed and walk to my dresser for some fresh clothes. I pull out an oversized t-shirt and some exercise tights.

"Nice boobs," I hear him mumble but instead of being mortified, I chuckle and simply step out of his view. "Aww," I hear him whine. "Why did you move?"

I giggle to myself and move back into his view when I'm fully dressed. I walk back over to the bed. He's still half asleep.

"You can keep sleeping if you want, I'm just going to quickly tidy the house before Mum and Dad get home. Where did you put the things?" I sat down beside him.

"Are you in that much of a hurry to put what we did last night in the past?" he jokingly says before becoming shy. "Don't worry about it. They're all accounted for in my bag."

I kiss his cheek and he smiles.

"And they're called condoms, Hayley!" I hear him call as I enter the kitchen.

I laugh to myself as I put the kettle on and get out two cups. I place the left-over pizzas inside Tupperware containers and put the pizza boxes in the recycling bin. Hunter doesn't take long in the shower and I start to prepare our drinks.

"Do you want a tea?" I ask as he walks into the kitchen.

"Is now a good time to tell you that I'm actually more of a coffee drinker?" Hunter leans against the bench and rests his arms across his chest.

My eyes go wide. What? Since when? How had I not noticed this?

"What? It's not like we've hung out at breakfast time a lot. You never would've known." He shrugs his shoulders. "I don't drink it often, but I prefer it over tea."

"I can't believe I didn't know this about you." I start to prepare a coffee instead for him. "What else might I not know about you?"

"That I am madly in love with you." He walks up behind me and gently pulls me around to face him. "I can't tell you how much last night meant to me." He kisses me slowly and when his tongue starts to playfully trace my lips, I start to pull away.

"My parents could walk through that door any minute, Hunter." I feel the heat rise to my cheeks. "Now, do you want milk in your coffee?"

Hunter gives me a look that sends a tingling sensation through my body. I know I'm going to pay for turning him down later. I couldn't believe how much sexual tension there was between us now. Had this always been there and we just didn't know what it was? Had we unlocked this power when we slept together? It all confirms that I made the right choice last night. I return to making the drinks and when I walk out onto the deck, I hear a familiar car pull into the driveway.

"See? Luckily we didn't do anything because they're just pulling into the driveway!" I say matter-of-factly to Hunter.

He laughs. "Trust me, if I needed to fuck you quickly, I'm sure I could manage."

His raw account of what could've been sends chills up my spine. It makes him sound all the more dangerous and bad-boy like, and I need to stop fantasising about him or otherwise my parents are going to catch us in the act right here on the deck. Hunter looks at me with a smirk on his face, like he knew where my mind just went.

I jump out of my chair and race downstairs, leaving Hunter wondering what was going on in my mind. Or to calm down himself. After all, for guys, it was much more obvious when they were aroused.

My parents are getting out of their car when I reach the bottom of the stairs.

"Wait, just so you both know, he's still here," I whisper.

"He who? Who's he? Antonio, do you know a 'he'? Honey! Is she still seeing people that aren't really there?" Mum jokes as Dad laughs.

"Ha, ha," I respond sarcastically as I roll my eyes.

Hunter meets us halfway up the stairs and offers to take the bags off my dad who happily obliges.

"Thanks, kiddo. How's your team doing?" They start to engage in a conversation about sports.

I follow Mum into the kitchen and start to help her make coffee and tea for her and Dad, before heading out to the deck where Dad and Hunter now were.

"So how was retreat?" Mum asks.

Hunter and I share a smile between us as we recount everything we had gotten up to on retreat. Mum and Dad listen enthusiastically and ask questions at the right times.

"And did you work out what you're going to apply for at university?" Dad asks as he finishes the last of his drink. "Are you going to do the dance teacher course or are you going to follow through with the audition for Dynamite Studios?"

I almost want to shoot Dad. Several weeks ago, Dynamite Studios saw a tape of one of the performances ACE Dance Studios put on and encouraged the dancers, me included, to audition for their school as a potential career path. Dynamite Studios was one of the top tiered performing arts schools in the country and I couldn't believe they were even considering me. I brushed it off as I didn't think I would be good enough and didn't want to miss out on applying for the local university here. Dynamite had followed me up last week to see if I'd be auditioning as I was stuck on what choice to make. The dance school also happened to be a two-hour flight away, which didn't seem that far, but resulted in a much higher cost for me to move and live there. I didn't know if I could commit to something like that yet.

I also hadn't told Hunter about Dynamite Studios as I didn't know what I wanted to do and I didn't want to scare him with the possibility of me moving away. We had grown so close over the last several months and I didn't want to derail our progress when I hadn't made a choice yet. Dad realises my discomfort immediately as I feel Hunter's eyes burning into me.

"I mean, you've still got plenty of time to decide what to do. Just make sure you pick something that you really want to do and make a career and a life out of," he tries to cover.

"Just ignore your father, Hayley. We just want you to do whatever makes you happy!" Mum interjects before quickly changing the subject. "How about you, Hunter? What are you going to study?"

"I'm not sure if I will go to uni actually," Hunter replies. This was no surprise to me. He hadn't shown an interest in a particular career path in the whole time I had known him.

"What will you do instead?" Dad asks. I can almost read his mind. His only child ending up with someone with no ambition. I shake my head at the negative thought and push it from my mind.

"Not sure yet. Maybe I'll just do an apprenticeship or something." Hunter shrugs his shoulders like it's no big deal.

"I didn't know you were considering an apprenticeship," I slip out. I didn't mean for it to come across in such an accusing manner but Hunter doesn't miss a beat.

"I didn't know you were looking at moving across the country," he snaps back.

I stare at him with a confused look at my face. Clearly, I had struck a nerve.

"Thanks for letting me stay the night," Hunter gets up. "I should probably go home now. I haven't seen my family all week."

"No problem," Dad responds, sharing a look with Mum. He mouths the word 'sorry' at me after Hunter turns his back.

I get up to follow him to my bedroom.

"Hunter, please stop." I go to take his hand but he steps out of my reach to grab his bag.

"Why didn't you tell me?" he demands in a whisper. "How come you've been sitting on this massive piece of news about Dynamite Studios that just so happens to be nearly two thousand kilometres away from me? When were you planning on telling me? Do you even think about a future with me?"

"Hunter, calm down. It's not like I've changed my whole plan. They approached ACE several weeks ago and encouraged us to audition. I'd never even considered Dynamite Studios. They have so many applicants each year and there's so many people that are way better than me. I'm still looking at going to uni here though. That hasn't changed." I rest my hands on his chest as I explain my decision.

He pushes my hands off. "Of course you'll get into Dynamite Studios," he scoffs. "Stop with your modest crap! You just didn't have the guts to tell me you wanted to move away!"

"That's not true." I try to argue quietly.

"Just don't, Hayley. These last twenty-four hours, hell, this last week, I've bared a lot of my feelings to you and you can't even tell me this. Fuck, how could I be so stupid? You're just like Abby!"

I didn't know the girl's name who hurt him but his context makes me realise he's just put me in the same category as her. That was the last thing I wanted. How did this spiral out of control so quickly?

"Hunter, please don't say that. I'm not like her. This isn't the same thing." I can feel the tears start to form as I watch him shove his stuff into his bag.

"Of course it fucking is." He spins around. "I slept with her because she led me on, then she left me. Now I sleep with you and I find out the very next day that you're going to leave me! Fuck this! I'm going home now. Don't try to stop me, I don't want to hear it, and if you do, I'll tell your parents what we did last night and then you won't be the perfect daughter they think you are!"

I feel like I've been slapped in the face. I couldn't believe the words that just came out of his mouth. I thought I could handle Hunter's outburst as I knew I could convince him that I wasn't like Abby, but having him throw our night of vulnerability and love back in my face purely to hurt me crossed the line. I slump down onto my bed as the tears start to pool.

"Hayley," he starts as he realises what he's said.

"Get out." My voice is low and cold. "Get out, now!"

He scoffs and shakes his head angrily as he walks out the door. I dry my tears away in the hope that I can pretend nothing happened when Mum quietly appears at my door.

"Guess he didn't know?" she asks.

"No. I didn't want to scare him with the thought of moving far away. Things have just been so good between us lately." I let another tear fall and she walks over and sits beside me on the bed.

"Hayley, let me be honest with you. This argument is not worth your tears. He doesn't deserve them. If he wants to be rude about it, that's on him. You focus on you. After all, it's your life that's ahead of you and you need to put yourself first. You can't give it all up for him." She gives me a hug and then gets up to leave. "And Hayley, I'm only going to say this once because I trust you to do the right thing, but female hygiene after 'it' is very important."

My eyes go wide. How does she know?

"Be safe," she says.

"We were," I whisper. She smiles and walks away.

Chapter 19

I decide to switch my phone off for the rest of the weekend. If Hunter wanted to act like a jerk then Mum was right. He didn't deserve my time. I knew the consequences of sleeping with him. We were safe. There's no reason to be concerned in that regard. It hurt me that he thought I was anything like Abby. Maybe one day he'd see that but it honestly felt like the damage was already done. Would he ever trust me again?

For the rest of the weekend I focus on my classes at ACE Dance Studio, finishing up assignments, helping Mum around the house, and building a small trophy cabinet with Dad for his award. I eventually cave and decide to turn my phone back on on Sunday night. A few messages come through. There is one from Kate asking how my night went with Hunter with a winking emoji and another follow up Saturday night with a question mark emoji. Disappointingly, there are no messages from Hunter. I open up Instagram and start scrolling through my newsfeed. I come across a post that Hunter has been tagged in. He went to some party last night and he's in plenty of photos. He seems to be enjoying himself and I can't help but feel jealous until I come to the last two photos on the post. I almost have to do a double take. The female pizza delivery driver is in the photos. She has her arms around his shoulders as his hands are wrapped around her waist, like they're dancing. It looks intimate. I feel my heart break.

CHAPTER 20

Kate meets me in the dance room at 7:30am on Monday morning and I fill her in on what happened.

"What?" she exclaims. "You two finally have sex, then get into an argument and he goes and fucks her!"

"We don't know that he did that, Kate." I'm trying not to cry.

"What a jerk! I know he's not the easiest guy to get along with but far out, he likes to make life difficult, doesn't he?" Kate is fuming. I've never seen her this mad. "I just want to punch him in the face!"

"Get in line, girl." I try to laugh as I pace up and down the dance room.

"He fucks with my best friend, I'll fuck with him!" She's pacing the dance room now too. "How dare he!"

In the end, it took longer for me to calm Kate down than it did for her to calm me down. I appreciated her anger on my behalf and it was good to know that she had my back. I knew that everyone would know that there was something going on with Hunter and I.

"Was he any good at least?" She puts on her hands on her hips.

"Like I have anything to compare him to, Kate." I laugh. "If we did it more than once, I think that says something."

She breaks into a laugh. "My little girl is growing up!" she cries dramatically. "Now, what are we going to do about him?"

I shrug my shoulders. "I really don't know, Kate. I feel like that photo says it all. Should I just wait to see what he does and follow his lead?"

"And have a silent argument with him? Hayley, if he upset you or even cheated on you, you need to do something about it. Either talk to him or show him what's he's missing." She winks at me with a hand on her hip.

I take a moment to think about what she said. I know I should really talk to him about it but I'm just so angry that I'll probably end up saying something I regret. I want him to see that I'm not bothered if he goes off with other girls. That I'm not a controlling girlfriend, or jealous ex-girlfriend, but that I was someone who could be wanted by someone else. I sighed heavily. *How do I do that?*

"I should just talk to him." I run my hand through my hair. That was the right thing to do.

Kate bites her lip but nods in agreement. "In my opinion though, he's the one who walked out on you. He's the one who needs to apologise. You did nothing wrong, so why should you be chasing him for an answer?"

"I know," I mumble back at her as I sling my backpack over my shoulder and follow her out the door and down the path to homeroom. I can't help but feel like everyone is watching me and it just makes me feel sick to my stomach that my problems with Hunter were now plastered over the internet. I must've looked upset as I see Theo stop what he's doing and walk over to me.

"You okay, Hayley?" he almost demands. "Did Hunter do something?"

"Why do you assume that it's Hunter?" I sigh. Theo talking to me was the last thing I needed. I didn't really want to stir the pot with Hunter, who knows what mood he was in, but Kate had a point. Why was I chasing Hunter for an apology? I had other romantic options. Just like he did with that pizza delivery girl.

"Fair, but it usually is him," Theo answers matter-of-factly.

"You know he'll probably be mad if he sees you talking to me," I try again. I don't want to be rude to Theo but who knows what mood Hunter is in.

"I couldn't care less anymore. What's the worst he can do? Yell in my face?" He shrugs.

"He could beat you up?"

Theo gently pulls on my arm, so I stop walking and face him. "You really think he would do that if you told him not to?"

He had a point. Regardless of how annoying Theo was in the beginning, he's the reason Hunter finally came to his senses. Plus, I'd never want anything to turn violent. Hunter, on the other hand, may need only a little push to start something. I turn and keeping walking as Ethan appears from one of the buildings on our walk back to the senior school area. He gives me a weary look as he takes sight of Theo. Clearly, he's looking out for Hunter.

"I don't know if Theo is the best person to be hanging out with at the moment, Hayley," Ethan whispers to me as we walk.

"Like Hunter cares anyway," I reply in the same tone.

He knows I'm right. "Don't hurt him, Hayley."

"I wish you would tell him the same thing about me, because he already has," I respond. "He should know better anyway, given his past."

His face drops. "You know about Abby?"

I nod. "If he knows pain, and that's why he didn't want to commit to another relationship, then why is he hurting me now?"

"I know, Hayley, and I am sorry. You know what he's like now though and trust me, I've seen him this morning and he's not in a good mood."

I sigh. "Theo ran into me and we stopped to talk. We're in the same classes. I can't just ignore him, that's rude. It's not in my nature. I thought things would be different after the retreat. They seemed to be getting along."

"I know, Hayley." He squeezes my arm. "I'm on your side here but I'll always look out for Hunter. He's my best friend."

"He's lucky to have you." I smile weakly.

"He's lucky to have *you*." He lightly nudges my shoulder.

"Well, he doesn't have me anymore." I can't help but retort so that Ethan knew the seriousness of what was going on.

"I know you're going to hear all sorts of crap today, but he didn't sleep with her. That's the truth," he responds before finding Kate's hand and leading her down the path.

I sigh as I watch them walk away. I didn't realise just how much Ethan and Hunter told each other. I wonder if Hunter had told Ethan to say something. I absentmindedly fall inline beside Theo and we make small talk about an upcoming assignment. I let out the breath I've been holding when I notice that Hunter isn't at the lockers.

"You know you never answered my question, Hayley." Theo leans against the locker next to mine.

"Hunter's not in a good mood today," I warn him again.

"I don't give a fuck." He smiles sweetly. "You're upset and I want to help you."

"I'll take it from here, thanks." I feel Hunter loom behind me. Theo's eyes search my face for an answer.

"Please don't," I mouth back at him.

Theo pauses for another second. "Whatever you've done, Hunter, you'd better fix it."

"Stay the fuck out of our relationship, Theo," Hunter spits through his teeth.

"Maybe you should tell that to the girl you seemed awfully close with at Tom's party," Theo smirks.

I turn to look at Hunter to gauge his reaction. My suspicions were right. It looked like everyone knew about the party. Was I the only one not there? Behind Theo, a small crowd is forming. Hunter's eyes are wide and full of anger.

"What the fuck did you just say to me?" Hunter demands. He seems to grow taller. It must be an intimidation technique.

"You heard me." Theo's voice is cold and hard. "It's all over Facebook too, just so you know. And I'm guessing that's why your girl is upset. Not that she told me anything. I'll never understand the loyalty she has to you, but you can't look me in the eye and tell me she's not upset right now," he demands.

"That's right, she is *my* girl, so stay out of it!" Hunter growls.

"What is all of this yelling? Get to class all of you!" a teacher shouts as she comes around the corner.

Theo shakes his head. "I'll see you in class, Hayls."

I knew that Hunter hated it when Theo called me by my nickname and I could see how tense it was making him. I had no words though. I silently grab my books and go to close my locker but Hunter stands in the way.

"Please look at me," he begs. He goes to touch my chin but I step out of his reach.

"Please don't," I whisper. His face drops. He knows what he's done and it's written all over his face. Having Theo throw the obvious truth in his face managed to crack him.

"I'll explain everything." The worry in his voice is obvious. "Please give me a chance."

Theo was starting to become a catalyst for change with Hunter.

"Just go to class, Hunter." I walk backwards and eventually turn around as watching his face breaks my heart. I flinch as I hear his fist slam into the locker.

Chapter 21

I feel like I'm on autopilot. I move between classes and sit quietly. I try hard to avoid Theo as well. There was no point adding fuel to the fire. Soon I would have to face Hunter in English class and at lunch break. I didn't want to do any of that. I just want to be alone. I decide to hide in the dance room for the first break and practice some routines. Then it would be time for English. Begrudgingly, I begin to walk to English class and run into my teacher, Mrs Yun.

"You're looking a bit tired there, Hayley. Are you okay?" she asks as we walk.

"I'm a bit drained to be honest," I reply pathetically as I will myself not to cry.

"How about you take this period to rest in sick bay? You're up to date with your work and we're spending this class working on your essays anyway. Rest is just as important as your education. You need it to do well."

I couldn't believe the timing.

"Thank you, Mrs Yun. I really appreciate it." I let out a small tear as I watch her write a note for sick bay.

"Email me if you have any questions on your essay." She smiles and walks off.

Thank god.

—◆—

Are you coming to English? It's Theo texting me.

No, Mrs Yun gave me a free period. It was a small extension of the truth.

Hunter looks miserable, if that helps.

Don't say anything to him.

I shouldn't be responding to Theo at all. I know it would hurt Hunter if he knew I was doing this. Sure enough, I got a text message from him.

Where are you?

I only hope that Theo isn't winding Hunter up. I don't know how to respond. I don't want to talk over text message, but it may calm him down, making it easier to talk to him later.

Dance room. Another lie, but I couldn't bring myself to face him. My courage from this morning had vanished.

But it's English period?

Yeah, I know

I need to see you

I want to cry but need to keep it together for the rest of the day.

Please, comes another message.

I decide to give him hope and that way I'll have time to talk to him somewhere private.

I'll meet you at your house after school.

Hayley, I have to see you before then. You have no idea what this is doing to me. Please. I'll meet you at lunch.

No Hunter. I'm getting cranky. I don't care what he is going through. What does he think I go through when he pulls shit like this? *That doesn't work for me. I'll meet you at your house after school.*

Please Hayley, I promise, once I explain it, we can go back to the way things were. I love you.

Like it's that easy, Hunter? Is he serious? Who even behaves this way?

No you don't. My sassy attitude gets the better of me and I hit send before I have a chance to think it through. I can feel my heart racing. What have I done? I turn my phone off and shove it in my pocket.

CHAPTER 22

I honestly don't know how I got through the rest of the day. I tell Kate during the final period what I messaged Hunter and her eyes go wide.

"Hayley, you're breaking that boy's heart," she sighs. "I watched him in English. I figured it was you he was texting. His face just gave it all away. He just got up and left. I don't know where he went and neither does Ethan."

I bite my lip. Shit. What have I done?

"He'll have gone home. That's where I told him I would meet him," I sigh. "I shouldn't have sent it, Kate. I know that. It was childish but I felt like I needed him to know how he made me feel."

"Has he sent you any further messages?" Kate asks when we're able to start working on our assignment.

"I don't know. I turned my phone off." I took it out of my pencil case. "Should I turn it on?"

"I would wait until after school. You've made it this far. It's only another 30 minutes. Are you going straight to his house?" she says.

"I was going to go home and change originally but now that I know he's gone home because of me, I think I'll just go straight there," I answer. "I'll catch the bus with Ethan. He'll tell me what stop to get off at."

"Maybe he can give you some pointers on what frame of mind Hunter is in. He knows Hunter the best."

Maybe, I think to myself.

—◦—

The bell rings and the school is buzzing with students grabbing their bags and heading home. I almost didn't notice him standing at my locker.

"I didn't fuck her, if that's what you think," Hunter declares as I get closer. This draws the attention of the people around me.

"If that's what any of you are thinking, I didn't sleep with that girl. I'd never cheat on Hayley," he announces to the people around us. "And Theo, if that's what you're walking around telling people, then you can go to hell!"

I didn't realise Theo was even in the same area.

"Hunter, please calm down." I touch his arm. "I don't want this to be a big deal and I definitely don't want to do this in a public place."

This seems to calm him down only slightly. "Get your stuff, we're leaving," he says bluntly.

"Don't talk to her that way, Hunter." Theo pushes Hunter's arm away from me, causing him to snap and shove Theo against the lockers. Great, this is exactly what I didn't want. I see Ethan and Charlie, one of Hunter's friends, immediately spring into action as they pull the boys away from each other.

"I've told you once and I'll tell you again, mind your own fucking business, Theo!" Hunter growls, struggling against Ethan's hold.

"Well, stop making your private business knowledge to the entire fucking world, Hunter," Theo spits back at him as he, too, tries to get out of Charlie's grip.

Hunter manages to break free of Ethan's hold, lunging at Theo.

Ethan grabs my arm. There's urgency in his eyes. "You need to get Hunter out of here, now!"

I have no idea how I'm supposed to get Hunter away. He was so tall and strong. I wouldn't stand a chance. I yank as hard as I can on Hunter's hand hoping my touch breaks him out of his rage. He swings around glaring before he realises it's me.

"Hunter, let's go. Right now," I beg. "Please."

"No, I'm not done here. It's about time I finally put that prick in his place!" Hunter shakes off my grip and lunges back at Theo.

"You must clearly care a lot about her if this is how you act when she asks you to stop," Theo taunts him. Theo was quick on his feet, and each time Hunter went for him Ethan or Charlie would attempt to restrain him.

"All you ever wanted was to take Hayley from me. She's mine so just leave her the fuck alone!" Hunter tries to take Theo by his collar, but he manages to scramble out of it.

The crowd is getting bigger and I know I need to get Hunter away from it all. I can see that Hunter is going to throw a punch soon. In a split decision, I've wedged myself between the two boys and throw my arms up in front of my face in case Hunter throws a punch before he's realised I'm there.

"Hunter," I squeak from behind my arms. It goes deafeningly quiet.

"Hayley, what are you doing?" Hunter's voice breaks and is full of panic as he gently lowers my arms to my side. "I could've seriously hurt you. Hayley, why?" His eyes search my face and my body for evidence that I'm hurt even though he didn't actually swing at me.

I let out the breath I was holding and lean back, feeling Theo's chest against my back.

"Whoa," Theo says as he realises I've leaned into him. He gently starts to push me off.

"Don't fucking touch her," Hunter's hushed voice spits at Theo. He pulls gently at my arms so I'm no longer leaning on Theo.

"I'm out of here," Theo growls as he steps away. "Stopping fucking with her, Hunter. She doesn't deserve it. You can't treat people like shit and get away with it!" He then turns to the crowd that has formed. "What the fuck are you all looking at?"

It goes loud again as people start to go on with their business.

"Move, Hunter!" I hear Kate shout as she shoves him out of the way. "He didn't hit you, did he?"

She searches me for signs of injury. I shake my head.

"No, Kate." I clear my throat. "He didn't hit me." I glance up at Hunter. He's standing just to the side of me, worry in his eyes. He's biting his lip and I can see that he is struggling not to reach out and hold me. "Hunter wouldn't do that," I say.

I look behind her. Ethan is fixing his uniform and Charlie is ruffling his hair. They're both laughing nervously at the prospect of this having gone a lot worse.

"What were you thinking, Hayley?" Kate demands. "Never ever do that again! Do you hear me? That was the dumbest thing you could've done. Hunter would never have forgiven himself if he hit you instead of Theo."

"Hunter would never do that, Kate, and you know it. If I hadn't done that they would still be fighting. I knew that I needed to get in Hunter's line of sight for him to stop," I snap.

"Kate, please relax," Ethan sighs. "What she did was dumb but she had to do something."

"Still," she bites back. "Don't do it again. And you!" She turns to face Hunter. "You need to sort your shit out. Honestly, Hunter. Don't fuck this up. She's the best thing that's ever happened to you and you know it!" Kate storms off.

Ethan shakes Charlie's hand before checking in on Hunter, who was now slumped against the lockers. "Mate, come on. You need to pull yourself together." Ethan grabs Hunter's shoulder and lightly shakes him. "She picked you. Stop fighting everyone and just trust her. She's not Abby." His voice is low.

Hunter's face drops in embarrassment. I wonder how many times Ethan has had to pull Hunter out of a fight or vice versa. I also wondered how often Ethan and Hunter spoke about Abby.

I sigh heavily. How on earth did it get like this? I feel like I'm living in a soap opera. What are people going to think of me tomorrow?

"Come on Hayley, we need to talk," Hunter says softly. He holds out his hand for me to take.

I look at his hand but don't take it.

Chapter 23

Hunter opens his front door and I follow him inside. I was always blown away by how fancy his house was. Which really surprised me considering how messy his room was. He closes his bedroom door behind us. I drop my bag just beside the door and watch him walk towards the bed. I can see the tension in his shoulders. In a split second he has me backed up against the door and is kissing me with such urgency that I almost forget why we're here.

"What are you doing?" I push him away angrily. Like hell was I letting him back in that quickly.

"I just had to do it, Hayley. I needed to calm down and you have that effect on me." He runs his hand through his hair.

"Well, I couldn't before, when you wanted to rip Theo's head off, and you certainly didn't want a bar of me at my house." I cross my arms over my chest.

"I don't know what the fuck you've done to me, but I've never begged a girl before in my life. I'm begging you to understand that I do love you and I know I fucked up."

"I want to know the whole story, Hunter. You told me you would explain." I stand with my hands on my hips.

"I just, I don't know," he starts. "Running into that girl was just an accident, Hayley. Please believe that. I had no idea that she would be at that party. And nothing happened. You saw what she was like. She just followed me around the whole night, taunting me about you and how we wouldn't work and she was better. The photos were snapped so quickly and she just went for it. I'm actually trying to push her away hence why my hands were on her hips but clearly the photo doesn't show that," he tries to explain. "I wish I never went to that stupid fucking party. I should've fucking run back to you the second I walked out your door." He hangs his head low.

"I understand that you were hurt before and I respect that, I really do, but when you used what we did as a threat, I was so repulsed by you. You were like some power-hungry tyrant. How do you think that makes me feel?"

"Please just stop," he whispers. He sounds like he is about to cry. "I know what I said Hayley and I'm so ashamed of it. You're nothing like Abby, I know that." He gets up and puts his arms around me. "Please, tell me what I can do to make you forgive me."

"Why don't you start with apologising, Hunter?"

"Hayley." He brings me over to sit on the bed. "I'm so sorry that I used us having sex against you. I really shouldn't have said that. I certainly didn't mean it. I shouldn't have gone to that party. I was looking for trouble by going there. I made a mistake, Hayley, and I shouldn't have done it." He throws his hands in the air in defeat.

"Hunter, you also fought with Theo." I see anger flicker through his eyes. "I told you not to and you did it anyway. You even screamed our private fight out to all our school friends. Were you looking for attention?"

"I didn't know how else to get through to you. You wouldn't talk to me and you weren't answering my texts. Fighting is all I know." He sighs. "I want to be better for you, Hayley. I want to be the first person you think of when you wake up, I want to be the person that brings that smile to your face." He touches my cheek. "I love you so much."

I let him kiss me gently. "We're going to need to talk about our future, Hunter. Dynamite Studios asked me again over the weekend if I'd like to audition."

"Yeah, I know, but not right now. I have plans for us right now." His lips move to my neck, and I know exactly what he wants.

"Hunter." I let out a giggle. It makes him pause and look at me.

"What?" he asks before returning to my neck. "You're telling me you don't want this?"

"We can't just have a massive blow up and then have sex." I don't make any move to stop him though.

"Please, I've heard make up sex is the best." I can feel his hands go underneath my shirt to unhook my bra. My hands move to unbutton his shirt and push it down his arms. I hear it drop to the floor. He responds by unbuttoning my shirt and pushing it down my shoulders. He pulls my bra straps down my arms before returning to kissing my neck. I let him move us to the centre of his bed.

"You're so sexy," he breathes. I let him pull my skirt and underwear off as he slid between my legs. I fumble for his belt buckle, and he helps by taking off his pants and underwear.

"Do you have a—?" I start.

"I know your rules Hayley, of course I do." He gets ready.

He's not wrong, make up sex does feel pretty good. Hunter goes slower than he usually does and it's not long before I'm begging him to go faster. He seems to thrive off this and tortures me for a little while longer. It then becomes too much for him and he collapses against me. He takes a minute to catch his breath and then rolls off me.

"Why the fuck did it take us so long to have sex? There were so many places I could've fucked you at retreat." He runs his hand through his hair. It sounds so rough when he talks this way about sex but it sends tingles up my spine.

"All I ask is that you don't pick fights with me just to get that result. If you want sex, you just have to ask," I say sheepishly.

Hunter rolls out of bed and I can hear him taking the condom off. I pick up my clothes and walk to the toilet to get dressed.

I come out of the toilet and Hunter is half dressed on his bed.

"Do you want to watch a movie?" he asks as he turns on the TV.

"Can we talk about Dynamite Studios?" I suggest.

"Not right now, maybe tomorrow. I think we should just be together right now." He pats the spot beside him.

I sigh.

"We will talk about it, just not right now," he tries to soothe me.

I try to shake off the annoyance I have that he doesn't want to talk about this after the big deal he made. It makes me wonder if he's hiding something.

CHAPTER 24

"What are you going to wear for the formal?" Kate asks as we sit eating our lunches at the outdoor tables. Formal was fast approaching. It was a night we all looked forward to as we celebrated the end of our high schooling career. The girls got to wear pretty dresses, and the boys got to wear nice suits. We were treated to a dinner and night of speeches, awards and dancing. It was going to be the best night ever!

"I'm trying to work out what colour dress I want first so I at least have a goal when I go shopping. I was thinking burgundy or something, maybe?" I reply.

I had been dreaming of this moment and wondering if I was supposed to assume that Hunter would be my date or if he had to be official and ask. If it was the latter, it was hard enough to actually get him to ask me to be his girlfriend so this would be difficult. I was hoping that maybe he was getting some inspiration from other 'proposals' that were happening. The boys, along with some girls, were already asking their partners, or friends, to formal in the most public of ways regardless of their relationship status. Of course, I could ask Hunter. I'm a strong independent woman after all, but at the same time, I was stubborn as hell. If he wanted to go with me, he had to ask me, just like in the movies. Sadly, he's not mentioned it once though.

"Cute!" Kate responds. "I think I'm going to go for a lilac colour as it'll compliment my hair."

I nod. Her dark hair would suit lilac really well. I think about my own hair and decide then and there that burgundy would be the way to go.

"That reminds me!" Ethan announces and turns to Kate. He pulls out a small party blower popper and hands it to Kate.

"How random," she giggles. I knew exactly where this was headed.

"Try it!" He sits, waiting.

Kate blows into the mouthpiece, and it shoots out its streamer. I can see what it reads from here, but I don't think she can.

"Does it say something?" she cries.

I smile at her and Ethan gets up on the table. He clears his throat and gets the attention of everyone sitting around him. "Kathryn Bellmont, will you do me the honour of going to formal with me?"

Kate's cheeks immediately go pink as she blushes and nods an over-excited yes. Ethan plants a kiss on her cheek and then sits back down brushing his hands off proudly. Kate squeals with excitement and she launches herself at him.

I look over at Hunter who meets my gaze but turns away.

CHAPTER 25

"What kind of change did you notice?"

"I don't know, he seemed a bit withdrawn at times but really happy, like his usual self for the majority of the time. He's really hard to read to be completely honest." I sigh. I was lying. I could read Hunter like an open book.

Dr Martin switches gears, but I could tell that we would circle back to this question.

"So, tell me about this fight with Hunter then?" Dr Martin asks. "Had you ever seen Hunter like this before? Was he always this aggressive with Theo?"

I scratch my jaw. How did I answer this without making it look like Hunter had these bad traits from a young age?

"Aggressive is a bit of a strong word, don't you think?" I try to be vague.

Dr Martin raises his eyebrows at me. I knew that look all too well. My answer was insufficient. Cocky bastard.

"He was a growing boy with testosterone. Surely you remember what that time was like?" I can't help but snap. Therapy was a fucking headache. This was going to be my last session. I'd had enough.

Dr Martin sits there silently whilst I recover from my outburst.

"I guess at that age, everything and anything could irritate you. Theo was no different. He knew how to push Hunter's buttons. So he never helped the situation and Hunter probably never felt at ease while he was around. He just didn't like him. Plain and simple."

"Is he the reason Hunter became a bit withdrawn at times?" And there it was.

"I don't know." I shrug and wrap my arms around me. "I don't know if he saw Theo as a threat. It was something else."

"Home life?"

"No."

"School life?"

"I don't know. He seemed fine to me."

"Most of the time though, not all the time?"

I roll my eyes.

CHAPTER 26

We were getting closer and closer to graduation. I felt very comfortable with how I was tracking academically and had set myself up quite well to have a relaxing few weeks before school was over for good. The only things stressing me out was my audition piece for Dynamite Studios and the fact that Hunter seemed to have no interest in formal whatsoever, or even just in me lately. Our text messages started to slow down. He stopped messaging me before he went to bed and when he woke up. He no longer sent detailed messages either, just a few words here and there. He also didn't ask to hang out as often anymore, and now he was no longer waiting for me at the drop off zone so we could walk into school together. When I eventually decided to walk down, I found he was already at the tables. It was the same this morning, and I decided if he wasn't already there, he wouldn't be there at all. Fool me once, shame on you, fool me twice, shame on me. Fool me a third time, well, it's just not going to happen.

I put my headphones in and start the walk down the hill. I could feel anger building inside of me. Why had his behaviour changed? It had been several months since we first had sex, and now I felt as though Hunter was bored of me. He didn't have to try anymore. He didn't have to impress me because we'd now had sex. He definitely wasn't stressed about school. He was actually doing quite well himself. It seemed as though he didn't want a bar of me. I was boring, obsolete, embarrassing myself by chasing someone who wasn't interested anymore. I decided on my walk to not go after him this morning. I wasn't going to play the game any longer. I was so happy before and now I wasn't so sure of myself. It was time I refocused my attention back to me. I'm the centre of my universe, not Hunter, and he needs to work his way back. I need to ensure a successful start to my future and not waste time waiting on Hunter to decide if he wants to be with me or not. I felt more and more confident in my decision to audition for Dynamite Studios with his recent behaviour. I had to at least say I gave it a go and didn't give up what could be the biggest opportunity of my life for a boy.

I get to my locker after going the long way around, so I don't see Hunter at the tables with everyone, if he was even there.

"He's done it again." Kate sees me as I approach.

"Yep," I reply coldly. "I think I'm done, Kate. I don't like feeling like this. I feel nothing from him at all. He just uses me whenever he wants."

Kate sighs. "Well, he hasn't said anything to anyone about it. He's made no comment that would alert me or Ethan that he wants to end things."

"That doesn't make me feel any better. His actions say differently and that's what I'm more inclined to go with. He goes out of his way to not see me or interact with me." I shrug. I told her some of the feelings I had when I was walking down the hill. "If he's scared about graduating, I wish he'd tell me. What if I do end up auditioning for Dynamite Studios and I actually get accepted? Is this his way of ensuring he doesn't get hurt if I move?"

"Well, first off, I think it's great for you to audition for Dynamite Studios. You definitely should. You can only give it a go, and they do second round offers for university so you'll always have a backup. Secondly, you sound certain that it's time to end this relationship, which I'm surprised by, but I want you to take the weekend to sleep on it and make sure it's truly what you want, because with a guy like Hunter, if you end it, I think that'll be it." Kate's working hard to keep her facial expression neutral but I can see her concern. It's been a long road to even get to this point.

"Ask me again at the end of the day," I say. I can feel the butterflies in my stomach even thinking about it. "I shouldn't have to chase someone who's not interested."

"True. I understand that. It sucks, that's all. You both just looked so happy when things were good." She gives me a hug. "Okay, act normal, Hunter is about to walk behind you."

I nod and keep looking in my locker.

Kate clears her throat. "What were you and Theo chatting about this morning?"

My eyes go wide at Kate and she nudges me. I couldn't believe she'd say that. I wanted to talk to Hunter on my own terms, not be pushed into it.

"Uh, nothing important, just school stuff." I try to keep my voice steady. I really wasn't prepared for a confrontation right now.

I hear a scoff and can't help but turn around. I see Hunter leaning against the lockers behind me. Of course he only cares about me when Theo's involved.

I take a deep breath and muster my confidence. "Sorry, did you say something?" I ask coldly.

His face is angry, and he scoffs again. "I'm not playing this game with you."

Instead of biting back, I close my locker and walk away. I was not even going to entertain this conversation if this was how it was going to be. I wish Kate had just let me approach Hunter myself.

"Hayley, wait." Hunter grabs my arm.

I sigh and turn around. "What?"

"Was Kate serious? Are you really talking to Theo again?" His face and voice are full of concern, but I don't want to buy into it. He won't change my mind. I refuse to be treated like a friend when I'm supposed to be so much more.

I decide to keep the small lie going. "It was just a brief conversation about something irrelevant. It's really nothing of your concern."

"What do you mean nothing of my concern?" he demands. "My girlfriend is talking to the guy I absolutely hate. Is this why you've been acting so differently lately? Because you're now in love with Theo?"

I'm shocked. Is that what he thought? Some nerve! "I beg your pardon?" I spit. "I'm the one getting treated like an outcast but I'm the cheater?"

I couldn't believe he just said that. My anger continues to rise. All of this built-up emotion is bubbling at the surface waiting to be released.

Hunter goes to reply but I cut him off. "No! You don't get to talk, Hunter. I'm not the one who has changed. I've been loyal and devoted and am trying to be understanding but you give nothing in return. You won't talk to me, you ignore me, you forget about me all the time. I clearly mean nothing to you anymore!"

"That's not true, Hayley." He tries to grab my hand, but I pull it away. Shock spreads over his face.

"Yeah, well your actions speak louder than words." I feel tears welling up. This is it, this is the moment I break up with him. "And I'm done, Hunter. I can't do it anymore. It was a mission to even become your girlfriend and it's becoming a mission to stay your girlfriend." The tears are flowing now. Hunter is silently biting his lip. Again, it's had to be for me to call him out on his behaviour for the truth to come out. "And I don't want that."

"You don't mean that, Hayley." He starts to panic. "Surely you don't mean that? Are you hearing yourself?"

"Yes, I am, Hunter, and believe me this is hard, because I thought we were stronger than this. I gave you everything I had, everything, and as soon as you got what you wanted, I got dropped. I should've known better, given your reputation."

"That's bullshit, Hayley, and you know it," he snaps, shaking his head. "We've been together for too long for you to pull this shit on me. Of course I love you, you know that. I didn't spend all this time with you just to get rid of you the moment we got into bed together."

"Then why, Hunter? Why have you been ignoring me? You see me and immediately look the other way. You seem completely disinterested in graduation. You never text me first or offer to hang out. You never want to discuss our future. You hardly wait for me in the morning or the afternoon, and when you do see me, it's like I'm just another girl walking past. Something has changed with you and I hate it! I'm over it. You and me are done."

"Stop saying that!" He raises his voice. "You're not breaking up with me. You're being silly. Just go to class and calm down." He turns to walk away.

"I'm auditioning for Dynamite Studios anyway and I certainly don't expect you to move two thousand kilometres when you can't even move to see me at school," I snap angrily, adding more fuel to the fire.

This stops him in his tracks. "What?" His voice is broken and his face drops.

"You heard me." I stubbornly cross my arms over my chest.

"Get to class, Hunter!" I hear a teacher call out from a classroom window. This breaks his gaze from me, and I take the opportunity to walk away first.

"Hayley," he calls after me.

"Now, Hunter!" the teacher yells again.

Begrudgingly, I see Hunter turn and walk in the opposite direction towards his classroom.

I'm bubbling with anger. He didn't address any of my feelings. It took me throwing Dynamite Studios in his face to get a response. I do something I never thought I would do. I go to sick bay with my backpack and fake being sick. Luckily, they buy it and before I know it, I'm at home in my bed with the weight of what happened on my shoulders.

CHAPTER 27

Dad takes a seat on my bed and feels my forehead for my temperature.

"Well, you don't have a temperature." He removes his hand. "Are you sure you're feeling sick?"

I look at him puzzled. How does he know?

"He's talking about Hunter." Mum appears in the doorway.

Don't cry, Hayley, don't cry, I will myself.

"I'm okay. I just needed to get away from everything. Just a bit stressed, you know, graduation is approaching." I try to laugh it off.

"Really? My little girl is graduating? My baby girl is going off to leave me all alone!" Dad acts dramatically.

"Hey!" Mum laughs. "I'm still here."

"You're my favourite, don't tell Mum," Dad laughs as he tries to whisper his joke.

I crack a smile. I admired my parent's relationship. They seemed to still be in the honeymoon phase, even 20 years later. I feel like Hunter and I passed that honeymoon stage after we slept together. Does this mean we're not right for each other?

"You'll be okay. You're strong, Hayley." Dad puts an arm around my shoulder.

I nod. It's so hard not to just burst with everything that has gone on between me and Hunter but I just need to get my head around it myself first.

"You're stronger though." I rest my head on his shoulder.

"Don't leave me out of this!" Mum pretends to race into the room and sits on the other side of me, wrapping her arms around me too. "I love my little family." She kisses my forehead and then Dad's.

"I'm going to audition for Dynamite Studios." I try to sound confident in my decision.

Dad's bottom lip drops in surprise as he shares a look with Mum.

"That's great, honey!" Mum beams at me. "I think you're making the right choice."

"Me too, even if that means my little girl is moving all the way across the country." Dad squeezes me tighter.

"It's only a short two-hour flight, Dad," I chuckle. It really wasn't that far away.

"And seeing as you lied and you're not actually sick, your punishment is to work on your audition for Dynamite Studios all day and all weekend." Mum pokes her tongue out at me before getting off the bed. "I'm so proud of you, Hayley." She plants a kiss on my forehead.

"Well, you heard the boss!" Dad gets up too. "Better start working on that routine."

I smile and push the covers away.

"That also means no Hunter this weekend. You need to focus." She gives me a look which makes me realise instantly that she knows something's up and is saving me from having to explain why Hunter wasn't coming around or why I wasn't going to see him. Not that he'd been around much lately anyway.

"What's for dinner, Mum?" Dad asks.

"Not sure. I'll have to do a pantry challenge," she laughs as she exits my room.

"Challenge accepted." Dad stands up straight and salutes, following Mum out the door. "Watch this space, kiddo, MasterChef at work."

I laugh. Dad was such a dork sometimes.

I pull out my phone. God only knows what storm I had created.

My feelings towards Hunter have been up and down. I go between anger and then confusion, and worst of all, I try to make excuses for his behaviour. I know in my head that if I have these negative thoughts about him, then I probably shouldn't be with him. I definitely needed to give it the weekend to determine how I really felt. I have several messages from Kate. Her last being that she rang my parents and they confirmed I was sick, but she calls bullshit and will be ready to talk when I am. I then go to my message chain with Hunter and scroll to where the new messages start.

We need to talk

Meet me at the lockers at break

Where are you?

Hayley! Seriously, where are you? It's lunch now and we really need to talk. Everyone is talking about us.

Hayley, please stop ignoring me. We really need to talk.

I'll wait for you.

Is this really it? You break up with me and then disappear? Maybe it's better that we are done.

I stop there. My tears are overflowing and it's so hard to read the other messages from him. I can see that he goes between apologetic and frustrated. Instead, I open Instagram to start mindlessly scrolling when I hear a loud thump.

"Antonio!" I hear my mum cry out.

I jump out of bed and race for my door. I run to the kitchen and see Mum crouched down beside Dad. He's lying face first on the ground.

"He's not breathing!" Mum cries.

I grab my phone and call for an ambulance.

CHAPTER 28

I never realised just how cold hospitals were. Or maybe it was just because I was fed up with waiting for the doctors to come out and give us some news that I was nit-picking a place that saved lives. Watching Mum have to pull herself together to get behind the wheel to follow the ambulance was tough but luckily, we didn't live too far away from the hospital.

The paramedics that arrived at our house managed to get Dad responding but he was constantly slipping in and out of consciousness. They kept firing questions at Mum about his health history but he's lived a relatively healthy life, apart from being a heavy smoker up until recent years. He wasn't a pack-a-day kind of guy though. Well, at least not anymore. I knew he snuck the odd one or two here and there, but maybe that odd one or two was in addition to three or four that I didn't see when I was at school. When we got to the hospital, the nursing staff told us we had to wait until the doctors had a chance to assess Dad and work out what had caused his collapse. We were directed to a waiting room just inside the emergency room. They said to sit tight but couldn't give us an estimate of how long we'd be waiting for.

"He's not going to die, is he?" My mouth moves without my consent, the words cutting deep as the enormity of the situation hit me.

"Honey, I've always been honest with you. I don't know. I don't know what happened. I don't know if he's okay but I'm keeping positive until we hear some news from the doctors." She hugs me tighter. "Do you want to call Hunter?"

Hunter. That's right. My *ex*-boyfriend.

"Oh, um, we broke up," I mumble.

"I know, honey." She smiles weakly at me. "You don't think I know a fake sickie because of a guy when I see one?"

I look at her sheepishly.

"Give him a call. He'll come through, regardless of what's going on between you two. I know he will."

I sniff and wipe my nose on the tissues that the nurses gave us earlier. Did I really want Hunter here? Of course I did. Was I scared to reach out to him after breaking up with him? Totally. He could reject my call. He could've blocked me since I'd been ignoring him. Hell, he could've already moved on with one of the girls from his past. But I would have to talk to him eventually so I may as well get it over with.

I stand up and stretch my legs before turning back to face Mum briefly. "If they come out, come and get me immediately."

She nods. "He's in the best place to get the best care, Hayley."

I walk out of the waiting room and take a deep breath as I tap on Hunter's contact card in my phone.

He answers nearly instantly.

"Hayley," he whispers.

I can't bring myself to say anything. I feel like my mouth isn't connecting to my brain and I can't seem to get the words out.

"Hayley, please talk to me." His voice his broken and I can feel my heart shatter more than it already has.

Be strong, I will myself. "It's my dad. He's in the hospital."

CHAPTER 29

"Mrs Gonzalez." A doctor finally emerges from behind the emergency room's sliding doors.

Mum and I both jump out of our seats.

"Thank you for your patience. I'm Dr Reid. We have managed to stabilise Antonio, but we need to run some more tests to determine the cause of his collapse," the doctor advises. She was a petite woman with short blonde hair that was peppered with grey. Her eyes were a piercing blue and if you stared at her too long you could almost see the trauma she had seen as an emergency room doctor seep out.

"Can we see him?" Mum asks, not even trying to mask the desperation in her voice.

"He's currently in the intensive care unit and on a ventilator, Mrs Gonzalez. You can visit but only one at a time," Dr Reid instructs.

"When will he come off the ventilator?"

"When we are certain that he will be able to breathe on his own. If he can't breathe on his own, we will make him as comfortable as we can."

The weight of Dr Reid's words hit me like a ton of bricks.

Dad could really die.

"Mrs Gonzalez, I'll take you through first if you like," Dr Reid offers before turning to me. "You can wait just outside his room."

"Hayley!" Hunter's voice pulls my attention away from Dr Reid. He rushes through the doors of the emergency department and wraps me in a hug.

I don't have time to respond to Hunter as Mum places a hand on my shoulder. "Hayley, come on," she says.

"Can Hunter come?" I ask Dr Reid.

"Of course," she nods in response. "He can wait on the bench with you while your mum sits with your dad."

Hunter takes my hand as we follow Mum and Dr Reid. I'd never been in an intensive care unit before, and it was terrifying. My heart was breaking to think that my dad was one of these people lying motionless in a bed hooked up to machines to keep him alive.

"You need to put this gown on, mask and gloves, Nurse Riley will show you how," Dr Reid directs Mum to a small woman at one of the nurse's stations who was already compiling the protective clothing she would need. "You two can sit here," the doctor finishes as she points to a bench outside of Dad's room.

"Hold him tight for me." I give Mum a hug and watch as Nurse Riley helps her prepare to go in.

I look at Dad for the first time. He looks like he's asleep but there's so many tubes and wires connecting his body to different machines.

Mum takes a seat next to Dad and I can see her hand shake as she reaches out to take his.

I sigh and slump on the bench. Never did I expect the weekend to go like this. First, I break up with Hunter, then Dad collapses. It was a rollercoaster that I really wanted to get off.

"How are you holding up?" Hunter places an arm around my shoulder.

"I don't know. Like, what the hell? This week has been fucked." I curse as I put my head in my hands.

I couldn't believe he'd answered the phone and that he managed to get here so quickly. I was thankful that he didn't try to argue with me on the phone. He just said he'd be there soon. It was a 30 second phone call. I didn't even give myself time to prepare to see him again. All I knew was that Hunter was coming for me, and he still cared.

"What did the doctor say before I got here?" Hunter asks, pulling me out of my thoughts.

I clear my throat. "They need to run more tests now that he's stabilised to determine why he collapsed. Hopefully we should know more throughout the day tomorrow." I wipe under my eyes.

"Okay, well we will keep positive until we hear from the doctors as to what's wrong." He squeezes me tighter.

I nod. A wave of tiredness washes over me. My eyes feel heavy but I need to keep going. I don't want to miss anything. Mum, and Dad, needed me.

"Hayley, I need to know the best way I can support you," Hunter says quietly.

I turn to look at his face and he's biting his lip again.

"Am I supporting you as a friend or as your boyfriend?" he mumbles. "I just need to know where I stand."

"Will you leave if I tell you we're just friends?" I snap unexpectedly.

His face drops. "No! I would never do that. You need me right now whether I'm here as your boyfriend or your friend. It just would be nice to know which...that's all."

I sigh. I knew I would have to face the music at some point so why not now? Why not get all the hurt out now? Then I can focus solely on Dad and getting him better.

"Hunter," I begin. "Today I expressed to you how you made me feel and you didn't listen at all. You told me I was being silly and to calm down." He puts his head down. "I told you that I felt ignored and forgotten, and like I was just another girl walking past you. You made me feel so small and unimportant. Why do you refuse to talk about your future? *Our* future? Why did you stop talking to me? You never want to hang out. Why? Why were you no longer waiting for me? Why did you brush it off when I tried to ask you? Why would you ignore me when you walked past me?" I rapidly shoot questions at him as my anger comes flowing out. "I don't think you even realised that it looked like I wasn't your girlfriend anymore and you were trying to get another girl."

"There is no one else, Hayley. Don't even think that," he says quickly before he sighs. "I don't know, Hayley. I don't know. I had a brain snap again, I guess."

"For nearly two weeks this has been happening and during that time I really thought I had fallen out of love with you."

He looks up, his eyes wide. Were they tears forming?

"I don't want us to break up, Hunter, but you just wouldn't explain yourself and I don't want to be with someone who only wants me when it's convenient for them. Do you not love me anymore?"

"I love you more than you know, Hayley." There's a hint of anger in his voice, like he's annoyed that I questioned his feelings. "I love you more than you love me. I just, I don't even know why I did it. Yes, I made the conscious decision to not wait for you. I guess I had a feeling of nostalgia where I wasn't the one being chased anymore. I was settling down. You have to remember, I was going to go through my whole high school and probably most of my twenties without a girlfriend. I enjoyed playing around and not having to commit but I'm not doing that anymore, I'm ready now. I don't want to go back to that, but I guess what I'm trying to say is I was scared. I was scared that things would change after graduation. You have ambition, you're going to do things with your life, and you have a plan. What do I have? An attitude and no desire to keep learning. You were going to go off with your university friends, or hell, even move across the country, and eventually I would get left behind. I let my mind get the better of me. The fear of getting hurt again is still strong within me. She's the sole reason why I am the way that I am. Until I met you." He sniffs and wipes a stray tear.

I sit silently and take in everything he is saying as he pours his heart out to me.

"I guess I was hoping you'd chase me, but you didn't. You didn't chase me before we started dating, so why should I have expected anything different," he chuckles half-heartedly and hangs his head. "I'm sorry, Hayley. I hate that I've made you feel like I don't care about you because I do. I care so much. I just got scared and it's a shit reason. I've never felt this way about anyone before, and I didn't want to lose what we have."

I make sure he's finished speaking before I start. He was very headstrong, so I knew that what he was saying was true. He got scared and decided to run from his feelings. Again.

"What made you feel this way? Is it because graduation is coming or is it because of Dynamite Studios?"

He nods. "Well, yeah. Graduation is coming faster than I would like, and up until several days ago, you hadn't even made a decision about Dynamite Studios. Change isn't easy, and then Ethan reminded me how much things *had* changed. We both would be graduating with girlfriends and having done not too bad academically. He then went on to tell me all his ambitions with Kate and how they were going to go through life after school, and I realised we never had a plan and now I could lose you forever if you go to Dynamite Studios."

"Well, it's not for a lack of trying, Hunter," I scowl. "You always told me we'd talk about it later. We could've discussed Dynamite Studios multiple times over the last few months. You didn't even give me the opportunity to ask you to come with me."

A small smile grows on his face as he thinks about what I've said before he shakes his head of whatever thought he was having. Hell, I don't even know what I just said. Did I just invite Hunter to come with me if I got into Dynamite Studios?

"Well, the point is, I'm ready now to talk about our future but I just don't think now is the right time." He looks over his shoulder at my dad. "I know that's what I always tell you."

I sigh again and decide to move on from it. He was right. I had more important things to worry about than what will happen in a few months. I move onto my next question. "Is that why you wouldn't ask me to be your date to formal?"

"Did you want a grand gesture from me to ask you to formal? I honestly thought it would've been obvious that we would go together. You're my girlfriend. I would be so hurt if you chose to go with someone else."

That's a very fair assumption. We are dating, *were* dating? I didn't know where we stood right now but I understood what he was saying. Why would we go with other people?

I decide to be honest, just like he has been. "As lame as it sounds, yes. I did want a grand gesture. I want people to look at our relationship and be jealous of what we have."

He smiles shyly at this. "Well, now is not really the right time for me to ask you about that either."

I sigh for what feels like the millionth time and I wipe my nose. "Hunter, I really wish you had come to me with these concerns instead of shutting me out. We could've avoided all of this."

He hangs his head. "I know, but at the same time, I wish you had told me about Dynamite Studios earlier."

"How could I though, Hunter? You were shutting me out. I had to use it to get your attention," I say truthfully. It wasn't the best way to bring it up, but I just couldn't get through to him that day.

It looks like he's trying to figure out what to say next. He goes to start a sentence a few times but stops himself. "All I can say is that I'm sorry, Hayley. I find it really hard to talk about these deep feelings. It took me ages to ask you to be my girlfriend, and I was bloody shitting myself when I wanted to talk to you about sex."

I let out a small laugh. "We are a sad pair, aren't we?"

"But we're in this together?"

I take a moment to think about what he's asking. He wants to know if we're in a relationship or not. Did I want that after all of this mess? Yes. If he had just told me all of this shit before, we wouldn't be in this position. I never wanted to end things with him. I felt like he had forced my hand, and I said it out of anger. But him being here, tonight, after everything, meant the world to me.

"Yeah, we are." I rested my head on his shoulder.

We sit there silently but comfortably.

"We have to make a plan for our future soon, Hunter," I eventually say. "But right now, I need to focus on my dad."

"I understand," he replies, placing a kiss on my forehead.

I stand up and look into Dad's room. Mum is talking to him, but I can't hear what she's saying. My heart aches to be in there with her but I know I need to wait and follow the instructions from the doctor. Mum sees me looking and I give her a weak smile.

Eventually Dr Reid lets me know I can go in too, but we don't have long left of visiting hours.

"Does he know that we're there? Can he feel us holding his hand?" I ask her on the way in.

Dr Reid pauses for a moment. "There's no scientific proof to say yes or no to that. Some people claim they can feel and hear everything, others don't. Ask him when he's off the ventilator and awake. He'll tell you if he could."

I hang onto the what the doctor said. *Ask him when he wakes up.* I need to run with this positivity because yes, Dad will get through this. He has to.

Mum looks up. I can see she is happy that I'm able to come in. It's hard to know where to hold Dad. He has tubes just about everywhere and I would hate to bump one by accident. I sit on the other side of Dad, unsure of what to do.

"Why don't you try talking to him? Tell him about Hunter or your graduation plans," she suggests.

"Uh, um okay. It might help to talk about Hunter. He's a lot to handle," I sigh.

"But he's here," Mum reassures me.

"You're very much team Hunter, aren't you?" I laugh and Mum joins in.

"He's just such a good kid, Hayley. I know he's a lot of work, but I think he's worth it. He makes you so happy," Mum replies, and I give her a look. "Well, most of the time he does but what's life without a few speed bumps?"

I start from the start. Mum and Dad pretty much know everything about my plans and they know of most things that happen between Hunter and me. He came over so often that they never really needed to get the information from me, Hunter would just tell them what they wanted to know. I tell Dad of some of the funny things Hunter and I had gotten up to and all the sweet gestures from Hunter that they may not have known. Mum smiles softly as I tell them about some of the petty arguments he and I had had and how we temporarily broke up only to get back together 24 hours later. I tell Dad how Hunter didn't even ask questions, he just came regardless.

"And now we're here, Dad, waiting for your body to heal at its own pace so that you can come back to us." I squeeze his hand so tightly that my mind plays tricks, thinking he's squeezing my hand back, but I know that he's not.

After what only feels like minutes, we're told it's time to go.

I feel my face drop. I want to keep talking to Dad because it feels amazing to get all this weight off my chest, but I understand why. Mum has the same expression on her face. It would be just as hard for her to leave Dad here. They were inseparable. Begrudgingly, we both stand and head back to the nurse's station to remove our masks, gloves and robes.

I'm relieved when Mum offers for Hunter to stay the night. I certainly didn't want to spend the night alone and I couldn't even begin to imagine what she was going through.

When we walk back over to where Hunter is sitting, he stands up and hands me and Mum a bottle of water each. I take one final look at the hospital before we leave. "We'll be back for you, Dad," I whisper.

CHAPTER 30

My eyes snap open. Have I overslept? What time is it? Is Dad awake? My mind is racing with all these thoughts. I sit up quickly before I realise it's still pitch black.

"Hayley," Hunter mumbles. "Are you okay?"

I look at the clock. It's been half an hour since we went to sleep. Damn it.

"I'm fine. Sorry, I didn't mean to wake you up." I lie back down.

It's no use though. Sleep doesn't come and I find myself checking the clock more often than not. After I watch nearly every minute tick over, I start to get frustrated with myself. I know I'm tired. I certainly feel it, but I just can't sleep. Poor Hunter probably hasn't slept much either, but he's remained quiet throughout my tossing and turning. He just adjusted his position every time that I moved. This night has been shit. This whole week has been shit. Why is everything so shit? Why is Dad in the hospital? What did he do to get this sick? Did he know he was sick? What if he never wakes up? What if he dies? What do I do? God my chest feels tight. Am I dying?

"Whoa, Hayley, calm down." I feel Hunter's arms wrap around me. "Just breathe, you've worked yourself up."

I force myself to take a deep breath. I didn't realise that I had worked myself into such a state. I take another deep breath. I feel like it's not working, I need a distraction. I know something that could take my mind off it. It worked in those romance movies. I saw Lydia do it to Stiles in Teen Wolf and it seemed to work, and she was smart.

I feel for Hunter's face and kiss him hard. At first, he's a bit surprised and then he accepts it. His arms pull me closer to him and instantly I want more. I reach for his shirt and start to tug it up.

"What are you doing, Hayley?" Hunter says through kisses as he grabs my hands.

"I need you to take my mind off it," I plead, wriggling to get free of his grip.

"Are you sure?" he asks, his grip still firm.

"Yes." I nod even though he probably can't see me.

"Are you sure you're sure?" he asks again.

"Hunter," I scowl.

"I'm trying to do the right thing by you and not take advantage of you," he laughs as he presses his lips against mine again.

"Hunter, I am of sound mind, and we've done this before. Now take your damn shirt off."

He chuckles. "Hold on, let me get a condom." I can feel him reach over the side of the bed before he sits back upright and I continue taking his shirt off.

His hands move to my shirt, and he pulls it over my head, matching my desperation to get things moving at a faster pace.

"We have to be quiet," I whisper against his lips.

"Easier said than done. Good luck with that," he chuckles softly.

His hands move to my pants, and he makes quick work of removing them before he takes his own pants off. He cradles my head in one hand while the other holds his body weight up.

He pauses briefly to brush a strand of hair behind my ear before he leans down to kiss me. "I love you, Hayley," he whispers.

I smile even though he can hardly see me. "I love you, too."

Things had an odd way of working themselves out. I was satisfied with what Hunter had told me. I truly believed what he'd said at the hospital. I just wish he'd said something instead of hiding from me. Hopefully now he realised he could come to me about anything so we could get through it together. Until I was able to drill it into Hunter's head that I wasn't going anywhere, he would always have a fear of losing me. I didn't know if that was a good thing or a bad thing.

◆

I can feel the sun streaming through the blinds. It's nice and warm. I stretch out and accidentally hit Hunter's chest. His muscly, bare chest. It causes him to stir and he slowly opens his eyes. Surprisingly, I managed to sleep soundly after having sex with him.

"I could get used to this," he yawns as his eyes look me up and down before landing on my chest. I then remember that we never got dressed after last night, so I pull the sheet up quickly. He laughs and tucks the sheet around me.

"Is that better?" He rests his forehead against mine.

I smile shyly in return but still can't bring myself to stand up and be naked in broad daylight. He notices my discomfort. "I've seen it all already. You don't need to be embarrassed," Hunter laughs but I give him a look until puts his head under the doona cover.

I race out of bed and go to my dresser, grabbing new clothes out quickly and dressing at lightning speed. Now I felt okay and comfortable.

"Much better." I walk back into view and see Hunter is now seated on the edge of the bed. He's put his pants on so far.

"I highly disagree with that," he smiles before reaching for his shirt.

I walk over to him and sit on his lap. "Thank you for last night." I kiss him gently.

"I would do anything for you, Hayley," he replies. "And I will do *that* anytime."

I blush and get up to brush my hair.

"Sex hair really suits you." He walks up behind me, taking the brush and putting it back on the dresser.

"It looks like a bird nest." I laugh and turn around to face him.

His hands travel down my back before he lifts me up onto the dresser. His lips find mine easily. "If you keep brushing your hair, I'll just do to you what I did to you last night, over and over."

I feel my stomach flitter with excitement. This was the Hunter I remembered from school retreat. I let Hunter continue to kiss my neck until my eyes land on a photograph of my dad and me, and the events of last night hit me.

"My dad is sick," I utter, and Hunter pulls away immediately. His face drops as he too realises the whole reason we're here in the first place. He quietly helps me off the dresser before he grabs his shirt and slips it over his head.

"Cup of tea?" he offers.

Hunter opens my bedroom door for me, and I lead him to the kitchen.

I can see Mum is sitting outside on the deck, a cup of tea already on the table. She's looking out over the backyard. Both the house phone and her mobile phone are beside her on the table.

"Do you want me to make you a cup of tea?" Hunter leans on the counter.

"I can do it." I smile and start to prepare a drink for each of us. Mum hears me and I see her wave.

"Good morning, you two." She smiles and returns her gaze to the backyard.

"Do you need a refill?" I call out.

"That would be wonderful, honey. I don't know how long I've had that cup sitting there."

That's when I realise she's in the same clothes as yesterday. I wonder if she had any sleep at all. I walk outside to her and see her cup is half full.

"How long have you been out here?" I ask as I pick up the cup. It doesn't even feel hot.

"Too long," she chuckles. "I don't think I've slept a wink. I was frightened that the phone would ring, and I would miss it."

Her eyes have dark rims around them, making my heart ache.

"Mum, I will man the phones for a couple of hours while you get some rest. Dad needs us to be strong right now," I offer.

She chuckles lightly at me and then lowers her eyes to her cup, as though she's weighing up her options. "Maybe I will, but you need to wake me up the minute the phone rings!" She gets up out of her chair and stretches.

I put both phones in my pocket and follow her back inside.

"Morning, Hunter. Did you sleep okay?" She smiles at him.

"As good as I think I could've, all things considered." He takes a sip of the drink I made for him.

"I need to call your mother and explain," Mum looks at me. "Can I have a phone?"

"Don't worry about it, Miranda, my mum doesn't really care. She's not a good mum like you. I sent her a text message just before. She's not bothered." He shrugs.

I'm surprised by this, greatly surprised. I didn't know he had those thoughts of his mum. My mum gives me a look, and I shake my head. I want to ask him more about the topic but Mum cuts me off.

"Are you sure, honey? I can call her. I'd hate for you to get in trouble," Mum replies warm heartedly. "We're still yet to meet your parents."

"There is nowhere else I'd rather be than right by Hayley's side. The more support I can give Hayley, the better support she can give you."

"Thank you, Hunter, for being here for Hayley," Mum says softly as she walks out of the room.

Now was my chance to ask him about his mum so I turn to face him. "What has your mother done to you?"

His face drops and I hope I've haven't ruined a good morning. "Don't even worry about it. She's just not as good as your mum," he says quietly.

"Why have I never known this?" I'm curious more than ever now. "We talk about your family all the time. Why is this the first time I'm hearing this?"

"Last night when I told Mum I needed her to drive me to the hospital, she gave me her credit card and said it was my problem to deal with, and I needed to be more careful next time. She didn't even ask why I needed to go there. She didn't ask who it was for, if everything was okay. Just here's the credit card, deal with it, like she thinks I got a girl pregnant or something." He shrugs again and looks out the window.

"Is this the first time this has happened?" I ask, taking a seat opposite him and trying hard to hide my desperation to know all the details about his mum.

"Let me ask you this, Hayley, how many times has she been around when you've come over? How many times have we actually had a proper conversation about my family? We just talk about general stuff, never anything too deep." He shrugs.

"I'm sorry, Hunter." I reach for his hand and he rubs my palm.

"It's not your fault. My dad's never around anyway and Mum has to put up with me and my brother. It's not like I'm the easiest kid to deal with."

"That shouldn't matter though," I respond but he looks away quickly. I need to choose my words carefully now as he's clearly upset by it. "Can I do anything?"

He chuckles. "Yeah, focus on your dad getting better. Don't worry about my family shit."

I look back at him, trying to gauge his emotions but he's giving nothing away.

"Another coffee, please." He holds his cup out to me.

I hated that he shut the conversation down, but I knew this was a battle that wasn't worth the fight, especially right now. He had a point though. I had never met his parents in the whole time I'd known Hunter. They were always out somewhere or on a holiday. I felt terrible that I had often breezed past the conversation of his parents, instead of paying more attention and realising that they weren't around. I made a mental note to check in on him regularly so that he knew I cared. I couldn't imagine growing up in a family where my parents didn't care about me like mine did. I knew that Hunter was difficult—he knew that he was difficult—but I could see that he must've tried to make things easier between him and his parents. It just hadn't worked. My heart ached for him, and I was even more thankful for the relationship he had with my parents. My dad was probably the only real father figure he had so he was probably just as worried as I was that we could lose him. I shake the thought of losing Dad out of my head though. I had to be strong.

CHAPTER 31

I stare out the window the whole drive to the hospital. We all remained quiet, not really sure of what to say or what we were about to walk into. We hadn't heard anything, but we were still allowed to visit. My stomach starts to churn as Mum parks the car. The weight of the situation dawns on me. Would he still be lying comatose hooked up to all of these machines? Would he be sitting upright trying to finish a sudoku? Would he be somewhere else?

As we enter the hospital and follow the same route as last night, Hunter keeps a firm grip on my hand. He is having trouble hiding his nerves though and I can see his eyes searching the hospital, taking in the severity of the situation.

We turn the corner to the intensive care unit, and I can't decide if I want to vomit or scream. Dad is sitting upright in bed with a cup of tea in his hand talking to Dr Reid. I hear Hunter let out a sigh of relief. Mum has tears in her eyes as the nurse helps her prepare to go into the room. I race up to the window of his room and tap on the glass like a child. He's still connected to a lot of cords but he's smiling back at me. He raises his hand slowly to wave and I can see it's taking a lot of energy. I fight back tears of happiness watching Mum carefully embrace Dad and sit on the edge of the bed. Dr Reid starts talking to them both and I strain to hear her through the glass.

"Easy," Hunter chuckles. "You're going to fog up the window." He gently pulls me back into his embrace.

I continue to stare into the room. Hopefully I would be allowed in soon if Dad was awake.

Dr Reid seems to finish up what she's saying and checks Dad's monitor one last time before exiting his room.

"Hi Hayley," Dr Reid smiles at me. "Your dad has not stopped talking about you and how proud he is of you."

"Is he okay?" I ask before I can stop myself.

"I'll let your parents fill you in and then you can ask me any questions after that." She pats my shoulder and turns and walks away. A nurse appears and helps me put on a gown and face mask. I race into the room the second she finishes and launch into my dad's arms.

"Careful kiddo," Dad laughs as he wraps his arms around me.

"Yes, careful please, Hayley," Mum chuckles. "I don't want to have to try and work out where all the cords go."

I let go of Dad and sit perched on the side of his bed.

"Hunter can come in if he wants." Dad smiles at me. That's when I realised Hunter didn't follow me into the room and was sitting outside.

"I think there's a limit, Antonio." Mum rubs his arm gently and his face drops slightly.

"What's going on? Are you going to be okay, Dad?" I ask eagerly.

"Well, eventually it was going to bite me in the butt but it's the smokes, honey. I've got emphysema." Dad's face drops as though he's a child being scolded by his parents. "It's not good at any level though so I need to stop entirely to make sure it doesn't kill me, because honey, if I keep going the way I am, it'll kill me earlier than I'd like. I did too much damage in my early years, it's catching up with me."

"Don't scare her, Antonio," Mum warns. "What he means is that he's kind of lucky if you think about it. We've caught it now, so he knows what he needs to do and how to stop it from getting worse."

"The next few weeks will be the hardest," Dad continues. "I'll be going cold turkey off the cigarettes so it'll be tough, but I can do this, kiddo, you don't have to worry about anything." Dad squeezes my hand.

"So what does it all mean? What does emphysema mean?" I struggle to pronounce the word.

Mum pulls a piece of paper off the table beside Dad, and she starts to read. "It's basically a lung condition in which the air you breathe in doesn't leave your body properly so it becomes trapped and therefore can't enter your bloodstream properly. Your dad wasn't getting enough oxygen, so he collapsed, but there is medication to help with this. It won't fix the condition, but it'll help slow progression."

"Will he collapse again?" I ask, trying to absorb all of the information.

"There is always a possibility, but if he keeps smoking then it's a higher chance." Mum puts the piece of paper back on the table.

"But I'm going to give up smoking, Hayley, and do whatever the doctor tells me to do." Again, Dad squeezes my hand and reaches for Mum's hand. She smiles faintly.

"You gave me a fright, honey." Mum presses a kiss on his forehead and his eyes close. A tear trickles down her face, but she clears her throat and quickly wipes it away. "He'll be in the hospital for another couple of nights and then he can come home." Mum smiles at me.

"That's a lot to take in." I stare at the ground. "Are you sure you're going to be okay, Dad?"

Dad and Mum both nod their heads.

"You've got nothing to worry about," Mum says. I want to believe her but sitting here in an intensive care unit room makes it difficult.

CHAPTER 32

Hunter stays with us for another night before Mum makes him return home to go back to school on Monday. I tell him everything that Mum told me about Dad's condition, and we spend time researching emphysema before I get upset, and then we do something else to pass the time. Mum rings the school to let them know what has happened and I get the week off.

I find it hard to sleep the first few nights without Hunter and opt to stay up later to ensure I sleep straight through until morning. It doesn't work though. Mum and I spend the time waiting to visit Dad by perfecting and filming my audition for Dynamite Studios. She then makes sure I dedicate time to my schoolwork so that I can just enjoy Hunter's company in the evenings.

Dad comes home Wednesday, after four nights in the hospital. His first night is peaceful and I feel myself start to relax and believe that he was going to be okay. I watch my audition video with him, and together we press send on my application to Dynamite Studios. He chimes in on a video chat to Hunter when I call to let him know I'd submitted my application.

The weekend finally rolls around, and I spend most of the day playing cards with Dad until he wants to lie down. I make him a cup of tea and get him his sudoku puzzle book before walking back to the kitchen where Mum is prepping for dinner.

"What time is Hunter coming again?" she asks as she slices the potatoes.

"Um, I think around 6pm?" I answer as I sit on the stool at the bench in front of her.

"What can I chop?" I ask.

"Nothing, you've done heaps for me today, honey." She looks up and smiles at me.

"There must be something I can do?" I whine.

Mum chuckles. "Why don't you go and be a normal teenager and play on your phone?"

I laugh. "And then in ten minutes you'll tell me to get off my phone and help!"

"I don't know, honey," she laughs. "Go have a shower or something. Tell Hunter to come over earlier and he can entertain you." She puts the sliced potatoes in the oven tray and starts coating it in the sauce for a potato bake.

"Message received, Mother. Don't you want my company?" I joke as she puts the potato bake in the oven.

"Honey, you have been at home for a week now. We've spent quite a bit of time together." She squeezes my shoulder. "I love having you around to help, Hayley, but your dad is going to be okay, so I want you back at school on Monday. We will be able to manage without you for the six hours a day you're at school." She smiles weakly. She looks so tired. I can't imagine what's been running through her head over the last couple of days. I imagine that every time Dad moves or makes a sound in his sleep, she wakes up, scared that something is going to happen to him again.

"Mum, if you keep telling me Dad is going to be okay, then I think you need to believe it too," I hop off my stool and walk around to give her a hug. She responds instantly and I can feel her body slouch and her breathing become uneven as she starts to cry. I squeeze her as tightly as I can. It only takes a few seconds before she slowly releases me, sniffs and then stands upright again. Her eyes are red from crying. She tucks her hair behind her ears.

"Thanks, kiddo." She pinches my cheek and returns to what she's doing.

"I think I will have a shower." I give her a reassuring smile before heading off to grab my things. I waste no time getting in the shower before sitting down in the bathtub and letting my emotions take over. I try hard not to make a sound as I cry. Watching your parents cry is one of the hardest things to do, knowing there's not much you can say or do to make it better.

Eventually I remember Hunter is coming over and I need to dry my hair still. I turn the taps off and get out of the shower. The mirror is all fogged up thanks to my hot shower and forgetting to turn the exhaust fan on. I use my towel to wipe the mirror and see my tired face looking back at me. I had until my hair was dry to stop from crying and making my eyes even more red. My mind wanders to random thoughts as I dry my hair. Given how thick and long my hair is, it takes a bit of time to get it to a point where I'm happy with how dry it is. I switch the hair dryer off and hear Hunter's muffled voice. How long have I been in the shower? I thought I'd left myself plenty of time. He must've come over earlier. I creep up to the bathroom door to listen better. Who is he talking to?

"What are your plans for after you graduate?" I hear my dad's voice. "I ask her, but she says you're still thinking. What's that all about?" My eyes go wide. I can't believe how candid Dad is with him. I can only imagine Hunter's facial expression. He's probably starting to get mad.

"I don't know, Antonio. I just don't want to get left behind, that's all." His voice is low and sad.

"Left behind? You'll only get left behind if you don't do something. She can't make that decision for you because then she will go off and follow her dreams and meet new people, and what will you be doing? Sitting in your room playing

PlayStation, waiting for her to come back? She has a real shot at Dynamite Studios, whether she chooses to believe it or not. At the end of the day, I want what's best for her and I'll encourage her to go with or without you."

My jaw drops. I didn't think Dad had a problem with Hunter but at the same time, I want to high five him. I knew that Hunter didn't have a strong father figure at home, so I bite my tongue and decide not to interrupt them.

"Well, what do I do then? I have no idea what I want to do with my life, and I don't want to sign up to some stupid course that I have to pay for and not like. I want to see the world!" There's an attitude in his voice but I can tell it's not directed at Dad. He's being confronted with the truth and he's trying to work out the answer.

"How are you going to see the world, Hunter? Travel costs money, kid." I can imagine Dad shrugging.

"My parents would just give it to me to stop me interfering with their lives." Hunter's voice drops. After our last conversation, I realised that Hunter probably had to raise himself. Either that or his older brother Trace had to, and I knew that Trace wasn't really on the best path in life. He partied a lot.

"Do you really want to live a life like that where you just waste Mummy and Daddy's money? Go build a name for yourself. Create your own wealth. Build an empire, for goodness' sake! Show them you don't need them."

I really thought this may cause Hunter to snap. The Hunter I knew would've been happy to waste his parents' money seeing as they didn't give him anything else.

"How though? I'm not interested in anything," Hunter says sombrely.

"Do you like fixing things?"

No, I mentally respond. Hunter certainly didn't like fixing things.

"Do you like sports?"

He likes watching sport and playing sports but it's probably too late to go pro, I respond in my head again.

"You like to talk though. What about sales or marketing?"

I almost laugh out loud. I couldn't imagine him doing that.

"What's talking got to do with sales and marketing?" Hunter laughs. I almost sigh with relief knowing that the conversation seemed to be going so well.

"Use that brain of yours and the words you put together to sell something or convince someone of something. You convinced my daughter to date you, after all. I know exactly who you were before she came into your life." I imagine Hunter blushing at Dad's comment.

"I don't know but I am intrigued, I guess," Hunter responds.

"Let me put it in a different way that your brain may enjoy. Use that head of yours to sell some poor sucker some overpriced piece of crap, like the next Xbox that does the same thing as the first one."

Hunter laughs hard at this and then the room goes silent. I wonder if he's actually considering this. How was it that Dad could get through to him when I couldn't?

"I could do that." Hunter's voice is so low I strain to hear it.

"You like video games? Go be a consultant or something, or a creator. You could build video games." There's energy in Dad's voice. He's thoroughly enjoying helping Hunter.

"I'm going to go look online. Can I use Hayls' laptop?" There's excitement in Hunter's voice. I want to hug Dad tightly. Then I remember I'm still in the bathroom with my shirt half over my head. I quickly finish getting dressed and hang my towel up.

Hastily I unlock the door and try to walk casually to my room.

"Oh, hey Hunter, you're early?" I try to act normal. He's sitting on my bed with my laptop in his hands.

"What's your password?" he asks, his focus solely on my laptop. I can almost see his brain ticking over.

"LuckyStar94," I reply. "What are you doing?"

I can feel my heart racing. I need to play it cool in case I scare him off or worse, he chooses not to tell me.

"I need to have a look at something. What university are you applying for again?" His fingers are flying over the keys.

"James Cook," I reply as I try my hardest to remain calm. This was finally it. He was creating a plan for his future, and it involved me.

"Antonio!" Hunter leaps up and takes my laptop with him as he walks out of my room. I follow him quickly so this time I can be included in the conversation.

"What's up, champ?" Antonio pats the spot beside him. Without hesitation, Hunter sits on the bed beside my dad and angles the laptop so he can see.

"Look!" he beams. "James Cook offers a business degree in marketing, and they also have one in graphic design!"

Dad puts his glasses on and angles the laptop screen to his liking. "See! There you go. Read up on it, kid, and see if it's something you want to do."

"If you don't want to do a degree, you could try a certificate or a diploma? Less of a financial investment," I blurt out. I want to show Hunter that I'm supportive and he has options, but I'm worried I'll scare him.

Hunter looks at me as though he's just realised I've been standing there. His expression then changes to puzzlement.

"Aren't you going to James Cook though?" he asks.

"Yes, well that is unless I don't get Dynamite Studios." I shrug my shoulders and lean against the door frame.

"You'll get in," he quickly says before returning his gaze to the screen.

"You could look at schools in the Gold Coast area?" I say quietly.

"Very true," he mutters as he types away. "There's Griffith University that's not too far from Dynamite Studios. Marketing is a three-year commitment and even entry level positions seem to pay a decent salary. Looks similar to what James Cook offers."

Hunter looks like he's trying to do the math to see if it's worth it. I glance at Dad and he gives me a reassuring look.

Give him space to think this through, is almost what I hear Dad's voice say.

"Looks like I can maybe get into them with average scores. I don't need to be the top of my class. That's good then. There's no chance I can go from my grades now to top of the class this close to graduation." He rubs his chin and leans back against the bed frame.

"Well, you're not doing too bad academically, from what Hayley tells me anyway." Dad's voice is so encouraging, so supportive. It was wonderful to watch this interaction unfold but at the same time, I wish I could've been the one to guide Hunter.

I stand silently, waiting for him to go through things in his head and, for some reason, with my dad. Every now and then he spits out a question directed at my dad, and calmly Dad responds. Hunter seems satisfied with each response and I can almost see a light in his eyes as he imagines a future he never thought he'd have. I almost want to cry. Hunter fits in with my family so well. Dad's probably stoked that Hunter is listening to him. Their chatter slowly turns to mumbled voices as my mind imagines what my life could be like if Hunter actually follows through with these plans: a house with a white picket fence, a ring, a baby.

"Dinner's ready!" I hear Mum call out, breaking me from my fantasy.

"We'll be right there!" Dad calls back. "Click that button and enter in your details there."

I really want to know what they're doing, but again, I'm worried I'll spook him.

"Is that all I need to do?" Hunter looks at my dad.

"Yep, that looks like it, kiddo. You'll get an email to confirm it all so check that it has gone through properly," Dad stretches his arms out in front of him and takes his glasses off, placing them on the bedside table. "All done," he swings his legs over the side of the bed and grins at me. I walk to his side and offer my hand for Dad to help him up. Dad's had a big day today so he takes my hand, and I help him to his feet.

"I can take it from here, kiddo," he says as he uses the hallway walls to guide him down to the kitchen. I turn to follow him.

"Hayley!" Hunter grabs my hand and pulls me back to him. He has a wide grin on his face. "I did it, Hayls. I made my decision."

"Yeah?" I slowly ask.

"I've applied to Griffith University and if you don't get in to Dynamite Studios, I've applied to James Cook!" he beams. "I can see it all, Hayley!" He plants an urgent kiss on my lips. "You and me! We're going to become super successful and super rich, and we won't have to rely on anyone. We'll have our own money that we can do whatever we want with!"

"Yeah?" I ask again but this time I let excitement come through in my voice.

"Yep, you'll be a world-famous dancer and I'll be the head of a top tier marketing firm!"

I smile with him and reach up to kiss him gently. His hands snake around my hips, coming to rest on my butt. I quickly shove his hands away.

"We're in my parents' room! They could walk in anytime!" I blush.

"I think I'll need a minute." He blushes as he looks down.

CHAPTER 33

I wake early Sunday morning and no matter how hard I try, I can't go back to sleep. I get up and check my phone for any notifications. There's a message from Hunter, wishing me a good night's sleep. I roll myself out of bed and walk to the kitchen. Dad is awake which is no surprise. He's sitting on the deck reading a book with a cup of tea in his hand. He smiles at me through the kitchen window and waves his cup in the air. "Make your old man another cuppa, please?" he calls out.

I grin and put the kettle on before walking out to grab his cup.

"Sleep okay?" he asks.

"Yeah, straight through the night." I turn to walk back into the kitchen to make the drinks.

"What's on your mind?" he asks, taking a sip of his tea. "Something seems to be bothering you still."

"Do you think Hunter was serious about uni?" I ask sheepishly.

"What makes you think he isn't?" His eyes narrow.

"I just feel like it was a snap decision. One second he had no idea what he wanted to do with his life, then he spends an hour with you and he has his whole life sorted out." I run a hand through my hair. "It just seemed odd to me and I'm worried it's not what he really wants."

"Hunter doesn't strike me as the kind of guy who does what other people tell him to. If he doesn't want to do it, he wouldn't have applied." Dad shrugs his shoulders. "Why sign himself up if he wasn't going to follow through?"

"I don't know. I guess it just came as a surprise. Talking about a future with Hunter was always a really tough subject. He didn't seem to want to discuss anything serious like that. It always got shut down." I take another sip of my drink.

"Maybe he just needed an adult to talk to?" Dad offers. "Maybe he needed guidance that you couldn't offer. He probably feels like he's the one who needs to have all of the answers. He's the male in the relationship—he's got a dominant personality. He may have felt a bit off having you tell him what to do when he's such a headstrong person."

"But he shouldn't feel that way," I sigh.

"It's not a bad thing. He's just a teenage boy trying to work out what he wants in life. Sounds like he may not have that authority figure or someone he can look up to, so his future was very uncertain to him because he had nothing to base it on. I would give the guy a break to be honest."

I finish the rest of my tea. "I need another tea."

"I'll do it," Mum's voice calls as she walks out to grab my cup. "Morning everyone. Want another cup, Antonio?"

Dad shakes his head. "Hayls just made me one. I can't drink boiling hot liquid as quickly as she can."

I chuckle at Dad's comment.

"Hunter asked to stay tonight so make sure your room's clean. Don't want my future son-in-law thinking you're a grub," Dad jokes. Mum laughs and shakes her head.

"I haven't spoken to him though?" I asked puzzled. "Did he ask you?"

"Yeah." Dad pulls out his phone proudly. "We're text message buddies now."

I must've still had a look of puzzlement on my face as Dad adds, "We thought it was a good idea to be able to contact each other if we needed to."

I just nod, still unsure how to feel about them potentially talking about me, or about Dad's condition, behind my back.

"He wants to make sure you actually go to school tomorrow," Mum laughs before changing the topic. "Does he ever talk much about his home life? I almost feel like he lives here."

"Not sure, Mum, ask Dad. Hunter seems to open up to him about that stuff." I turn to walk back inside.

"Someone's a bit bitter," Dad smirks.

"I'm not bitter, Dad." I snap back around and he raises his eyebrows at me. "Okay, maybe a little, but you can use this to your advantage. See if he'll tell you. I'm sure he'll tell me when he's ready and knows what to say."

"Does he say anything though?" Mum persists.

I shake my head no. "Sometimes he'll drop a comment that his mum doesn't really care and his dad is never around. It just sounds like they had a busy life before they had kids and now that the kids are old enough to take care of themselves, they're back to living the high life without them. It's actually quite sad. I think that's why he's got this big tough exterior but is a sweetie on the inside. Well, at least with me he is."

"Poor kid, that must be tough." Mum's face drops.

"Well, he's always welcome here and we trust you to pass that onto him," Dad adds quickly. I smile gratefully at my parents and walk back to my room.

CHAPTER 34

Graduation Day was finally here. Twelve long years of schooling were coming to an end. In true high school formal fashion, Kate and I had gone shopping with both of our parents to find our formal dresses for the dinner. I even had a tie made for Hunter in the same colour material so we'd match. Kate's older sister, Alice, was in charge of hair and make-up as she was currently studying to be a cosmetologist. She certainly fit the description of a hair and make-up artist. I could've sworn that every time I had seen Alice, even briefly, she had different coloured hair. Currently, it was aqua blue and pulled back in braids. Her eye make-up and lipstick colour were nearly identical to her hair. Kate had a nice girl look to her, whereas Alice had a tougher appearance. Her numerous facial piercings probably didn't help, but she was absolutely lovely and made me feel so at ease that I knew she'd do a great job on my hair and makeup. She knew in great detail all about Kate and Ethan's relationship and I knew that Kate would've told her a bit about my relationship with Hunter, having met him several times in the past as well. Like the other girls in my grade, Alice was amazed that Hunter had finally committed to a relationship and that she was glad he'd met someone like me. I still couldn't believe the extent of Hunter's reputation sometimes, but it made me proud to think I had managed to attract him. As I waited patiently for my turn, I couldn't help but be amused at the interesting dynamic between Kate and Alice. They bickered constantly but it was tasteful and kind of funny. It definitely helped settle my nerves. Kate's parents were having drinks with my parents on the deck. Occasionally, either my mum or Kate's mum would come in check on us. Both Hunter and Ethan would arrive at 5:00pm so we could get some photos and then go to the formal.

I sat nervously in my chair when it was my turn for Alice to work her magic on my hair. I couldn't shake the feeling that Hunter would pull out at the last minute though. He had been so great in supporting me while Dad recovered but his face screwed up whenever we spoke about formal and graduation, even after all of our discussions about being more honest with each other. I tried to make the conversations light-hearted and not so serious. He was still concerned about the possibility of things changing between us after graduation. Luckily, I was starting to be able to read his cues, and I knew when to pull back on the conversation.

I was amazed at how talented Alice was. She had neatly braided my hair from a side part around to the back before gathering the remainder of my hair in a bun. She pulled a few strands out to add some curls and had neatly tucked a few diamante pins in the bun.

"How are you feeling, Hayls?" Kate asks. "Still worried Hunter won't show up?"

I nod. I didn't think I would feel better until I saw him in an hour or so.

"Ethan promises me he'll be here. You just need to trust him." She squeezes my hand.

"I just can't help it," I continue. "I'll be so embarrassed if he doesn't show up. You know what he's like when he has to deal with serious situations. His fight or flight instinct is strong. I don't think he's ready for graduation."

"He is and he'll realise that soon enough. He won't be forced to wear a uniform, or to be somewhere at a certain time. He won't have teachers forever breathing down his neck."

"No, instead he'll have university lecturers doing it," I sigh.

"He's a big boy, Hayley. He will be okay. He's got you after all." She smiles as she takes a sip of her drink.

I smile back at her. I knew I was being silly but only time would tell.

⋯◆⋯

I look at the clock, time was flying! We had only 15 minutes to get dressed, put our shoes on and have Alice do any touch ups before the boys arrived.

Breathe, Hayley! I urge myself.

Kate's lilac dress suited her so perfectly. It was strapless and had some silver rhinestones scattered all up and down the first layer of tulle.

"Well, go on! Go and put yours on!" She beams and gently pushes me into the bathroom.

I look at my dress on the hanger. The burgundy colour was stunning. It was an A-line satin gown that slipped slightly off the shoulders. The bodice had a layer of lace that was beautifully detailed, and the remainder of the dress had a layer of tulle over the satin. The bottom of the dress had a sprinkling of gold glitter. I was in love with the dress and I really hoped Hunter liked it.

"Zip me up," I try to offer with the same enthusiasm as I walk back into the room. If Kate sees right through my facade, she doesn't say so.

"Alright, shoes!" She takes a seat on the bed beside me and starts doing up the straps of her silver platform heels. "Hayley, lighten up, please, you're dampening the mood! Hunter will be here, I promise!"

I mentally slap myself in the face. I didn't want to ruin this moment with Kate. It was my celebration too. My whole world didn't need to revolve around Hunter. I was allowed to enjoy this moment.

"You're right," I say and sit beside her, reaching for my simple gold stilettos. I had opted for slip on heels, an option I was hoping wouldn't backfire later in the night when my feet would swell. "This is going to be a great night regardless!"

"That's the spirit!" She grins and buckles her strap.

"Ok, let me look at you both!" Alice analyses both Kate and I and flits between the two of us making small touch ups here and there. When she's happy, Kate and I both squeal in excitement.

"Mum!" I called. "We're ready!"

"Let me get the camera, honey!" I hear her call back. "Hunter and Ethan are here. They're just having drinks with me and Naomi!"

I turn to face Kate. I could feel the butterflies in my stomach. *He came!*

"I told you so!" She grins.

"Why did I doubt him?" I say out loud.

"Who knows? He's Hunter, after all. Now let's go!" She shrugs her shoulders. "Mum!" she calls to Naomi. "I'm coming out now."

I watch as Kate walks out to the deck with confidence.

"Wow," I hear Ethan exclaim as he finally lays eyes on her.

I knew I needed to just follow Kate outside, it wasn't hard, but I felt the nerves kick in. I felt very embarrassed. Everyone's eyes would be on me. What if my dress was actually hideous, or Alice had picked the wrong shade of foundation?

Dad eventually appears in my view, as though he had sensed my unease from out on the deck. He goes to say something but stops and smiles instead. A tear glistens in his eyes.

"Don't you start," I warn him with a light chuckle.

"You look beautiful, honey," he says as he offers his arm for me to take and leads me outside.

I look up nervously as Mum lets out a gasp. Hunter's bottom lip drops.

"Doesn't she look beautiful!" Dad exclaims as he beckons both Mum and Hunter over. "Here we are, kids, your formal night. You're going to have such a good time. I couldn't be more proud of you, and you as well, Hunter." He lets go of my hand and reaches out for Mum.

"You look stunning, Hayley." She places a quick kiss on the top of my head.

Hunter still hasn't said anything though and I can't help but feel worried again.

"Have fun tonight, kids, but not too much fun. Remember, I'm too young to be a grandfather." He winks and claps Hunter on the back as I roll my eyes.

"What a charmer you are," I say as he walks away, proud of himself.

I turn to look at Hunter who reaches out to hold both of my hands.

"You look incredible," he stutters, his cheeks turning pink.

"You came," I blurt out and confusion spreads across his face.

"Of course, I came," he says, puzzled. "Did you really think I would do that to you?"

I feel the embarrassment flood my face. I couldn't believe I had just blurted that out. He was exactly right. Why wouldn't he come? He had no reason not to come. He had been so good lately and I doubted he would want to miss this experience, especially when the whole senior class was doing it.

"Sorry," I mumble.

He smiles back at me. "I have this insane urge to kiss you, but I don't want to ruin your makeup."

I giggle at his admission and give him a quick peck on the lips. "I can always reapply lipstick."

"Alright, photo time!" Mum announces.

"I got you this." He holds out a plastic box with a corsage in it. He was already wearing the matching buttonhole.

I watch as he takes the corsage out of the box and places it on my wrist. Seamlessly, once the corsage is on my wrist, he pulls my hand to his chest and the other wraps around my waist.

"You look insanely beautiful," he whispers, and I smile again.

"You look pretty handsome as well," I admit.

"Well duh, what did you expect?" he jokes, and I shake my head in laughter. "As beautiful as you look though, I can't wait to take that dress off you," he whispers in my ear, and I feel my heart start to race. He has a mischievous grin on his face and I'm about to tell him off for making such a joke around my parents when Naomi interrupts.

"Come on! Outside into the garden. That'll provide a better backdrop for some photos," she instructs, leading the way out to the garden. I share a quick glance at Hunter, but he just grins and follows Naomi out.

"I only speak the truth, Hayls." He turns around quickly and pokes his tongue out before falling into step beside Ethan.

Once out in the garden, Naomi tells us where to stand and what to do for poses. Kate said she was in her amateur photographer era and to just go with it. Hunter stands stiffly behind me for the first round of photos and eventually he starts to relax, joining in with Ethan's jokes. I almost want to tell my mum to delete any of those photos from the beginning.

"Give her a kiss, Ethan!" Naomi jokes as she holds her camera out.

"Mum!" Kate groans. "He'll ruin my makeup."

"We're so in love, can't you tell?" Ethan laughs and she elbows him in the ribs.

I turn and give Hunter a peck on the lips again, much to his surprise.

"Love always finds a way." I turn back to Ethan, and he continues to laugh.

"Way to show us up, Hayls," Ethan says.

"This is showing you up," Hunter jokes as he puts an arm around my waist and dips me back. I feel like a girl in a movie as Hunter delicately kisses me before drawing me back upright.

"You've always got to one-up me, man." Ethan lightly punches him in the arm. "Come here Kate." Ethan reaches for her, and she squeals in excitement as he twirls her around the garden.

"Alright kids. Let's go. Time to have the night of your lives!" my dad calls out.

CHAPTER 35

The four of us arrive at the formal and are taken aback by how well the school had done with choosing a venue and decorations. It was at one of the local hotel's ballrooms and the whole space had been filled with fairy lights and artificial greenery. There were balloons spelling out the word graduation. It was beautiful. We settle in with the rest of our group of friends.

"What do you think Hunter?" I ask.

"It's really nice," he responds, clearly nervous again.

"Hey, this is going to be a fun night. Try to push the purpose of the night out of your mind and just have fun. We can freak out together on Friday when we are actually graduating."

"You're right!" He fixes his jacket. "Why waste tonight? It's no different to anything we've done before. Come on, let's go to the photobooth!"

I let Hunter lead me towards the photobooth and it was amazing to see him finally relax. The formalities would begin soon and then we could really let go and have some fun. I let Hunter pick who we spoke to and what we did until we were seated for dinner. I wanted to make sure he did what he wanted to do because I knew I'd enjoy whatever it was so long as I was with him. He was the class clown, the one everyone liked to be around. I couldn't remember the last time I had laughed so much.

CHAPTER 36

"So you say that you started to notice a change in Hunter just before graduation?" Dr Martin presses me for information.

"Yeah, he was scared. I don't think he really knew what to do. He was just doing what people told him or what he thought sounded good. I don't think he was convinced of what he wanted to do," I reply.

"Did he display any odd behaviour at the formal you told me about earlier?"

"Not really. He was nervous for sure, but I think she managed to calm him down. She always had a calming effect on him. It took him about ten minutes to settle when we got there and then he was normal Hunter. You could just see how much he loved her. He was either holding her hand or had his arm around her waist or his hand on her knee. He was happy."

"How did she reciprocate that?"

"She was hanging off him. She felt the same way about him. She loved having his attention." I shrugged my shoulders. I didn't know how to respond. It made me hurt inside knowing what life used to be like.

"Tell me more about that night." He crosses one leg over the other.

"Well, we had dinner, which was really nice, and then the speeches started. That's when I think Hunter started to get a bit nervous again as people were talking about life after school, but Hayley brought him back. Like she always did. Then we had the student council speak and they gave out some silly awards. I don't know how they got away with it. Kate and I got 'most likely to get married and have children after graduation'. Hayley and Hunter got 'best couple'. There were awards like 'most likely to become prime minister when they grow up', 'most likely to get arrested', and 'most likely to end up in jail'."

"Who won those awards?"

"Not Hunter. He got 'best athlete' though."

Chapter 37

I couldn't sleep last night, my mind filled with thoughts of graduation, and the knowledge that today was my last day of school, ever. We would have our graduation ceremony this morning and then that was it. We were free kids on the verge of adulthood. Once school was over, I had full control of my life. I could do whatever I wanted, whenever I wanted. If I didn't get into Dynamite Studios, Hunter, Ethan, Kate and I would move in together for our first year of university. We would be responsible for paying rent, utilities, groceries, any bills that came our way, any take-out food we wanted. We would be entirely responsible for ourselves. It scared me a little bit, but I was excited and felt more than ready to take this next step. Especially with Hunter. Either way, we were going to live together after school, whether that was here or on the Gold Coast.

I walk amongst the crowd of seniors looking for Hunter, or Kate and Ethan. We had to sit in alphabetical order by surname in the auditorium for graduation. That meant Hunter and I couldn't sit next to each other. He was a couple of rows behind me. Ethan would be a couple of seats to my left and Kate was a couple of rows in front of us. The spacing meant that I would be able to see at least Kate and Hunter walk on stage and get their certificates. I had hidden my phone in my graduation gown and would sneakily try to take photos of Hunter if his parents ever wanted to see them, just in case they didn't come.

Finally, I could see the tall frame of my boyfriend. He's standing with Ethan and his face lights up when he sees me.

I leap into his arms, and he spins me in a circle.

"The day is finally here!" I beam at him. He kisses me softly as he puts me back on the ground.

"Thank god! I was getting worried when I couldn't find you." He smiles down at me and keeps his arm around my waist. "All I can think about is tripping over when I walk up the stairs or across the stage."

Ethan laughs. "You'd be the only person who'd be able to get away with tripping. You'd make a joke out of it. All of us poor suckers will be remembered as the idiots who can't walk properly."

"Where's Kate?" I ask as I search around us.

"Taking a million family photos." Ethan shrugs.

"Doesn't she want you in her photos?" I ask, puzzled.

"Hayls, I've been here for ages. As soon as I saw Hunter I snuck away and that was about a thousand photos in," he answers as he fluffs his hair up.

"Alright everyone!" our year coordinator calls. "Time to take your seats!"

Ethan and Hunter do their signature handshake, and Hunter gives me one more kiss before walking off to find his seat.

Ethan grins at me. "Ready?"

I nod and take a deep breath.

He gives my shoulder a quick squeeze. "We made it!"

⸺◦⸺

I sit nervously in my chair as the principal went through their address to the school. Then it would be the year coordinator's turn and then we would receive our high school certificates. I have an overwhelming urge to cry but I keep it together. I wonder how many times the principal's address had been used at previous graduations. Did the teachers recycle their speeches too? Our year coordinator's speech is actually pretty amusing. He managed to weave every high school student's name into his speech. It made me feel all warm inside. Finally, it was time. The principal calls out Kate's name which snaps me back to reality and soon I notice my row being called to walk towards the stage. Ethan gives me a thumbs up as we stand and move towards the stage. I look back to see if I can find Hunter, but we move too quickly. I feel the energy start to pump around my body. This was it!

"Hayley Gonzalez." I hear my cue to walk up to get my high school certificate. The auditorium breaks out in the standard applause each student received. I hear a whistle thrown in there too. I look into the audience and see my dad standing up with two fingers in his mouth. Another whistle comes and he grins. I put my head down in embarrassment and try to focus on walking in a straight line to the principal.

I finally met the eyes of the principal who smiled back at me. He holds one hand out for me to shake and the other hand held out my certificate. Like Dad said, I paused for a moment for the photo and then it was over. The biggest day of my life, gone in a blip. I blink away the tears quickly. Now was not the time to get emotional. Not yet anyway. I focus on walking back to my seat and counting each step to take my mind off the seriousness of the day.

"Hunter Woods." His name being called out draws my attention back to the stage and I watch as Hunter walks confidently across the stage to receive his certificate. I quickly get my phone out and take a few photos. I hear the whistle again and turn around to see Dad standing up again clapping. Hunter looks out into the audience, and I see the smile grow on his face when he notices my dad.

"There's my girl!" Dad beams as I run into his arms. Mum joins in the hug as well. I hear her sniffling. She must be crying.

"Get in here too, kid." Dad motions to Hunter who must've appeared behind me.

I feel Hunter join the hug for a moment before he clears his throat. We all break from the group hug and that's when I notice two people standing awkwardly behind him. They must be his parents. They actually came. I had seen them in photographs throughout Hunter's home but never in person. Amanda was stunning. She had perfectly styled blonde hair and a full face of Kardashian style makeup. Her fingers were donned with gold rings and a massive diamond sat on her ring finger. She had gold bracelets around each wrist and a chunky necklace to match. Wearing a vibrant orange pant suit and gold platform heels, Amanda looked very out of place. Steven was dressed in a plain charcoal business suit and white collared shirt. He was a tall man, a clear indication of where Hunter got his height from, and very broad. He embodied the word arrogant though, another trait Hunter must've gotten from him. He had piercing blue eyes and sadly looked like he'd rather be anywhere but here.

"This is my mum and dad, Amanda and Steven." He looks at the ground as he introduces his parents. "Mum, Dad, this is Miranda and Antonio, and this is Hayley."

It goes quiet for a moment.

"Well, it's great to meet you, Amanda and Steven." Dad breaks the silence and reaches out to shake their hands. Mum follows suit.

"It's great to meet you too," Amanda replies. "And Hayley, we've heard so much about you!"

I want to raise my eyebrows at Hunter. I really didn't think there was much conversing at that house, but I decided to run with it. I only wish I could say the same back to Amanda.

"It's lovely to meet you." I reach out to shake her hand and Steven's hand too.

"Wasn't today great!" Dad exclaims, always the conversationalist.

Steven doesn't look as amused as Dad. I had the feeling he had already been scolded by Amanda at least once today for checking his watch.

"I'm so proud of Hunter." Amanda beams at her son. I couldn't tell if she was being genuine or if she knew that we knew that they weren't really around.

"So am I." I chime in and put an arm around Hunter's waist. He feels stiff like he doesn't want to be here. Either that or he doesn't want my arm around him. Amanda smiles softly at Hunter and I. There's a hint of sadness in her eyes. I had been around for so long and this was the first time I had met Hunter's parents whilst he seemed at home with mine.

"Thanks," he replies to my admission before turning to his mum and muttering just loud enough that I can hear. "You can go if you want."

Amanda's face drops. Maybe it wasn't all true what Hunter said. Maybe she did want to be part of his life, but he was the one that didn't want her.

"Well, we're going to go out for lunch," Mum announces. I'm not sure if she heard what Hunter said. "You're welcome to join us?" Mum offers to Hunter's parents. He was always going to come with us even though he wouldn't give us a straight answer if his parents would be there.

At this, Steven finally pipes up. "I really wish I could, but I do need to get back to work. I've got a big project meeting today. We're really far behind."

I almost feel like Hunter relaxes at this statement.

"Well, I don't have to be back at work for another hour, so I can always stop by for a coffee at least," Amanda offers. "We can meet you there?"

Mum and Dad, looking satisfied with themselves, continue to engage in conversation with Amanda about where we were going to have lunch.

"Alright Hunter, I'll see you at home tonight." Steven claps Hunter on the back.

"I was going to stay at Hayley's tonight," Hunter answers.

Steven's eyes narrow and he glances quickly at me. I could almost see Hunter in him. It was very clear where Hunter got his arrogance from.

"We're going to have a family dinner and then you can go to Hayley's. Trace will be there too," he says firmly.

"Well, we had plans," Hunter responds tersely but his dad gives him a stern look. He takes a deep breath and turns back to me. "I guess I'll be over after dinner then."

"The day is yours, Hunter. Do whatever you would like to do." I try to lighten the mood. "You're welcome to come over whenever you want."

I catch Steven rolling his eyes. There were definitely similarities between the two of them. I only hoped that Hunter didn't end up like him.

"I'm going now. Amanda, I'll see you later," Steven announces and gives Amanda a quick peck on her cheek which makes her smile. "So great to meet you all," he says, but it feels more like a general statement rather than a genuine comment.

I watch Steven walk away and finally, Hunter pulls me close. I try to give him a reassuring smile.

CHAPTER 38

I couldn't work Amanda out. Was she a lovely human being or was she a spoilt trophy wife? Was she a mother or was she a guardian? For a moment, I couldn't understand why she was with a guy like Steven, but the way she dressed and the expensive jewellery she wore, and the holiday destinations she talked about, made me realise why. Steven made a lot of money and with the many childless holidays Amanda spoke about, it made me think that they had Trace by accident and decided to give him a friend to entertain him whilst they were out gallivanting around the world. I squeeze Hunter's knee under the table every now and then, but I could tell he was eager for her to just drink her coffee and leave.

Amanda was a chatterbox, though. Mum and Dad chime in when necessary but otherwise they couldn't really get a word in. Amanda told us so many things about her and Steven but nothing really about Hunter and what his childhood was like. It made me wonder why she even came, if not to look good in front of me and my parents. She talked about flying business class to places like Bora Bora, Venice and Paris, but not one thing about Hunter. I wondered how he felt in this moment. Embarrassed? Ashamed? Neglected?

"Well, this was lovely. Thank you for the invite," she says as she takes the last sip from her cup. "We will have to do this again!"

"Definitely," Mum quickly chimes in before Hunter could make an excuse.

"See you at home for dinner, Hunter." She ruffles his hair and places a kiss awkwardly on the top of his head. This makes him snap around to look at her in shock. "Don't be embarrassed." She tries to shake off his attitude before walking off.

"When was the last time she did that?" Mum asks softly once Amanda was out of ear shot.

"I don't even remember," he shrugs his shoulders and again I squeeze his knee underneath the table again. He smiles weakly at me, but his eyes tell a different story.

"Now, let's eat!" Dad rubs his hands together as the waiter puts his plate in front of him.

Timing really was everything.

CHAPTER 39

My phone buzzes with a notification. My heart stops. It's an email from Dynamite Studios.

"I'm just going to the toilet. I'll be right back!" I say as my heart starts to race.

We were just about to sit down for dinner. I hadn't heard from Hunter since we said goodbye after lunch, and I really hoped that his family dinner was going well and he could still come over later.

"Dinner's just about on the table, so don't take too long, Hayley!" Mum calls. "I don't want it going cold."

I rush to the toilet and try not to slam the door shut in anticipation of what the email could possibly contain. I lean against the toilet door as I fumble to unlock my phone and read the email.

I didn't get in.

I let out the breath I was holding as I skim read the rest of their email wishing me well and encouraging me to continue dancing. I don't know why I thought I had a chance anyway. It was something I never seriously considered up until the middle of this year. I never had my heart set on attending Dynamite Studios, but it was still hard to accept that after all of their encouragement and follow up calls that they still declined my application. I give myself an extra minute to see if a tear will fall so I can process the news and move on, but nothing happens. Maybe this was a blessing in disguise. I wasn't as upset by the news as I thought I'd be. At least I could plan things now. I could tell Kate and Ethan that we could move in together. It also meant I could stay close to home. Close to Dad. I can still be there for him.

I unlock the toilet door and head back to the dining room.

"Everything okay?" Mum asks as she dishes food onto my plate.

I take a deep breath. "I didn't get into Dynamite Studios," I say as I pick up my knife and fork.

My parents share a glance between themselves.

"It's okay guys, really," I say earnestly. "I never had my heart set on it, remember," I try to explain. "It was just a nice surprise to have them interested when I wasn't really trying."

I can see the look on their faces as they process this information. They can't work out how to react. I did put a lot of effort into my audition, and I'd be lying if I said I wasn't a little bit excited about the possibility of going to Dynamite Studios. I found myself dreaming of what it'd be like living on the Gold Coast. I even had a look at where Hunter would've gone to university and where we could potentially live. There was nothing wrong with James Cook University though. I would still have the opportunity to teach dance anyway and that was my ultimate goal. I was okay with this, truly.

Dad gets up from the table and walks towards the hallway cupboard. He returns with a cap on his head. I smile when I see the James Cook University logo on it.

"I've had this since we first discussed what you'd do after school when we moved to the area, and before you were approached by Dynamite Studios." He grins and continues eating his dinner. "So long as you're happy, kiddo, that's all that matters to me."

"It means you get to stay here and not move all the way to the Gold Coast," Mum chimes in, "That's a long way away, honey. I don't think I'd be able to cope with you living that far away," she sniffs in a joking manner.

"It also means you're well and truly stuck with me now." I grin and lightly nudge Dad with my arm.

Throughout dinner I realised I was truly at peace with being rejected by Dynamite Studios and my attention shifted to Hunter. I hadn't heard from him since lunch. I hoped his family dinner was going well. I didn't want him to come over angry, but I still wanted him to come over regardless. Any little thing could upset him and today was too important to ruin.

"He'll message you as soon as he can, Hayley," Dad tries to reassure me as he cleans away our dinner plates. "Leave him be with his family. God only knows how long it has been since his whole family had dinner together."

"I know." I look down at my plate. "Can we save him some dessert? Even if he doesn't come, he can eat it next time."

"Of course we can, honey." Mum smiles and moves towards the kitchen.

I sneakily check my phone while Mum and Dad are in the kitchen. I knew that they didn't like phones out at the dinner table, but I wanted to know that Hunter was okay. Disappointingly, there was no message from him, and it was nearly 8:00pm. I try to push him out of my thoughts. Why couldn't I just be happy for myself? Today was my celebration too. After twelve long years, I had finally graduated from school. I let my emotions take over and feel the smile grow across my face. I didn't *need* Hunter to celebrate my win, although I would *like* it. I shake the thought from my head too.

No, I urge myself, *be happy for yourself. This is your moment as well.*

"So, we have passionfruit cheesecake, cookies and cream flavoured ice cream, and jelly. Take your pick." Mum's voice distracts me, and I look over to where she is showcasing the dessert selection on the kitchen bench.

"Who says I have to choose one?" I poke my tongue out.

Dad chuckles. "Well, you're certainly my daughter. One of each, I think, Miranda." He rubs his belly.

"Do you want a cup of tea to go with it?" I ask my parents.

"That would be lovely." Mum smiles as she gets four bowls out and starts scooping them up. It makes me smile that she was so inclusive of Hunter. I didn't know when he'd actually be around to eat it though.

"Yeah, I'll have a cuppa too please," I imagine Hunter answering as well. His voice was loud and clear in my head, almost as if he was in the room.

I snap my head up and see Hunter standing beside my mum in the kitchen. They both have a massive grin on their faces. I jump out of my seat and launch myself at him. He chuckles as he stumbles back at my force.

"You made it!" I beam at him.

"Of course I made it." He puts me back on the ground.

"You two knew he was coming, didn't you?" I turn around, pointing a finger at my mum and dad. They both grinned back at me.

"Of course we knew!" Dad laughs and gets his phone out, waving it in my face. "Hunter texted me and told me what time he would be here!"

I almost want to cry at the sweet gesture. This year has been so tough. It was a roller coaster of emotions. Regardless of what happened throughout the year, Hunter stood by me and here he was now, standing right in front of me at the end of such a big day for us both. He was the guy that didn't want a relationship because he was badly hurt in the past, the guy that, for some reason, chose me, out of everyone, to be with. The love of my life. Nothing could compare to this moment. Not graduating, not hearing Hunter say I love you, nothing. I was here, with my parents and Hunter. All the people that mattered to me most. Life was perfect. Soon, Hunter and I would be accepted into the same university, and we would start our lives for real. We would be adults tackling the world together and I couldn't think of anyone better to do it with.

~ PART 3 ~

CHAPTER 40

It had been over three months since I last heard from Hunter. That was March. It was now June. He didn't answer phone calls; his social media accounts were inactive, and no one seemed to know where he was. His mum and brother didn't even know where he was. I had gone through the most part of the first six months of university thinking I was in a relationship and turning away really nice guys even though Hunter was gone without a trace. Today was the day I was going to completely wipe Hunter out of my life and finally focus on me. To celebrate the end of an era with Hunter, and the end of our first semester at university, we were having a house party. I was going to burn every picture that had Hunter in it and throw away anything that reminded me of him. I was also going to ask out Jethro, someone I'd met on campus. He still seemed keen even after Hunter punched him when they first met. That was an awful encounter. Hunter was acting like his normal protective and jealous self but took it a step too far. It was like meeting Theo all over again. Only this time when Hunter told him to back off, Jethro bit back and it resulted in Hunter throwing a punch. I didn't speak to Hunter for two days after it happened, I was so cranky with him. I even went back home, just to get away from him. Yet, surprisingly, it didn't deter Jethro. He texted me several hours later apologising for winding Hunter up and causing the outburst. He also checked to see if I was okay. I didn't hear from Hunter at all. I should've seen the signs that it was the only the beginning of Hunter slowly pulling away. Jethro didn't back off either, he was just more careful when he chose to talk to me. It was nice to have his attention as I wasn't getting much from Hunter anymore, yet I still couldn't see that I was slowly losing Hunter.

When I looked at Jethro, it was clear how different he was from Hunter. He wasn't much taller than I was, and he had shaggy black hair. He also had nicely tanned skin and dark brown eyes. He was a bit more laid back than Hunter. He was the kind of guy that was happy to go with the flow, and everyone seemed to gravitate towards his kind nature. His signature look was cargo pants, a t-shirt and a sleeveless hooded jumper. He came across messy when compared to Hunter, but not in a bad way. He was just different to what I was used to and that was okay. Today was going to be a fresh start for me.

"I'm proud of you." Kate squeezes my arm. "I know this hasn't been easy. Ethan assures me that Hunter is okay doing whatever it is that he's doing."

"Do you believe that?" I can't help but ask.

Kate shrugs. "I have to, for both your sake and Ethan's sake. My boyfriend and my best friend were abandoned by the same person. How many dead ends will you follow before you start to go insane?"

Kate had a point. I had tried everything to find Hunter. I tried talking to his parents, his brother, our group of school friends, anyone I could think of. No one knew where he went and what bothered me the most was that no one seemed to care.

"It's just messed up, Kate! Who even does this to a person?" I rip another photo of Hunter in half and chuck it into the fire pit that Ethan had purchased for our party tonight at the house we were renting, not far from the university and close to the many beaches that scattered the coastline.

"Well, that's what tonight is all about! Welcome to your new life, Hayley. We're going to throw a sick party and dance your old life away!" She takes a swig of the beer that she's been cradling for the last hour. "I can't believe we've survived six months of uni."

"I wish Hunter was here to enjoy it with us." I smile weakly.

Hunter and I spent the better part of our formative years together. Every good memory I had was with Hunter, and now he was gone, and I was heartbroken.

"No, you don't, Hayley." The anger rings through Kate's voice. "You need to move on from Hunter. If he wants to disappear, he is not worthy of your time. I honestly cannot believe what he has done. This is really, really out of character, even for him." She relaxes back in her chair again.

"I agree with Kate, Hayley," Ethan joins us from inside with a bowl of chips. "If he wants to be a dick, then he can deal with the consequences."

"Do you think he thinks of me, wherever he is?" I ask quietly.

"Do you want the hard truth, Hayley?" Ethan asks, shovelling another handful of chips in his mouth.

"Not really." I rub my forehead. Why did I even have to ask that? Of course he doesn't think about me. Why would he leave me?

"Just forget about him, Hayls. Move on. It's for the best," Ethan replies anyway. I knew what that meant though. It meant Hunter didn't think about me at all.

"Get with that Jethro dude," Ethan continues.

After nearly three months with no contact with Hunter, I started leaning into the idea that I was in fact single, and I could do whatever I wanted with whoever I wanted, and that's where Jethro came in.

"Is Jethro coming?" Kate leans forward excitedly. "You did invite him, right?"

"Yes," I say. "And you're right. Tonight's the night." I stand up and throw the remaining pictures of Hunter into the fire pit. It was time to go and pick out a killer outfit.

CHAPTER 41

"So, are you enjoying uni life so far?" Jethro shouts in my ear. The music is loud and pumping. I can almost feel his heartbeat, he's that close to me. It feels nice to have someone this close again. I almost forgot what it felt like to be wanted by somebody.

"It has its perks," I flirted back.

He grins back at me as he realises I'm not trying to awkwardly stand at a safe distance from him. I lean into him instead and occasionally reach out to touch his arm when he says something funny.

"I guess Hunter's not coming tonight then?" he asks sheepishly.

"Hunter who?" I respond, a cheeky smile playing on my lips.

He grins again and goes to brush a strand of hair out of my eye. This was it! Jethro was going to kiss me, and I was going to finally move on from Hunter. Jethro leans in for the kiss, but I'm distracted by a voice.

"Why do you have your hands all over my girlfriend?" Hunter's voice breaks through the noise.

Jethro recoils quickly. Hunter was more than happy to get in people's faces and throw words around. He was that confident. And arrogant.

I stare at Hunter in shock. It's been so long since I last saw him. He's built more muscle and seems to have grown an extra inch. His face remains the same though and his hair is still spiked up so not everything had changed.

"I'll take it from here mate. Maybe you can learn a thing or two." Hunter storms over to me, pushing me gently, even with his apparent anger, against the wall behind us, pressing his lips against mine. I almost melt against him. Almost. My brain kicks in and I shove him hard in the chest as Jethro comes to my aid.

"What the fuck, Hunter?" I shout in fury. Kate and Ethan are by my side in an instant and it's almost like the music has been turned off. Everyone was now watching, just great.

Hunter looks smug with a wide grin on his face, like this was all a big joke. "Oh, please, Hayls, I haven't been gone long, let's not be irrational here. You're still my girl. Now come here and give me a hug."

"I think you've had a bit too much to drink, mate." Ethan steps in to pull Hunter away but he steps out of reach, like it was a game to him. Hunter always loved the attention, no matter how he got it.

"I don't think I've had enough to be honest. The party's just getting started and I'm here to see my girl." Hunter walks towards me and I try to flatten myself against the wall. This new Hunter was edgier than I would've ever imagined he'd become. He had a look in his eyes that screamed danger to me, but I couldn't get past the fact that I was still attracted to him. I still wanted him. Even after all that he'd done. I was in deep trouble. I didn't know how to be strong. I was still in love with Hunter.

"Hunter, stop. You're scaring her," Jethro interrupts my thoughts, noticing the fear that must've been spreading across my face.

"She should be bloody scared. She's kissing you when she's still with me," Hunter snaps at him.

Was he trying to intimidate me? It was certainly working. But my god, he just looked so good.

"Hunter, stop." Ethan and Jethro both square up in front of me almost like a human shield.

"Come on, Hayls, say something." Hunter looks past the two men in front of him. He then looks properly at me. "Oh, I'm just joking, Hayley. I didn't mean any of it. You know it's just the alcohol talking. Let's get out of here and catch up." He starts to gently push between Jethro and Ethan.

I don't meet his gaze as he stands in front of me. I muster up all the confidence I have to confront him. "You can't just show up and demand to hang out or even assume we're still together." I start to feel the anger bubble inside of me. "You left me! For three months I had no idea where you were, what you were doing, who you were with. No one did. Then you just turn up out of the blue," I challenge him.

"I never meant to hurt you, Hayley. I owe you an explanation, I know that. It's you that I want. It'll always be you. Please come with me, Hayley, so we can talk." He holds his hand out to me.

He says those magic words I had been dying to hear. He still wanted me.

As much as my brain and the faces around me begged me not to, my heart wins and I take his hand. I let him pull me away from the party and follow him upstairs to my room. Well, *our* room.

"You better have a good reason for disappearing, Hunter. I was just learning how to be without you." I cross my arms over my chest once we enter the room.

"What's time anyway, Hayls? What was it? A month?" He grins.

"Try three months, Hunter!" I snap back.

He pauses for a moment like he was only just realising how long he had been away for. He then nods his head. "Yeah, that's right. Geez, it's been a while, hey? Let's make up for lost time then."

He walks over to me and tugs at the bottom of my shirt.

"Don't, Hunter." I smack his hands away, much to his surprise.

"Come on, Hayley!" he cries out in frustration. "I'm out living my life, isn't that what you wanted me to do? I'm not going to sit and wait for you to come home every day like some pathetic loser. I'm bored. I don't want to be stuck in this life."

"Stuck?" I was shocked. Where was all of this coming from? We were going so well. He just disappeared without even a hint of being unhappy. "You think you're stuck with me? Well, by all means Hunter, I can make things very easy and end it all now for good! If you don't want this life, then leave!"

"I did leave, Hayley!" he snaps. "Or did you forget that I was gone?" he smirks.

His words are like a slap across the face. "So that was you breaking up with me?" I try to stop my voice from cracking.

"No, I just needed a break from everything. I just couldn't be bothered with this shit." He smacks the back of my desk chair and watches it spin around.

"So, you needed a break from me but just didn't want to tell me?" I try to work out his logic. I couldn't believe how childish he was being. He was so mature in our relationship with how he approached sex and how he really stepped up when my dad got sick.

"It doesn't matter anymore, Hayley. I'm back now. You're mine. It's been too damn long, so please just take off your shirt or I'll do it for you." He reaches back for my shirt.

I'm just as stunned as he is when I slap him across the face.

"Get out. Now!" I cry.

He bites his lip at me which is all it takes to break my anger. There, standing in front of me, was the love of my life, Hunter. The one who stood by me through high school. The one I needed to be careful with as he frightened easily. The one who told me he didn't want a girlfriend as he'd been hurt badly before. He must've gotten frightened with adult life, so he ran. Like he always did in school. Maybe this time, I'll let him come back.

I close the distance between us quickly and grab his face, pressing his lips to mine. I can feel his smile growing and he responds by tangling his hand in my hair and grabbing my waist.

"I love you, Hayley," Hunter mumbles between kisses as he walks us over to the bed. More magic words spill from his mouth, and I love it. "I've been waiting for this. I've missed you so much." He grins as he takes his shirt off. He's definitely been working out whilst he's been away. His abs were more defined that I remembered. I can't help but reach out to touch them. A smile slowly grows across his face. It almost looks like he's blushing. He lowers himself down on top of me slowly and starts to kiss me again. I feel my body relax more and more at his touch. This was my Hunter. I needed to show him that I trusted him and that we would be okay. That he was safe with me and could come back to me.

"This is going to be quick I think," Hunter groans in my ear. "I forgot how good you felt."

I giggle and let him take control. He's not wrong though as it doesn't take long before we're both on our backs laughing.

"Holy fuck." Hunter runs a hand through his hair as we both catch our breaths.

Eventually he says, "So, you're going to give me another chance?"

"Are you going to tell me where you went and why?" I ask carefully. I need to know why he left. It was going to drive me insane until he told me.

He groans and rolls to his back. "Why do you care so much?"

I didn't understand why he was being so difficult. The Hunter I knew was honest, most of the time, because he didn't care what people thought, and any mind game he played he usually gave up quickly.

"Hunter, imagine this," I try to start explaining. "You and I have just started our lives outside of school. We're having fun, getting into routines, meeting new people. Then all of a sudden, I just disappear. I don't call. I don't text you. I don't make any contact for weeks, even months! What would you do?" I don't mean for my voice to have such a tone, but I can't help it. I was angry and it was taking everything in my willpower to handle this delicately. I don't want him to blow up at me after he seems to be willing to talk about our future.

It almost looks like he's thinking about his options before he reaches out to touch my chin, guiding me to look at him. "I'd go to the ends of the earth to find you. I would stop at nothing." His voice is cold. "Which brings me to you: why didn't you go to the ends of the earth to find me?"

"You're kidding, right?" I push his hand away from my chin, unable to hide how annoyed I was. I sit up straight, eager to get away from him and disgusted that I let him back in so easily. "I don't have the resources available to me to even know where to start. I spoke to every member of your family. Every friend that I could remember you talking about. That damn pizza girl that came to my house that one time! Even your bank! No one knew anything about you or could even give me a hint as to where you were. It drove Kate and Ethan mad! I spent so much time trying to find where you went, Hunter. What did you expect me to do? Chase my tail in circles grasping at straws? I had nothing to go on!" I've worked myself up to the point of crying and he moves to hold my face in my hands. "You were just gone, Hunter. I thought we were in this together!" I let a few tears roll down my cheeks.

"We are in this together, baby." His thumb rubs the tears away. "Why don't we get some rest?"

I couldn't take another heartbreak but at the same time, I still had to be strong.

"I don't think so, Hunter." I climb out of the bed and start to get dressed again. Confusion spreads across his face. "There's a party going on downstairs that was to celebrate the first six months of uni, and to say good riddance to you, actually. So, I'm going to go downstairs and re-join the party."

"You really threw a party for me?" He smirks as he too makes a move to get dressed again.

God, how had I forgotten how arrogant he could be?

"No, it was for Kate, Ethan and I to celebrate our first semester of uni. It just so happened to be a good opportunity to move on from you, Hunter. You left me, remember?" I snap at him before fluffing my hair and walking towards the door.

He stands up off the bed to pull his pants up. "It's none of their business, and I don't give a fuck what people think. You should know that."

"You should care what I think." My voice is low as I open the door. I can't look at him. "You still refuse to tell me where you went, Hunter. How can I trust you again?"

Hunter responds by shrugging his shoulders. I roll my eyes in frustration and walk out the door, slamming it in his face.

"Hayley!" I hear his voice growl through the door and it's not long before he's by my side.

Gently, he grabs my arms and backs me against the wall in the hallway, placing his hands on either side of my head on the wall behind me. "Hayley," he breathes as he rests his forehead against mine. "I want you to trust me. I love you, Hayley, only you. I'm ready to settle down."

He said those magic words again, *settle down*. He wants to be with me. He still sees a future with me. I have to keep going. Whether he tells me where he went or not. What's three months out of a lifetime of happiness?

CHAPTER 42

"So you're back now?" Ethan asks sheepishly from across the table. It was the next morning, and Hunter had managed to bring the party back to life. He kept a hand around my waist for the rest of the night. It felt like old times. I was even used to everyone's eyes being on me. I probably looked pathetic though, so desperate for love that I gave someone like Hunter another chance. Jethro gave me a look of disappointment before excusing himself and leaving.

"Yep," Hunter says as he hands me the tea he made for me.

"Where did you go?" Ethan tries. If Hunter tells Ethan and not me where he went, I will be pissed.

"Just away. I needed to get away." Hunter shrugs his shoulders. Ethan shoots a disapproving look at me.

"What about Hayley?" Ethan demands as one hand slams down on the table. "You just left her."

"Why don't you worry about your own girlfriend, and I'll worry about mine," Hunter spits through gritted teeth.

I had never seen Hunter and Ethan argue. It made me uncomfortable, and I knew that I would hear about it later from Kate.

"He won't even tell me, Ethan. Don't waste your time." I sigh.

"You're kidding, right?" Ethan looks between Hunter and I. "You're just going to accept that, Hayls? And Hunter, you don't worry about Hayley. If you did, you wouldn't have left her." Ethan pushes back in his chair so abruptly that it falls backwards when he stands up.

"Ethan!" I call after him as he storms up the stairs.

"Someone's in a bad mood," Hunter smirks as he reaches for me.

"Just stop with the games, Hunter." I lean away from him and his face drops slightly. "It was annoying yesterday trying to get the information out of you. If I have to go through this again, I'll scream."

"I just don't get why it's such a big deal. I went away for a bit. Who cares what I did?" He draws circles on the table with his finger. "I didn't kill anyone, so can everyone just chill out about it?"

I groan. Now that I'd slept on it, I couldn't shake the feeling of anger towards Hunter and his carefree attitude. I couldn't understand why he didn't want to tell me where he went, and it would eat me alive until he told me.

As if he could read my mind, he says, "You're not going to let this go, are you?"

I sigh, feeling the weight return to my chest. "I don't think I can, Hunter. I just want you to be honest."

He shakes his head in frustration. "I'm going for a run," he announces as he hastily walks out the door.

"Hayley," I hear Kate yawn as she comes down the stairs. Ethan is following behind her. He looks grumpy and I can tell I'm about to get a talking to.

"Save it, guys. I know what you're thinking." I hang my head in my hands. I didn't need a lecture. I already knew how pathetic I must look.

"It's not good enough, Hayley!" Ethan's voice is cold. He was so angry, but I couldn't blame him. "It's completely disrespectful. You shouldn't have given in so easily. You're digging your own grave by letting him come back without a reason."

"Ethan!" Kate scolds him before turning back to me. "What he's trying to say is you need to know why he left Hayley, or otherwise he'll keep doing it."

Ethan speaks before I can respond. "I can't keep having the same conversation with him, Hayls. I want to know where he went too, and I'm sorry but this is not just your house. If he can't treat me and Kate respectfully, he can't stay here."

I look at the ground. They were right. This wasn't just my house and Hunter needed to be respectful of them too. Ethan shakes his head, clearly disgruntled and not satisfied with the resolution.

"I'm going out the back to clean up some stuff." Ethan pushes the door open with such force it hits the wall before slamming shut.

"He's hurting a lot, Hayley," Kate says as she pours herself a cup of coffee. "He didn't just walk out on you. He walked out on Ethan too. They've known each other a lot longer."

"I know. I just don't know what to do, Kate. He doesn't want to tell me." I take a sip of my tea. Hunter made it just the way I like. He remembered.

"You're a woman for goodness' sake! Use those seductive charms!" Kate laughs.

"Blow him," Ethan says bluntly as he comes in to grab a bottle of water. "If he doesn't tell you then, he's probably gay."

Kate and I burst out laughing. At least Ethan seems to have calmed down.

Chapter 43

"Hunter!" I call out, excited to tell him about my results from the first semester of uni. I had received glowing comments from my professors, and I was offered an internship at my old dance school for the summer program as a choreographer.

While I still couldn't get Hunter to talk about where he went during those three months, he changed his tune and was the Hunter we were all used to. He was funny, polite, and even helped around the house. He also paid for some new things for the house as a way to make up for leaving. I knew that Ethan hadn't necessarily forgiven him, he was just happy to not fight with Hunter anymore and things started to feel like old times.

"Hunter!" I call out again, looking around the house for him. I couldn't hear him anywhere. Maybe he was asleep. I walk into our room but he's not there. Instead, there's a note on my pillow. My heart almost stops. Not again.

"Not here?" Ethan asks, appearing at my doorway. I can feel the tears brimming in my eyes.

I open the note and plop down on the bed to read it.

I can't do this anymore — H.

I let one tear escape before reading the note again. I let my new reality sink in, and the tears started flowing. It had only been a few weeks since he came back and now he was gone again.

"You okay?" Ethan approaches me before taking the note out of my hands and reading it. "Fuck," he mutters. "I'm sorry, Hayley." Ethan sits on the bed beside me, wrapping an arm around my shoulders.

"Why?" I cry. "Why does he keep doing this to me?"

"I don't know, Hayley," he responds, rubbing a hand up and down my back.

"You know, I thought I could be happy without him. I met a guy and everything. He just comes in, ruins it and then fucks off again." I wipe the tears away, but they keep coming.

"Maybe Jethro will understand?" he offers. "If you talk to him and explain it all? Hell, I'll even talk to him if that'll help."

"Why? So Hunter can just come back and fuck it up again?" I snap. "I can't help it, Ethan. I love Hunter, and I probably always will. I'll be that old lady that's pining for her playboy lover who does god knows what when he leaves her."

"If he comes back, show him what he's missing." I hear Kate's voice draw nearer as she walks into the room. "Go and find another guy who doesn't want something serious and muck around. You're at uni. Have fun!" Kate jokes as she kneels beside me.

"Hey!" Ethan lightly pushes her shoulder back. "Stop stealing my thunder, I'm giving her advice this time." He laughs.

Kate laughs and shakes her head. "Hayley, Hunter was our friend too, but what he's doing isn't right. Go find another guy and move on. He's not worth your time."

"Right, I can do that," I try to say confidently. "I mean it's not like I've spent the last two and a half years with someone who I thought I'd spend forever with."

I can see that I'm frustrating her.

"Doesn't matter how long you've been with him. You need to focus on yourself and your future, and clearly he doesn't want to be part of it." Kate stands up.

I know what Kate is saying is right. "But it just hurts, Kate, it hurts so bad." I continue to cry.

"I still think my approach was working better," Ethan tries to joke as he gives me a quick squeeze. "All you're doing is making her cry, Kate."

She looks at her watch and then back at me. "Right, you've got two hours to cry and get it out of your system, then we're going out tonight! Me and Ethan will be your wingmen and you're going to get laid tonight by some guy that will rock your world harder than Hunter ever did," and with that she turns on her heel and walks out. I don't even have time to argue.

Ethan gives my arm one last squeeze before he gets up and leaves, closing the door as he goes.

I sit quietly on the bed, looking at some of the things Hunter left behind and let the tears consume me. Kate was right. Cry now and get over it with. Hunter was now just a blip in my hopefully long life. What's three years out of ninety-seven? This was the old Hunter coming back. Forever being secretive and unable to be held down. Why should I put up with that? Angrily, I jump off the bed and start to grab all the items he's left behind: an old jumper, a shaver, some socks and his cologne. I chuck it all into one pile. I rip any remaining photos of us I can find into a million pieces and throw them out the window. Ethan would kill me later when he found them but right now, I didn't care. I was single and in my prime. It was time to go out and have fun, just like Kate said. I just needed to make one phone call. He wouldn't answer anyway, and I doubt he'd check his voicemail.

The phone dials and I almost drop it when I hear his voice answer after two rings.

"I don't want to talk to you." Hunter's voice is angry but hushed. An image of him in bed with another girl flashes across my mind only fuels my anger.

"Good, you can just listen. Just so you know, I'm going to be okay, like I always am, and tonight, I'm going to go out and find some guy that will fuck me better than you!"

"Hayley—" I hear him growl, but I end the call.

I feel like I can accomplish anything. I feel so powerful that I was able to tell him how unaffected I was by his decision to leave me again.

My phone starts to vibrate, and I'm surprised to see his name appear on the caller ID. I decline the call but he just calls again. I let this one ring out. I feel giddy inside. This is what it felt like to be wanted. My heart drops. He still wants me. How was I going to move on now, knowing that he still wanted me?

The phone rings again and again, and each time I decline the call. A text message then follows after the fourth call.

Answer your phone now! his text message reads.

Maybe I could enjoy this. I could go off and be flirtatious with whoever I want. Maybe he'll realise what he's missing and come back for good. Another text message from him comes through.

Hayley! Call me back now!
What the hell are you doing?

If Hunter wanted to be a jerk than I was well and truly going to flaunt myself in front of him. I had nothing else to lose.

I then hear a knock at my door and Ethan comes in with his phone in his hand.

"What have you done?" He looks confused but I can almost see the wheels turning in his brain as a grin slowly spreads across his face.

I can't hide the smile on my face. "I did what Kate said to do."

He shakes his head and laughs. "Fuck yeah, he wants you. Look." He hands his phone over to me so I can read the messages.

Are you with Hayley?
Are you going out tonight?
If you see her, tell her to call me back. I need to talk to her.

I feel so proud of myself. I've shown Hunter I don't care and he's realised he's made a mistake. I wasn't going to lie though, I was kind of interested in flirting with a stranger to see where it ended up. After all, Hunter left me. Let's see what it takes to bring him back.

CHAPTER 44

It's been nearly an hour at the nightclub, and I haven't seen or heard from Hunter. Part of me is sad to think that I wasn't enough to get him to come back but the other part of me is excited to just have fun and see where the night takes me.

"Another drink?" Kate offers me one of her glasses. She always double parked herself but never ended up getting to the second drink.

"Sure!" I take it and continue dancing. I still didn't like the taste of alcohol but tonight I didn't care. Ethan is at table with a few of his mates from uni and their partners. Kate and I are swaying around on the dance floor. It's still a bit early for the club to be packed though.

"Is that who I think it is?" Kate whispers in my ear and turns me around to show me who she was talking about.

It was Theo.

I hadn't seen Theo since school. He went to a different university to us where he did a lot of remote learning. It was probably to get away from all of the drama that followed Hunter. He hadn't changed too much, except he was clearly a gym junkie now. He's leaning on the bar with a few guys around him. Was this a sign? Was I meant to run into Theo tonight? He was kind and caring when we first met. He was open with his feelings towards me whereas Hunter and I played cat and mouse for over a year. Maybe I was supposed to be with Theo this whole time?

"What do I do?" I panic and turn to face Kate.

"Go talk to him!" She pushes me gently in his direction.

I turn back around to face him, and he looks casually in my direction. His eyes widen as he realises who I am, but he breaks into a grin quickly. He pushes himself off the bar and walks towards me. My heart skips a beat. He looks really good.

"Hayley? Wow, it's been so long!" He wraps his arms around me. He feels warm yet uncomfortable, almost like we don't fit together. I shake the thought away.

"Kate and Ethan are here too," I blurt out, not knowing what to say.

He looks behind my shoulder and nods in their direction. "So, the whole gang is still together?" he asks sheepishly.

I feel my face drop. I knew what question was coming next.

"Where's Hunter?" he asks bluntly.

I quickly try to regain my composure. "Oh, Hunter? He's old news. We broke up," I say as casually as I can manage.

Theo raises his eyebrows at me. He always could see straight through me.

I shrug my shoulders, avoiding eye contact so I don't fall apart. "Yep. I don't even know where he is to be honest." *Well, at least that wasn't a lie.*

"Sounds like he hasn't changed a bit since high school." Theo smirks. "I honestly have no idea what you saw in him. He was such a tool. I thought you were better than that."

Theo's words sting slightly because there was some truth to what he was saying but I also got the feeling that he didn't really want to talk to me. I probably hurt him too much back then and he was smart enough not to keep pushing. Or maybe he thought that Hunter would appear and he just wasn't interested in whatever drama ensued.

"So, Hunter's gone?" he asks again carefully.

I nod, feeling a shift in his energy.

"He hasn't got some sidekick in the shadows who will kill me for talking to you?"

"He's not the mafia, Theo." I try to laugh but his face is cold. "Like I said before, I don't even know where he is."

"Are you going to tell me what happened between you two?" His eyes narrow. I can see he's sceptical. He wasn't past the drama, clearly.

I screw my face up. "I don't think it's even worth repeating, to be honest."

"Well, I can't say I'm not intrigued, Hayls." His demeanour changes. *Was he flirting with me?*

I lead him over to the bar stools so we could sit. I tried to give him the basic details of what happened, as I didn't want to scare him off but the more and more I talked to him, almost as though he were a stranger, the more I just kept opening up. Theo just made me feel comfortable and validated. He nodded politely and shared his disbelief at some of the things Hunter had done. Every now and then he would reach out and gently touch my knee or shoulder when he was responding. His touch was gentle and caring, whereas Hunter's was always urgent and desperate.

"Sounds like he needs someone to just put him in his place and make him realise how shit of a person he was to you. Clearly, he's got some power over you and you'll just cave because he's what you're used to. God I'd love to see him again to do just that," he bluntly says.

"It's really not worth any of the drama or your time." I sigh and brush a strand of hair behind my ear.

"Well, a guy can dream. Imagine if he did turn up here." He turns back to the bar and finishes the rest of his drink.

"Let's not go down that road. I know what I'm like. You said it yourself, I'd probably just follow him out the door." I feel frustrated and ashamed for having just admitted that. I started off the night so strong.

"Let's find out then," he says through gritted teeth. "He's fucking here."

I gasp in shock and sit up straighter. I tried to casually look around the room but I was starting to panic. "Are you serious?" I had started to think that he really wouldn't come. "What do I do?" My heart was racing and I fumble my drink on the bar, nearly knocking it over.

Part of me wants to turn around and watch his expression when he saw me with Theo. I knew he'd be fuming. I also knew that it would hurt him but I had to remind myself that he had hurt me, repeatedly.

"Well, I could really rock the boat and kiss you?" He raises his eyes at me, noticing my desperation.

"Maybe a last resort," I laugh nervously. "This is Hunter we're talking about."

Theo rolls his eyes. "I'm not scared of that twat."

I almost burst out laughing at this brash comment, but I keep it together. "Ah, how about you tell me a story to distract me and we'll just see if he approaches us?"

Theo obliges and starts telling me a story about some camping trip he went on recently and I try to listen intently. My heart is beating fast with the thought of what could happen next.

"But then it just appears right behind me." He squeezes my knee inconspicuously and looks briefly behind me. "Like just out of nowhere, he's right there. It's a shock."

It takes me a second to understand what he's saying as it doesn't fit with his story but sure enough, I feel someone standing close behind me and I recognise the cologne almost instantly. I know it's Hunter. He actually came.

I see Theo's lips move but I can't work out what he says. He moves closer to whisper in my ear. "I really enjoyed seeing you tonight. We should do this again."

I almost feel Hunter stiffen next to me. Theo was teasing him on purpose. I had to think quickly about how to handle the situation. I wanted Hunter to see that I was a desirable woman. I could do whatever I wanted with whoever I wanted. We weren't a couple anymore and I didn't have to play by his rules.

"Hunter? Is that you?" Theo cracks first though. His pride must've gotten in the way and he wanted to get on Hunter's nerves. "Wow man, I haven't seen you since high school. Hayls and I have been catching up all night."

This was it. This was the moment I would come face to face with Hunter and he could make his decision from there.

"The fuck you are," Hunter's voice booms and I swivel around in my chair. His face is angry, and his eyes are shooting daggers at Theo.

"Oh hi, Hunter." I try to act unfazed. Hunter's eyes meet mine and then he looks me up and down, his eyes going wide.

"Holy fuck, Hayley, what are you wearing?" He's surprised by my low-cut purple sequinned top, short, black leather skirt and leather jacket. "Fuck, you look incredible!"

I almost melt at his words. He still found me attractive. He was still drawn to me. *But why does he keep leaving you?* my brain asks my heart.

"Can you not talk to her that way? She's not a piece of meat," Theo snaps, abruptly standing from the bar stool. How did I not see this coming? Theo was probably looking for any reason to fight him.

This breaks Hunter's gaze from me and his eyes revert back to Theo. "I can talk to her however the fuck I want. She's my girlfriend so get the fuck away from her." He jerks his finger behind him before reaching for my jacket and pulling it closed.

I smack his hand away, much to his surprise, and his bottom lip drops. "You have no right to touch me, Hunter. You broke up with me, remember?" I demand.

Hunter scrunches up his face. "Don't be silly, Hayls, just drop this stupid game. I don't want to play. You made your point. I want you. Now, let's get out of here." He tries to reach for my hand but I pull away, unconsciously leaning into Theo. Anger spreads across Hunter's face.

"Hayley," he growls, taking a step towards me. "Think about what you're doing."

"I am." I snap back and in a split decision I grab Theo's face and pull it to mine.

His kiss is gentle and intimate, like how it felt when I first kissed Hunter.

"Hayley!" Hunter growls again, lightly pulling at my shoulder which causes Theo to break off the kiss slowly.

"I think she's made her decision," Theo smirks as he looks up at Hunter, his arms still wrapped around my waist.

Hunter pulls my hand so I face him. He's upset. It's written all over his face. "Why?" he demands. "Why are you doing this to me?" he pleads, bending slightly to look me in the eye.

"You know why." I rip my hand away from him but he just grabs my waist instead pulling me close against him. We just fit together, there's no denying it. His gentle touch made me remember what we used to be like and it made my heart break.

"Hayley, please stop. This is killing me, please." I can almost see tears in his eyes. "Please don't leave with him. I get it, okay? I really do. I love you so much. I promise I'll be better. Please, just please give me another chance."

Theo laughs, having heard everything Hunter has said. "Manipulation. Same shit, different year with you, Hunter. You treat her like shit. You tell her you don't want her. She moves on. Then you just say what she wants to hear so she'll come running back."

Hunter's eyes snap to Theo, and he grabs at the collar of his shirt. "Who the fuck do you think you are?"

Theo just laughs and pushes Hunter's hands off him before turning to look at me. "The decision is yours. Just remember what you spent the last hour telling me."

I look back at Hunter and worry fills his face. He knows I'm considering going with Theo.

"Don't, please, Hayley, don't go with him. Stay here with me," Hunter pleads again.

"You promised me you wouldn't leave last time." I feel tears fill my eyes as I slowly back away from him and into Theo's outstretched arm. Hunter's face falls.

"I mean it this time, I swear!" He reaches for me before looking back at Theo. "Get your fucking hands off her!" he yells.

"The more you yell at him, the more I want to leave with him tonight!" I spit out. I don't even know where it came from. I said it to hurt him.

Theo laughs again and Hunter's face drops.

"You'll regret this," Hunter warns.

"No, I think what we're going to do next, I'm going to enjoy." I turn to walk away.

"I was talking to your new toy," he snaps and gets in Theo face. "She'll always want me so don't be surprised when she's back in my bed tomorrow night, calling out my name."

I pull at Theo's arm to keep walking towards the exit.

"What an asshole," Theo exclaims as the fresh air hits our faces.

I burst into tears, holding my face in my hands.

"Hey, it's okay." Theo takes my hands away from my face. "He's an asshole, Hayley. He always has been. You should be proud of yourself. You need to break the hold he has over you."

"I know, it just hurts so bad. I didn't even recognise the person I was in there. She's not me. That girl in there is not me at all. This—" I point to my outfit "—is not me."

"You're not the first girl who dresses differently to get the attention of their ex, and you won't be the last," Theo laughs. "Zip your jacket up and you'll start to feel a bit normal."

I let him pull the zipper on my jacket up. He hugs me as I cry lightly. I was trying to process what just happened. I take a few shaking deep breaths when I feel like I'm done crying.

"What do you want now?" Theo's voice is stone cold.

"I just want to talk to her." Hunter's voice is strained. "Please, I can't let it end this way."

"Do you want me to get rid of him?" Theo whispers in my ear.

"Don't leave me alone with him," I pleaded, looking into his eyes. I know what'll happen the second Theo walks away. I'll let Hunter back in, like I always do.

"I'll wait right here for you." Theo rubs my cheek. He makes me feel warm inside and I don't want to lose this feeling. I turn back to face Hunter and slowly walk towards him.

"If you want to fuck him, just go and do it. Get it out of your system. I know you're angry with me." Hunter kicks at the rocks on the ground. I can hear Theo scoff.

"You can't honestly want that?" I ask, shocked.

"Of course I don't want you to fuck another guy, Hayley, and not fucking Theo, of all people, but if that's what it takes for you to realise that it's me that you want then just do it." His voice is urgent, and I can see it's taking all of his power not to just take my hand and lead me somewhere private so he could show me what I'd be missing.

"You're so twisted," I said, a sense of disgust rising within me. "What I want is to feel wanted by you and to not have you just up and leave me again. I'm so sick of this behaviour. All you do is break promises, Hunter, and manipulate me into letting you come back without an explanation."

Hunter groans. "I honestly don't care who you fuck because you'll realise no one can replace me."

I walk up to him with confidence and get close enough to whisper in his ear. "So you don't honestly care if Theo touches my skin, my body, in places that only you have touched?" I try to make my voice sound seductive as I trace my finger down his chest, stopping just above his belt.

"No." His voice starts to shake, so I continue, my tactic clearly working.

"You don't care if Theo kisses my lips, down my neck, my chest?" I let my finger keep tracing all the way down and then back up from his thigh.

"Fuck, Hayley, just stop." His breathing is heavy and he wraps his arms around my waist. He tries to kiss me but I tease him by moving in different directions. A smile creeps slowly onto his face.

"Well, seeing as you don't care, I might just go and do exactly as you suggested." His body freezes. "I'll finally know if Theo's better than you." I push away from him, his face shocked and tinged with sadness. I try to ignore it though as I turn and walk back to Theo who holds his hand out for me to take.

"Hayley!" Hunter cries out but I ignore him. "Hayley!" he yells again but I keep walking with Theo.

"Wow, look at you go. Not going to lie, you kind of turned me on." Theo laughs as we walk away from the club.

"I like you. I think I'm going to keep you around this time," I grin.

I was so proud of myself. I did exactly what I set out to do.

CHAPTER 45

Theo takes me back to his place and offers a t-shirt and track pants so that I'm not sitting in my ridiculous outfit. He said he shared an apartment with his cousin who was a year older than us. It was very basic, unlike my house with Kate and Ethan. Theo just had the necessities. The only thing that stood out to me was the massive television with what looked to be several different Play Stations and Xboxes neatly arranged. I didn't care though. I felt like I was on cloud nine.

"I feel like I could run a million miles!" I beam as he hands me a bottle of water.

"You should be proud." His smile widens as he takes a seat beside me on the plush couch.

"Thank you, Theo." I squeeze his hand.

He scoots closer to me and reaches out to hold my face with one of his hands.

"Glad I could help." He smiles and after a moment or two of hesitation, he kisses me gently again. He felt so different to Hunter. It wasn't a bad different. He just wasn't Hunter. Eventually I can feel his tongue slowly trace my lips and I oblige. He certainly knew what he was doing. I felt his strong arms wrap around me and I press against his body. Instinctively, I reach for his shirt and he helps pull it over his head. I start to pull my shirt over my head but Theo stops me, breaking the kiss.

"You don't have to do this, Hayley." His breathing is heavy as he rests his forehead against mine. "It's only been a day, and I really don't want to be something you regret."

"Oh." I pull away, somewhat relieved but also completely embarrassed for coming on so strong. "You don't want this?"

He scoffs. "Believe me, I want this and knowing Hunter saw me kissing you made me incredibly happy with all the shit he causes, but I want you to sleep on this. I feel like this whole night has been completely out of character for you. This isn't the Hayley I remember."

"How can you still be this kind to me after all the crap that's gone on?" I sit back, fixing my shirt. High school wasn't that long ago and Hunter and I, to an extent, probably caused a lot of unnecessary issues for Theo.

Theo shrugs and leans back on the couch. His body is strong with muscle in all the right places. He had changed for the better compared to Hunter.

"Are you alright there, checking me out?" He grins.

I blush but don't hide it. "You have a very nice body."

"What can I say? This is my party trick to get the girl into bed," he smirks as he puts his shirt back on. I laugh at him and take a sip of water. Theo had a different energy to Hunter. Why couldn't I see that at the start? Why did I pick Hunter over Theo, who was a genuinely nice guy?

"What do I do, Theo?" I sigh.

"I think you need to work out what you really want. If that's not me and it's him, that's your decision to make, but you'll always know where to find me, even if you just need a friend." He smiles but there's a sadness behind it. He brushes a strand of hair behind my ear. "But Hayley, just be careful. He seems a little bit unhinged at the moment. Something's changed since high school."

"He's just a power tripper." I shrug my shoulders. "Like everyone knows, he says what I want to hear and I cave, and he knows it."

"He's obsessive," Theo corrects me. "But you know him better than I do."

I look at my phone for the first time. There're messages from Kate and Ethan. Then there's one from Hunter.

I love you so fucking much it hurts, but you'll never love me the same. Come home and let me prove it, it reads.

"I should probably go," I say and reach for my clothes.

"Regardless of what you choose, I had fun tonight and would do it again if you need me."

I squeeze his shoulder. "Why couldn't I have met you first?"

"Maybe in another lifetime." He pulls me into a hug and I hold him as tight as I can. "I'll drop you home."

"Thanks Theo, for everything." I don't want to leave his apartment and return to my normal life, but I knew I had a mess to clean up. A life with Theo seemed simple and I know my friends and parents would love him. Well, maybe not Kate and Ethan as I think they'll always look out for Hunter. I still wanted Hunter though, even after everything he had done. I started to become consumed with the thought of how badly I must've hurt him as I tried to make him jealous. After all, that's what the aim of this whole night was. I hurt him just like that girl did when we were younger. Something he told me he was scared would happen again, yet I purposefully hurt him anyway by kissing Theo and going home with him. But what was he doing when he went away? Was he kissing or sleeping with other girls? Why wouldn't he tell me?

CHAPTER 46

It's nearly 2:00am when Theo drops me home. Before he pulls away, we exchange phone numbers and then I watch as he drives off. I wondered if I would ever see him again. It would depend on whether Hunter came back for good, I guess. I walk up to the front door and Kate yanks it open. She's still dressed from our night out.

"Where have you been?" she demands. "We've been worried sick!"

I wasn't in the mood to be lectured so I walk past her and into the house, my eyes searching for Hunter even though I had no idea if he went home with them. "I was with Theo, remember? You pointed him out to me. What has Hunter told you anyway?" I demand and Kate's eyes go wide.

"Nothing, Hayley! He won't tell us anything," Kate exclaims.

"He's here, isn't he?" I feel anxious to see him so soon after what I did at the club.

"Hayley!" Ethan's face lights up when he sees me. He races down the stairs and gives me a big hug.

"I just wanted to make sure you were safe." Hunter's voice comes from behind Ethan. His voice is strained, and his face is visibly upset. My heart wants to break at how sweet he could be. Deep down he had the traits to be a wonderful boyfriend and even husband, I knew that from our time together in school, but something had changed. He wasn't the same Hunter I fell in love with and that's what I had to remind myself of. Hunter had changed and I was still holding onto the old him.

"Let them talk, Kate," Ethan says as he pulls gently at Kate's hand to leave us be.

"You owe me an explanation!" Kate points her finger at me. "And you—" she spits at Hunter, "—either sort your shit out or fuck off. What you're doing is wrong. I don't want to have to pick up the pieces for a third time."

With that, Kate turns on her heel and storms upstairs. Ethan looks at me and shrugs. "I've tried to talk to him, Hayls." He squeezes my arm. "It's up to you now." He follows Kate upstairs.

I look at Hunter but he's staring at the floor. He looks so young and innocent in this moment, like he was a kid who knew he was about to be told off for bad behaviour.

"We didn't have sex Hunter, we just talked." I cross my arms over my chest.

I needed to start this conversation off right, rather than drag it out. I know Hunter would've been desperate to know what I did with Theo. If I wanted Hunter to be honest with me, I needed to show him that I could be honest with him.

"Is that his shirt?" he mumbles, still looking at the ground.

"Yes." I look down at the shirt I was wearing. "Theo kindly offered me something to wear so I would feel better."

"So, you didn't fuck him?" he asks as he takes a step towards me.

I take a step back though and shake my head. "He said no."

Hunter scoffs loudly. "What guy in his right mind would say no to having sex with you? What an idiot." He lets out a light-hearted chuckle.

Why would Hunter say all of these things when he just kept leaving? His comment still makes me blush though.

"He said we shouldn't rush as he knows this was out of character for me and that I really needed to sort out what I wanted."

A smile creeps onto Hunter's face. How cocky could he be?

"But he said I'd know where to find him if I needed him," I add, which makes his smile disappear again. It then goes silent for a minute or two. I don't know where to go from here. I don't know what I want.

He moves quickly and is standing right in front of me. He takes my hands in his. "Let's start over, Hayley, let's start from the start," he pleads, desperation written all over his face.

"Why, Hunter? Why should we even bother?" I feel a tear escape and I look away from him.

He lightly guides my chin so I'm looking at him. "Because we're meant to be together, Hayley, we're just going through some issues right now, but we can talk about it and work out a plan to get through it. Hayley, I'll do anything to get you back. Please, let me show you." His voice breaks and I can see there are tears in his eyes.

I hastily wipe my own tears from my eyes. How many times would we go through this? We really just needed a fresh start. "You can't live here anymore, Hunter." I decide on the spot. "Either you move out or I will," I say as my brain starts working out a plan on how to move forward with Hunter.

He thinks for a minute. "I don't understand how this will help us when I can't be with you, Hayley."

"I want you to move out Hunter, and then we'll go to a bar and I want you to pick me up." I see confusion flood his face. I wasn't sure where this was headed either but I kept going. "I want you to impress me and ask me out on a date." I put my hands on my hips. "We don't know each other at the bar. We're starting from scratch. Which also means we can't live together."

Hunter starts to smile as he slowly begins to understand what I'm asking of him. "I think I can do that."

"I'm being dead serious, Hunter. We're not together anymore. You broke up with me yesterday so we're not a couple right now. Which also means you're going to have to work for it if you want sex. Clearly, I don't suit the slutty type and can't sleep with someone on the first date." I finish my rant and start to feel a bit more confident that I could actually still have a future with Hunter.

"Will you wear that outfit again?" His grin is full of mischief.

"No, because that's not me, Hunter, and you know it." I cross my arms again. "If that's the kind of girl you want, then we're really done here, because I'm not going to pretend to be someone I'm not."

"Can you at least give me the pleasure of ripping some other guy's clothes off your body?" He playfully teases the hem of Theo's shirt. "It's the least you can do after you got me all hot and bothered before ripping my heart out and leaving with Theo, of all people."

I think about his request for a moment. I guess he needed to get something out of this deal. Maybe I could let him have one win so he remembers what he's working for?

"Hmm," I pretend to think. "How about this, you can take one piece of clothing off when you tell me where you've been and why?"

"Well, that sounds like two pieces of clothing." He bites his lip.

"You left me twice, Hunter," I snap. I don't expect my words to come out so forceful but they do.

He ignores my attitude and gently pushes me back against the front door. "I'm never going to leave you again, Hayley. I love you." His voice is low and he bites his lip before he gently presses kisses against my neck. I can feel the urgency behind his kisses grow as his tongue grazes across my skin. No matter how strong I try to be, Hunter makes me weak. He had a way of making me want more and tonight was no different.

"Upstairs, now!" I demand. He swoops me up which makes me giggle as he carries me to our bedroom. He lays me gently on the bed and starts kissing me with a passion I'd never felt from him before. He starts to tug at the bottom of my shirt.

"No," I tell him between kisses. "Remember our agreement." I grab his hands and try to pin them down, but he was stronger than I remembered.

He groans. "I can't think about anything else while you're in that fucker's clothes. I need you to take them off now!" He breaks free of my grip and reaches for my shirt again.

"No," I repeat firmly as I sit up and push against his chest but he hardly moves. "You'll get what you want when I get what I want."

With a huff, he sits back, running a hand through his hair.

"Where did you go the first time you left, Hunter?" I cut straight to the chase, even moving away from him so I could see his face and work out if he was lying at any point.

I can see he's getting angry, but I wanted to know. I *needed* to know. I can't have secrets anymore.

"I was with my brother," he says. "In Melbourne."

I am shocked that he's actually just told me something but at the same time, I know he's lying. I spoke to his brother face to face several times. He was always easy to find and therefore couldn't have been in Melbourne.

"Doing what?" I demand as I try to see how far he'd stretch the lie.

"Nothing. We were just partying and doing shit we shouldn't have been doing." He hangs his head. "Wasting my life away as you would probably call it."

"For three months? And you couldn't tell me any of this so I at least knew you were okay and not dead in a ditch?" I snap.

"Oh, no. This isn't how the game works," he growls seductively. "I told you where I was and what I was doing, so come here and let me get what I want." He holds his hand out to me with a devilish smile.

I sigh. He had a point. He told me where he was and what he was doing. Whether it was the truth or not was another story.

I crawl over to him and let him take my hand as I climb onto his lap. "You're not lying to me, are you?" I keep my hands firmly on his chest.

His smile disappears and he groans. "Why would I lie?"

I sigh again. This wasn't working. "Because I spoke to your brother and he said he didn't know where you were and he was still in town," I reply, much to his disgust. He just rolls his eyes and shakes his head, clearly calculating his next move.

"Please don't lie to me, Hunter. I don't deserve it," I say quietly as I move to get off his lap.

"Don't start, Hayley." He grabs my waist to stop me from moving. "The only thing I can think about right now is Theo having his fucking hands all over you in the most jaw dropping outfit I've ever seen you wear. All I want to do is have sex with you right now. Let me just have my way with you and I'll talk after," he pleads. "Please."

It's my turn to roll my eyes. This was always going to be pointless. I had to accept that he was never going to tell me the truth. This was just a game to him. It was time to finally call it quits.

"Just forget it." I shake my head and get off his lap, pushing his hands away as he protests. "Just get out."

Hunter scoffs and gets off the bed, beckoning me to come back to him. "Come on, Hayley, you can't be serious. We were making progress."

"And then you ruined it, like you always do, because you can't tell me the truth!"

"For fuck's sake, Hayley! Why am I not enough? What is it that you want from me?" he shouts.

His anger makes me crack. He had no right to be mad at me. He was the one in the wrong. "How many girls have you fucked whilst you've been away? Is that where you were after you wrote me a note—*a fucking note*—to break up with me?" I snap even though I didn't know if I really wanted him to answer.

"None, Hayley! How dare you think I'd do that to you? You're the unfaithful one in this relationship, not me!"

His words are like a slap in the face. I would never cheat on Hunter, but I couldn't say the same for him. I certainly didn't cheat on him with Theo. He had broken up with me with a damn note.

"You're a liar!" I snap. "You just keep lying to me."

"I fucked five girls. Are you happy?" he roars at me.

I can feel my heart shatter. *Five girls?* He was gone for three months. Did I mean anything to him at all? My bedroom door swings open, banging loudly against the wall. It's Ethan and he's seething.

"Get out, Hunter!" he shouts. "Get the fuck out of this house!"

"Fuck! I don't know why I said that, Hayley. It's not true. I didn't sleep with anyone else. I promise! I just said it out of anger." Hunter rushes towards me but Ethan grabs the hood of his jacket and pulls him back and away from me.

"Just cut the bullshit, Hunter. Where have you been?" Ethan pushes Hunter against the wall. "You do know we've all been worried about you, right? Imagine if Hayley left and you were in her shoes right now and she refused to tell you the truth? What would you do, huh?"

"Hayley, don't do this to me, please." Hunter looks around Ethan at me. "I'm begging you. Can we just forget about all of this and just start again like we talked about, please? We'll start over just like you said. You can trust me this time."

"I don't know what to believe anymore, Hunter." I feel the tears fall down my face as I back away from him. "I'm sorry but this is over. We're not good for each other."

He pushes past Ethan and gathers me up in his arms.

"No, we can work this out, please." Hunter holds me tight, cradling one hand around the back of my neck and the other around my waist. "Hayley, please don't do this, please! I love you. I swear I do and I'm going to show you. Please let me show you. I didn't sleep with anyone else, please believe me. I know you didn't sleep with Theo, I believe you. You wouldn't do that to me, just like I wouldn't do it to you. I went away for a while and now I'm back. I'm not going to leave you again, I promise."

"Stop feeding her lies, Hunter!" Ethan rips me out of his arms and lightly pushes me towards Kate who pulls me away. Ethan then grips Hunter by the scruff of his shirt. "I said, get out!" he shouts.

Hunter struggles against his grip but manages to break free to take a swing at Ethan who luckily avoids it. I didn't realise how strong Ethan was against Hunter.

"Don't make me call the police, Hunter!" I can see how hard this is for Ethan and soon he will crack and just let Hunter back in. This must be how I look to everyone around me.

Hunter's face drops as the realisation of our situation sets in. We had all had enough of his behaviour and he knew it.

"Can I please just say goodbye?" I hear Hunter whisper.

"If you try anything funny, I will rip your fucking head off," Ethan warns before releasing his grip on Hunter's shirt.

"Hayley." Hunter tries to reach for me, but I turn away from him.

"Don't touch me." My voice comes out croaky from crying. "Don't make this harder than it needs to be."

A tear falls from his eye and I want to wipe it away. This was really it. The end of an era.

"We belong together, Hayley. I'll give you your space, but I'll be waiting for you," he mumbles before he turns and walks out of the room.

CHAPTER 47

It's been over a week since Ethan practically threw Hunter out of the house and my second semester of university was set to start the following week. I felt lonely and guilty, like I was the cause of all this pain. I should've just waited for Hunter to come back. Instead, I had to poke the bear. I tried to call Theo for an outsider's perspective, but he never answered, and he never called me back. I tried to stop by his apartment, but no one ever answered the door. Maybe Hunter was right. Maybe we just needed time apart, on mutual terms, to live our lives and decide if we really wanted each other. I missed the old Hunter so much. Maybe we could try again. When things were good with us, it was amazing. I had one last shred of hope that the old Hunter was still in there. I had to give it one last shot. He said he really was serious this time. I could hear it in his voice and see it on his face. I pick up my phone and pull up Hunter's number. I hesitate though and put my phone on the floor where I was sitting in my room.

"Just call him," Kate appears in my doorway. "Clearly you still have some stuff you want to get off your chest."

Ethan appears behind her, offering a supportive smile.

"I'm so sorry to put you both through this." I force myself not to cry.

"He was our friend too, Hayley. We're in just as much pain as you are." Ethan was visibly upset too. They were supposed to be best friends. His interaction with Hunter had really rattled him. I don't think they'd ever had a physical fight before; sure, they'd thrown words around but never fists. Ethan was probably hurt that Hunter took a swing at him.

"Will you sit with me while I call him?" I was embarrassed to even ask.

They both nod and sit on the bed behind me while I dial Hunter's number. An automated voice lets me know that the number has been disconnected. My heart breaks as I realise Hunter was well and truly gone this time.

CHAPTER 48

Time moved slowly for the first few months after Hunter left. He was a ghost to nearly everyone, except me. I desperately wanted him to appear again, to tell me he loved me and then stay with me until the end of time. I'd take him back in a heartbeat. I loved him and couldn't work out what I had done wrong. I wallowed for the first week or two, disappointing both my parents and Kate and Ethan. Jethro went on some humanitarian trip overseas and I never heard from him again, not that I wanted him like I wanted Hunter. He was a distraction to me. I even struggled to contact Theo again. It's almost as though everyone had deserted me.

What a selfish view to have!

When I finally snapped out of my depressive state, I had something else to worry about. Dad.

He wasn't getting any better; if anything, his health was declining. As awful as it sounded, his health distracted me significantly and I transferred all my energy to helping him wherever I could and making sure he was proud of me. The last thing I needed was for him to worry about me now that Hunter seemed to be well and truly out of the picture. To prove even further to my parents that I was serious about leaving Hunter in the past, I changed my phone number and email address, and made new social media accounts in an effort to reduce all further contact he could've made. I changed my privacy settings, so I had control over what photos I was tagged in and was very selective in what I posted, rarely showing my face or location. I did a deep clean and threw out absolutely anything of Hunter's I could find. Any last remaining items of his like jumpers, any hidden pictures, jewellery, anything that even reminded me of him. I even threw out the ballerina charm which was harder than I thought it would be. I deleted all of our photos and videos from my phone and laptop. He was officially gone from my life, and I hoped to become a ghost to him. I needed to start fresh. I dived into some of the university social clubs and built a wonderful friendship group. I started to feel like myself again. I had earned a high achiever award at university, and was even awarded a scholarship which helped pay for some of my student loans in my second year of university. Things were looking up. Once the new year came around and my second year of university had started, it had officially been eight months since Hunter left, and by this stage I was ready for someone new.

Enter, Rhys.

~ PART 4 ~

THREE YEARS LATER

CHAPTER 49

Rhys is the complete opposite of Hunter, and I love it. We met in the June of my second year of university. When we started talking and hanging out after we both went to grab the last box of cookies at the bakery, I was so worried that Hunter would show up, like he did with Jethro, but he never did. I had finally seen the last of that boy. *Good riddance.* I didn't even tell Rhys about him until I was certain there was a future with him. I didn't want to scare him off, thinking I had this insane ex-boyfriend that would hunt him down because I knew that Hunter would actually go to that extreme. His incessant need to feel like I was his property only became apparent when Ethan spit the dummy the last time I let Hunter come back, only to disappear again.

Rhys was so different from Hunter. It made me wonder why I was ever attracted to Hunter. Rhys was taller than me but not a giant. He was well-built, not skin and bone with muscle. He had blonde hair and blue eyes. Nothing compared to the dark features Hunter had. It almost felt like I could breathe again with this fresh, new, colourful and light person. Hunter was making me suffocate with his dark energy, appearance and spirit. I just couldn't believe it had taken me so long to realise it. The genuine interest Rhys showed in me was so deeply attractive. When I talked, he listened, and he recognised that there was a time for jokes, and time to be serious. I felt like for the first time I wasn't chasing my tail, trying to work out where I stood. I could've kicked myself at how much time and energy I'd wasted on Hunter when there were guys like Rhys out there. After only weeks of meeting, Rhys and I were officially a couple, nothing like the yearlong wait I had with Hunter. I guess you just know when you've met *The One.*

Everyone approved of Rhys. But they probably would've approved of anyone so long as they weren't Hunter. Mum and Dad were thrilled to see me happy. Rhys was there when I got the fateful phone call from Mum to say that Dad had passed peacefully, but unexpectedly, in his sleep at home. I thought I'd lost a piece of my soul. In the wake of Dad's death, I sometimes felt so desperate to talk to Hunter as he and Dad were close and then I'd have to mentally slap myself. Why would I want him back in my life? What would that accomplish? I told Ethan how I was feeling and he refused to talk to me for three days. He was so angry at me for even thinking of trying to reach out to Hunter. But Ethan didn't understand. How could I talk to my dad the day before, and then all of a sudden, he was gone? He wasn't displaying any symptoms. He was getting frailer, but the medical team made it sound like emphysema was a slow progressing disease. The only person who could understand what I was thinking was Hunter. Another mental slap. Why? He wouldn't understand at all. Hunter was a boy who thought sex was the answer to everything. I opened up to Rhys, and it felt good to be able to talk about something without the end result being sex. I think that's when I really knew he was the one I wanted to spend the rest of my life with. Rhys would always make me a cup of tea and then listen to whatever I had to get off my chest. I must've been doing something right though as he got down on one knee, on the six-month anniversary of Dad's passing. That's when I realised that everything would be okay. On Dad's birthday, I married a wonderful human being in the company of my loving family and friends. Nothing could ruin this high that I was on. After graduating from university with a bachelor's in education, I secured a role as a teacher at one of the local high schools. I taught dance, drama and English to the senior students and I loved it! Some of the students were kids I taught when I was at ACE Dance Studios, so it was nice to have familiar faces. It made my job a lot easier, and I wasn't so nervous when I first started. I also picked up a role with the local eisteddfod company in mentoring and judging each June and July school holidays. It meant I was kept busy though and I really needed that after my dad died. I felt like I was finally in my element, and I was content that this was where life had taken me.

CHAPTER 50

I was grabbing a quick hot chocolate to take away when I accidentally stepped back into someone, spilling both their drink and mine.

"Oh my goodness, I'm so sorry!" I feel the blood rush to my cheeks. I bend down to start cleaning up the mess, apologising profusely and highly embarrassed at the mess I had just made.

"Hayley?" His voice makes my heart skip a beat.

I slowly look up into Hunter's face. It had been nearly three years since I last saw him. He had definitely matured but I could see it was the same old Hunter.

"Hunter," I stutter, struggling to comprehend that he was standing right in front of me. "What a surprise."

He smiles shyly, the same smile I fell in love with all those years ago. "Tell me about it, it's been a while." He offers his hand out to help me back on my feet. Instinctively, I take his hand and let him help me up. Even his skin felt the same. I must've pulled a face though as he helps me up because he quickly adds, "I know, you don't need me to remind you of how long it has been. For what it's worth, I'm sorry I put you through all of that, Hayls."

I nod slowly as I try to convince my heart to slow down at the sound of his voice saying my nickname. I couldn't believe he was standing in front of me. "Thanks, I guess."

"Can I buy you another drink and we can catch up? Only if you've not got somewhere to be, of course?" he offers.

I check my watch. I've still got time before I meet up with my friends to go through my wedding photos. Was I actually considering going with him after everything he'd done?

"Okay." It comes out as a whisper, as though I don't want anyone to hear that I've agreed to spend time with him. Deep down I knew I'd always wonder why he did what he did. I still longed for answers.

I stand back quietly as he orders our new drinks, and we stand in silence whilst we wait for them to be made.

"Want to walk and talk?" he asks as he collects the drinks from the barista.

"Sure, I guess we can go for a walk," I reply as he leads the way.

At least I wouldn't have to stare at him the whole time. I could focus on walking. I inhale deeply and take a sip of my drink.

"Wow, who's the lucky guy?" he asks half-heartedly as he takes sight of my diamond engagement ring and wedding band.

I feel so shy telling my ex-boyfriend about my husband. It was very awkward, but I push through it. I had nothing to be ashamed of. "Someone really amazing. I've never felt love like this before."

Technically I had with Hunter, but he didn't need to hear that. With the look on his face, I can tell he's upset by what I've said. Surely, after all this time, he didn't think I'd wait or that he'd still have a chance?

"Right," is all he says. He looks heartbroken.

"For what it's worth, I'm sorry, Hayley. I really am. I didn't expect you to wait for me each time, but I'd be lying if I said I didn't think we'd make our way back to each other and live happily ever after. I've changed. I've grown up now. I know what I want. I'm just sorry it took me so long to realise it." He tries to brush a strand of hair out of my face but my reflexes take me by surprise and I grab his arm before he has the chance. I can see sadness spread across his face.

"Oh right. I guess I can't do that anymore." He looks down at his shoes.

"It was nice seeing you again, Hunter, but I've got somewhere to be," I say quickly. Hunter was going to be Hunter again. I could see it coming this time and I wasn't going to let him win. I give him a quick smile and turn to walk away.

"Can I meet him?" His voice is strained.

I snap back around to face him. "No! Absolutely not. You can't meet him."

"I just want to see the guy who stole you from me." He shoves his hands in his pockets.

Stole me from him? This was crazy talk. Sure, I may have fallen for his ways before when he'd disappear and then reappear. I used to think his bad boy ways were attractive but now I was disgusted by it.

"Just asking." He shrugs his shoulders. "I think you owe me that at least."

"I don't owe you anything," I spit through my teeth. "Have a nice life, Hunter."

I turn on my heel and walk away from him. I feel my anger boiling to the surface. What an unnerving experience. I feel my breathing getting faster as my pace increases. I don't even know where I'm going. I just let my anger take me wherever it wants to go. I think back to all of the experiences I've had with Hunter. My mind travels back to when we were in school. The words Hunter used; *mine, stole you from me,* even the way he described sex. It was as though I was a piece of his property. I had managed to go three years in the same town we grew up in without running into him and now when I'm finally truly and completely happy, he shows up.

"Hayley, where are you going?" Someone grabs my arm and pulls me back to the present.

I whip around to find Ethan.

"Whoa, are you okay? What's wrong?" He holds me by my arms, searching my face and body for signs of trauma.

I don't even know what to say to him. As far as I knew, Ethan hadn't heard from Hunter either. Hunter had disappeared from Ethan's life as much as he had from mine.

"He's back, isn't he?" Ethan whispers. "He found you."

"Did you know he was back, Ethan?" I demand, tears forming in my eyes.

"What? No!" he shouts. "I haven't heard from him in as long as you haven't. He deserted me too, Hayley. I honestly never thought I'd see him again."

Hunter's behaviour and disappearing act had hurt Ethan too. He was just much better at hiding it.

"Ethan, what did you mean by *he found me*?" I'm so frustrated. "His behaviour, now, and everything that's happened in the past is so bizarre. Do you think I need to be worried?"

"You have nothing to be afraid of, Hayley." Ethan squeezes my arm. "You know all too well what he's like. He's always had you wrapped around his finger and now that he doesn't, he's trying ways to flick the switch and make you go back to him."

"I'm not going back to him," I spit.

"Did I say you were? Hayley, I'm not the enemy here. Stop getting snappy with me." He runs his hand through his hair.

I was frustrating him and it wasn't fair to treat him this way.

"You didn't give him your number or anything? He doesn't know where you're going? You'll be late to meet the girls so let me walk you there."

"No, he doesn't know." I let Ethan lead the way. No doubt he just dropped Kate off. "Should I tell Rhys?"

"You mean Rhys doesn't know about Hunter?" Ethan's shocked.

"He knows about Hunter, yes, but I just haven't gone into detail about him. I was trying to move on when I met Rhys." I wipe the tears hastily from my eyes. "Hunter was nothing but a memory. He wasn't a discussion point."

"You need to tell him, Hayley. This is too big of a secret. You're married after all," Ethan says bluntly. "It's not fair on Rhys."

"I know." I feel like a child being scolded but Ethan was right. It was time I finally told Rhys everything about Hunter. It was the right thing to do. Hunter was back and who knows what he was going to do.

⸺•❖•⸺

I toss and turn that night. I couldn't relax. The thought of Hunter being back and what he could possibly do scared me, but I was even more scared to have to tell

Rhys that he was. I didn't want him to worry. Things had been going so smoothly with us; we rarely experienced a hiccup. Hunter was going to derail everything. Rhys working late tonight didn't help either. Apparently, something urgent came up and he had to stay late. I didn't mind. I was used to this. It was just the nature of his role, not that I fully understood it. He seemed to be at the beck and call of his clients, almost like he was on call 24/7, not that I could understand why they'd need to call him at all hours, but he said they weren't always in the same time zone. Business is business and he wanted to get ahead, so he was trying to impress management.

By the time he gets home, I relax slightly, already feeling safer with him around. Sleep finally overcomes me. Thoughts of Dad start to fill my head and how he was so supportive of Hunter when we were together. How he acted like a father figure for him, how he helped him pick a career path, taught him to build things, talked sports with him. And now they were both gone. How could Dad do this to me? I needed all of those things still. I needed his support, I needed his help to build things, I could talk sport with him. Hell, I'd sit and watch paint dry, just to be in his company again.

I shake myself out of the dream, breathing heavily at the state I worked myself into. Far out, it was only 2:00am. What a restless night.

"Are you okay, Hayley?" I hear Rhys stir and roll over.

A wave of comfort rolls over me at hearing his voice.

"I just had some weird life-like dream about Dad. It was rough," I try to explain.

He sighs, an unusual response to what he usually does.

"Sorry, I didn't mean to wake you," I apologise. I can't see his face but his sigh made it sound like he was frustrated.

"At some point, Hayls, you need to get over this and just go back to sleep. I don't always have the energy to talk in depth about it. I'm exhausted and it's been over a year now. You need to learn to work through it by yourself".

I feel like I've been slapped in the face. I never expected a response like this in a million years from Rhys. He was always kind and supportive no matter what.

"I need to sleep, Hayls. Can we just talk about it later?" he tries to recover.

I don't know what to say. All I manage to do is apologise quietly and lay back down on my side. I wait to hear his breathing even out and then I start to cry.

CHAPTER 51

I sat with my book, taking in the sunshine and watching my engagement ring and wedding band sparkle in the sunlight. I break my gaze away from my hand to turn the page of my book, trying to focus on the words on the page whilst I wait for Rhys to come back from the toilet. We hadn't spoken about the other night where he snapped at me for waking him up after I had a vivid dream about Dad. He was normally the first to approach a difficult conversation, but he didn't bring it up and I decided he was probably just tired and didn't mean it. He was the one who suggested to come here today though. That had to account for something.

"I knew I'd find you here one day," Hunter's voice calls from across the grassed area.

"What are you doing here?" My heart was racing.

"Waiting to see you." He casually walks towards me. "Is Rhys here?"

"How do you know his name?" Fear was setting in. This was the last place I wanted to run into Hunter.

"Got it out of Ethan. He caved." He shrugged. "Eventually," he adds with a wicked grin, before taking a seat beside me on the bench.

"What did you do?" I ask carefully with the fear of what he could've done to Ethan flooding my mind.

"Nothing. Mind if I sit?"

I'm speechless at how brash he's being. My mind struggles to focus on what's happening as I watch him take a seat beside me.

"Now, what are you doing here?" I feel like his eyes are looking directly into my soul.

"If you're here then you already know," I mumble.

"I want you to tell me. I want to hear it from you," he demands.

"Why are you doing this?"

"I'm just asking a question, Hayley. Now, what are you doing here?"

"My dad died, Hunter." My voice shakes.

"Why didn't you tell me?" he growls.

"Because—" I start but am interrupted.

"Oh, so you're Hunter," I hear Rhys's voice. *Thank god.* Hunter grins at me and stands up, offering his hand out for Rhys to shake. Rhys was confused by Hunter. I can see him trying to work him out. I want to tell Rhys it's no use, but I don't want to cause a scene at a cemetery.

"Yes, I am," Hunter proudly answers. "I see you've put a ring on her. You sure are a lucky man. Better treat her right though, you never know how easy it could be to steal her away from you."

"I'm pretty confident it won't be as easy as you'd like to think." Rhys's voice is cold. "We're married, after all." He waves his hand at Hunter, showing off his own wedding band.

"You never know. I won her over before and then over and over again. What's time anyway? Doesn't it make the heart grow fonder?" Hunter smirks and then walks off.

I see Rhys hesitate, like he wants to go after him but instead he turns to face me.

"What the fuck? Who the fuck does he think he is?" Rhys's anger takes over.

"That's Hunter," is all I manage. *Here we go again.*

"Did he always talk about you like that?" He starts pacing in front of where I'm sitting.

"Once we left school, he became more intense." I ran my hand through my hair.

"Intense? That boy is obsessed with you, and not in a healthy way." I can see the concern over his face.

"I saw him a couple of weeks ago," I say quietly.

Rhys's eyes go wide. I know I should've told him earlier. I should've known better.

"I know. I'm sorry I didn't tell you," I say quickly. "I just wanted to forget the whole experience. It was every bit as unnerving as today's encounter."

"And you haven't seen him again since?" he asks as he sits back down beside me.

"No, I swear!"

"It's okay, I'm not doubting you. I just think his behaviour is really odd." Rhys pulls me into his arms. "Are you okay?"

"Rhys, I'm scared," I finally admit as I feel the tears form in my eyes. "He was such a pest last time and he just messed everything up. He's going to say anything he can to make you mad or to doubt me. He's a compulsive liar. I promise that anything you ask I will always tell you the truth." I really wanted Rhys to trust me. I knew what Hunter was like and how quickly he could derail my marriage.

"Tell me everything about your relationship with Hunter, Hayley, from the start," Rhys asks. "I want to know everything."

I take a deep breath, wondering where to even begin.

CHAPTER 52

I can feel myself falling asleep. It had been a long couple of weeks. Rhys and I had spoken at length about Hunter. It actually felt good to talk about everything that happened. It was like I was officially closing that chapter of my life. It was now out in the open with Rhys. He knew everything about Hunter, what our relationship was like, and what happened when it all fell apart. He listened patiently and made me feel appreciated in ways Hunter never could, but I could see how frustrated Rhys was, like he never would've gotten with me if he'd known the whole truth about Hunter and what he was really like. Rhys was reluctant to leave me home alone after that day in the cemetery. He wanted to be by my side at all times, but his work was starting to ramp up and it required him to travel frequently to finalise some of his projects. Ethan promised Rhys that he would keep an eye on me, and I promised Rhys I would call him every morning and every night. Still, when I dropped Rhys at the airport, he wasn't convinced. Once he got back, we were going on a much-needed holiday to Fiji. I was so excited I had already started packing once I dropped him at the airport.

I was nearly about to get into bed when my phone starts ringing on the bedside table. *Who on earth is calling at this time of night?* I had already said goodnight to Rhys so it likely wouldn't be him. I pick up the phone and see Ethan's name on the caller ID. I instantly start to panic. Kate was now a few months pregnant, so I hoped nothing had happened to her or the baby for Ethan to call me this late at night.

"Ethan, is everything okay?" I answer.

"Hayley, are you awake?" He sounds scared. Poor thing, it would be very daunting having your first baby.

"I was just about to go to bed, why? Is everything okay?" I ask as I settle back against the headboard in bed.

"Can you meet me at the pier?" There's urgency in his voice.

"Ethan, it's nearly 10:00pm. What's going on? Is Kate okay?"

"It's Hunter. He's threatening to throw himself off unless you come to him."

I nearly drop the phone. I honestly thought I was done with him after the last time I saw him.

"Hayley! Are you there? Can you come or not? I really need you here! I don't know what to do!" I can hear the fear in his voice. Never did I think it would come to this. Sure, Hunter was always the bold type, but never would he take his own life. What had happened to this boy? What made him change so much?

"I can come," I blurt out without thinking. I knew that Ethan needed my help regardless of the situation, but I'd be lying if I said a part of me didn't want to know what Hunter was doing. "I'll be there soon. Hang on."

My heart was racing. I jump out of bed and change into some warmer clothes to go out in. It's so dark outside and my gut is telling me not to go but I knew I had to. What would I do if I didn't go and he actually was trying to kill himself? I don't want to be the reason someone dies, and I didn't want to live with regret. I also didn't want to put Ethan in that position either.

The pier is a 20-minute drive from my house and, of course, I catch every red traffic light. I can't help but drum my fingers on the steering wheel as I wait for each light to turn green. There are butterflies in my stomach as I pull into the parking lot near the pier. Ethan's car is there and there's another car which I assume is Hunter's. After I park, I sit for several minutes before I convince myself to get out and head over to where Ethan was standing. I don't want to look like I'm rushing to Hunter's aid as I don't want to give him false hope that I cared for him the way he wants me to. I try to stroll up casually beside Ethan. He looks wrecked, like it had been a long day of dealing with Hunter. Ethan really didn't need this extra stress. He had Kate to worry about. He squeezes my arm but doesn't say anything, he just turns to face the railings on the pier where Hunter must've been standing.

"Hunter?" I call out and he steps into the light. He's standing on the other side of the railings. There's a bottle of vodka in his hand.

"Well, look who finally showed up," he slurs. "I knew you'd come to save me. You just can't stay away."

"Hunter, what are you doing?" I ask cautiously as I approach him.

"When you got married, was it everything you ever wanted? Did you smile in your photos? Did you kiss what's-his-name?" His face drops. "Did you wish it was me?"

I look back at Ethan. This was worse than I thought. I wasn't sure I'd be able to handle this. Hunter had well and truly lost the plot now. I needed to be strong though. Now was not the time to be weak. He needed a reality check and someone to give him the hard truth.

"Hunter, why don't you tell her what you were telling me? Let her know how you feel?" Ethan tries to get him to talk. Clearly, he's said a lot to Ethan in his drunken rampage.

"Talk to her?" Hunter exclaims. "That's all I've been trying to do since I saw her again in that coffee shop. She doesn't want a bar of me!" he cries before looking at me. "What changed?" he demands. "Why are you no longer giving me chances like you used to? So, what? I went away for a while! I never stopped loving you though. We were meant to be! You said you loved me!" He was so far gone and had worked himself into such a state. It was like he was stuck in the past, unable to move forward.

"Hunter, do you realise it's been three years?" I ask carefully. Maybe something was seriously wrong with his mental health?

"Three years? Is that how long I was away for? Were you counting?" He grins but then it disappears. "We were in this together! Do you remember at your father's bedside in the hospital? We said we would be in this together!"

His words sting. I wish he would've left my dad out of it. He has no right to talk about my him.

"Do you realise the shit you put me through each time you left and came back? Where were you when you left me, Hunter?" I finally snap, the anger bubbling inside me. I was trying hard to remain cool, calm and collected but *god, he just irritates me*. How did he possibly think he could get away with this?

"You know where I was." He grins as he takes a sip from the vodka bottle.

"Where were you?" I demand again. His grin flickers for a second.

"Out living my life," he smirks as he replies.

"Damn it, Hunter!" I explode. "Where were you when you left me?"

His face turns to shock.

"Tell me!" I scream, rage taking over. "Tell me where you were right now or so help me god! What? Hmm?" I throw my hands out in frustration. "You think you can just demand to be back in my life? You can't even tell me the truth!" It felt so good to finally get my anger out.

"It's none of your business what I was doing, Hayley. What were you doing whilst I was away? Getting cosy with other blokes, that's what!" he tries.

I almost feel smoke come out of my ears and I let my anger get the better of me as I storm over to where Hunter's standing.

"Hayley, don't!" Ethan tries to grab at me, but I push him away. I was on a war path now.

"Stay away, if you come any closer, I'll jump!" I hear his voice but all I see is red. I was not letting go this time. He had no right to question me and my loyalty.

I reach out and grab at his shirt, ready to yell at him some more. Given his state, I was prepared to be hit with the smell of alcohol but I can't smell anything. That's when I realise he's not drunk at all. He's faking it. He sees me eyeing the bottle and throws it into the water.

"Just do it then, Hunter." I'm almost shocked at the words that come out of my mouth. They were harsh, but I was so tired of his nonsense. "I cannot be bothered with this narrative anymore. I'm so done with you and all of your bullshit. I've had enough. I refuse to be blackmailed by you. I don't love you anymore!" I tighten my grip on his shirt. I had nearly past the point of no return. "If you think that I will give up everything I have to save you, then you're dreaming. I gave you chance after chance. If you truly loved me like you say you do, then you would let me be happy!"

His face drops. I can see his body slouch against the rails. "I do love you, Hayley. So much it hurts! Why won't you come back to me? Why can't I have one more chance?"

"Because you don't deserve it, Hunter. You can't even tell me where you were and what you were doing." I let go of his shirt and wipe a tear away. "I became a shell of myself because of you. I didn't know if I would ever be happy again. How was I meant to trust again when the person I thought I was going to spend the rest of my life with starting disappearing on me, lying to me and manipulating me?"

He wipes another tear away from my cheek as he takes my face in his hands. I don't fight him, but I look away.

"What the fuck have I done to you?" Realisation spreads across his face, and for the first time since high school, I think I'd had finally gotten through to him.

"You broke me into pieces, Hunter, every single time you left me. I was miserable waiting for you to hopefully come back and then had to live this half-life when you did, thinking each time it'd be different, and maybe one time I would actually be enough to make you stay. You could've been there for me when my dad died." I watch a tear fall from his eye and I realise just how close we are. I jerk away from him which surprises him. "But what you don't realise is that by you leaving me, I found myself. It was the best thing you did for me because it let me rebuild myself into a stronger and happier person. I found Rhys because of you."

I drive the final nail in. "So, I'm going to go home now to the life I'm proud of and to a husband who loves me and treats me right. Whether you decide to end it tonight or not, I do hope you find peace, Hunter. There will be someone out there who will love you. It's just not me."

With that, I turn and walk away.

"It will always be you, Hayley," he calls out after me. "Please! Can we talk? For real this time? I promise I'll tell you everything!"

"How many times have I heard that before?" I throw my hands in the air without turning back to look at him. "I don't trust you anymore, Hunter."

"Please, it'll be different this time, I swear!" he cries out.

"Yeah, I've heard that before too." I keep walking away from him, away from Ethan, ignoring the burning desire inside to run back to him and do whatever I could to help.

CHAPTER 53

It's been nearly three months since the incident at the pier. I hadn't seen Hunter since that night. I was beginning to believe that maybe he really was gone for good this time, but then again, I thought that last time too. As much as it pained me to lie to Rhys, I didn't tell him about the incident at the pier with Hunter. I didn't want him to worry. Otherwise, he would turn down the work trips which could have an impact on his career overall. I developed a habit of checking every lock twice, something Rhys put down to being alone due to his frequent work trips. I also found myself often second guessing someone's motive, worried that they would be some sort of spy planted by Hunter, giving him the perfect opportunity to wriggle his way in when I least expected it. Ethan would call more frequently as well. He claimed he was just being friendly, but I suspected it was because he wanted to make sure Hunter hadn't reappeared. I didn't want him to worry though. Kate was only weeks away from having their first baby. He had enough to worry about. I didn't bother Kate with it either. Mum was the only other person who knew about the issues I had been having with Hunter, and I think it was because she had a sixth sense. She disagreed strongly when I decided not to tell Rhys about the pier, but I stuck to my decision. Like Dad, Mum was shocked at how Hunter and I ended things, and the person Hunter became. I think they were relieved to hear that I'd moved on and met Rhys. They were even more thrilled when it had been so many uninterrupted years without Hunter creating havoc. It made me proud that I was strong enough to pull away from Hunter for good and make something of my life, particularly after that night at the pier. I had a loving husband, a beautiful mum and my two best friends, Kate and Ethan, were having a baby. Life seemed to be getting better and better, and hopefully Hunter would become a distant memory for all of us.

"Hayley!" I hear Rhys call out, pulling me out of my daydream. "Can you come here please?"

"Coming!" I call back and walk in the direction of where his voice came from. I walk outside into the warm sunshine and towards the shed in our backyard. Rhys seemed to be talking to someone, but I couldn't work out if he was angry or upset. Then I notice another person leaning against the car.

Hunter.

CHAPTER 54

"Do you know what happened? Do you understand what happened?" Dr Martin asks.

I feel like this session has gone on for longer than an hour. It's so draining and now this fucker asks this question like I'm stupid.

"Yes," I snap. "Of course, I do."

"Tell me, in your own words, what happened, Ethan?"

I take a deep breath, forcing myself to remember that day. My stomach starts to churn. I can feel my blood pressure start to rise. I make a mental note of how close the trash can is to me.

"He killed her," I whisper.

"You can speak louder. This is a safe space."

"Hunter killed Hayley."

~ PART 5 ~

CHAPTER 55

It had been over a month since Hayley's funeral. It was a beautiful service. Many of her friends from university and the dance studio came, as well as friends from high school. I even recognised some of the teachers from high school. Her mum, Miranda, sat there blankly. My heart hurt for her. First, she'd lost her husband and now her only child. Tears streamed down her face, but she sat motionless, staring ahead at her daughter's coffin. I looked at the photographs of Hayley. Her beautiful smile felt like it was pointed directly at me. A smile that would now just be a memory. There's a photo from her wedding with Rhys. I look at him, sitting next to Miranda. He was staring at the ground. Rumours circulated for weeks after Hayley's death. We all knew who did it. There was an eyewitness after all. The newspapers reported that Hunter just sat there and screamed her name over and over, trying to make her come back to him. I was surprised to hear that Rhys hadn't beaten the shit out of him when he realised what he'd done but he probably wouldn't have had time if he was trying in vain to save Hayley's life. The trauma that Rhys would have to live with for the rest of his life would run deep, but he held his head high. God only knew what happened behind closed doors. Kate and I ended up naming our baby after Hayley and gave her the nickname Haze. She would've shown strength and courage right until the end. Hayley wouldn't have known what was going to happen and I don't know if it that was a blessing or a curse. After all, we still don't really know what happened that day and due to the ongoing investigation, Rhys wasn't allowed to say anything. To be honest, he was doing remarkably well. I never saw him cry. He always wore a stone-cold expression on his face, but he looked tired, like he was haunted by the memories of that night. I would catch myself thinking back to the memories I had of growing up with Hunter. He was my best friend. Never in a million years did I think he could murder somebody. It was a hard truth to accept but his behaviour leading up to Hayley's death was disturbing. I should've done more to protect her, but I guess I just never expected Hunter to do something like this. No one did. That's why I was even more surprised to be called as a character witness as part of Hunter's defence. I felt sick to my stomach being asked to discuss how great Hunter was after learning he killed one of my best friends, but he was my best, best friend. We met when we were six or seven years old and clicked instantly. We were inseparable. He was like a brother to me. We had the same interests, and we always had each other's back. There wasn't a single thing I didn't know about him. I knew all about his love life and his reputation. He was like an open book with me. He knew he could trust me as I knew all about the girl who broke his heart in the beginning. He told me the same day he met Hayley that he was interested in her. She was a hard egg to crack but slowly, we worked on how to win her over. She never would've known, but I knew everything that went on in his head because he told me everything. He asked me how he should go about asking her to have sex with him. He was so nervous, but he knew that he was ready to take this kind of step with her. He told me how happy she made him but that he was getting scared that she was going to leave him when we finished school. He told me what she said when she broke up with him and how worried he was when he couldn't get a hold of her, only to find out her dad was in the hospital. He cried on the phone to me when he got home after spending the weekend with her, thinking her dad was going to die and how he didn't want to lose the only real father figure he had. I knew *everything*. But what Hayley also didn't realise was that I knew how she felt when he left her, because he left me too. I couldn't lean on him as I started to worry about what kind of father I'd be. I couldn't talk to him about wanting to ask Kate to marry me. The Hunter I knew was gone and I missed him terribly.

When I told Kate that I'd been called to testify, she started to cry. She knew that after everything we had been through, Hunter would drag me into this. I asked the attorney for a couple of days to think about it. The trial would take months. Originally, we all thought that Hunter would be charged with murder but increasingly, the reports were now on manslaughter. His lawyer must've done some serious bargaining to get a manslaughter charge. My mind started wandering one night while I was doing the dishes. Kate had taken Haze upstairs to put her to bed. We were tense after I had told her about being asked to be a character witness. She was so frustrated that I was even considering it. I thought back to the time when Hunter and I would get into a fight, usually over something silly, and Kate would provide sympathy and tell me he was no good. Then a couple hours later, she would tell me to stop being stupid and go and make up with him. There wasn't a memory from my childhood, teenage years and early adulthood that didn't have Hunter in it, good or bad. I thought back to when Hayley first started at our school. Hunter was immediately infatuated with her. She was the first girl I'd seen him feel this way about since Abby. There was just something about her. I always thought they'd end up married with children by now. He really did like her, hell, he was in love with her before I think even he realised he was in love with her. I couldn't believe I got to play witness to two people falling in love. It was magical. Then it became a nightmare. Hayley was dead. Yet, Hunter was fighting a manslaughter charge. Something wasn't right.

Chapter 56

"I'm going to do it, Kate," I announce the next morning at breakfast. Kate looks at me, puzzled. Her hair was all frizzy and I knew she was dying to wash and blow dry it properly. I make a mental note to take Haze out for a walk so Kate could have some time to herself. She would probably want that after this conversation.

"Do what?" she asks as she takes a sip of her coffee.

"I'm going to be Hunter's character witness," I reply confidently.

Her eyes widen, her bottom lip drops.

"Kate, I can explain," I start.

"No," she cuts me off quickly. "I don't want to hear it!" she shrieks as she jumps out of her chair. "Hayley is d—" She takes a minute to compose herself. "She is dead! He's not your friend, Ethan! How didn't we see the signs earlier?"

"When?" I demand. "When should we have seen the signs? Okay, sure, he displayed unusual behaviour in the months leading up to her death but, Kate, we can't sit here and think we could've done more for Hayley."

"She was my best friend," Kate cries.

"And dammit, Hunter was mine!" I slam my hand on the table and sure enough, I hear our child start to cry.

Kate sighs and looks at me.

I take a deep breath before I speak. "Look, I'm sorry but something is not right, Kate. He was charged with manslaughter, not murder, which means there is evidence of some kind that he did not intentionally kill her." I try to keep my voice calm. "Hunter tried to reach out to me for help not long before Hayley died. I just didn't get it." My voice trails off as the realisation hits me. He needed help and I abandoned him.

Kate scoffs and turns to walk off.

"I'm going to do this, Kate, whether you support me or not." I try to be strong but my voice cracks at the end.

Again, Kate sighs.

"What if he's innocent, Kate?" I whisper.

"He's not," she replies and walks out of the room.

CHAPTER 57

Walking down the halls of the remand facility scared me. I still had no idea what it all meant. I didn't really envision having anything to do with this side of the law, so I was still learning. Signing in as a visitor made me feel exposed and vulnerable. Even though I hadn't done anything wrong I felt like one wrong move would see me in here for the rest of my life. Who knows what kind of real criminals were behind these walls? Were there real criminals here? Seeing as Hunter wasn't convicted, yet, they were all probably charged with something and hadn't yet faced trial. Who knows how dangerous they were? I couldn't imagine how Hunter felt trapped here. He wasn't offered bail, so he had to spend the entire trial in a remand facility until he was convicted. I had to see him though. I needed to talk to him and see him before I agreed to be a character witness. I needed to see if the old Hunter, the one I grew up with, was still there or if he was well and truly gone. I sat on the cold steel framed chair in the visitor's hall. I looked around the room and saw other people waiting anxiously for their loved ones. Some remand prisoners were already seated, their orange jumpsuits faded. I wondered how long they had been waiting for their trials. The door to the visitor's hall beeped open and Hunter is led in. He looked like he hadn't slept in days. His eyes search the room before he breathes out heavily at the sight of me. I feel tears spring to my eyes as memories flash before me of when he would look at me the same way when either one of us got into a fight that they needed the other to help them with. He needed help and he needed me. Hunter was innocent. I knew it.

CHAPTER 58

Something big was coming, I could feel it. They kept postponing Hunter's court date so I could only assume it was because they were trying to find more evidence or maybe they had more high-profile cases that took priority with the judge. I didn't know what it was, and they wouldn't tell us either. Each day I would either call or visit Hunter and each day he looked and sounded more and more defeated. I tried to tell him stories that I thought he would laugh at, but he didn't. I even tried to have a heart-to-heart with him and told him how I had gone to therapy at Kate's request after Hayley died. I told him all about Dr Martin and how frustrated I felt talking to this stranger. I got *a* chuckle out of him but otherwise I think I made him feel worse about how badly he'd messed things up. Sometimes, we would just sit in silence. I wouldn't push him to talk. I think he just liked having a familiar person around. Someone he could relax around. There were a few days I wasn't allowed to visit on medical grounds, and when I finally could see him, he had bruising on his face. He wouldn't tell me what happened though. He requested I don't visit as frequently as I did. He said a phone call was fine, but he didn't want me going out of my way for him.

"I'm probably going to be locked away for a long time, I don't want to get used to a frequent visitor," he mumbled one day.

I felt terrible. Even his own family had disowned him, not like they cared for him anyway. They distanced themselves from him the minute he got arrested and he tried to phone for help in securing a lawyer. He told me that it was easy enough to disassociate themselves with him. Their surname was common, they hardly took him on holidays or to social functions. It would be merely a coincidence that they shared the same name. It was rough to hear him recount this but I had seen the way they treated Hunter throughout the years. He pretty much lived at my house when we were younger. I was watching my best friend go through a harrowing ordeal and I was all he had. He wasn't allowed to talk about the case with me either, for obvious reasons. He really had no one. Just his lawyer, Jerry, who I saw every now and then when I was visiting. I never spoke to him though. He was often coming or going when I saw him. No matter what Jerry was telling him, Hunter was starting to lose faith in the justice system. I was worried for him. I even felt like I had no one. Kate didn't want to hear it, and my parents were disappointed that I'd chosen to do it so I felt like I couldn't talk to them either.

"Don't say that." I would try to argue with Hunter, but it was no use. It was his word against Rhys, and unfortunately his behaviour prior to Hayley's death meant everyone had no reason to doubt Rhys. Begrudgingly, I accepted Hunter's wishes and started to drop my visits down to once or twice a week for several weeks, until it became once a fortnight. All I could do was support him however he wanted me to. What got me through all the harrowing visits and seeing the old Hunter fade away, was that I knew that if he didn't kill Hayley, Rhys did, and the truth would come out eventually. I couldn't work out why Rhys would do that to her. Why did he do this to Hunter? He could've sought a restraining order or something against Hunter, he didn't have to kill Hayley to teach him a lesson. Occasionally, I'd see Rhys around town, and I wanted so badly to storm up to him and demand to know the truth. I knew that I couldn't though. I didn't need a criminal charge brought against me. Instead, I just did whatever Hunter needed me to, which was really nothing.

CHAPTER 59

"Am I speaking with Ethan Charlton?" the unfamiliar voice on the other end of the phone asks.

Puzzled, I answer that I was. I had no clue who this person was. The number was unfamiliar.

"It's Jerry McLaren. I'm the lawyer representing Hunter Woods," he says.

My heart drops.

"Is he okay?" is all I ask.

"He will be. Look, I need you to come in for a meeting with Hunter and I. There's been a development in his case, and he has agreed to have a support person with him when I deliver this news. Can you come in at 10:00am?"

I check my watch. I'm meant to be in a meeting for work at that time.

"What's the address?"

An hour later, Jerry is leading me to a room at the back of the police headquarters. It was a strange place to meet but there must've been a reason. I enter the room, and Hunter is sitting there in his orange jumpsuit. He was slouching in the chair. Whatever this was mustn't be good. He looked like a man who had lost hope. It takes a moment before he realises I've entered the room. He looks up and breathes out a sigh of relief.

"Thank god. Do you know what's going on?" he asks desperately before running his hands through his hair.

I shake my head. "I just got asked to come in here and that there has been a development in your case."

"Yeah, they asked if I'd like a support person and I asked for you," he answers quietly.

I clap him on the back, trying an old school trick to calm him down. "We'll deal with whatever this is. Maybe there's new evidence?"

"You can say that again," Jerry interrupts as he enters the room. He places his briefcase on the table before starting to pace back and forth, like he's trying to find the right words to say. "Never in my career has this happened," he begins. "I didn't even think shit like this happened, but it has."

Hunter and I share a puzzled look between us. Eventually Jerry stops pacing and leans his hands on the back of the chair opposite Hunter.

"Hunter, I want you to know that I really did believe in you," he begins and I see Hunter's jaw drop. Jerry was about to deliver the final blow. I could sense it. We had run out of time. Hunter was going to jail for life.

"But I will no longer be defending you," Jerry says, and I hear Hunter gasp.

Jerry really was Hunter's last chance at beating this and now he was dropping him.

"What? Why" I demand.

"Let me finish," Jerry says putting his hands up to settle us. "There has been a wider operation going on that I had no knowledge of and the team responsible is ready to bring it to a close. We were basically strung along so that everyone assumed justice was being served and that a murderer was being sentenced, which is also why they kept pushing your court date out. Hunter, I've always hoped I'd be able to say this to you and now I can. Your case has just been dismissed," he almost chuckles like a madman. "It's all over, you're a free man."

"Wait, what? What do you mean?" Hunter and I both ask at the same time.

"Well, it's very hard to charge someone with murder when the person you allegedly murdered is not actually dead," Jerry responds, rubbing his forehead.

Hunter's head snaps up at Jerry's words. *What the fuck?* Something was definitely going on. A knock comes at the door and Jerry signals for them to come in. A tall gentleman enters the room first followed by another person. The room starts spinning and I almost want to throw up.

"Hayley," Hunter gasps as she walks slowly into the room. She looks like a deer caught in headlights. There are tears in her eyes but it's definitely her. She was small to begin with but now she looked like a shell of her former self.

"What have they done to you?" Hunter's voice is strained as he takes in the love of his life. He's trying hard to hold back tears. Even I want to cry.

Hayley looks up at Jerry and he nods. Slowly, she walks towards Hunter and reaches out to touch his face.

CHAPTER 60

Her hand is smooth and warm, just like I remembered. I want to embrace her, but I'm frozen in place. *Was this a dream?* She strokes my cheek, taking in my whole face as though she were trying to memorise me.

She then places both of her hands on my chest and looks up at me, her beautiful brown eyes beaming. I let a tear escape which she quickly wipes away.

"Hunter, you're going to be okay." Her voice breaks as she repeats the same words I said to her as she lay dying in my arms. It's all it takes for me to fold her into my arms. I hold onto her tightly, taking in her scent and the warmth of her body.

"You were dead," I mumble into her hair. "I thought I'd lost you."

"Hayley," I hear Ethan whisper. I had forgotten there were other people in the room.

Hayley breaks away from me, much to my disappointment. I only just got her back and there was no chance I was letting her go again.

"It's okay, Ethan. It's really me, I'm here." She holds her hand out to him, and he cautiously walks over and takes her hand.

"You're alive." Ethan's voice breaks as he fights back tears. He looks at me. "Hunter, she's alive."

Ethan starts to chuckle before he breaks down properly, the emotions consuming him. Hayley pulls him into an embrace, wrapping one arm around Ethan and one arm around me. He stays for several moments before clearing his throat and stepping away. "Oh my god." He takes a seat in one of the chairs and hangs his head in his hands.

I hold Hayley out at arm's length. Her eyes are all puffy from crying but she's still the same. The love of my life was still in there.

"Let's get started, shall we?" Jerry interrupts our reunion. He shares a glance with the tall gentleman who then starts talking.

"Detective Brown from the Major Crimes Division." He was the one who entered the room before Hayley. He had tired eyes, like he hadn't slept in days. He wasn't wearing a wedding band so I could only assume he was married to the job. His jacket was faded but I could just make out the word 'police' on the pocket.

"Please." Detective Brown motions for us to sit down.

Like glue, Hayley does not leave my side. She nearly sits on me, she's that close, and it takes everything in my power not to pull her onto my lap and continue to hold her. Now that she was in fact alive, I never want to let her go. Instead, she takes my hand and squeezes it.

"Hunter, formally, your case has indeed been dismissed because the person whom you were charged with killing is miraculously still alive." There is no amusement in Detective Brown's voice which means he knew all along that she was alive. "Hayley has been part of a wider police operation as we've been closing in on notorious fraudster and—due to the events that took place at your house, Hayley—attempted murderer, Rhys Centino."

My jaw drops and I feel Hayley cower at the words Detective Brown has just said. I squeeze her hand tighter and shuffle closer to her. She's starting to shake so I wrap my arm around her. I look at Ethan who's looking just as shocked as I am.

"So, we made Hayley disappear," Detective Brown continues. "In order to really nail Rhys, we needed him to crack. So, when we heard there had been a domestic incident at Hayley's residence, we swooped on the opportunity. Paramedics made it seem as though they were unable to save her when in fact, she was just unconscious."

My mind becomes flooded with images of Hayley from that day. She looked somewhat peaceful as her eyes slowly shut as she began to drift away, and I had honestly thought I'd lost her. I couldn't stop the bleeding and Rhys—what he did was absolutely fucked. There's no other way to put it.

"And with usual protocol, no one is allowed to touch the dead. Especially one that had been murdered. Don't get me wrong, Hayley is still a victim here. She was still very much shot and had very serious injuries, but she has, as you can see, recovered, somewhat."

"So, Rhys tried to kill you?" Ethan looks at Hayley, shocked.

"Rhys tried to kill Hunter," she answers quickly, her face and voice stone cold. "He then pinned my 'murder' on Hunter. Who were they going to believe when the only eyewitness was dead?"

"It took longer than we had hoped to have everything prepared to bring Rhys up on charges as we wanted to nail him on every piece of evidence we had," Detective Brown interrupts. "We have a secret weapon though that only Hayley knows about, and she is not to disclose it to any of you," he says sternly.

"Couldn't Hayley's statement alone have been sufficient for you?" Ethan demands. "Why put Hunter and Hayley through all of this bullshit?"

"It's okay, Ethan," Hayley's voice is soothing. "Why get him on one thing, when they could get him for all the bad things he had done? He was a bad person. A very bad person. He will be going to jail for the rest of his life, not just 25 years or whatever they claim *life* means. I knew that Hunter would be able to deal with this." She turns to look at me. "I knew you were strong enough. I knew you could do it. Detective Brown asked me to give him six months to get his ducks in a row," her voice changes as she continues, "after all the shit you put me through, Hunter, I was still angry so I agreed to do it."

I wince at her words and her face drops. It made sense why she did what she did. It forced me to grow up and hopefully be the man she once fell in love with.

"Hunter, you will be compensated for the time you spent in jail." Detective Brown brings me back to the present. I would be walking freely soon, and it was all because of Hayley. She was the reason I was there in the first place, but I had to overlook that. I put her through months, years even, of hell.

"But right now, Hayley, you need to go back to the safe house until Rhys goes to trial. We haven't come this far for someone to see you. You will be a key witness to his crimes. Your testimony will be the final nail in his coffin."

"Where do I go?" I choke out, hoping he doesn't say that I'd need to go back to the remand centre until Rhys goes to trial too, in order to keep up the act. But knowing Hayley was alive, I would stay in there if it meant I got to see her again.

Detective Brown looks at Hayley and she nods.

"You will be able to stay with Hayley if you want to. Otherwise, a separate safe house will be sourced. As far as everyone knows, you're still locked away. And you," Brown turns to Ethan, "seeing as you have been privy to this conversation, we will also be recommending you go to a safe house for the time being. Rhys has other contacts out there and we hope to nail all of them with this one operation. If they get wind of this, they'll turn into ghosts. I understand you have a wife and a child?"

Ethan nods. "We've actually separated." He drops his head.

"What?" Hayley's eyes go wide as she turns to Ethan.

"She didn't believe that Hunter was innocent, and it caused a lot of fights, so we decided to separate until the trial was over." Ethan gave me a weak smile.

I knew they had separated due to this case. It hurt knowing that Kate thought I was capable of murder. I had caused so much pain. If I had just left Hayley alone, we wouldn't have been in this mess. But then if I had, I wouldn't have her back in my arms now. If I just behaved liked a normal person, a normal boyfriend, I never would've lost her in the first place either. I should've leaned on Ethan when I started to get scared, but I didn't and now look what I'd done to him and Kate. I hung my head in shame.

Hayley starts crying but before I can comfort her, she jumps up.

"How much longer is this going to take, Detective?" She starts pacing the room. "I've been waiting so patiently and am drip fed news every couple of days. You're ruining our lives by locking us away." She looks between Ethan and I, like she was hoping one of us would offer a better solution. She was scared though. Scared of whatever could come of this case and the possibility that Rhys could be found innocent or the danger she would be facing if one of his accomplices went on the run. I wondered how much questioning she went through to try and get the truth about Rhys. She would've had to go through their entire life together for detectives to pick at little plot holes. She clearly had no idea what Rhys was doing behind her back.

"Just a little bit longer." Detective Brown tries to calm her, but she makes a move towards the door.

"That's all you ever say!" she spits out. I don't think I've ever seen her like this. Maybe once, at the pier. I shake away the memory.

"Just a little bit longer!" she continues. "I'm sick of hearing that. I've been locked away this whole time while you sort your shit out. The people I love think I'm dead! Look what it did to Ethan and his wife, they have a child! Look at Hunter, he's spent all that time in jail! And my mum, hasn't she been through enough? I want to see my mum, now!" she demands and goes to yank the door open. Before she can turn the handle, Detective Brown grabs her arm and she cries out. I immediately jump to her defence. Ethan pushes the detective's arm off Hayley, and I snatch her quickly into my arms, copping her flying fists as she struggles to break free. As small as she was, she had a lot of power. I pick her up and walk her to the corner of the room where I place her down gently. She's trying to catch her breath. I can see the frustration all over her face.

"I just want this over with," she whispers as the tears stream down her face.

The damage that this whole ordeal had done to her was evident. The strong-minded girl I fell in love with was replaced by a skittish, scared girl. She knew the truth though and she knew exactly what Rhys was capable of. Who knew what else Detective Brown had shared of Rhys' dark past. I would be scared too.

"I know Hayley, but you need to remain calm. We will leave soon, and you can go home." I try to settle her down.

"I don't have a home," she sobs into her hands. "I married a murderer. Hunter, he tried to kill you. I'm so sorry," she whispers.

"You have nothing to be sorry for." I wrap her in my arms and turn back around to face Detective Brown. Ethan is now standing beside him, his eyes going between Hayley and I and the detective. While I know that probably wasn't Detective Brown's intention—he's put months, maybe even years into building this case against Rhys—I still didn't want him to touch Hayley again. All he does is sigh at her outburst. I'm guessing she wasn't the first witness to behave in this way. He would've dealt with plenty in his career.

"What's the next step, Detective?" I ask calmly, trying to move forward with the conversation so I could get Hayley away from him.

"You will all be escorted out of this building and to your safe house. Ethan, you and Detective Randall, who's just outside, will travel to your house to get your wife and child," he instructs.

"What do I tell my family? I can't just up and leave. They'll want to know if everything's okay with my daughter," Ethan asks. There's a slight bit of annoyance in his voice.

"Your cover will be going on last minute vacation to get away from the media hype surrounding this case. You can call your parents and tell them that's what you're doing. We need to make it look legitimate. Once a criminal such as Rhys or his accomplices get wind of even the smallest hint that they're being investigated, they will vanish. I've not spent this long on this case to ruin it now," Detective Brown explains to Ethan.

I understand what he's saying. It's really just for their safety, but it would be hard to convince Kate of that.

"We expect to bring charges against Rhys in the next several weeks. Once the charges have been laid, he will be taken into custody, along with his accomplices. We believe they'll all be within the same vicinity soon, so once we have them all, Ethan, you and your family will be released. Hunter, Hayley, you will stay hidden until the case goes to trial."

Hayley sighs beside me. "Can I at least call my mum now? She'll want to know why the case against Hunter has suddenly stopped progressing."

Detective Brown considers her proposal for a moment, and I can almost see the clogs ticking in his brain. He looks tense at the same time too, like he wanted us to get moving straight away to avoid any risk of Hayley being seen.

"Sit tight, Hayley. The more people who know you're alive means more people are at risk. Things can get messy," he says evenly.

I see her face drop. For a second, she had hope. She nods and shrinks away from him, defeated.

"So, can we go to the safe house now?" I ask, wanting Hayley to be safe again. "I think we could all use some rest."

"Yes, I'll be taking you and Hayley to the safe house. Ethan, you can drive back home and Detective Randle will follow you there." Detective Brown points to a man who had just come into view through the small window in the door. "I'll just alert the team to do a final security check, and we'll get moving." He leaves the room.

Hayley takes a deep breath beside me and presses the palms of her hands against her eyes. She looks worse than when she first entered the room.

"This is where I will be leaving you, Mr Woods." Jerry gets up off his chair. I almost forgot he was there. "You don't need me anymore," he says.

"Thanks for everything, Jerry. I really appreciate it," I say sincerely. For a while there, Jerry was all I had until Ethan agreed to be my character witness. "Can you help Hayley in any way?" I ask.

Jerry laughs. "I wish, but it looks like that's already sorted out. Rhys will source his own defence and as entertaining as I might find it, I will not be defending a guilty man."

"You'd make a fortune though." Hayley's voice is small.

Jerry laughs again. "Hunter told me about you. You're still a firecracker!" He reaches for his briefcase and walks towards the door. He stops and turns back to us. "If you need advice on what you might be in for now that you'll be part of the prosecution's case, give me a call on this number." He scrawls a number on a piece of paper and Ethan, closest to him, takes it.

"Thank you," I reply as I shake his hand, and Ethan does the same before Jerry leaves the room.

Once the door is shut and it's just the three of us, I wrap Hayley back in my arms.

"I can't believe you're alive," I breathe into her hair. I notice Ethan standing awkwardly behind her and motion him forward. "Get in here, Ethan."

He joins in, wrapping his arms around Hayley and somewhat around me. I don't know how long we stand like this for but long enough that Hayley's breathing evens out.

I jump when the door opens, and I try to shield Hayley away from whatever is coming. Detective Brown has returned along with the man who I assumed was Detective Randall.

"This is Detective Randall," he says, confirming my suspicions. I looked at the man. He did not look like someone I wanted to mess with. He had a shaven head and dark blue eyes. He was smaller than Detective Brown but had a Jason Statham vibe. He looked dangerous.

"Right, Ethan, let's get going." Detective Randle beckons for him to follow.

Ethan turns to look at Hayley and me. He reaches for her hand and squeezes it before patting me on the arm. "See you soon," he says and follows the detective out the door.

"Let's get going, you two," Detective Brown says.

I take Hayley's hand and lead her out the door behind him.

"You're a free man now, Hunter." Hayley smiles weakly at me.

Chapter 61

The safe house is your average family home on a normal family street in the middle of suburbia. I actually didn't know this part of town existed. I had never been here before. It looked like all the other homes on the street. Some sort of timber exterior in neutral shades, a front garden and a small porch. I wasn't a builder so I really had no clue how else to describe the place. I guess it was picked as it didn't draw attention by being over-elaborate or too run down. Detective Brown pulls the car into the garage and shuts the roller door before letting us out of the car. Hayley's face immediately drops. You could tell she was disappointed to be back.

We follow Detective Brown through the internal access door after he's entered a code into the lock pad. I'm greeted to an open plan living, dining and kitchen area. It was styled nicely, similarly to what my mum probably would've done. The couch looked comfortable. The TV was huge and the kitchen had nearly every appliance you could want sitting under the island bench. It actually looked like the kitchen had never been touched but I knew Hayley was a clean freak, so she was probably just keeping it tidy seeing as she had nothing else to do. Hayley points out which room is hers. Then she points out which room I can have. I feel my face drop that she didn't ask me to stay in her room but then I have to remember everything that she has been through. She will probably need some space still. I couldn't assume that she'd want me with her immediately, or at all. She sits on the couch while I sit at the table and listen to Detective Brown as he goes through some of the rules of the safe house. Most are pretty standard safety measures like keeping noise to a minimum, not approaching the door if someone knocks, leaving all windows and shutters closed, that kind of thing. He also puts forward a document outlining the compensation on offer for my time in the remand facility and suggests I take some time to read it and think it through. By the time he's finished explaining it all, an alarm goes off. Hayley doesn't seem panicked by it but it sure scared me. It sent my mind straight back to my time in remand and how long it took me to get used to the different alarms.

"Don't worry," Detective Brown reassures me. "That's just Detective Randle arriving with Ethan and Kate."

Hayley jumps off the couch in anticipation and I go and stand with her. There's excitement on her face as she prepares to see her best friend for the first time in months. I can hear Kate's voice floating through the safe house before coming into view.

Kate takes one look at me and one look at Hayley.

"What a shit show," she mutters as she adjusts the baby capsule she was carrying in one hand and storms past us into an empty room.

Hayley's face drops as she watches Kate walk straight past her. I didn't care so much. Kate thought I was guilty and a part of me was hurt that she honestly thought I'd do something like this that I didn't care if she didn't speak to me ever again. I cared how she treated Hayley though.

"Just give her some time," Ethan says calmly. He sighs heavily as he collapses into an armchair across from where Hayley is standing.

Hayley slumps back down on the couch whilst Detective Brown does another run through of the rules for Ethan. I see Detective Randall in the corner talking in a hushed voice on the phone.

"All sorted?" Detective Brown asks as Randall finishes his phone call, nodding in response. "Hayley, after many discussions with our team, unfortunately we're not prepared to compromise this case by allowing you to speak to your mother. I do hope you understand, Hayley. We've come too far to lose it all now. I really do mean it when I say not much longer." He follows Detective Randall back out the internal access door and the door locks mechanically.

You could see Hayley was trying to show that she wasn't affected by his words but once she started fidgeting, I could see it was her way of masking her true emotions. God, he was so damn brutal with her sometimes. He really needed to work on his delivery. He builds her up only to bring her down. I want to comfort her but I'm worried I'll suffocate her, so I move to sit at the other end of the couch. I lean my forearms on my knees and look at Ethan, unsure of what to do or say next. He pulls a face, almost reading my thoughts.

Hayley picks up on our silence. "Please stop tiptoeing around me," she announces to Ethan and me. "I'm fine, I'm just frustrated. I've been alone for a while. You try being locked away and unable to see anyone or do anything—" She stops her rant when her eyes land on me. "I'm sorry, Hunter. That was really insensitive of me. Of course you know."

"I don't want you to pity me, Hayley. If I was an outsider, I probably would've thought I'd done it too." I hang my head.

"I just, I'm just—" Ethan tries to start as he gets off the couch. "I don't even know what to say, Hayls. I'm just so happy that you're alive."

"I'm not a ghost, Ethan." She offers her hand out and he takes it, tears forming in his eyes. "Sit with me," she says to him. He collapses on the couch next to her and starts crying big heavy sobs. I feel awkward just sitting there watching so I turn to the kitchen for a drink. It felt so good to be able to do whatever I wanted, whenever I wanted. I wasn't scared for my life anymore. I could finally relax.

When Ethan finally pulls himself together, he gets up off the couch. "Anyone want some lunch?" he asks as he heads towards me and starts opening cupboards.

CHAPTER 62

After lunch, Hayley excuses herself and goes to lie down.

"Let's go check out the rooms," I suggest to Hunter. "Not sure Kate is in the mood for company right now, so I'll leave her alone for a bit."

Hunter nods and I follow him into his room. I watch as he flops onto one side of the bed and rubs his hands over his face. He was still in his orange jumpsuit.

"What the absolute fuck?" he mutters. "What a rollercoaster of a day."

"She's okay, Hunter. Hayley's okay." I sit on the edge of the bed trying to reassure him.

"And you—" Hunter sits up. "—You believed in me. When no one else did." I can see the tears he's trying to choke back. "I can't tell you what that means to me."

I shake my head. "Don't start, Hunter." I was not one to cry and I felt like I'd cried a whole lifetime of tears in several hours. I didn't want to get dragged into another sob fest. It gave me a headache.

"You might lose Kate over this," Hunter whispers.

Just like Hayley had all those times before, I had put Hunter first too. I really hoped that it didn't affect Kate and I long term. She really was the love of my life, and I wanted to share everything with her so I had to be patient now and follow whatever cues she gave me to reconcile. He and Kate always had a sibling-type relationship where they bickered constantly, but deep down they had love for one another. I was really lucky for that. She would come around and I knew that I needed to put Hunter's mind at ease.

"She'll come around, Hunter. I know it. It's all so fresh in her mind, it's probably really hard for her to comprehend and now that Hayley's actually alive, she just needs to process it all," I try to reassure him whilst also defending Kate at the same time.

"Thank you, Ethan." His smile is weak, and I can see the fine lines that had started to form around his eyes.

"We'll get through this Hunter, like we always do," I try to calm him down. He had been through such an ordeal. Yes, he acted odd, but he was on the path to prison. That's no holiday. "Why don't you get out of that damn thing?" I say referring to his jumpsuit.

"I'll burn the damn thing, I swear." He gets up and follows me to the wardrobe.

Much to our surprise it's got men's clothing in it. They must've been planning this for a while. Or Hayley asked for him to stay with her. Hunter was also coming straight from the remand facility. Who knew where the rest of his belongings were? I watch as he pulls out some jeans and a fresh white shirt. Then he starts pulling off the jumpsuit.

"Whoa! What are you doing, dude? Just wait until I turn around!" I laugh.

"Mate, I've been locked away and treated like a criminal. I couldn't care less if you see me in my underwear. I've had complete strangers see me in less."

His admission stuns me and makes my heart pang. Jail was certainly not on my bingo card for any of us.

"Hey." He grabs my shoulder after he finishes getting dressed. "It could be worse. I could be in there for the rest of my life and Hayley could still be dead. But I'm out and she's alive." He takes a moment to compose himself. "They were all probably jealous of my incredibly good looks anyway."

There's the old Hunter. The one I hadn't seen since high school.

"Still so humble?" I laugh.

His face drops and I can almost tell what he's thinking.

"You need to give her time, Hunter. I have no idea what frame of mind she's in but give her time. You hurt her, and here she is, still saving you."

"Do you think she'll ever forgive me? After everything I put her through?"

I think for a moment. When they were good, they were so good. Maybe one day they could be good together again. "You have a lot of work to do, I think. You need to be honest with her, really honest. Then she might see that you just hit a speed bump."

He grabs a hoodie and puts it over his head.

"We hit a fucking mountain," he mutters.

I can see he's a bit stuck on what to do next. I know he's probably dying to check on Hayley.

"Go and see her," I encourage him. "You two have a lot to talk about".

CHAPTER 63

I'm struggling to rest with the thought of Hunter being so close to me. I almost want to leave my room to find him, even if it's just to be around him and Ethan while they talked. I finally had someone to talk to.

A light knock at the door startles me. It would take some time getting used to that again.

I'm surprised when Hunter pokes his head around the door. "Can I come in?" he says.

"Sure," I gulp. This would be the first time we've been alone together in years. What do we do? What are we meant to talk about?

Hunter sits on the edge of the bed. I can see how hard this is for him. He wants to be close to me, but he doesn't know how. Hell, I don't even know what I want. I'd spent the last six months thinking about the moment I'd be able to see him again. Our fight at the pier was intense. I basically told him to follow through with his suicide attempt. Who even says something like that? I guess I was so desperate to get through to him that I didn't care. But far out, I cared. Rhys may have had a point. I just wanted Hunter to be happy. Whether that was with me or someone else. I just couldn't handle the games anymore. We had come too far. The disappearing acts were childish and unsupportive. I could've really used him when Dad died. He would've known exactly what to do. Hunter would let me wake him up in the middle of the night just because I couldn't sleep, only for me to throw myself at him. As time began to pass after Dad died, Rhys grew less tolerant of my talking about him. He wanted me to just move on. I had a bad dream one night and I woke Rhys up as I just wanted to talk about it, but he told me I was being silly and childish and to go back to sleep. How had I not seen these traits in Rhys from the start? At the time, I just thought he was really tired from work. How did I get so deep as to marry this psychopath? Why didn't I just stick it out and wait for Hunter to come around? *Because he never would have*, the voice of reason appears. We needed something catastrophic to bring us back together. What would people say about me? I ended up with the guy that my husband tried to convince the world had killed me. Did I even want to deal with that? Or was I just looking for closeness after being alone for so long? I didn't really know what it was like to be alone until now. I'd had

Hunter for so long and then I met Rhys. I was never alone for long periods of time. Hunter was familiar. He was a constant in this nightmare. Hunter was safe. Was he? Wasn't he? Did I even want that? God, my behaviour today made it seem like I wanted him. I needed to be careful.

We sit in silence until I work up the courage to speak. "Where were you?" I ask.

CHAPTER 64

"Where were you?" Her voice is soft and tired.

I bite my lip. This was my time to be truthful. This could win her back. If I was just honest with her, at least she can then make a fully informed decision as to whether or not she wanted to get back with me. We could start fresh. It was time to come clean, no matter the consequences.

I patted my pockets before realising the slip of paper I was looking for was still in my jumpsuit in the room next door. I get up off the bed.

"What are you doing?" she asks quietly, and I turn to look at her.

"I need to get something from my room. I'll be right back."

I quietly knock on my door in case Ethan was napping, which he was. I tiptoe over to the jumpsuit and take the whole thing with me so I wouldn't wake him with the ruffling of paper and clothing. I walk back into Hayley's room, shutting the door behind me. She's still sitting where I left her. She stares at me wide-eyed in disbelief that I was finally going to tell her the truth. I take a deep breath. This was going to be hard but after what she'd been through, not just with Rhys but with me over the entire course of our relationship, she deserved to know why I did what I did. She deserved to know why I left her so many times only to come crawling back and mess up all the progress she had made in trying to build a life for herself.

"I wrote this, Hayley." I show her the paper. "I had hoped to convince someone to let me visit your grave and I was going to tell you everything. Better late than never I guess," I say half-heartedly. "So, if it's okay, I'd like to read this to you. I spent a lot of time writing it."

Hayley pats the spot next to her on the bed but instead I sit at the foot of the bed. I needed to have some distance from her as I read my letter out to her.

I take a deep breath. "I'm here. I have no idea how I managed it, but I guess they granted me one last wish? I'm in an orange jumpsuit that doesn't fit me properly and the guys here all look at me funny. I'm the only guy my age here. I'm scared, Hayley." She hangs her head on hearing my admission. "I'm so scared of what my future holds. I cannot believe how fucked up this whole situation is. And now you're gone. What I wouldn't do to take your place—" I stop to wipe my eyes, and she crawls forward to sit closer to me. She hesitates before placing her hand on my knee. I clear my throat and continue, "I have no right to be here but at the same time, I have every right to be here because I owe you an explanation. It's time I finally came clean. I'm just sorry it took you dying for me to open up." I glance up to watch her expression and she gives me a reassuring smile. "It's true, Hayley. I did leave you because I wanted a break from us. I wanted to see if there was a better life out there for me. I felt like I was stuck and going nowhere. I hated uni and I struggled to meet new people. I was out of my comfort zone whereas you were flourishing. I felt that it was too good to be true to marry your high school sweetheart. When I told my brother about how I felt, he convinced me to at least see what single adult life was like. Stupidly, I followed his advice. He told me where to go and said he could help me just disappear. I wanted to tell you so many times where my head was at, but I didn't want to lose you. It made me sick to my stomach when I decided to take Trace up on his offer and just disappear for a week or two but as you know, I went for much longer. I knew how you felt about me, and I was adamant that you'd forgive me when I first did it. I loved you and I loved spending time with you, but I just couldn't be the person you wanted me to be. So, I kept leaving, only to realise how much I loved you and how much I missed you, so I'd come back. Obviously, I could stay away for long periods of time and sometimes, not very long at all. Alcohol was my best friend during those times—" She has tears in her eyes as I read, "—My parents just gave me a credit card and didn't even care what I did or how much I spent. I went about living my life, but without you. I tried to date other girls, but it never stuck. They just weren't you. I did sleep with a few girls over the time I was away." She scoffs lightly at this. "I know I said I didn't, and I promised that I didn't, but I lied. Again. I don't know why I kept lying. It just made it easier. I also don't know why I couldn't be upfront and just tell you everything. I kept it a secret and made it a game. I don't know why. I probably thought it spiced up our relationship. It kept things interesting. Well, it kept things interesting for me, not you. I can't believe I was such a dick. Hayley, I'm going to do right by you and keep trying to clear my name. I didn't kill you. Only you, Rhys, and I know that. I just need to figure out a way to make Rhys talk because I didn't kill you and you didn't kill yourself."

"You said you loved me—past tense," she mumbles. "Do you not love me anymore? After what I did to you?"

"No, Hayley, not at all." She lets me wrap my arms around her. "Hayley, I will always love you. It will always be you. I'm just sorry it took me so long to sort my shit out. We could've avoided all of this…" I rest my forehead against hers.

"Hunter, I'm done." She pulls away and my heart sinks, but she holds her hand up to stop me from speaking. "I'm done with what happened in the past. All it causes is heartache, a pit in my stomach, and regret."

"What parts do you regret?" I ask before I can stop myself.

"A lot of things, Hunter. I often think of the 'what ifs' but what's the point?" She shakes her head. "I don't understand how I feel about you, Hunter, but right now I just want to be close to someone. I really was alone for six months so having other humans around has been really nice." She leans away from me. "And that's not fair to you at all because it's misleading and you and I don't do casual. It never works."

I understood her, but at the same time I wanted to at least try and see if we could be something. I would stay away if that's what she wanted though. I try desperately to keep my expression neutral.

"For what it's worth, Hunter," she continues, "I am sorry that you got wrapped up in Rhys' bullshit and had to go to that terrible place. I hope, one day, you'll forgive me."

"I have nothing to forgive you for, Hayley," I say quickly. "What you did—me going to jail—was out of your control. I can see that there was a bigger plan in place to get Rhys. I really get it. I did a lot of personal growth in jail. It was fucking harrowing, and I didn't think I'd ever have a future again, but then you appeared. I had hope. I will be here for you however you want me to be, even if that means that after this is all over, you choose to go off on your own."

"Do you really think you've changed, Hunter?" she asks. "Or will I regret letting you back into my life?"

"I would do anything to be back in your life, in whatever way you want me to be," I try to reassure her. "I'll respect your decision this time even if you don't want me in your life at all." It pains me to say these words, but I want her to hear how serious I was this time around.

She gets up off the bed and walks over to the window frame, pushing open the curtains to reveal a brick wall. She chuckles. I wonder how many times she had opened the curtains, wondering if a view would ever appear.

"You don't want me," she laughs again. "I'm not the girl you fell in love with."

"But you are," I answer quickly.

"I'm not!" she snaps, spinning around to face me. I was shocked by her sudden outburst. "Look at me! I can't even remember the last decent meal I ate. I feel like I haven't seen the sun in months. I don't even know what fresh air smells like anymore. And look!" She unbuttons her shirt hastily, exposing her chest and bra. "Look!" she demands again as she storms towards me pointing at the scar on her chest.

I gasp. I didn't realise how big of a scar a bullet would leave. It's raised and pink around the edges and it looked like it still caused her pain, even after all this time.

"See!" she cries. "Even you think it's hideous! How can I ever return to a normal me?"

I get up slowly and walk towards her, but she backs away until she's against the wall. Without saying anything, I calmly reach for her shirt and button it back up. This whole situation had damaged her so much. She needed help but instead she was locked in here with her thoughts, all alone. Hayley and I really were alike, as much as she probably wouldn't admit it. We'd both gone through this alone.

"Hayley," I held her face in my hands. "You could be completely disfigured, and I'd still love you. You're beautiful inside and out. It's just a scar. It'll disappear. We'll do whatever it takes to get you back to your old self. I will help you—just like you tried to help me—because I love you, Hayley."

She stretches up quickly, pressing her lips to mine. I feel like fireworks are going off inside me. She feels exactly the same way as when I first kissed her in high school. Her lips fit mine perfectly. Her hands twist in my hair, pulling me down to her. I wrap my arms around her and for the first time, notice that I could feel more bone than her usually toned body. I ignore it though. I would help her to get on track. She needed me.

CHAPTER 65

I gasp. I can't believe I just kissed him. I look down shyly.

"I'm sorry," I whisper. "I don't know where that came from."

"Don't be sorry." He brushes a strand of hair behind my ear.

"I'm not going to have sex with you, Hunter," I blurt out.

"I don't expect you to have sex with me now, or ever," he chuckles. "I'll never force that on you."

"I'm still married," I mumble.

"We'll get you a divorce," he answers without missing a beat.

"How?" I ask. "I'm stuck in this shithole until that bastard goes to trial." I can hardly look him in the eye. I was so embarrassed.

"We'll figure it out. Maybe we can call Jerry, and he can help research it while we're in here."

"How do you have an answer for everything?" I sigh, rubbing my forehead.

"Because I spent six months locked away where I had to grow up very quickly," he tries to laugh it off and that's when I finally look at him.

"I feel like I'm the one who owes you, Hunter. You nearly went to jail for life because of me." I move to sit back on the bed, but he stays where he is. "Do you want to talk about your time there?"

He shakes his head. I can see that it is hard for him to talk about. "Not today. Maybe one day." He turns away from me, clearly upset at even the thought of having to recount his experience.

I nod but I stay where I am. "I understand. I want you to trust me though, Hunter. I know you couldn't before. I didn't realise you were struggling so much. But I'm listening now, I promise."

"Thank you," he replies as he turns back around to face me and runs his hands through his hair. "Surprisingly, I think it changed me for the better."

"I doubt you'd be saying that if you were still in there."

"But then you wouldn't be here." I can see panic start to cross his face. "Wait, this is real right? I'm not dreaming this. You're here in front of me and I'm free?"

"Yes!" I jump up and close the space between us quickly, reaching out for him in the process. "Here, I'll pinch you so you'll know it's real."

He pulls me close and rests his forehead against mine as he takes several deep breaths.

"I'm here, Hunter. This is real. I'm alive. I didn't die but you did spend six months in a remand facility," I try to snap him back to reality. "I'm going to help you, like you said you'd help me."

Instinctively, our lips meet again, and I can feel him relax.

A knock at the door makes us jump apart, like we were scared to be seen together so quickly after all that had happened. Ethan pokes his head around the door.

"Kate's ready to talk to you," he says.

Chapter 66

I can see the hesitation in Hayley. She'd had enough of having to talk to people and needed a proper rest.

"Maybe this could wait until tomorrow," I suggest but Hayley shakes her head in protest.

"I just want to start tomorrow as a brand-new day," she says. "The people I care about most now know that I'm alive, and tomorrow we can start to move forward." She ruffles her hair and wipes under her eyes as though I hadn't just had my arms wrapped around her as I kissed her just a few minutes earlier. "But Hunter is coming with me and if she's not okay with that just yet then I can't see her. She owes him an apology too."

I love how much she is defending me. She's standing up for me, like she always has. Like she would've done when she continuously got back together with me. Now it was my turn to fight for her the way I should have back then.

Ethan looks stumped. I could almost guarantee that Kate didn't want to see me.

"Hold on," he says and then I hear him call out to her. "She wants Hunter to come as well."

I can hear Kate groan, and I feel the anger start to build. I was frustrated that she still couldn't believe that I was innocent.

"I need you to remain calm." Hayley notices how tense I am.

I let out the breath I'm holding. Any sentence she started with 'I need you' meant I was going to listen this time.

Ethan's head ducks back around the door. "Look, I'm not going to say she's thrilled with this. She has a lot of shit to work out in her mind, but don't worry Hunter, it's two against one, and there's living proof that you're not a murderer. She can't argue with that."

He too looked frustrated but we had to make this situation work. Who knows how long we would all be stuck in this small safe house.

Hayley takes a deep breath and follows Ethan out into the living room. Hesitantly, I follow her, staying close behind. Kate was less likely to have a go at me physically if Hayley was in front of me.

I couldn't remember the last time I saw Kate. I always tried to avoid her during my attempts to find Hayley. I only ever went to Ethan, hoping to clutch at the last remaining pieces of our friendship to get him to help me. Looking at Kate now, she looked tired and aged. I guess that's what having a child does to you, on top of the stress of thinking you'd lost your best friend and possibly your marriage.

Kate gasps at the sight of Hayley. She won't look at me though. Slowly, Kate gets out of her chair. "Hayley?" she breathes.

Begrudgingly, I let Hayley step out of my reach to hug Kate.

Kate almost collapses against Hayley as she sobs into her shoulder. I put my hand out to steady Hayley. She was so small now. Kate's eyes land on my hand and they dart up to my face. Her expression changes almost immediately.

"So, you didn't kill her?" Kate says coldly.

I want to reply with something snarky. *Clearly*, I didn't kill Hayley. She was standing right in front of her.

"No, I would never hurt her," I opt for instead.

Kate scoffs. "Bullshit! The emotional shit you put her through still caused pain, Hunter. You still hurt her. She has a bullet wound, I would presume?"

"I'm right here, Kate." Hayley draws Kate's attention back to her. "Rhys shot me—not Hunter," she says bluntly.

It was the first time I had heard Hayley be this open about what had happened.

Kate's eyes go wide and then she looks at me. "But you were acting so bizarrely. It made sense that you did it."

I want to hang my head in shame. As true as her words were, I don't think it would ever stop hurting when I heard what people thought I was capable of.

"Look," Hayley interrupts again. "I'm actually not supposed to talk about the case, and neither can Hunter, so that's all I can say. We're the only two witnesses in this case and they need to charge Rhys first before the truth can come out. All I'm going to tell you is that Hunter didn't do it. I was there, Kate. Believe me. Yes, Hunter was acting strange, so I understand why people would assume that's what happened. But it isn't. Only Hunter and I know what happened and we're both telling them the same story." She holds Kate at arm's length. "As if I would go to all of this trouble, stress and anxiety if Hunter had truly intended to kill me."

God, I loved her. Even in these trying times, she still knew exactly what to say.

Kate starts to cry again. "How are you talking so openly about this?"

"Because, Kate, it's not in my nature to frame an innocent person. Hunter's behaviour terrified me, yes—" I stiffen at her words. "—but never in a million years did I think he would do something like this. Deep down, you know that too."

Kate stares back at me and Ethan moves to comfort her.

"I nearly lost my relationship because I believed you were guilty, Hunter," she says and then looks at Ethan. "I nearly lost my family because of this."

"You haven't lost anything, Kate. I'm still here," Ethan replies as he pulls her face to his. I want to leave the room while they made amends, but I would stay out there as long as Hayley was. I didn't want Kate to get in Hayley's head and make her think she couldn't trust me.

"Are you going to make me say it?" Kate whispers to Ethan.

He has a smug look across his face. "I kind of think you should. At least to Hunter anyway. He's more deserving of it."

Trust Ethan to always have my back.

She sighs before looking at me. "I was wrong, Hunter, clearly. I'm sorry I doubted you, but can you blame me?"

I shake my head. I guess that was as close to an apology as I was ever going to get from her.

CHAPTER 67

"Look who finally decided to join the party," Hunter smirks. He was running his hands along all of the tools that Rhys had displayed neatly on his work bench.

"What do you want, Hunter?" I ask carefully. I had no idea what frame of mind he was in and was cautious that he could take anything I said in the wrong way.

I truly thought I had seen the last of him that night at the pier. I thought I had finally gotten through to him that what we had was over. I was emotionally drained and he was clearly unstable. I could only hope Ethan had dropped him to a hospital so he could get some help.

"Just thought I'd check in and see how the happy couple is." He was sounding crazier every time I saw him. I couldn't help but wonder if he was just pretending though like he was at the pier.

"We're doing swell, Hunter," Rhys snaps. I can see the frustration in his posture.

I almost want to scold Rhys. Now was not the time for anyone to be losing their cool with Hunter given the state he was in, but Rhys didn't know him like I did.

Hunter chuckles. "Guess I got under your skin quickly. It took Hayls about a year to work out how to deal with me."

"Well, here's hoping that I don't need to get to know you like Hayley used to," Rhys snaps again.

Hunter was clearly enjoying Rhys' reaction to him. "Ouch." Hunter grabs at his heart, pretending to be hurt. "Must be fun to be around him," he says to me.

"Hunter, what's wrong? Why are you here?" I ask again, trying to keep him focused.

"I was just checking in." He looks casually at his nails, like he has no idea how uncomfortable he's making everyone. "I thought it had been too long between visits. When was the last time I visited? Oh, that's right, at the pier?" He has a devilish grin on his face.

"What?" Rhys demands, his head whipping around to face me. My decision not to tell Rhys about the encounter at the pier was proving to be the wrong choice but I didn't want him to worry. I could handle this, and I didn't want Rhys to ruin his career by having to stay at home and babysit me.

Hunter thrives off of this revelation though. "Oh, you didn't tell your husband about me?" He walks towards me but I take a step back. "That's okay, I'll tell him for you."

"Hunter, stop it," I plead.

"No, go on, Hunter." Rhys's response surprises me. "Tell me all about it, seeing as my own wife couldn't. I want the truth! Are you sneaking around with him behind my back?" Rhys challenges me.

"No!" I shriek at the same time Hunter chuckles and says, "Maybe."

Great, he was trying to plant doubt in Rhys's mind. What was wrong with him? Why couldn't he just let me be happy?

"I think you were away or something, but I needed her and like she always does, she came running," Hunter taunts.

"Hunter, just stop!" I yell desperately. "Rhys, I'll tell you everything. He's twisting what happened." I rush towards Rhys but he steps away from me, his hands up in protest.

"That fact is that it happened, Hayley. That's what annoys me!" Rhys yells.

"Rhys, please," I try again as I reach for him but surprisingly, he slaps my hand away.

This seems to change something in Hunter.

"*Do not* speak to her that way." Hunter straightens himself up, a serious look creeping over his face.

"She is my wife, Hunter, and you won't leave her the fuck alone," Rhys shouts as he slams his hand on the table. "And you—" He points at me. "—you're lying to me! I know you said Hunter could do this. He can twist words but you said you'd always be truthful. Maybe you're the one who's been the problem the whole time? You're leading us both on. Only I was dumb enough to marry you."

"That's not true, Rhys," I plead again. I couldn't believe this was happening. How did this turn back on me?

"No, what's true is that you just cannot get over Hunter. Just admit it, you love it when he reappears. It sparks something inside you that I can't give you. I gave you diamonds and a roof over your head, and what has he given you? Huh? All he is is a window to the past."

"Rhys—" I let the tears fall. "Please stop saying all of these horrible things. They're not true!"

"I think you're crossing a line." Hunter steps in front of me, putting distance between me and my husband.

Rhys laughs. "Do you even hear yourself? You're the one that just shows up randomly! You're purposefully trying to ruin our lives, and you think it's funny. Yet, I'm the one crossing a line when I'm trying to get answers."

I see Hunter's posture change. He slouches as he can't argue with Rhys. Was this finally his turning point?

"I'm going to leave now," Hunter said. "Hayls, you've heard it from me so many times, but I am sorry."

Why did he suddenly choose now to change? God, it was like he had bipolar disorder or multiple personalities. Something medical had to explain his behaviour. Was there something that I had never picked up on before? He could be sweet one minute and then angry the next.

"Hunter, what's wrong? Are you okay? I think you need help." I try to wrap up the conversation so that he would leave and I could sort things out with Rhys. I made a mental note to talk to Ethan about Hunter's mental health later. Maybe Hunter really did need help, the medical kind. I shake the thought away so I could focus on the present. Rhys was my priority right now.

"No, Hayley! I'm not okay!" Hunter turns around briefly, like he was trying to conceal his emotions. "I'm losing my fucking mind, and no one seems to give a shit. Not you, not Ethan, and god knows my parents don't fucking care."

A flood of memories hit me, and I remembered how I would always run to his side to comfort him in these moments. But I couldn't do that anymore. And certainly not in front of Rhys. I shouldn't even be thinking about helping Hunter. He had clearly gotten in my head again.

"He's faking it," Rhys groans.

I shake my head. "I don't think he is this time, Rhys. He needs help. We need to get him help."

"*We* don't need to get him anything!" Rhys slams his hand down on the table again. "He's not our problem!" He storms away back towards to the house. I was actually surprised he'd left me alone with Hunter.

I look over at him. The desperation was written all over his face. He was clearly at rock bottom with no one to turn to and nowhere to go.

I walk over to him as he slumps against the wall of the shed. "We're going to get you help, okay Hunter? Everything is going to be okay," I try to soothe him without touching him.

"No, it's time I end this for all of us." I hear Rhys' voice come around the corner and I turn to look at him to argue.

"Get behind me, Hayley." Hunter jumps up off the floor, pushing me behind him.

That's when I notice the gun in Rhys's hand. My hand covers my mouth to block my scream, but nothing comes out anyway.

"I'm leaving, okay?" Hunter puts his hands up in defence. "There's no need to point that thing at anyone." His voice is shaking but he doesn't move.

"What are you doing, Rhys?" I finally managed to say as I try to push around Hunter.

"Everyone is so sick of Hunter's bullshit. It's time to make it all go away." There's a deranged look in Rhys' eyes. I was more scared of Rhys now than I had ever been of Hunter, who hadn't ever been violent towards me.

"What do you think killing me will do to Hayley?" Hunter asks, trying to mask the fear in his voice. "You're prepared to leave her all alone while you rot in jail for murder?"

Rhys scoffs as he scratches his head with the barrel of the gun like a mad man. "Yeah, right. No, I won't be rotting in jail." He slowly walks towards us, the gun now pointed at Hunter, who moves us backwards until we hit the wall of the shed. "Because I'll be right by her side as we live out the rest of our lives. Everyone knows how you feel about Hayley, Hunter. Everyone knows that you would do anything for her. Everyone knows that you have been harassing her over the last three years. Everyone knows that you can't live without her—so why live at all?"

"You're going to make it look like I killed myself?" Hunter asks. His voice shakes as he realises the position he's in.

It was almost like Rhys had thought this all through. It would almost be too easy. Hunter had really dug his own grave. Who would believe me? Rhys would twist my words, and it was his word against mine. He could even claim self-defence. Who could argue with the crazy behaviour Hunter had exhibited? Everyone knew what he had been like. No one would believe me.

Ethan's voice rings through my head as memories of the past come forward. *You need to get him out of here!*

I look for possible escape routes and think it would be harder for Rhys to shoot at a moving target. As I try to pull Hunter with me to run for cover, he lunges forward to tackle Rhys.

It feels like time slows down. The sudden pain in my chest, the blood coming through my shirt, the wave of disorientation. My vision, whilst blurring, could see Rhys staring in disbelief as Hunter races towards me as I fall.

Rhys stays where he is as he watches Hunter lower me to the ground and apply pressure to the wound. I had been shot. Rhys had shot me.

"Call an ambulance!" Hunter shouts at him. "You're okay, Hayls, you're going to be okay." I could see the fear on his face as he looked down at me. I'd never seen him so scared. "Stay with me!" he urges. "Call a fucking ambulance!" he shouts again at Rhys.

My eyes were getting heavy, the pain becoming too much. I watch as Rhys walks calmly towards us, forcing the gun in Hunter's hand as he tries to protest.

"What have you done, Hunter?" Rhys shouts. "What have you done to her?" he continues to exclaim as he pulls his phone out of his pocket and starts dialling. "You've killed her! I need to call an ambulance!"

CHAPTER 68

I jolt upright in bed, forcing the nightmare to end. This was standard for me now. Reliving the same scene every night that would startle me awake after only a couple of hours of sleep. I can feel the sweat soak through my clothes and so I did what I did nearly every night, I head for the shower. Sleep would not come again tonight unfortunately. I try to be as quiet as possible so as not to wake my friends. I couldn't believe that I finally had company, and after all this time it was Hunter who I wanted around during this whole ordeal. I couldn't distinguish if I kissed him by accident or on impulse. I needed to be very careful. Would it be so wrong to get back with Hunter though? He had made quite a mess of my life but maybe this was the turning point we both needed? I knew deep down that I would always care for Hunter. Hell, I would probably always love him. He was my first love. That had to count for something right?

I slowly turn on the shower and wait for the water to heat up when I hear a door open. I almost jump out of my skin, forgetting momentarily that I had people living with me now. I peek my head out the bathroom door and see Hunter stumble out of his room, rubbing his eyes.

"Oh, it's just you." He yawns. "You okay?" he asks.

"Yep, just showering," I answer.

"It's like three in the morning?" He yawns again.

"I'm very much aware of what time it is," I snap.

"Are you okay, Hayley?" He walks slowly towards me. "Talk to me, please," he whispers.

"No," is all I respond before I shut the door again.

⊱⋅⊰

After nearly half an hour in the shower, I finally get out. I wrap the towel around me, mentally scolding myself for not bringing a change of clothes in with me. I guess that's what happens when you spend so long alone. I peek my head out the bathroom door and sigh when I see Hunter with a cup of tea and a cup of coffee at the dining room table.

"I think you and I should talk," he says gently.

I take a deep breath. I knew this moment would come. I needed to sort my feelings out though. It hadn't even been a full day since Hunter came back into my life.

"I need to get changed," I mumble pathetically before walking quietly to my room.

I put on some shorts and a singlet. I catch sight of myself in the mirror and want to cry. My mind was playing tricks that the scar from the bullet was still gaping with blood. My mind instantly transports me back to that moment. The pain, my god, it was unbearable. I didn't want to die but I needed something to put an end to the white burning sensation. Those first few weeks felt like torture. So many random healthcare workers checking on my wound, and while they were making sure it was healing, I felt like I didn't have the right to my own body, they just demanded to see it whenever they wanted. I could hardly lift my arm above shoulder height. It was agony and the relentless thoughts that my husband was the one to cause me all this pain made me vomit on more than one occasion. The violent force of throwing up sent waves of pain through my body. I'd truly been to hell and back. I try to fight off the tears. I didn't want Hunter to worry. I thought I was starting to get over what had happened. Lord knows I've had plenty of time to come to peace with it. I slowly rubbed my hand over the raised scar, reassuring myself it was not gaping, it was healing and I was okay.

"Does it hurt?" His voice startles me.

"It's all in my head," I answer bluntly at his reflection in the mirror. "I'll be right with you."

He doesn't say anything further as he leaves the room. I shouldn't be so hard on him anymore. He was not the enemy for once. He was far from it.

I pull a cardigan on and meet him at the dining room table. He pushes my drink slowly towards me, like he was scared he'd do the wrong thing after the way I just treated him.

"It doesn't hurt so much anymore," I start, trying to make up for earlier. "It took a while to get over the sensitivity but then it healed as good as new. It will take time to stop looking so inflamed though. The doctors gave me some scar treatment stuff."

He nods silently but doesn't look up at me.

We both sit in silence, unsure where to even begin. It really hadn't been that long since this whole ordeal began. It wasn't like it had been years; it had only been six months.

"Hayley, I just want to set the record straight," Hunter begins. "I am so sorry. For all the bullshit I put you through. I honestly mean that this time. I've been forced to really reflect on my life choices while in remand and I truly do mean I'm sorry. I hope one day you'll be able to forgive me for what I did to you. If I wasn't so fucked up, we probably wouldn't be in this situation."

"Rhys was always a criminal though, Hunter. I don't think that would've changed," I try to explain. "Like I said yesterday, I'm done with the past. I just want to move on from it. There's no use going back saying things we would've done differently. We can't change any of it, no matter how much we might want to."

"I know, but I just don't think I can ever stop apologising." He hangs his head.

Now was my chance to ask one of the questions I had been dying to ask since that day. It was the one question I had been trying to work out how to ask politely and without offending him over the last six months. I really had no idea what frame of mind Hunter would be in when I saw him again, but he really seemed to have changed. If he told me the truth, maybe it would help me determine how I felt about him.

"Was it all an act, Hunter? Or were you, or are you still, having mental health problems?"

He looks a bit puzzled. "What do you mean?" he asks.

"The whole showing up randomly thing, the odd behaviour—" I start to list the things he had done. "The night at the pier?"

"Oh." His face drops and he stares at the table. He takes a deep breath before speaking again. "I don't know, Hayley. I thought it was funny in the beginning to be honest. I remember I was super random with you when we first met, and you seemed to find it charming then, but this time was different. To me, it was like a game of cat and mouse."

Again, I'm amazed at how honest he was being, and I just knew he was telling the truth. He had hit the nail on the head though.

"I did whatever I thought would grab your attention, but that night at the pier really changed something within me."

"And yet you still showed up at my house?" I ask as I try to understand his mind frame. "Why would you do that if something changed?"

He hangs his head again and runs his hands through his hair. "I don't know." He was getting frustrated now. "I don't know, Hayley. I just couldn't stay away regardless. I don't know. I didn't know how to move forward. Lord knows my parents never cared. I pissed Ethan off with what I did to you. I had no one to turn to. I trusted you and I just couldn't get through to you. I didn't know how to show you or tell you I needed help with how to get my life back on track. It was like I was stuck in time. Everyone else was moving on and growing up, except me."

"For someone who always claims to go after what he wants, when it really came down to it, you were nothing but talk." I don't mean for my words to come out so harshly, but they do, and I can see the pain all over Hunter's face.

"I know." He breaks into a big sob as he drops his face into his hands. "I'm so sorry. I fucked everything up, Hayley."

It breaks my heart to see him this way, but I also feel like a weight is slowly being lifted off me as I unravel each of Hunter's layers and get the answers I so desperately wanted. The old Hunter was still in there and I was determined to find him. He deserved a better life than this. I move out of my seat and hug him from behind until he clears his throat and moves to wipe his eyes. When I sit back down, he looks exhausted, and I remembered what time it was.

"Maybe you should go back to bed and try to rest," I offer seeing as I'm lost for words as to what to say after everything he'd told me.

"Is that all you have to say?" he asks carefully. "There's nothing else you want to know?"

I think about what he's asking me. He told me the truth about where he went every time he abandoned me. He told me the truth just now about why he acted the way he did. Was there really anything else I was desperate to know? If he hadn't left me, we would still be together and nothing would've changed.

"I'll always tell you whatever you want to know. I promise you that." He offers his pinkie finger out and I wrap my pinkie around his.

"I'm scared," I admit finally.

"Of what?" He reaches out and squeezes my hand. "You have nothing to be scared about. You're safe here."

"Not of Rhys. Of you—" His eyes widen at this. "I'm scared that you think I'm someone I'm not. I'm scared that it was you all along and I should've just waited. I'm scared that I won't fall for you again because I never stopped loving you. I'm scared of what people will think of me. I'm scared of the damage this has done to you. I'm just scared. Everything seems so uncertain right now..." The words come out of nowhere and I feel slightly embarrassed to have been so candid with him.

I can see Hunter trying to conceal a smile though. I couldn't imagine how it felt for him to hear those words after all this time and after everything he'd told me within the last 24 hours.

"So, do you understand why I'm trying to keep my distance?" I ask. "It's a lot to work through and I've been alone for so long by myself here, I don't want you to get the wrong idea or to think I'm using you."

"I don't care, Hayley." He moves towards me and kneels in front of me. "I just want to be a part of your life again, in any way that you want."

"So, if you slept in the same bed as me, if I cuddled into you, if we slept together, then after our time in this house is over and we can live normal lives and I went off on my own, you'd be okay with that?" I ask suspiciously.

"If that's what it came to." He looks away.

"Because it didn't work last time we ended things," I reply.

"I'm a different person now. I'm on a better path now. I had six months in a fucking jail cell to sort my life out," he says bluntly before pushing back up to a standing position. "I'm sorry, I don't mean to be so rude. I'm just frustrated. I don't know what it will take to make you believe that I really have changed but I want you to let me show you. You can then make that decision once this is all over. I'm asking for one more chance, Hayley. The ball is in your court now."

I sigh. I didn't know what I was waiting for either.

"Plus, I won you over once before in high school, I'm confident I can do it again." He smiles. "Properly this time though."

"What will people think?" I sigh again.

"Who gives a fuck what people think, Hayley?" He gets frustrated. "You'll never know happiness if you keep caring what people think. Is it so wrong that I could make you happy?"

"No, Hunter, that's not it at all. I just don't want to get hurt again."

He groans before composing himself. "I get that but—" He stops himself from saying whatever was going to come next. "I'm going back to bed. Talk to me when you've figured it out." He turns and walks back to his room.

"Hunter, wait," I panic, jumping out of my seat. I didn't want to fight with him. I just wanted to be as honest as possible with him. I didn't want any blurred lines.

He turns slowly. "What is it?" he asks.

I don't know what to say to him. I know I won't be going back to sleep but he was probably tired. He probably hadn't slept well in the last six months, like me. Maybe he would be the answer to my sleeping problems. He was when my dad got sick. I could only try.

"I might do some sudoku to see if it helps me fall asleep, but you could stay in my room for the rest of the night, if you wanted to?"

A smile slowly creeps onto his face, and he nods.

I leave our cups on the table and walk to my bedroom. He waits at the door for me before opening it. I walk in and move towards the bed. He stands awkwardly at the door. I could almost read his mind. He wanted to be close to me but he couldn't work out how. He didn't understand what I was looking for. Hell, I didn't even know what I was looking for. I had told him exactly how I was feeling though. I told him of my concerns, my fears. It's a lot to work through after everything that had happened. I never thought in a million years I would have the option of getting back with Hunter. We just ended things so badly last time. What I failed to realise back then was that he was struggling and he needed help but didn't know how to get it. Like I was now, Hunter had been trying to work out how to move forward with his life, without me. He said he was stuck and everyone had moved on except him. He said he had no one and didn't know which way was up. I couldn't imagine how horrible that would've been. At least I had a loving family to turn to. His family abandoned him long before I had even met him. Hunter had been truthful with me earlier and answered every question I had about why left me to begin with. It wasn't because he stopped loving me. I wasn't excusing what he'd done by any means, but I believed him when he said he still loved me. What harm could come from getting back with him? He cared so much about me, even now after all the rubbish he went through in the last six months, he still wanted to be with me. That had to mean something, right?

I lie on top of the covers and turn the bedside lamp on before pulling out my sudoku book. Hunter remains at the door, unsure of himself.

"Are you coming?" I ask quietly. He nods slowly and turns the light off. Even in the dim light of the lamp I could see that he had become shy. He copies me, lying on top of the covers.

"Why don't you try to get some more sleep too?" He yawns, before hesitantly offering his arm for me to lay against him.

I bite my lip, now unsure of whether this was the right thing to do. I always enjoyed being in his arms, but I was concerned I'd be leading him on if I did. A good night's sleep did sound appealing though and he knew the risks of only being with me while we were locked away in this safe house. God knows I could use a decent sleep.

With as much confidence as I can muster, I put my sudoku book back on the bedside table and lay my head on Hunter's chest. His arm curls around me instantly. I hear him breathe out slowly, like he was finally relaxing as well.

I feel an instant sense of peace. I couldn't remember the last time I felt this safe. Before I realise what I'm doing, I snuggle in against his chest and body. I feel a light chuckle rumble in his chest and his arm tightens around me in response.

We lay in silence, and I can feel myself growing tired. Hunter's breath evens out as he drifts off. For once, I don't try to fight sleep, and it slowly overcomes me.

CHAPTER 69

I wake to the sound of a baby screaming. I groan as I catch sight of the digital alarm clock on Hayley's bedside table. It was 6:00am. Here I was hoping that after my first night of freedom I would've been able to sleep in for a bit longer. It didn't help that Hayley had woken me up so bloody early but that wasn't really her fault as she didn't make that much noise. I was just a light sleeper these days and I had to make sure she was okay before I attempted sleep again. I squeeze my eyes shut, hoping to force my body to go back to sleep, but Hayley stirs in my arms. She looks so peaceful. I rub my hand up and down her back, trying to soothe her back to sleep. I can see her trying to fight her restlessness and soon, her eyes fly open. Her beautiful brown eyes stare up at me and I can't help but place my hand under her chin in an attempt to kiss her. I pause, realising my actions, but in her daze she closes the distance between us, softly kissing me before breaking away and rolling onto her back.

"Morning," she says through a yawn. I chuckle. I couldn't remember the last time I felt this good in the morning. Here I was, lying in bed with the love of my life. She let me hold her last night and she kissed me this morning. Things were finally starting to look up.

"Morning, Hayley," I whisper. "How did you sleep?"

She thinks for a moment. "Wonderfully," she replies before rolling back onto her side to face me. "I haven't slept like that in a really long time." Sadness crosses over her face at her admission.

"Neither have I," I admit. "Except I've never been woken by a crying baby. Maybe by a crying criminal, but never a baby."

She frowns. "I want you to tell me about your time in the remand centre. Will you tell me?"

I shake my head. "I don't want to ruin this moment, Hayls. I'll tell you after lunch today, I pinkie promise." I offer my little finger out for her.

She thinks for a moment. I know she's heard me say those words a million times before only for me to never follow through. I don't know what else I can say to assure her that I will tell her, just not right now. I will tell her though, I was certain of it. I needed to talk about my experience. It would make me feel better. After a few moments, she smiles weakly before locking her pinkie around mine. "Deal."

"Come on, let's go out and face the day." I try to change the subject. "The sooner we deal with all of this, the sooner we can move on with our lives." I roll off the bed and hold my hand out for her to crawl off behind me. Without hesitation, she takes it and keeps hold of my hand as we walk out into the kitchen.

"Now there's a sight I never thought I'd see again." Ethan grins from a chair in the lounge room, his child sucking on a bottle in his arms.

Hayley lets go of my hand as she makes a beeline for Ethan on the couch. Kate had hidden herself away for the rest of the afternoon yesterday and that meant the baby went with her.

"Do you think Kate would let me hold the baby?" she asks quietly as she sits beside Ethan on the couch.

"She's my child too, Hayley," Ethan says bluntly. "So, if I want you to hold her, you can."

I watch the joy flood Hayley's face as Ethan places the baby in her arms and sets the bottle again once she's comfortable. I see tears form in Hayley's eyes.

"What's her name?" Hayley whispers without taking her eyes off the baby.

Ethan clears his throat, standing abruptly. I knew that look. He was fighting off emotions and I knew exactly why. I cried too when he told me what they had called their daughter.

"Hayley." He finally turns around. "We named her Hayley. After you."

A tear rolls down her cheek. "Really?" she whispers.

"We knew you would've shown strength to the end. We only hope our baby girl will be as strong as you are." Ethan sniffs before taking a seat back on the couch next to Hayley. "But we gave her a nickname. We call her Haze."

She smiles softly. "I love it," she says as she continues to stare down at the baby. I can see the bottle is almost finished.

"I'll make us some drinks," I offer. I felt pained to see Hayley with the baby. To think she nearly had her whole life taken away from her upset me greatly. She nearly didn't get to experience motherhood. Watching her with this baby, I had no doubts that I wanted a family with her one day. I wanted to live my whole life with her, if she let me. I needed to show her, now more than ever, that I was serious and I wanted this to work. I'd buy her a ring tomorrow if I knew that's what she wanted.

I try to make our drinks quietly so as to not disturb Haze now that she was peaceful.

"Need some help?" I spill the hot water I'm pouring for Hayley's drink at the sound of Kate's voice.

"Oh, um. I'm okay, thanks though," I say, quickly wiping away the excess water. I had never felt shy around Kate before and her watchful eyes made me feel even more ashamed of everything I'd done.

"Well, you can't carry all of those cups in one trip," she persists.

I really didn't know what to say to Kate. We didn't leave things in the best way yesterday. I didn't want to upset her as it would upset Hayley.

"Do you want a drink?" I offer instead.

"A cup of coffee would be great, please," she answers as she leans against the kitchen bench. "Lord knows I could use one."

"Tell me about it," I let slip out.

"Did you get coffee wherever it is they took you?" Kate asks hesitantly.

I nod as I continue to make the drinks, still unable to look her in the eye. "It was the instant coffee though, not this fancy stuff," I answer, referring to the fancy pod machine on the bench.

"I guess it was something," she shrugs before realising what she's said. "Sorry, I didn't mean that to come across wrong. I really shouldn't comment at all. It was a jail, not a hotel."

"It's okay," I reply. I knew I'd be fielding comments like this for a while and particularly from Kate until she calmed down.

"Why didn't you fight harder for yourself, Hunter?" she asks quietly. "If you were innocent, why didn't you fight harder?"

I want to snap at her. I bloody well tried. It's not like Judge Judy. I have to sit at that table in handcuffs, listening to people I don't know tell me false stories of what happened that day and lies about who I was as a person. I can't sit there and argue every point raised. I didn't have the opportunity to defend myself. I was charged and awaiting trial before I even knew it. My bail was denied, and I was immediately placed in the remand facility. The girl I loved with my whole heart was dead. I witnessed it, but no one would believe me. I lost hope.

"Why live in a world when Hayley wasn't in it?" My voice is so quiet that even I can't hear it. It was the first time I had ever admitted that to anyone and I turn slowly to look at Kate. There are tears in her eyes as she analyses what I've just said.

"You really loved her?" she asks as she lets a tear fall.

"I still do, and I always will, Kate," I say firmly. I didn't know what further I could do to prove to Kate that I cared about Hayley. All I cared about was making Hayley see that I had changed and I would do whatever it took to get her back.

"You didn't hurt her that day?" she presses, I can almost see the clogs in her brain ticking over. She was asking specific questions to get the answers she needed for it to all make sense in her brain. Baby brain had gotten her good.

"No, I tried to protect her from him." I drop my head as the memory comes flooding back of catching Hayley in my arms as she fell. "Clearly, I couldn't though."

Before I know it, Kate is wrapping her arms around me, sobbing. Slowly, I hug her back and stay in her embrace until she's ready to let go. I catch sight of Ethan, and he smiles.

CHAPTER 70

I feel anxious waiting for Detective Brown to bring an update on the case against Rhys. Hunter tries to get me to calm down but he didn't understand how it felt waiting each day for this information. Some days I received no updates other than 'just a little bit longer' and some days I'd hear nothing but some journalists' opinion on the news.

"Just sit down, Hayls, he'll be here soon," Hunter tries to reassure me as I pace around the living room.

"I'm so sick of hearing that!" I snap. "That's all people have said over the last six months. 'Just a little bit longer' or 'just be patient'! You have no idea how frustrating it's been!"

"Actually, I do," he says calmly. "You try sitting in a real jail cell, not some fancy safe house."

I begin to retaliate when Kate interrupts. "Come on you two," she says. "There's no need to get nasty about who had it worse."

Kate was right. It was clear that Hunter had it worse being locked up and I needed to stop feeling so sorry for myself. This was all for a good cause.

"I'm sorry," I mumble, knowing very well I was in the wrong. Hunter just smiles weakly. His response almost shocks me. Usually, he would be more verbal and argue. Maybe he really had changed?

Hunter stands up, walking over to me. "I think you need to talk about what happened to you, Hayley, and what you've been going through these last few months," he says, his voice low so Kate and Ethan didn't hear. It was far from the demanding Hunter I remembered.

"You know exactly what happened and probably know better than anybody what time alone can do to someone." There's anger in my words, but I can't help it. I just want to move forward.

He goes to say something but refrains. Instead, he gets up off the couch and runs a hand through his hair. I know I should apologise but I don't have the energy for any more emotions right now. I wanted to have a clear mind when Detective Brown visited so I could fully absorb any updates.

The familiar alarm signals his arrival, and the door opens.

"Hello," Detective Brown greets us as he enters the living room. "I trust you enjoyed your first night of freedom, Hunter?"

Hunter nods in response. "Guess it'll take some time to get used to how quiet it's supposed to be at night."

I drop my attitude immediately at Hunter's admission. How could I be so tough on him after what he went through? I dealt with silence. He dealt with possible murderers and psychopaths.

"Let's sit down. I've got a bit of information to go through." Detective Brown pulls up a dining room chair next to the couch. "You two can stay to hear this," he advises as he catches sight of Kate and Ethan.

I sit next to Hunter on the two-seater couch, across from Kate and Ethan who were on the other couch with Haze. I take a deep breath, hoping desperately for good news.

"You'll be pleased to hear that yesterday we arrested Rhys Centino on the following charges: one count of attempted murder in the first degree of Hunter Woods, one count of grievous bodily harm of Hayley Centino. He will face separate charges for felony fraud and that is being handled by another detective."

I let the words sink in. This whole ordeal was finally coming to an end. Hunter breathes out beside me as he relaxes into the couch.

"Wow," Ethan says quietly.

"He's a dangerous guy. You two are very lucky to still be alive," Brown says gravely.

Holy shit. They actually did it. I look around at my friends. We were all rendered speechless but I had one question on my mind.

"So, when can we leave here?"

CHAPTER 71

I almost want to punch Detective Brown in the face as he chuckles at Hayley's question.

"You've been very patient so far, Hayley, but you need to keep going for just a little bit longer."

I squeeze her knee, hoping she doesn't have another outburst like she did yesterday. Disappointingly, she jumps at my touch and brushes my hand away.

"I gave you six months, Detective. It was six months yesterday," she says sternly.

"And Hunter is free," he replies bluntly. "That's what the deal was."

"Don't twist my words," she snaps back. My heart races and my mind floods with thoughts of knowing she had been fighting for me this whole time, like she tried to on that fateful day.

He chooses to ignore her and keeps speaking. "Rhys is currently sitting in a jail cell. He was not eligible for bail. Based on his charges he is considered a flight risk. We were also able to arrest most of his accomplices. One engaged in a shoot-out with police and was pronounced dead at the scene."

Ethan claps his hands together loudly and we all look at him. "I'm not even sorry. They all deserve it," he says smugly.

I couldn't even believe Rhys was associated with someone who would do such a thing as shoot at a police officer. It made me want to be sick and I hang my head in my hands. Hunter places a hand lightly on my back and starts to rub circles between my shoulder blades.

"You okay?" he whispers in my ear, and I nod in response.

"Right now, the state and Rhys' lawyer have six weeks to prepare to go to trial. Now that we have eyewitnesses and you, Hayley, we don't anticipate the trial taking too long. The state will be putting pressure on Rhys' lawyer, as we have all the evidence we need to nail him. So, we'll be pushing to move as quickly as we can to get you out of here as soon as we can," Detective Brown explains. "Kate and Ethan, now that he is in a remand facility and so are his accomplices, you will be able to go home, but you will have a security detail at all times, just in case there're others out there that we don't know about. We don't believe you're in any danger, but we would rather be cautious."

Kate and Ethan look hopefully at each other. This would be the fresh start they needed. They could get their relationship back on track.

"You will be able to leave tomorrow," Brown continues, and Kate breaks down quietly. "Hunter, you do have the option of going to a separate safe house still, if you want," he says carefully.

"No!" Hayley's head bolts up. "You can't leave me here alone again for six more weeks!"

"I'll stay with her," I say swiftly in an attempt to avoid a meltdown on Hayley's part.

She whips around to face me. "Are you sure?"

"You're not asking, I'm offering," I reply softly, and I can see her start to relax.

"Remember, just because you get along now, doesn't mean you will always get along in this confined space, so I'd recommend putting some boundaries in place," Detective Brown says carefully.

Chapter 72

Kate takes Haze back to her room with Ethan as they prepare to leave tomorrow. I wanted to be happy for them, I really did, but it hurt knowing they got to leave, and I had to stay. I remain seated on the couch when Detective Brown leaves. I feel defeated again even though I know I shouldn't. Hunter had a point. The end was in sight now. I could keep going. I needed to be strong. Justice would be served.

"Do you want a drink or something?" Hunter offers as he gets up off the couch.

I shake my head. Surprisingly, I just wanted to be alone. After all this time, I needed to process this on my own. They had arrested Rhys. All the pain and suffering would be over soon.

"Do you want to talk about it?" Hunter tries again but still I shake my head no. I felt like I was in a daze.

"Talk to me, Hayley, please," he whispers as he kneels in front of me. "You can't bottle this up."

I can almost feel his words go in one ear and out the other. I just didn't have anything to say. Nothing had really changed. I was still stuck here.

"Hayley," he pleads again, resting a hand on my knee.

"Hunter," I snap out of my daze, leaning back abruptly on the couch, crossing my arms over my chest.

"Don't be like this," he says weakly. "Remember how cranky you were at me before Detective Brown got here?"

"I wasn't cranky."

Hunter smiles at my response. He was purposefully trying to get a rise from me. "I'm fine, Hunter. What will it take for you to believe me?"

"You don't act fine, that's why," he replies, concern written all over his face. "I know it's hard to see it now but you're doing the right thing. It'll all be worth it in the end. I know you're hurting."

"Of course I'm hurting, Hunter!" I can't help but rudely cut him off. "I got shot with a fucking bullet from someone I thought I could trust!" I hurl at him. "How do you think that feels? I thought I could trust you, and you fucked off. I thought I could trust Rhys and he did this," I point at my scar. "The two people I know I can trust I can't talk to at all! And if I do talk to one of them, people think I'm crazy because Dad is dead! How do I trust anyone?" I didn't realise how much I had been holding in about my time in the safe house.

He rests his hands on my knees, waiting for me to finish my outburst.

"Yesterday was the first time in six months I had been allowed out of this hell hole, and it was the first time I was seeing you. I didn't know how you'd react when you saw me alive. We left things so violently on the pier, and then of course at my fucking house."

His face drops. "You don't have to remind me. That night at the pier was my fucking lowest point, I think."

"It may have been your lowest point, but I also think it was your turning point. I just wish you realised you needed help earlier."

"Well, I can't change the past, Hayls," he growls, dropping his hands from my knees. "I don't want to talk about that night."

"But here you are making me talk about my experience." I cross my arms over my chest again.

He scoffs. "It's not even remotely similar, Hayley."

"How so?" I argue, leaning forward. We were so close to each other in this moment. I watch as his eyes search my face as he tries to come up with an answer.

Instead, he angrily pushes up off his knees. "Whatever." He walks away to the kitchen.

I sigh and get up off the couch to follow him. "Hunter, I'm sorry. I don't mean to keep getting so angry."

"I just don't want to reminisce about all the shit I put you through, Hayley." He turns around and I can see how frustrated he is. "I regret all of it. I acted foolishly, like a complete fucking idiot. I hate myself for what I put you through. I really do. And now I have a chance to make it right, but you won't trust your gut and follow your heart. You said it yourself yesterday."

I open my mouth to argue but he turns his back on me and leans against the kitchen bench.

I can't help myself. I want to comfort him. I wrap my arms around his waist and lean my cheek against his back. Slowly, I can feel his body relax.

"I don't think you realise the effect you have on me," he whispers, his head hanging low.

"We're sad, aren't we?" I say quietly. I didn't want to ruin this moment with him. It felt so right.

"But we're in this together?" he asks, looking over his shoulder at me.

Again, my mind flashes back to the hospital with my dad, when we first said we'd always be in life together. Hunter would always be a big part of my life, regardless of whether he was my boyfriend or friend. He was part of so many memories I had with Dad, memories that were joyful and that I didn't want to forget.

"Together," I agree but I knew, deep down, I still didn't know what that meant.

CHAPTER 73

Hayley invites me to sleep in her room again tonight. She told me it was nice having me around but not to read into anything. She gave me so many opportunities to go back to my room or to move away from her when she came near but I couldn't. I craved her touch more than anything in the world. I didn't care how she felt about me. I would fulfil whatever need she had for me if it meant I got to be with her. Even if that meant losing her once this was all over.

"Hunter?" she asks as she settles back against the pillows on the bed.

"Mm?" I respond as I shut the door and turn the lamp on before turning off the ceiling light.

"Will you tell me about what it was like in the remand centre?" she asks quietly.

I pause. I didn't really want to talk about it but I owed it to her to always be truthful and to tell her whatever she wanted to know. I promised her this morning that I would tell her. I wouldn't make the same mistakes I did in the past. It was time to show her that I had grown up and could be the man she deserved.

"It's very hard to talk about," I say carefully. "But I suppose it wouldn't hurt to get it off my chest."

"You don't have to." She sits up quickly. "I was just wondering. I don't want to push you if you're not ready."

"No, I think I should." I nod and take a seat beside her on the bed. "I don't even know where to start though."

"Just when you're ready, and wherever you want to start." She rests her hand cautiously on my thigh and it sends an electric current through me.

I take a deep breath. "It was fucked." My voice shakes as I force myself to remember things that I wanted to mentally block out forever. "I saw you everywhere I looked, not just in my dreams. Every time I looked around the corner, you were there. Hauntingly there, like a ghost. Just staring at me. I tried to ignore you at first and walk through you, but my mind would get the better of me and I would end up walking around you." I peek up at her. Her eyes are wide. "I remember that the other men there thought I'd lost the plot. They'd ask me who you were and why I kept shouting your name in my sleep. I let my anger get the better of me one day. I woke up in the infirmary a day later having had the shit beaten out of me."

"Oh, Hunter." Her tears overflow at my admission, and she moves to sit on my lap, resting her head against my shoulder as she squeezes me tightly.

I keep going. It actually felt good to get this off my chest. "We're all innocent until proven guilty, right? But some of them were clearly dangerous people and you'd do whatever you could to stay out of their way. There's definitely a pecking order there. People were coming and going so frequently as their trials started or ended but everyone told everyone each other's business. When news got out that I was awaiting murder charges, that's when things started to change. People would steer clear of you or try to get you to talk about your crime in hopes it'd get them a better deal if you slipped up. It was incredibly isolating. I tried to reach out to my family. It became evident that my dad blocked my calls. Mum visited once."

She takes a sharp intake of breath. I couldn't imagine what it felt like for her to hear my story.

"She cried the whole time we sat together before explaining to me that our family couldn't be associated with someone like me and that one day she hoped I understood. She said she was sorry for failing me as a parent." I can't help but break into a cry but as Hayley reaches for me, I get up and pace the room, trying to compose myself, before sitting back down. "I started to see you regularly, not just when I was dreaming. You would stare blankly back at me and occasionally, you would point at the bullet wound on your chest that gaped at me. A sickening snap back to reality. One night, I couldn't take it anymore and I tried to scream at you to leave me alone. I'd had enough. I really was losing the plot. You started to talk back to me that night. You asked me why. Why should you leave me alone? You said that I didn't do enough when Rhys shot you. I should've done more. I shouldn't have taken the fall for something I didn't do. You begged me to fight harder for myself." I wipe away a tear hastily. "Like when I fought for you."

"I know you would've fought as hard as you could and done anything to get through the days." She leans back to look at me.

"I've always been a strong-minded person, Hayls," I reply gently. "You know that with how persistent I was with you in high school. It's like it all just faded away. I couldn't be strong without you around."

"We're going to fight this, Hunter, and we're going to win," she says confidently.

"Well, your hope gives me hope." I pull her back into a cuddle and she rests her head on my shoulder. "Questioning is going to be tough though, Hayls. You need to be prepared for them to make you feel so small and so inadequate. They'll do anything to discredit you."

"I know. I'm ready," she says firmly. She had been waiting a long time for this. "We're going to be okay, Hunter."

I rub my hand up and down her back as we sit in silence. I gasp when I feel the cool of her hands slip under my shirt. She's doesn't seem phased though and gently rubs up and down my spine. I couldn't remember the last time she had done this. It was obviously years ago when she could actually stand to be around me. Back when she truly loved me. I feel her start to push my shirt up and I pull away from her, allowing her to pull my shirt over my head. I try to keep a neutral expression. She then returns to leaning her head on my shoulder, her hands travelling slowly up and down my back. There was no doubt that she could feel my heart racing. I want to say something to her. I want to take her shirt off and feel her skin against mine, but I didn't want to ruin whatever was going through her mind. Ever so lightly I feel her lips against my neck, and I feel goose bumps rise.

"Hunter," she mumbles against my skin, breaking the silence and pulling me back into reality.

"Yes, Hayley?" I hope she can't hear my voice shaking.

"I want to take your mind off it all."

I pull away from her quickly and look at her face. I knew exactly what she meant. *Sex.* My mind flicks back to when she used to ask me the same thing when she was going through all of that stuff with her dad. Stuff that I wasn't around to continue to help her with when he died. I want to fight back tears, knowing I wasn't there when he passed. I should've been there. I hold her face in my hands. "Are you sure?" I can't help myself. I need to know that she really wants this.

"Please," she responds.

I still hesitate for a moment before I pull her against me and the covers up over us.

CHAPTER 74

I wake to the sound of a baby crying once more. I chuckle when I hear Hayley groan.

"I've been alone for so long. That is a sound I'm not used to hearing and especially not having it wake me up," she mumbles against my bare chest.

I can't help but smile as I think about last night. I was surprised that she wanted to have sex but I certainly wasn't going to say no. We fit together perfectly, like missing pieces of a puzzle once again united. She felt exactly how she used to, albeit she was now just skin and bone. I wanted to relive the moment over and over again. I hear movement outside the room, and it reminds me that this would be the last time I saw Ethan for a while. I had pushed the thought out of my mind intentionally. I was enjoying being around my friends. I had craved friendship for the last couple of years after pushing everyone away. Having Ethan back was great. He truly was my best friend. I also had Hayley. Life was looking up but I couldn't help but let my mind wander as I remembered why I was here in the first place. I didn't hurt Hayley and I needed to prove that Rhys did. Now was my turn to fight.

"Where are you going?" Hayley mumbles as I gently move away from her.

"I'm going to go make us some drinks, I'll be right back." I jump off the bed and feel her eyes on my naked body.

"Wow," she says.

Her gaze makes me feel shy. We had seen each other naked before but now we were both so different. This is what women must feel like when men stared at them. Before I can walk away from the bed, she pulls at my arm. I turn back to face her. She's now sitting up in bed but the sheet is covering her chest. I can see down her back, the bones protruding from her spine. She keeps pulling my arm so I lean over her so she can rest her head once more on my shoulder.

"Last night was fun," she breathes against my skin. I feel goose bumps rise again at what might happen next. She always knew how to tease me and I was glad she hadn't lost her touch.

"Yes, it was," I reply with a smile. "Do you want a drink?"

"I think you know what I want..." One of her hands snakes down my chest, before stopping too high for my liking.

"And what's that?" I decide to tease back but gasp as her hand reaches the right spot. Without showing too much desperation, I wrap one arm around her and move us both onto the middle of the bed. She giggles, driving me wild, before she takes control.

"Fuck, Hayley," I groan into her neck, causing her to giggle again. My lack of human connection in the recent months is not on my side and before too long, we're both on our backs laughing like kids.

Hayley runs her fingers through her hair and I see the scar on her chest again. This time it doesn't make me gasp. I knew I needed to be careful about her scar as it would upset her again. She must see me staring and pulls the cover up.

"Are you going to be okay, Hayley?" I ask. "You know, when Kate and Ethan leave?"

Her face drops and I feel like I've ruined the moment. She wouldn't see them again until she was called to testify.

"I guess I'll have to be." She shrugs her shoulders.

"I'll always be there for you, Hayley." I kiss her cheek gently before getting out of bed.

This time she lets me get dressed but I feel her eyes on me the entire time.

"Do you mind?" I joke as I pull a t-shirt over my head.

She blushes. "You've changed a bit. You've gotten very muscly. It was about time you filled out." She pokes her tongue out.

"Well, being locked up does that to you. What else is there to do?" I shrug my shoulders.

I must've had a tone as she quickly says, "I didn't mean to offend you."

"You didn't offend me," I laugh. "It's just the truth. I'm learning to be more truthful, Hayls. All this bullshit could've been avoided if I was just honest with you."

"We can't think about what could've been, Hunter. We need to live in the now." Hayley sits up straight, the sheets falling away from her. I take notice of her scar again.

"And you need to learn to live with what has happened to you, Hayley," I reply bluntly. "You should wear that scar with pride. You survived being shot."

I feel like I'm scolding a child with the way her face drops. Once more she pulls the sheet up around her.

"Are you getting dressed or are you going to stay in bed all day?" I ask as I ruffle my hands through my hair.

"I just need a minute," she says quietly. I could already tell she was upset with me, however I didn't regret for a minute what I said. That scar should be worn with pride with what she had been through. I leave the room without saying anything further.

CHAPTER 75

Hunter was right. I hated him for being right, but he was. My scar was something I should be proud of. I survived attempted murder at the hands of my husband. I slowly move to the cupboard to see if I had any singlets or something that wouldn't hide the scar. Perhaps with Kate and Ethan leaving today I could try wearing one around the safe house and see how I felt. I would make an effort to look at it in the mirror so I could get used to seeing it. Hunter was supportive so I would be comfortable having him see the scar regularly, but I wasn't sure I was ready for Kate and Ethan to see it. I end up finding a singlet with thick straps and finish getting dressed. I step in front of the mirror and take a deep breath before looking at my chest. The scar is slightly hidden behind the straps of the singlet but I felt like I could see straight through the fabric. I knew what it looked like. It was burnt into my memory.

A knock at the door startles me and I step away from the mirror quickly. Hunter pokes his head around the door. He smiles gently, as though he knew exactly what I was doing.

"Your drink is going to go cold," is all he says. I couldn't help but feel like he was staring at my scar. Everyone was going to. I would forever be that girl with the bullet hole.

As though he can read my mind he says, "It's not as noticeable as you think it is."

He enters the room and walks over to the cupboard, pulling out a light cardigan. "Here, you can wear this and do it up when it all gets too much for you."

I take the cardigan quietly and put it on.

"Feel better?" he asks, and I nod pathetically. "Come on, let's start the day. Then it's one less day until you can go home."

I was getting used to having Hunter be the mature and sensible one in our dynamic. I didn't *not* like it, either. It was nice to have a voice of reason. He says *you* as well, instead of *us*, like he's finally putting me before him.

"Are you coming?" he asks from the doorway.

I muster up a smile and follow Hunter into the living room and kitchen.

"Morning," Ethan looks up at us and smiles. He's feeding Haze a bottle of formula on the couch. "I take the morning shifts and let Kate sleep in," he explains.

That pair truly were soulmates, forever moving in unison. Like my mum and dad. I look away quickly to stop any emotions from taking over.

The whole time I'm in Ethan's view his eyes never land on my scar, and I almost wonder if Hunter said something to him about how I felt. I bury an urge to snap and tell Ethan to just get it over with. *Go on, have a look at the scar from a bullet, ask your questions, tell me I was brave.* How cynical of me.

"Here's your drink," Hunter interrupts me from the kitchen. Again, I felt like he could see straight through me and knew I needed to be distracted.

"Morning," I respond quickly to Ethan and go to meet Hunter in the kitchen. He hands me my cup of tea.

"It looks good, Hayls," Hunter says as he takes a sip of his coffee. "The outfit, I mean. Just see how you go, if it becomes too much, just get changed into a t-shirt. You don't have to tackle this in one day."

"Should I just show everyone and get the questions over with?" I ask as I take a sip as well.

He shrugs. "It's completely up to you. I just don't want you to jump into anything you're not ready for."

"So, you think I was ready to have sex with you last night?" I whisper over my cup. "It's only been six months after all."

I watch his face drop but he recovers quickly. "You had sex with me twice, Hayls. I feel like at least one of those times you were in the right frame of mind. Well, I hope you were in the right frame of mind both times, otherwise I'd feel like shit."

"I feel like I should feel guilty about it," I admit. "Like, how did I do this so quickly with you after everything we've been through?"

I watch as he works out what to say next. "Maybe that's why you did it, because of everything we've been through?" he says as leans against the kitchen bench, his hand cradling his cup.

There was truth to his words, and I was glad he wasn't angry with me for even bringing it up. Again, I see the changes in Hunter, but it still felt odd to me. He was different but in a good way. I really don't know how to feel about what happened last night and this morning. It just felt normal to me. It wasn't like Hunter and I hadn't had sex before, so I wasn't concerned about a rising number of sexual partners. *God I was such a mess.* I had been with Hunter for a long time, even when we were stuck in an on/off relationship. When he disappeared for good, I then found Rhys. Then the whole world turned to shit when Rhys shot me, and I had no one. It was like I didn't know how to be alone, so being close to someone—anyone—was all that I was craving. In the end, was that what it came down to? Was I just using him because I knew how he felt about me? This wasn't fair to him.

"I don't think we should have sex again," I quietly say.

Hunter sighs, clearly getting frustrated. I couldn't blame him, the poor thing was probably so confused.

"Well, you did warn me at the start you weren't sure what this was." He shakes his head as he walks across the kitchen to stand against the bench opposite me. It was like he needed to be away from me. "But you're right," he continues. "It's probably for the best that we don't sleep together again or even sleep in the same room."

I feel my face drop. I still wanted him close but he couldn't be close to me the same way I needed to be close to him.

"Hayley—" He puts his cup on the bench behind him and walks over to me, holding my face gently in his hands. "I will always love you, you know that. I want to be there for you however I can but now that I think of it, and we actually had sex, I don't think I can be *just* friends with benefits with you. I can't keep losing you." He places a kiss on my forehead before letting go. He was finally drawing a line in the sand.

"Hunter—" I try to start but he stops me.

"What we did last night—and this morning—was fucking amazing." He looks so defeated. "But I know what I want now. I'm just sorry it took me so long to realise it."

"Hunter, I'm really sorry," I try to explain but as I take a step towards him, he takes a step back.

"Today sucks as it is with Kate and Ethan leaving, Hayls, I really can't do this with you right now." He turns and walks away quickly.

I slump against the bench. He was right. Again. It wasn't fair what I was doing to him. I needed to keep my distance properly this time, just like he said. No matter how vulnerable he is with me or how vulnerable I am with him, we were just friends trying to get through this ridiculous ordeal. I knew deep down that there was a good chance I would end up in Hunter's bed tonight, or him in mine, but I needed to be strong and just support him as a friend, like he said.

"How much of that did you hear?" I say quietly as I walk into the lounge room where Ethan is now burping Haze.

"Most of it," he replies without looking at me.

"Hit me with it then, tell me I'm an idiot and what I need to do to get through this." I slump in the armchair next to him.

Ethan chuckles and puts his daughter on the floor to play. "Well, let me just say, I'm not surprised you two got it on. That was inevitable." He grins. "But I understand where he's coming from. He's always loved you so it's probably confusing and hard for him to get you back just to potentially lose you again when you get out of here. I think you've made the right call to not keep leading each other on though. He needs to learn how to just be your friend and that may take some time."

"If I got back together with Hunter, what would you think of me?" I ask hesitantly.

Ethan stops to think about my question. "I don't know what I'd think to be honest." He pauses as he tries to articulate his thoughts. "If you're soulmates, you'll eventually find your way back to each other—but who's to say you are soulmates? I think you need to really think about what you want in life, Hayley. At the very least, who you want in life. Do you want to spend however long to see if there's someone else out there for you, or do you want to give Hunter another chance knowing very well he's ready to commit?"

"Did he say that?" I ask quickly.

Ethan laughs. "No, but I can see a change in Hunter, and you'd be lying if you said you didn't. Even Kate can see it. I've seen something in him that I've never seen before. This whole ordeal really did a number on him. Imagine thinking your whole life would be confined to a jail cell. I think he's really reevaluated his life. He knows what he wants and that's you. He wants the wedding, the children, everything—with you. But you're the one who needs to figure out what you want. I can't tell you that, and neither can Kate or your mum."

"Wow." I exhale. It's not like I didn't ask for his honest opinion, but he gave me something to think about. Did what Ethan say change anything? Did Hunter really want those things? Did I want those things? Did I want those things *with Hunter*?

Ethan moves to pick up Haze from the floor and heads back towards his room. He turns around before he opens the door. "Hunter lived by one rule in high school," he says, "and that was not to care what anyone thought of him, so long as he was happy doing what he was doing."

I chuckle. I remembered his mantra all too well. The question was, would I be able to not care what anyone thought about *me*?

CHAPTER 76

Hayley was miserable for the rest of the day after Ethan and Kate left, and went and hid in her room. Detective Brown came just before lunch time to escort them out and back home. I left her alone, as hard as it was. I didn't know how to make it better. I'd probably just end up sleeping with her again, even though we agreed that we needed to just be friends. I needed to be strong regardless of what I wanted. I was putting her first. Tonight was going to be challenging. I wanted to comfort her, but I didn't know how to be close to her without having her in my arms. How do you just be friends with the girl you love? How do I help her as a friend? I opened the fridge to see what would be on the menu for dinner tonight. When Detective Brown collected Kate and Ethan, he also delivered a truck load of food. We wouldn't go hungry, that's for sure. I saw lasagne and decided that would do. It was Hayley's favourite food, and I remembered her eating it on our first date so here's hoping this would coax her out and get her to eat something. Or it could backfire and upset her.

I take a deep breath before knocking on her door.

"Hayley?" I say hesitantly as I open the door. The poor thing looked like she had cried herself to sleep. I want to rush to her side but instead I tiptoe into the room and reach for the blanket to cover her. I turn her lamp on and turn the bedroom light off.

"Hunter?" she mumbles and stretches out on the bed.

"Yeah, it's me. I was just checking to see if you were hungry, but I'll let you sleep."

"I wasn't sleeping," she yawns.

I chuckle as I go to leave the room. "Okay then."

"I wasn't!" she calls again.

"I don't mind what you were doing. Are you hungry now that you're awake?" I stand in the doorway keeping my distance.

She thinks about this for a moment. "I think I am."

"Okay, well dinner will be ready in about ten minutes." I smile as she sits up and stretches again.

"Another one of Brown's pre-made meals?" she asks. There's a bit of humour in her tone.

I nod. "Maybe I'll try my hand at cooking tomorrow instead."

"That'd be nice." She smiles. "Hunter?"

"Mmm?"

"It's been a really hard day. I miss my friends. Can you just sit with me for a moment?" she whispers. "Please?"

I sigh. "You have no idea how much I want to. I want to be close with you. I want to wrap you in my arms, but I can't because then I'll want more."

"You can't just try? It's just the two of us for six weeks," she says quietly as she crosses her legs.

"I don't know if I can," I reply honestly. "Can we please just have dinner? That way I know you have food in your stomach and can make an informed decision."

She crosses her arms over her chest. "Well then no, I'm not hungry. I don't want food right now. I want my friend."

CHAPTER 77

He takes a big breath in. He was so frustrated by my behaviour. I knew I would cave eventually and crave his attention, his touch, anything. I just didn't think I'd cave in under 12 hours. I felt so pathetic. Six months ago, I was trying to force Hunter away from me and now I was trying to force him on me. I needed to respect his decision, and I wasn't making this easy for him.

"I'm sorry," I mumble. I felt so embarrassed. "This isn't fair on you. I'm sure it's not too late to change your mind. Detective Brown is just a phone call away."

He runs his hands through his hair before closing the distance between us. "I'm going to fucking hate myself in the morning for this," he growls and closes the distance between us in just a few short strides. His lips crash against mine and I feel myself melt at his touch. He just felt so right. Why did I keep hesitating?

"Are you sure?" I break away but he just moves to my neck.

"No," he answers between kisses. "But I'm gonna do it anyway."

His brashness makes me giggle, and I let him take control. I can feel his anger as he moves quickly in taking our clothes off. He's frustrated with himself. I can feel it but he couldn't resist. We were perfect disasters. Falling apart to become better together down the track.

"Why can't I just say no?" he groans as he rolls onto his back once it's over.

I bite back a laugh. Now was not the time.

"Why can't *I* just say no?" I repeat back to him as I turn onto my side to face him. "We're in the same boat."

"Then what are we doing, Hayley?" he asks bluntly as he sits up. "You told me this morning you wanted to be friends with benefits. I told you I couldn't do that. Yet here I am again, in your damn bed."

I can't help it this time. I laugh. This breaks the tension and he starts laughing too.

"I'm sorry Hunter, I know this isn't ideal. I'm just making it worse. It's not fair for you."

He sighs. "I get it. I really do. I want to be with you, believe me. Old Hunter would've jumped at the friends with benefits thing, but this time I'm for real. I want to be your boyfriend, I want to be everything you need, I want to be the father of your—" He stops abruptly as I sit up straight at his words.

"What?" I ask, begging him with my eyes to continue.

"Nothing. I don't know…" He jumps out of bed, pulling his clothes on quickly.

"Please finish your sentence." I reach out to grab his hand but he pulls away.

"No, I can't Hayley. I don't want what I want to cloud what you want. Just because I'm finally saying the words you've always wanted to hear doesn't change our current situation." He pulls his shirt over his head and walks quickly to the door.

"Hunter!" I call and wrap the sheet around me to follow him. "Please, don't walk away."

"I need to, Hayls." He turns to face me. There are tears in his eyes. "Please don't make this harder than it needs to be. I want so much with you and you can't even tell me if you want to be with me for real or if it's because you're lonely."

"Hunter, we can talk about this. Remember we said we'd be more open with each other," I try to plead with him.

"I fucking have been!" he shouts back. "I've been so open. I don't know what else to say. The buck stops with you now. You need to work this out. I'm going to bed. Please just leave me alone." He leaves the room and I hear a door slam.

I stumble back, falling onto the bed. I had royally fucked this whole thing up.

CHAPTER 78

She was really messing with my mind. I felt so weak around her. My judgement was so clouded with thoughts of what could be that I hardly slept that night. How could I be so stupid as to admit everything I wanted with her? I was far too open. I probably spooked her with how serious I was. At least now she knew where I stood, and it was up to her if she wanted to be with me. If we could just start again, make a plan for our future, these next six weeks would be amazing. We could get to know each other again. I just had to be patient.

When I eventually decide to get up in the morning, I can hear what sounds like reruns of Friends on TV. I strain to listen through the door to hear if she's crying. She could be sitting zombie like for all I know. I open the door slightly but I can't see her. A man has got to get a drink or go to the toilet at some stage though. I couldn't hide in here forever. I open the door fully and her head snaps up at the sound. She looks fine, like she hasn't been crying at all.

"Sorry, is it too loud?" she asks, reaching for the remote. There's not even a hint of sadness in her voice. Was that a good thing or a bad thing?

"No, it's okay," I reply and head to the kitchen for a drink.

"I'm going to make lunch at 12pm if you want anything, then I'm planning my dinner for 6.30pm if you want any. Just so you know."

"Um, okay, yeah. If I'm hungry, I'll pop out." I try not to make promises. My insides are screaming, *Yes! I want to join you, anything to be part of your world!* But I know that this is probably for the best. Her attention doesn't stay on me for long and she returns to watching the TV.

So, this was how it was going to be.

CHAPTER 79

It had been a week of trying to make sense of my feelings and only speaking to Hunter when necessary. I was giving myself two weeks to figure it out. I already knew after one week what I wanted but I needed to stay strong and really give myself the best opportunity to make sense of my emotions. Each day, I would write in my journal how I was feeling about Hunter, and each day I felt like I was writing the same lovey-dovey crap. *Surely, that had to be a sign?* He respectfully worked around me. We seemed to silently work out that I would get the TV in the morning and he would get it in the afternoon. We'd eat dinner together in the evening and then go about our separate business. I usually went back to my room and did my sudoku book and I was certain that he stayed up watching movies. Conversation was limited to polite chit chat. It felt like I was on autopilot. This was going to be a long six weeks.

CHAPTER 80

She moves silently around me, trying to stay out of my way. I wish I could let her use me for whatever she needed but I knew that it would just end in disaster. I wouldn't be able to let her go. I couldn't let her go last time and look at what happened. I needed to be strong in so many ways. We never really had the chance to live together. I had always fucked off to go and mess around in another city with different friends and other girls. I mentally slap myself. How could I be so stupid? Why did I mess around with other girls? They all dressed the same. Short, skintight skirts, boobs on full display, a face full of makeup. They were so different from Hayley. They even felt cheap. I'd be filled with regret when I woke up the next day and saw all their shit covering the floor and on the bedside table, their makeup staining the bedsheets. Yet I still did it, sometimes the same girl, sometimes a new girl.

I vividly remember leading a girl on to the point she had come home with me, but she was all business. She just wanted to sleep with me. She didn't want to get to know me, like all the other girls did. Her name was Olivia. She just wanted to sleep with me and move onto the next guy. She didn't waste time asking me about my family and friends. It was probably why I was interested in sleeping with her. The other girls were so desperate to share their life stories with me, hoping it would trigger some kind of emotion in me and I'd ask them to be my girlfriend. I felt so used by Olivia, just like how Abby had used me all of those years ago. So I made the decision to go home, find Hayley, and prove once and for all that we were meant to be. When I found out that she had moved on and was even married to some project management guy, I went on a bender for almost a week. Waking up in a pool of your own vomit was fucking foul and I knew that I needed to do whatever it took to get her back. Hayley and I were meant to be together. We had been through too much for it to end like this. I had always been an intense guy, she knew that, and following some of the pick-up lines or behaviours I used to use to pick up chicks at the bar, I assumed my tactics would be irresistible to her. Turns out I was just frightening her and pushing her further away. If I came to her and laid all of my emotions out so she knew how I felt, she could've made her own decision and maybe even have picked me. I was stupid to think that any of those plans could've actually worked though. This wasn't some Hollywood movie. People don't just snap their fingers and switch their emotions. If I hadn't pushed though, would I be here with her now? Would she be sitting in the room next to mine contemplating a future with me? Would I have felt the warmth of her body as I pressed it against mine in our times of pleasure or the spontaneity when we kissed for the first time after several years? Things happen for a reason and whilst I may have acted like a dickhead in the past, I will make up for it.

I sit up abruptly in my bed. I know what I need to do to win her back. I need to charm her and impress her again. Get to know her, like we did when we first met. It's not a grand gesture, but it is a starting point.

Chapter 81

"I saw the new Marvel movie is on Netflix. Do you want to watch it after we've finished eating?" Hunter asks randomly as we sit across from each other during dinner. We had a silent deal that we would just rotate through who cooked at each mealtime. I felt myself returning to a state of somewhat normal. I obviously didn't have any plans for after dinner tonight as I couldn't go anywhere except to the dining room, lounge room, kitchen or my room and I certainly wasn't about to take a field trip to Hunter's room. We were in a civil place at the moment. I didn't want to ruin that.

"Okay, yeah. That sounds like a good idea." I nod and he smiles at me softly.

Had I just given him false hope? I push back in my chair quickly and take my plate to the sink. He follows me silently.

"It's just a movie, Hayley. I didn't mean anything by it. I just thought you may be interested. I'm going to watch it anyway." He says it quietly, but I can tell he was hurt by my lack of emotion.

"Marvel was one of the first movies we watched together." I can see his eyes shine with hope as a smile grows on his face.

"You remembered?" he says softly.

I chuckle. "I'm surprised you did actually." I turn my back away from him. "Of course, I remembered," I say quietly.

"Do you want some popcorn?" he asks shyly as he ruffles through the cupboard.

"Ah, sure, if we even have any," I answer, scratching at my arm. I felt awkward around him all of a sudden. The same way I felt before going to the movies with him that first time. Butterflies chased each other around in my stomach.

"I can get the drinks?" I offer, trying to be helpful and not just stare at him.

I watch the muscles tighten in his arms as he reaches for a bowl for the popcorn, then his casual nature as he places the kernels in the bowl and then puts it in the microwave.

"Enjoying the show?" he jokes. It reminds me painfully of how good we had it so many years ago.

"Sorry," I mumble, and walk to the fridge to get the drinks. *How embarrassing!* He caught me staring at him. I knew what it felt like to have Hunter stare at me, so

I didn't take notice of it but now I did. I felt his eyes on me as I got the drinks. He was probably trying to work out what I was thinking. Just like I was trying to work out what he was thinking. I jump as the popcorn starts to pop.

"You okay?" he asks, eyeing me carefully.

"Sorry," I say again. Surely, I knew more words than that. "Just deep in thought".

I half expected him to ask me what I was thinking about but instead he says, "Trying to come up with more ways to entertain yourself? If you have any ideas, please enlighten me. I was kept to a routine in the remand centre," he admits as he jumps up to sit on the bench.

"What would you do on a standard day?" I ask slowly. I know he didn't like talking about his time there, but I was hoping, day by day, he may open up about it. It would do him the world of good to talk about his experience, but I wouldn't press him for details tonight. He already shared how hard it was but I was dying to know more. It's not like you meet someone often that had spent time in a remand facility, and as someone who considered herself to be a law-abiding citizen, I was curious what it was like and if it was really like what you saw in the movies.

"Well, they woke you up about 5:30am on most days. Sundays you got to sleep in until 6:00am, if you could sleep in that is. Then the blocks kind of rotate through shower time and breakfast. Then you get to go off to a 'job'." He uses air quotes. "So I went to the kitchen and learnt a thing or two. You were able to learn from real chefs, so that was interesting. Then you had lunch." His eyes remain focused on the popcorn, like he was counting each individual pop of a corn kernel. "I would go back to the kitchen to help with dinner prep and then I'd get yard time. Again, we'd rotate with the other blocks for showers and dinner. Then it was kind of like free time. We usually played cards."

"Oh, okay." I think about my response. "Very regimented then. I can see why you need some suggestions."

"Yeah, it was particularly bad when a real criminal came through. You could tell he was guilty just by his reputation," he continued as though he didn't hear me. "You just had to play it cool. Innocent until proven guilty, after all."

I can feel a tear escape my eye. He would be traumatised for the rest of his life.

"Do you want me to see if Detective Brown can get you someone to talk to?" I offer quietly. I didn't want to spook him.

He whips around to look at me. "I want to talk to *you* about it, Hayley, because I trust you. I just don't know how but I'm getting there slowly. I hope you can see that."

I'm slightly surprised by his words, and I don't want him to stop talking so I say, "I can, and I'm grateful that you want to share this with me. I know it must be tough." Instinctively, I reach out to touch him.

It was almost like an electric shock for the both of us and I quickly let go.

"I'm sorry," I apologise for the third time that night.

I can see him fighting an urge to reach out to me. "Come on, let's watch this movie."

CHAPTER 82

On week three, the prosecutor arrives to talk to both Hayley and I, accompanied by Detective Brown. The prosecutor's name was Harvey Winter. I stare at her for a moment. I'd never met a female Harvey but with such a masculine name, I hoped she would kick ass in a courtroom. She was quite tall and had a really strong build. Her tailored suit fit her perfectly and the skirt sat at just the right length. Her eyes were cold and grey, living up to her surname. Her blonde hair was neatly pulled back into a bun, and it was like she used makeup to highlight her very cold dark eyes. Hayley seemed thrilled to have Harvey on the case. Harvey alluded confidence and the right amount of arrogance. For the first time, I saw real hope in Hayley's eyes. Hayley liked and trusted Harvey so I would like her and trust her too. We had to speak to Harvey individually though. Harvey had requested to speak to Hayley first as she would take the longest. She had been married to the psychopath after all. I try to give Hayley a reassuring smile as she follows Harvey into the study. She turns to give me a thumbs up before closing the door behind her. That's a good sign. I slump on the couch. I wish we could've talked to Harvey together but I know that's not how this goes. I switch on the TV and scroll through Netflix before landing on reruns of the Big Bang Theory. I decide to start at Season One even though I preferred the later seasons. We had another three weeks in here anyway so this would kill some time.

After about twelve episodes, Hayley and Harvey finally emerge from the study. Hayley has a bunch of tissues in her hand and I can see she has been crying.

"Don't worry, Hunter, they're tears of happiness." Harvey smiles, giving Hayley a squeeze on her shoulder. It's the first sign of warmth I had seen from Harvey.

It doesn't make me relax though. The only person I would believe about Hayley's wellbeing was Hayley and when she nods in agreement, I let out a sigh of relief.

"Lunch?" Hayley offers to Harvey.

"Yes, I think I could use a bite to eat but I'll just eat some stuff I brought and take a breather before my next round of questioning." Harvey returns to the study and closes the door again.

I follow Hayley into the kitchen. I knew she couldn't talk about what was discussed but I was dying to know what went on and what I would be in for.

"So that went well?" I opt for instead of asking what I really wanted, which was *tell me everything*. That would allow for a vague response, right? She sees straight through me though.

"I like her Hunter," she says. "I think we're going to be okay. Just be honest with her. Answer her questions as best as you can. She's on our side and she's going to help us." She gives me a reassuring smile as she looks through the shelves in the fridge.

"I know." I lean against the bench. "Hopefully we don't have to be in here the whole six weeks."

"You don't like my company?" she asks with a frown.

I laugh at her. *She couldn't be serious?* We were finally starting to get to a place where I felt close to her, without physically being close. I had stuck to my plan of trying to win her over and I felt like I was making good progress. It took nearly a year or so to win her over the first time and now I knew what to do here's hoping it wouldn't take that long again.

"I just would've thought you'd want to get out of here as soon as you can." I try to cover my tracks.

She just shrugs in response. "Well, I must admit, having a roommate has definitely made it a lot easier."

I feel my heart beat faster knowing I was having a positive impact on her.

"I can make you something for lunch if you want?" I offer in an attempt to keep her talking to me.

"Are you sure?" She closes the fridge door and looks up at me. "You've got a big afternoon ahead of you. I'm actually going to try and have a sleep after the morning I had. It's a bit intense but I know it'll be worth it."

I resist the urge to reach out and pull her into a cuddle. Instead, I say, "I'll make us some lunch and you can clean up then, how about that?"

She smiles softly. "Okay, sounds good. Thank you."

"How about a burrito bowl from yesterday's leftovers?" I suggest as she hops up to sit on the kitchen bench.

"Yum!" she beams. "It's so handy having a chef in the house." She pokes her tongue out at me as she references my story from working in the kitchen at the remand facility.

I can't help but look at her with such appreciation. I always knew I was in love with her but at this second, I felt more in love with her than ever. She looked genuinely happy, and we were in such a good place. *My plan was working.* I hoped she could see how much I had changed.

"What?" she asks, and I could see how shy I was making her. Just like I did in high school.

"Nothing." I try to hide a smile.

"What's wrong?" she continues.

"Nothing's wrong, Hayley." I laugh as I start to pull the ingredients out of the fridge and place them on the bench.

"Where did your mind go?" Her eyes narrow. She was still as persistent as ever.

"Nowhere, Hayls, don't worry about it." I try to busy myself with making the burrito bowls. I didn't know how long of a break Harvey needed before I was called in.

"It went back to high school, didn't it?" she says quietly. "It kind of feels like the old us, doesn't it?"

I freeze. God, she just knew me so well.

"Well." She jumps off the bench. "If my memory serves me correctly, it took you a year to win me over." There's a cheeky smile on her face and I am instantly transported back to high school.

I feel like my heart has stopped. No, it definitely hasn't. I'm still standing. I can feel my face break into a big grin and decide to just go for it.

"Here's hoping it doesn't take me that long this time," I say as carefully and as casually as possible, trying to hide any excitement in my voice.

"One can only hope." She pats my arm and walks out of the kitchen.

So this is what real happiness feels like.

CHAPTER 83

Now I knew how Hunter felt waiting for me. I swear he had been in there for ten hours but really, it had only been two. I tried so hard to sleep like I said I would but the look he gave me in the kitchen that reminded me of how good we were in high school, and the retelling of my story to a complete stranger, had electrified me. For the first time since reuniting with Hunter I had hope, and I felt like we would be okay. We could make it work. I could trust him. I could see it in him. I was confident that he had really changed and that he had learnt from his mistakes. He wanted to make this work—make us work. I felt more and more confident with my decision to give him another chance and just see where things ended up, whilst also knowing that it really came down to me. I could leave anytime. I had a chance of real happiness, and it was like Hunter was the key to unlocking it. The trial was also moving forward. Harvey had given me inspiration to look forward to the future. The fact that there would even be a future for me drove my determination to get through this rough patch. When I was with Harvey, she told me she would come back a couple of times in the lead up to the trial, particularly if she had more questions. She would then come daily in the week leading up to the trial. Hunter would go with Harvey to court in three weeks and that would be it. He wouldn't be returning to the safe house. I would need to remain here until I was called as a witness. Harvey was hoping that it would be the next day so I would only need to spend another night here alone. I was okay with that, if it meant all of this was coming to an end.

Finally, I hear the study room door open and Hunter appears at my doorway.

"Harvey's leaving now," he says. He looks so drained. I can only imagine the heartache he would've had to endure, retelling his story to someone like Harvey and trying not to look crazy.

I get up off the bed and meet Harvey at the front door. Surprisingly, Detective Brown is there too. I didn't even hear the alarm signal his arrival. Even after nearly eight hours here, Harvey looked just like she did when she'd arrived. Not a single hair out of place.

"Well, it was nice to meet you both and get an understanding of your lives and stories. I trust you know that you still cannot discuss the case," Harvey says sternly, eyeing us both.

"Yes, we understand," I answer for both of us.

"I'll see you both in a week. That's when I'll return." Harvey smiles and Detective Brown lets them out.

Once she's out the door, I look back at Hunter and he sighs loudly.

"You okay?" I ask.

He looks so defeated. "I'm going to go for a shower and then have a lie down, I think."

I had come out of my time with Harvey feeling positive and ready to tackle the world whereas he seemed to have the opposite experience. I suppose the information he had to tell her was a lot more shameful than mine.

"Okay, I'll make us some dinner and then you can just relax." I try to spark some life back into him.

"Thanks Hayley." He squeezes my arm and walks towards the shower.

"Hunter?" I call.

"Mm?" He turns around, scratching at his jaw.

"I do hope you're okay."

He smiles weakly. "Thank you."

CHAPTER 84

I let the hot water scorch my skin. I wanted to melt away the embarrassment of having to tell Harvey about my reckless behaviour towards Hayley in the years leading up to this mess. She didn't bat an eyelid at anything I told her though. I could only imagine that she had heard worse. She was tasked with defending me against a real criminal. I knew I had nothing to worry about. The evidence was there to put Rhys away for life. Harvey had told me continuously that she needed to know everything so when the defence tried to poke holes in my story, or share things to shock the jury, she would be ready and not look like an idiot. So, I was. I was so truthful with Harvey. Anything she wanted to know, I told her. I had never felt so vulnerable before. I had never bared my soul like that to anyone other than Hayley. I knew Hayley was concerned for me when I finished with Harvey so I needed to put her out of her misery and get out of the shower. The thought of Hayley being concerned reminded me of our conversation in the kitchen. She was open to me winning her over again. I needed to let that consume me now, not the grilling I had by Harvey. It was time to kick it up a notch.

I turn the shower off and dry myself quickly. I use the towel to wipe the fog off the mirror and am surprised to see how exhausted I look. I really did just want to lie down and close my mind off to everything that had happened. Maybe Hayley would be open to watching the Big Bang Theory? That way I could still be around her but not have to talk.

I open the door and she is sitting in the lounge room watching the TV. She has some rubbish show on. I don't know why she likes it, but she said she got hooked before I showed up so now she needed to finish it.

"That was just what I needed," I announced to let her know that I'm coming up behind her so she doesn't get a fright.

She bolts upright anyway, turning the TV off in the process.

"Good," she beams. "I'm glad that made you feel better."

I plop down on the couch opposite her. She looked like she had been sleeping whilst I had a shower.

"Hungry? Thirsty?" she asks quickly, trying to be helpful.

"Yeah, I'm ready for dinner." I smile, hoping that I wasn't imagining the change between us and that there really was hope she'd take me back.

"Dinner shouldn't be too far away." She looks at the clock on the wall. "Chicken and hot chips, my lazy meal."

"Sounds good to me." I rest my head back on the cushions, closing my eyes.

We sit silently and I almost worry that she has fallen back asleep. I open my eyes slightly to steal a peek but she's flipping quietly through a magazine. The beeping from the air fryer makes her jump up off the couch and I can hear her moving around the kitchen. I know I should offer to help but I was just so tired.

"Here, we can continue watching TV if you want?" She places a tray of food down on the coffee table before going back into the kitchen for our drinks. She's got an array of sauces to go with the chicken tenders and chips. I feel my stomach growl. I didn't realise I was that hungry.

"Sure, so long as it's not that crap you've been watching," I chuckle.

"Hey!" she calls from the kitchen. "It's entertaining!"

"Right... Well, the Big Bang Theory is more entertaining if you want to watch that?"

She comes back with our drinks and sits down on the couch next to me, so close that our legs touch and she makes no effort to move.

~ PART 6 ~

CHAPTER 85

It felt odd being sat in the gallery of the courtroom instead of up the front in the defendant's chair. Rhys now took my place in a case that had well and truly shocked our community. Rhys was put in front of a jury for attempted murder and grievous bodily harm. He would face the fraud charges later. From what I understood, his trial had started a day before I was called as a witness. I slept a little better last night having given evidence yesterday. I was able to stay with Hayley for her final night but I wasn't able to calm her enough to sleep through the night. She didn't sleep well at all and the thing we used to do to get her to calm down, was a big no-no for us right now. The sex wouldn't have even been enjoyable. Instead, we moved a mattress out into the lounge room and put the Big Bang Theory on for the majority of the night. Now it was her turn to show everyone she was still alive. Luckily, she didn't have to hear all of the snide comments from Rhys's lawyer, Alistair, wondering how I felt to be on the other side of the law now. At least I was on the right side of the law, unlike his client. He reminded me of Danny DeVito when he played the dad in Matilda. Was this guy truly the best Rhys could find? I would've thought someone like him would have connections. Alistair continuously reminded the jury that I had not long ago been charged with Hayley's murder and now here I sat as a key witness. *What were the odds?* His nasally voice did my head in. I knew we were the real winners though, considering Hayley was alive and well. Or at least as well as she could be. During her cross examination today, Harvey told her told that she would likely be required to show her scar to the jury to prove she had indeed been shot and where. She would then be asked to give an accurate account of the struggle between Rhys and I when the gun went off, just like I had to. Here's hoping that her account and my account matched. It was one topic we steered clear of so as to not get ourselves into any trouble.

"I'd like to call in my next witness," Harvey announces. There's almost a smirk on her face. "Hayley Gonzalez."

The jury and audience gasp. Rhys' jaw drops so fast I nearly cheered. Miranda breaks into a sob. I wanted to sit with her so badly to support her. This would be the nail in Rhys' coffin. No one knew to this date that she was alive. I was surprised Harvey didn't have to disclose her as a witness to Alistair—but Hayley needed to be kept safe in case one of Rhys' accomplices tried to finish the job so maybe that's how they got around it? I take a quick look at Judge McLaren. He was an older man with grey hair and looked wise beyond his years. Everything about him was sharp, the creases in his robes, his eyebrow, his jawline, his lips that did not seem to move. Surprisingly, he didn't look shocked, and I wish I knew more about the legal system to better understand how this was all set up.

The bailiff led Hayley in and sat her in the witness box. I see her mum in the row in front of me clasp her hands together at the sight of Hayley, no doubt holding in her emotions and her desire to jump up and hold her daughter. Miranda should be so proud though. Hayley looked so small yet so powerful. She was ready to get this over with and move on with her life. You could tell by her posture. The bailiff handed her the bible, and she was sworn in as a witness.

"Questioning may begin," Judge McLaren says.

"Objection!" Alistair jumps up out of his seat. "Permission to approach the bench."

I can't hear what they're talking about but Alistair honestly looked like the little animated guy who trained Hercules from the cartoon. He looked like a mad little man. Harvey on the other hand, kept her composure. She almost had a smirk on her face like she had provided information on Hayley but either Alistair never received it or didn't read it properly. Either way, Judge McLaren sends them back to their corners. Alistair was absolutely fuming.

"Hayley, can you tell the jury where you have been for the last six months?" Alistair begins his cross examination.

"I have been in a safe house whilst the Major Crimes Division gathered evidence about Rhys Centino," she answers.

"I'm sure you can understand that I'm having trouble processing that you're sitting in front of us when you were pronounced dead six months ago." Alistair clasps his hands together as he walks closer to her.

"By who?" she asks and I watch Alistair falter for a moment.

"The medical experts." His eyes narrow.

"Do you have a death certificate?"

"I think I'll do the questioning here, Mrs Centino." Alistair narrows his eyes at Hayley. I could tell he was using her married name in an attempt to get a rise from her.

I just wanted her right now. She was turning me on with how cheeky she was being. She was like a bull ready to charge.

"Were you aware that a funeral had been held for you?" Alistair changes gears.

"Um, relevance?" Harvey interrupts.

"If you're making a point, do it now," the judge orders Alistair, who quickly recovers.

"What made you go into a safe house, Hayley, leave your family behind and put an innocent man in jail?" Alistair rests his hands on the frame of the witness box in front of her.

"Again, relevance? Isn't that what we're here to fight?" Harvey jumps in.

Alistair ignores Harvey and continues on. "Hayley, you are witness to the accusation that my client attempted to murder Hunter Woods. Can you please explain what happened that day?"

Finally, we were starting to get somewhere other than this ridiculous line of questioning.

"I was at home. It was Saturday afternoon. I heard Rhys call out for me from the garage. When I went to the garage Rhys was there and so was Hunter," she recalls once more.

"Can you please provide the full names of the other people in the garage?"

"Rhys Centino, the man sitting right beside you, and Hunter Woods." She points at Rhys when she says his name and it's the first time I see her look at him. She swallows quickly, fear fleeting across her face.

"Thank you for clearly identifying my client. Is Hunter in the room then, seeing as you're more than happy to point people out?" He tries to act smug but I see right through it, and hopefully so could Hayley.

"Of course I can," she snaps, before pointing behind Rhys at me. "That's Hunter."

Rhys turns ever so slightly in my direction and I lock eyes on him. I want him to see me looking at him. He was going down.

"Can you explain your relationship with both men?" Alistair continues.

"Rhys was my husband at the time and Hunter was an ex-boyfriend."

"What was Hunter doing there? That must've been an awkward situation."

I watch Hayley closely. I knew she would tread delicately around this. She had absorbed every tip and trick that Harvey had given her, and she was incredibly smart in her own right.

"Hunter was troubled," she says carefully. "He was struggling to find his way in life after we separated. He had reached his limit, emotionally. He needed help but didn't know how to get it, so he came to me. One of the few people he thought he could trust to help."

"Was there a history of Hunter showing up unannounced?"

"Yes, he had randomly appeared several times before."

"Didn't this seem strange to you?"

I already had a hunch about what Hayley might say but again she surprised me.

"At this start I thought it was a coincidence," she explains. "We were living in the same town so why wouldn't we run into each other from time to time? What I came to realise after was that they were cries for help."

"So, it didn't seem strange to you?" Alistair tries again for a concrete answer.

"No, I wouldn't consider it to be strange. We grew up in the same town. Why wouldn't we run into each other?" she repeats.

I almost felt like this was turning into a tennis match. Each opponent trying to outsmart the other. I was thoroughly entertained and so proud of how well Hayley was holding her own.

"Unless he had planned it that way." Alistair tries to create doubt in the jurors' mind on what happened. This is where the jury could start to look at things in a different light. He would twist Hayley's words, highlighting grey areas in her version of what happened, just to sway the jury's opinion.

"Speculation!" Harvey jumps up out of her chair.

"Sustained," Judge McLaren says.

"So, what did Hunter want during those unannounced visits?" Alistair moves on quickly.

"They weren't *visits*. As I said, we ran into each other. We never planned to see each other. Hunter only ever came to my house once and it was that Saturday."

"And what did Hunter want?"

"Hunter was trying to get my attention." She breathes out in frustration. "He wanted to know how I was going, if we could catch up."

"So, you believe that was Hunter's only intention on that Saturday?" Alistair pushes her for clarification.

"Hunter was trying to get help on that Saturday. He said it himself. He was a mess. Hunter always had trouble communicating his feelings."

I try to suppress the emotions rising inside me upon hearing Hayley describe what happened in a kinder and more compassionate light to what everyone had shrouded the story in.

"Did you rebuff him each time you saw him?"

"Yes, I did," she answers. "I told him it was not a good idea to see each other anymore."

"But he kept coming back? That's a bit obsessive." Alistair looks at the jury whilst he says this, his eyebrow raised.

"Speculation, your honour!" Harvey calls out quickly. She had certainly brought her A game.

Hayley has an answer before the judge can call 'sustained' or 'overruled'.

"Or it was someone who'd never had strong parental figures in his life trying to find ways to express he needed help. Imagine having these thoughts of not knowing what's next and not knowing who to turn to," she says quickly.

"I always know my next step," Alistair responds matter-of-factly.

"You're a lawyer," she snaps. "It's literally your job to make people believe twisted stories, so how do we know you're even telling the truth?" She was almost trying to ruin his credibility to the jury. Again, I was taken aback by how her fighting nature made me all the more attracted to her.

"Let's move on as to why we're all here." Alistair clears his throat, clearly annoyed at her.

"Finally," she mutters loud enough to hear. I don't bother to hide my smirk, and Ethan claps me on the back.

"She's doing well," he whispers.

"What happened when you walked into the garage, Mrs Centino?" Alistair's question pulls my attention back to the front of the court room.

"I would prefer if you called me Hayley, Alistair," she states. "And that's been recorded now."

Alistair shoots daggers with his eyes at her.

She was being a smart ass, and I was here for it. She moves on, answering his question. "Hunter and Rhys were in there. Once Hunter saw me, he started up the conversation. He wanted to know what I was doing, how I had been. He was trying to make Rhys doubt my love for him. This frustrated Rhys but then Hunter kept avoiding the question about what he wanted, and I knew something wasn't right," She kept to the facts rather than using too many emotive words.

"How did you know something wasn't right?" Alistair asks. "I don't believe humans have achieved mind reading."

He really was irritated with her. Either that or he used this as an intimidation technique because he was shit and couldn't do his job.

She doesn't miss a beat though. "If they had, Alistair, I don't think we'd need lawyers."

This gets a chuckle from the courtroom causing Judge McLaren to bang his gavel down several times. Alistair was absolutely fuming now. She was making him look like an idiot. Harvey looked totally relaxed on the other hand.

"Please enlighten us then, Hayley," he says through gritted teeth.

"I spent two and a half years with Hunter. I think you would agree that that was long enough for me to pick up on someone's cues. Surely you would understand that as a married man?" She pauses as though she's making a statement rather than asking a question. "So, when I started to try and understand what was going on with Hunter, Rhys appears with a gun in his hand. He said he was going to kill Hunter and make it look like an accident."

"Can we just go back to the part about Rhys questioning your love. Why would he be questioning you?"

I want to jump up and shout *you're missing the most important part—he was going to kill me!*

"I had visited Hunter one night when he needed help. He seemed suicidal and I was not going to be the person to just leave someone alone in that situation. I didn't tell Rhys about it, but Hunter brought it up in the garage." She makes it sound like it was no big deal. She had changed gears again and was using words that would stir emotion in the jury. It was quite impressive. She was like a mini-Harvey.

"What made you choose not to tell Rhys?" Alistair leans against the banister of the jury box.

"I was concerned that he would want to stay at home and not go on work trips anymore. I thought that could impact his career. He was chasing a promotion, and it required him to do a bit of away work."

And he was lying about what he did for work anyway! I want to scream but at that point we didn't really know who Rhys was or what he was capable of.

"So, you lied to Rhys?" Alistair detracts from her answer.

"No, lying is when you intentionally do not tell the truth. Rhys never asked me if I saw Hunter whilst he was away and I made the decision not to bring it up," Her statement seemed to stump him again. She had a point after all. She didn't lie.

"Were you keeping any other secrets from your husband?" He quickly shakes off the embarrassment.

"No, I was not."

"What happened after Rhys started questioning you about your deceit?"

She bites her tongue at his choice of wording.

"We're waiting," Alistair demands, and Harvey throws her hand up in the air in disgust.

"Rhys started to get angry. He started accusing me of being a liar and unfaithful." I can see the sadness spread across her face as she remembers the pain she felt once Rhys started verbally attacking her loyalty to him. "He was quite rude to the point even Hunter tried to get him to calm down."

"Were you ever scared of Rhys that day?"

"Yes, I was more scared of Rhys than I ever was of Hunter."

"So, Hunter was trying to protect you?" he asks stupidly, as though he was siding with us.

"Yes, Hunter was trying to protect me. Like he always did."

I can almost see Alistair mentally slap himself. This was quite amusing. Even Harvey had a grin.

"So, Hunter comes in with a gun?"

"No," she answers quickly. "I just said that Rhys came in with a gun. Not Hunter," she corrects. "Rhys wanted to kill Hunter to put an end to it all."

"What makes you believe that's what his intention was?"

"Because he said so," she responds.

"Can anyone else confirm this?"

Harvey scoffs.

"Yes, Hunter can. You can call him back to the witness stand if you'd like?"

Alistair rolls his eyes at her. "Did Rhys say anything else that made you think he was going to kill Hunter?"

"He described how he would make it look like an accident to the police. He said everyone knew how Hunter felt about me, and everyone knew how he would just appear out of the blue over the last year. He said it would be too easy to make it look like Hunter had committed suicide because he couldn't live without me."

I watch the jury whilst she answers. Some are writing down comments and others look hooked on every word she is saying. I couldn't tell which was better.

"You ended up getting shot, didn't you, Hayley? Can you please tell us who shot you then?"

"Rhys did," she responds promptly.

"A claim which he denies," Alistair states.

"You have another witness though?" Hayley questions him.

"We don't know that you're both not lying."

"And yet you're trying to convince everyone that Rhys isn't lying. What sets us apart? How does the jury know that Rhys isn't lying?"

I couldn't believe how feisty she was being.

"Your honour?" Alistair finally caves.

"Please rephrase the question," Judge McLaren says bluntly.

"Why would Rhys shoot you, Hayley? You're his wife," Alistair accuses her.

"Well, he was aiming for Hunter, not me."

"It's your word against Rhys." Alistair clasps his hands together again.

"Yes, and it's Rhys' word against mine. Only thing is, there was another witness there that afternoon," she fights back.

Hayley didn't need representation. She was doing so good on her own

"Hunter's fingerprints were on the gun," Alistair responds quickly.

"So were Rhys'," she argues. Harvey looks back at me and shakes her head with a smile. Hayley was doing her job for her.

"Why would Rhys shoot his wife? The woman he promised to love and cherish till death do they part?"

"You'll have to ask him that. He's right there, too."

Alistair looks defeated. Surely he knew that taking on this case wouldn't fare well for him. I knew Harvey's success rate. Alistair was struggling to even nail Hayley on a statement to plant doubt in the jurors' minds. She had an answer for everything.

"Rhys verbally told Hunter and I that he would make Hunter's death look like a suicide. I guess I was just collateral damage."

"So, you truly believe that Hunter was not there to kill you that night?"

"Yes, I don't even believe Hunter is capable of murder."

"Do you believe Rhys is capable of murder?"

"In that moment, yes, I did. He also told us that that was what he was planning to do. The look in his eye was pure evil."

Alistair walks away from the witness stand and towards the jury box, clearly defeated. "There is reasonable doubt that you need to take into consideration." The lawyer speaks directly to the jury. "Rhys had no motive to kill Hunter or Hayley, whereas Hunter had been obsessive and acting strange in the months leading up to that fateful day. The evidence is stacked against Hunter who had a motive to kill and, like Hayley always did, she let him back in to do that."

CHAPTER 86

We finally broke for a lunch break after what felt like hours of sitting in the witness stand. As I sat in a secure room by myself to eat lunch and regroup, I felt drained but proud of myself. I was so irritated by Alistair but I kept myself restrained for as long as I could, trying to poke holes in the defence. I hoped it was enough to show that Hunter and I weren't lying. It was two people's stories against one. I look down at the egg sandwich in my hands and take a deep breath before taking another bite. It was hard to swallow. I just wanted this to be over. I knew this afternoon would be a bit easier as it was Harvey's turn to question me.

You can do this, Hayley! My dad's voice in my head chants at me. *You'll be okay, kiddo.* His voice is so clear, as though he was right next to me. *Just a little bit longer and then you'll be free.*

"Don't break now, Hayley." I urge myself as I reach for the tissue box.

A knock at the door interrupts my thoughts. It's the guard, who advises that I have five minutes left until I'm to be escorted back to the courtroom. I force myself to take another bite and then throw the remainder in the bin. It was like chewing cardboard. I run my hand through my hair quickly and wait for the guard to return.

I take a deep breath as he leads me back into the courtroom and I immediately feel all eyes on me. I try not to look at anyone as I didn't want to crumble under Mum's caring eye, or Hunter's concerned expression. I needed to be prepared to be smashed again with questions from what I considered to be the dumbest attorney to ever walk the planet. I wasn't sure where Rhys found this guy, but he was shocking. He must've known he was going to lose so he hired the first guy from the Google search. We go through the court formalities and Alistair is off and rearing to go.

"So, we've now heard what happened on that fateful day when a gun went off, injuring Hayley Centino, but let's dig deeper into the motive behind it, shall we?" he starts, and I almost want to roll my eyes. I would be reiterating what I said this morning. How exhausting.

"Hayley and Hunter, as we know, had a romantic relationship several years before she met Rhys. They kept in contact; they lived in the same town. What were the chances of them running into each other again and again?" He pauses for dramatic effect. "Unless it was planned."

I try hard to keep my composure. I knew exactly where this was headed.

"What did you and Hunter talk about when you would catch up?" Alistair asks.

"Catching up implies it was planned. I can assure you, they weren't planned catch ups. We ran into each other. It would be a maximum of 10 minutes spent in the same space as the other."

"There are other ways to communicate though, Mrs Centino."

"I changed my mobile number and was very careful who I shared it with. I deleted social media. I didn't even have a LinkedIn profile."

"What about email?" he smirks.

"I have provided access to my accounts if you'd like to see what's in there."

"But somehow the star-crossed lovers got to be the winners in the end."

"Speculation!" Harvey jumps up from her seat. She looks fed up with him and we had only just started again. "Your honour, permission to approach the bench!"

Judge McLaren looks between the lawyers, before sighing and signalling them both forward.

"Are you absolutely kidding me, Alistair?" Her voice is low and aggressive. "You're really clutching at straws here. This isn't the trial for Hunter and Hayley accused of killing Rhys and what their motive was. There are two key witnesses, for goodness' sake! How long are you going to let this nonsense go on for, McLaren? Let me have my turn so we can all be home to watch the 6:00pm news."

Judge McLaren starts stuttering out a response.

"I know it's your job to get him off the hook but come on Alistair. The kid is doomed. Accept his fate," Harvey says before she pushes herself away from the bench as Alistair argues back with the judge. She catches me staring and winks at me.

"If you have a point, Alistair, you need to make it within the next ten minutes, or I'll wrap you up myself and hand it over to Harvey for her final round of questioning. You can then prepare for your closings tomorrow."

Harvey clicks her tongue and walks back to her table, satisfied with the outcome.

"Judge McLaren, come on, there could be more to it," he whispers as hard as he can but I can still hear him.

"Ten minutes, Alistair, then it's Harvey's turn."

I feel my mouth drop open. I couldn't believe what I was hearing. Was this normal for a court of law?

"Give me a moment with my client please," Alistair sighs. I watch him walk back to Rhys and he starts whispering to him. For the first time all day, I lock eyes with Rhys. He looks scared but it doesn't stir a single bit of emotion in me. Instead, I feed off it. It was the burst of energy I needed. I was ready for whatever came next.

Alistair stands up and waltzes back over to me.

"Do you think the jury has reason to be concerned by your romantic history with Hunter and now all of a sudden, your current husband is on trial for attempted murder?" he asks.

"I'm sure most of the members of the jury have experienced an ex that was difficult, or was the difficult ex," I respond.

"As a reasonable person though, it seems pretty suspicious that your ex was charged with your murder in the first place and is now a witness for charges against your husband," Alistair turns his attention to the jury. "Could it not have been the plan all along to get rid of Rhys? Except it backfired, didn't it?

"There are two sides to every story and seeing as you're determined to disprove mine, how about I explain this a different way?" I answer. "Hunter was a little odd leading up to the events that Saturday afternoon so, Rhys, a jealous husband, acted dangerously and murderously. Think about that while you're trying to spin another lie."

Alistair looks down at Rhys, who hangs his head in clear guilt.

"No further questions, Your Honour."

CHAPTER 87

Harvey stands up almost immediately, ready for her final round of questions.

"Hayley, I'm going to ask something quite personal of you." She approaches calmly. "Can you please show the jury your scar?"

I watch Hayley hesitate. She was so conscious of her scar. This was going to be hard for her.

"That's it, come down with me and we'll give the jury a closer look," Harvey coaxes her down from the witness box.

Slowly, Hayley rises, and I can see her start to unbutton her cardigan. Her face remains stone cold. Harvey walks her up and down the length of the jury's sitting area, stopping occasionally so they can have a better look at her scar. I watch Harvey mouth something to Hayley and slowly, she leads her over to where Rhys is sitting.

"Do you see the damage of what was done that day?" Harvey breaks the silence as she stops in front of Rhys.

Rhys refuses to look at Hayley and I watch his lawyer elbow him, forcing him to glance up. Surprisingly, he starts to cry. As if that wasn't an admission of guilt. This fucker was going down. Hayley starts to do up her cardigan when her eyes land on me. I try to give her a reassuring smile and she stops what she's doing, leaving the cardigan half opened, her chest still exposed and her scar on full display.

"Hayley, can you please do me a favour and stand in the middle over there?" Harvey points to an area on the floor. Hayley stands silently, waiting for the next direction.

"Can you please tell the courtroom where Rhys and Hunter were standing that day?"

"Hunter was on the floor beside me—" She points next to her. "—Rhys was standing probably about where you are, maybe a bit closer."

"So, when the gun was pulled, where was everyone standing?"

"In the same spots. I don't know where the gun came from. Rhys left the garage while I tried to talk to Hunter on the floor. He came back with it."

"Then what happened?"

"When Hunter realised what Rhys was holding, he stood up immediately, trying to shield me. I made the split decision to push him out of the way and ended up getting shot. Hunter fell to the floor."

"That's all, thank you Hayley. You can return to your seat." Harvey turns to face the jury. "So, now that you've all seen Hayley's account of what happened, let's have a look at some of the other evidence. The gun that was used had both Hunter's and Rhys' fingerprints on it. Why would Rhys' fingerprints be on it at all, if you believe his account of what happened? A reasonable person would conclude that he had no reason to touch the gun, unless he was lying. There has been no mention of struggle and if you remember, Hunter told us that Rhys forced the gun into his hand after the shot was fired. Rhys was cunning and calculated. Need I remind you that the gun was registered in Rhys' name, not Hunter's, so any reasonable person could make the assumption that Hunter knew nothing of the gun, nor where to find it. So, let's review those crime scene photos again, only this time my team has added animation to further support what really happened that day."

Harvey directs their attention to the screen. My stomach starts churning and I'm worried I'll throw up. I wish I had known they had this. I really didn't want to see the scenes of that awful day again, regardless of the fact it was fake. It shows the animated me jump in front of Hayley as the fake Rhys points the gun at us. I jump in my seat as the gun goes off, my hand covering my mouth as I watch the animated Hayley fall into my arms on the screen. There are a few audible gasps from around me and I feel Ethan's hand squeeze my shoulder. Hayley's eyes study the floor, but I could see the tears pooling.

"Happy to play it again if there's still doubt in your mind," Harvey says, almost smugly at Alistair. "Now, if you still need convincing, I'll give my closing statement. This is the trial for Rhys Centino, charged with the attempted murder of Hunter Woods and grievous bodily harm of Hayley Centino. This is not a trial for Hunter and it's not a trial for Hayley. They are the witnesses, meaning they saw the crime and are here to provide evidence to ensure the accused is reprimanded. Need I also remind you that Hunter has believed Hayley to be dead for the last six months so when would they have had time to corroborate their stories? Hayley has done a miraculous job in highlighting the truth of what happened that night, so much so, she's done most of my work for me. With Hayley's statement matching Hunter's, and forensics confirming the distance between the shooter and the victim, the fingerprints on the gun used, which need I remind you, was also registered in Rhys' name, I feel this is an open and shut case. I can't argue with real evidence folks, can you?" Harvey sits back down. "No further questions."

~ EPILOGUE ~

I stare across the sand and watch the waves crash against the shore. The sound was electrifying. I hadn't been to the beach to just listen to the waves in so long. I lay back on my beach towel, wishing the sounds of the surf would put me to sleep. Instead, my mind wanders. What a whirlwind of a year. I couldn't believe everything that had happened. Life was so different at the start of the year and I never pictured it turning out this way. I wanted to fall in a heap when the judge read out Rhys' verdict. I had an overwhelming urge to throw up. It was all over now and it was time to move on. Knowing that Rhys would spend the rest of his life behind bars made me happy but then I would think about Hunter and how he came so close to being in that situation. I remember I couldn't stop him from jumping to his feet when the judge read out the guilty verdict. I had to pull him back down but after all, Rhys was trying to kill him, not me. His smile was contagious and I felt all my worries disappear. The nightmare was finally over.

My mind wanders back to my first night of freedom. I spent it with my mother. We visited Dad's grave and shared a bottle of wine. It felt so good to sit outside in the fresh air. I almost wanted to set up a tent and sleep under the stars. I made a mental promise to myself that I would do that one day.

Hunter and I never got around to exchanging contact details. We went our separate ways when court finished and were escorted by police back to our nominated residences. I waved goodbye to him and watched the sadness fill his eyes, unsure of when we would see each other again. It's not like we had made a plan to reunite or move in together—or do anything together for that matter. The only time I saw him was on the news on TV. I made sure to watch any news story that came up on TV, just to hear the guilty verdict read out over and over again. Slowly, the case started to disappear from the news and so did Hunter. I knew what I wanted now and I was so grateful that he gave me the space to figure it out. Eventually I found out where Hunter was and I shouldn't have been surprised. Kate and Ethan took Hunter in so he could get back on his feet. He got a decent compensation package and was currently looking for a place to buy. He wanted it to be near the water somewhere as a reminder that he was free and not locked up in a cell. I messaged Kate to see if it was okay if I came for a visit, but also if she could keep it a secret from Hunter.

I wanted it to be a surprise. When I arrived at Kate's house, she opened the front door. Ethan was in the kitchen and Hunter was playing with Haze on the floor. The sight melted my heart, and I knew instantly that I made the right choice.

"Hayley," he breathed as he looked up. I smiled back at him, blinking away any tears that had formed while he stood up. I quickly bound into his arms and he squeezed me tightly.

"Hey, you." I pulled back so I could smile at him.

It doesn't last long though. He squeezes me once more before letting go and turning his attention to Haze.

"Look who's come to visit!" Hunter tells the baby as he sits back on the floor with her.

"Hayley!" Ethan beams as he enters from the kitchen. "Never thought I'd see the day," he says in reference to Hunter with Haze. She was nearly one now.

Hunter was helping her build a block tower. Then she'd knock it down and he would just start again, like he never got tired of the game.

"I actually think she prefers him over us now," Kate chimed in. "He plays with her a lot and always offers to help which has been so good as she's nearly walking now and it can get tiring chasing a baby everywhere."

Haze was actually growing right before my eyes. I didn't want to miss a thing now that I was free to do whatever I wanted. I sat down on the floor next to Hunter and almost cried when she held a block out to me instantly with a big grin, like she already knew who I was. Every now and then I would look up and see how happy Hunter was, which brought a smile to my face. I wanted to try and get him alone to talk, but Hunter didn't seem to pick up on any of my hints. Nor did he reach out and place an arm around me or put his hand on mine like for some reason I thought he would. Maybe this whole experience really had changed him to the point that our chance at being together was well and truly gone. I tried to shake the negative thoughts out of my mind.

Eventually, it was time for me to leave. I had promised to see a movie with my mum that evening. As I said my goodbyes, Hunter shyly asked if he could have my number. I felt my heart skip a beat as I nodded and entered my number into his phone. I then sent a message to myself from his phone, so I had his number too.

"Can you two just save us all some time and get back together now? None of this waiting crap that you pulled in high school?" Kate cheekily called out.

I felt my cheeks go red instantly and Hunter chuckled awkwardly. I took my opportunity and placed a kiss on his cheek. I didn't want to waste any more time. He smiled instantly and wrapped an arm around my shoulders.

A seagull squawks loudly, bringing me back to the present. For once, it felt like life was going to be okay. I had my family and friends back. I felt like I could finally breathe. I sit back up and look across the water. It was so nice to be free and I was becoming more and more accustomed to being alone, knowing that I was now free to do whatever I wanted.

I look over my shoulder, smiling at the world around me.

"Thought I'd find you here," Hunter smiles, taking a seat beside me on the towel. He hands me a hot chocolate in a takeaway cup, complete with a biscuit on top. "I haven't seen you in a few days. Your mum gave me a hint as to where you were."

I laugh as I shake my head. Of course Mum told him where to find me. This was starting to become my morning ritual so he was bound to find out at some point. I watch as he takes a sip of his coffee. He didn't look like he'd slept much now that I'd had a good look at him.

"I was actually hoping to have a chat to you about something," he says nervously.

I wondered what it could be. We were so honest with each other these days, sometimes too honest, but I felt like it was just making us closer. Any question I asked was met with an honest and serious answer by Hunter. He wasn't keeping secrets anymore.

"Go on," I say, a sense of worry filling me as to what he was potentially keeping from me.

He takes a deep breath and reaches for my hand. He won't meet my eye. "Hayley, I need to tell you something."

ACKNOWLEDGEMENTS

This book has been a dream in the making for many years. For the longest time, I found excuses not to pursue this chapter of my life — pardon the pun! — but one day, I finally decided it was time to share it with the world.

To my husband, Nathan — thank you for giving me the time and support to write, edit, and chase this dream.

To my mother, Michelle, and late father, Joseph — I hope this makes you proud. Thank you for always encouraging me to pursue my passions and for the support and loving home you provided.

To my sister, Mardi — thank you for reading my very first final draft and providing feedback, for sending editor recommendations and self-publishing guides, and your overall support. Maybe one day this book will find its way onto a library shelf where you work.

To my good friend, Alexis — thank you for reading that same draft, for helping me shape the ending, and for your encouragement and willingness to help along the way.

To Sarah (All In The Edit) — thank you for taking a chance on me and transforming my manuscript into the polished story it is today. You handled everything behind the scenes with such passion and patience, especially as I stumbled through the process as a total novice. I've learnt so much from you.

To my Maximus Prime and Luna-Balloona — thank you for your patience between each ball throw. You waited while I wrote, and I threw while you waited. The perfect partnership between a girl and her dogs.

To the lights of my life, James and Ava — never be afraid to share your creativity. The world will always need more magic and wonder.

And finally, to the authors who inspired me to write — your stories ignited a dream and encouraged me to put pen to paper, and I am in awe of your abilities to bring stories to life. I hope one day my work can sit proudly beside yours.

ABOUT THE AUTHOR

Telicia McSwan is a fiction writer who swapped city lights for country skies when she moved from Brisbane to Longreach, Queensland. What began as a creative outlet during maternity leave quickly turned into a passion project with the release of her debut novel, Hunted—a bold first step that opened the door to the many stories she's been waiting to tell. A lifelong dreamer with a soft spot for make-believe, Telicia has been crafting short stories since childhood. When she's not writing, she's off on an adventure with her husband, two kids, and a pair of fur-babies who are convinced they run the household.

Find me on:
Facebook : **Telicia McSwan – Author**
Instagram : **@telicia_mcswan_author**
Website : **www.teliciamcswan.com**